PENDULUM
of JUSTICE

By

D. K. Halling

ISBN: 1491264225
ISBN 13: 9781491264225

Advanced Praise for
Pendulum of Justice

"Whenever the legislators endeavor to take away and destroy the property of the people, or to reduce them to slavery under arbitrary power, they put themselves into a state of war with the people."

John Locke

Table of Contents

Prologue

The cab slid to a stop on the long circular run before the large, brightly lit glass doors. The cab door refused to open. *Fuck.* He looked for a lock—none. *What the fuck?!*

"Hey buddy, just a minute—pay me and I'll unlock the door." This was calmly spoken in precise English by the cabbie, whose full dark beard and tawny skin made his white turban seem to glow in the dark.

He tried to slow his breathing. Dazed, he pulled out his wallet and handed over a twenty. This went smoothly—an action performed a million times almost without thinking. He turned and rammed his shoulder against the door as he pulled the handle down. The door fell open quickly against the weight of his body and he stumbled out into heat so humid that it was as if someone was shoving a velvet scarf down his throat. *The door. Get through the door.* He willed his body to move the thirty feet into the light. He felt his heart beating out of his chest. His lungs were burning and straining his ribcage. He had the absurd thought that his organs would get there before him, leaving his body there on the driveway. The doors opened and he adjusted to the bright light. People were moving with efficient purpose and he looked first one way and then the other, seeing long, unmarked hallways—unproductive. Then he looked to the front and saw a sleek shiny wooden desk and a grey-haired woman with glasses hanging on her shelf of a chest, like a necklace. She looked him in the eye and willed him forward. "Name of the patient you are here to see?" she inquired calmly. His heart and lungs and love for the only one he truly needed in this world were already at the elevators ahead.

"Janine Rangar—Nelson, Janine Nelson," he said. *Whose voice was that?* It sounded like a child's unsure answer in a room full of attentive adults.

"Room 1115, intensive care. Take the elevators to the eleventh floor. They will help you find her." Necklace Lady pointed surely to where the first set of hallways began.

Find her, find her, find her—the mantra beat low in him, replacing his heart, which was probably already on the third floor. *Fucking traitor.* Now he had nothing and no one. He stopped at the elevator and willed the doors to open. They didn't. He waited, shutting his eyes and listening. He thought about how the Otis safety elevator worked. Flyweights spun by centrifugal force, pushing against brakes that engaged a rail. Soon, improvements in microprocessors connected to an accelerometer would sense when to brake more efficiently. The cable systems of most office elevators were faster than hydraulic systems—still too damned slow. The elevator bell sounded faintly; he opened his eyes and stepped into the metal box. Without Otis safety brakes there would be no skyscrapers, he thought. He punched a slightly worn silver button labeled '11' and felt the lurch of the elevator. His heart leapt into his throat. *Welcome home, traitor.*

The elevator braked and the doors parted. He walked forward and looked right, down a hallway full of marked doors. Seeing the directions 'Rooms 1101-1120' written in black on a small white sign, posted almost inconspicuously, he strode purposefully that direction.

A couple of nurses and two or three aides were busy at their nine-to-five, only it was past midnight. Then he saw Mark coming around the corner at the other end of the hall. Styrofoam cup in hand, his wrinkled blue button-down shirt was coming out of old khakis, his bare ankles anchoring scruffy loafers. Mark's tired eyes rested on him, almost unseeing, and then recognition lit and Mark moved quickly toward him. "Hank, oh God." Hank Rangar embraced him and looked toward the open door of 1115.

"I need to see her," he said unnecessarily. He released Mark and went into the room. He saw her small form laid out prone on the high bed. Tubes and wires were running out of her mouth, her arms, and her chest. They plugged into the ports of several machines, low-volume alarms beeping, and subdued lights blinking different colors. Hank did not look at the machines. He walked up to the bed and looked down at his sister's chalky face. He felt the hot tears well up. They spilled down his face, falling onto Janine's body run by machines. He lifted her strangely warm hand to his wet cheek and the tears continued to leave him. He noticed a nurse speaking the language of machines with her fingers, pushing buttons, writing down numbers. Like every science, medical language is a combination of numbers and words. Hank knew a little about all scientific languages and was fluent in many. He looked back at Janine's face, relaxed and pale. Her arm was pliant but heavy. He gently returned her hand to her side. "Where are Tristan and Jess?" he asked the room.

Mark's gravelly response brought Hank around. "They're home, with my parents. They know what is going to happen." Then he paused, "They can't be here all the time but they want to be. I waited for you—oh, God—I waited—and now—just tell me. Tell me, there's no choice—no way to reverse..." His voice trailed off.

Hank turned and said firmly, "There's no way to reverse it. It's done. They've killed her as surely as if they'd put a bullet through her heart."

Chapter I

"Hi, I'm Hank Rangar; that's Ranger with an A." He was standing before the partners of Kramer and Packard, a venture capital firm that had been around for decades. He felt uncomfortable in his new Brooks Brothers suit, and he had to consciously remind himself not to tug at his tie, which he felt was tightening by the second. "Houdini Security was incorporated eighteen months ago." His voice, loud to his own ears, seemed to echo off the walls. "Our technology is cutting-edge and can be used by home businesses and large corporations alike."

It had been Hank's dream to start a business from the day he entered engineering school. He wasn't interested in starting just any business. Only one built around a new technology—like Edison built GE around the electric light bulb, or Steve Jobs built Apple around the personal computer. Houdini Security was just that sort of business.

"Let's skip the incorporation details and get down to it, if you would, Mr. Rangar," grunted a slightly greying man on the left side of the conference table. Hank quickly glanced at a little cheat sheet he had made with everyone's name. John Smith, he noted. Hank was good with this as well.

"Houdini's technology is built on a new principle of linear algebra that revolutionizes hashing codes. This allows us to scan for incoming threats thousands of times faster than today's processors. Think of it like this: As a water filter on your kitchen tap absorbs minerals and particulates, it clogs, and over time, the flow of water lessens. It's that way with all of the current antiviral security software. The speed of your computer slows while the software is doing its job. Houdini software will not slow the speed of the computer, but will take on computer risks at a rate far surpassing current technology."

"I thought it had been mathematically proven that all hashing codes have collisions and their lookup speeds decline with the number of stored signatures." Hank consulted his sheet—Chris Branlo.

Smiling, Hank explained to Branlo how his software would avoid this problem.

"All right, enough geek talk already. We only have a limited amount of time this morning. Every company we see has great technology," a well-dressed partner,

Mike Holloway, interrupted. According to his accountant, Holloway had brought in a huge investment from Harvard's endowment, which entitled him to a larger vote than other partners. The room appeared to be split down the middle—the left side casually dressed, the right side more formal. *Ah, old school vs. new-line banking elite.*

"Hey Mike—we've heard your 'good ideas are a dime a dozen' speech before. The electric light bulb, the cotton gin, polio vaccine, the microcontroller, hell, the CAT scan, were all a dime a dozen," John interjected. He had started a semiconductor company in the late seventies and sold out to Intel for an impressive hundred million dollars. His sarcasm was not lost on anyone, including Mike, who scooted back in his leather seat, much like a petulant child. John Smith looked back at Hank. "Go on."

Hank didn't want to piss anybody off, and he could feel the underlying tension between financiers and engineers. He needed them all on the same page.

"You are well aware that this industry sits at five billion today, but will grow to a hundred billion by the end of the decade. We are in beta test with a Fortune 500 company as we speak and our technology positions us to capture a significant portion of the market." He tapped his computer keyboard and the next slide appeared. "Our projections show Houdini having sales of $150K this year, growing to $450K next year, and $1.5 million the following year. By the end of the decade, we should be sitting at $350 million."

Chris Branlo, who had founded an encryption startup that went public within five years, sat forward in his chair and gave a meaningful look to the other partners. "That's consistent with our understanding of your market."

"What about your management team?" asked Franklin Muntz, who had gone to work for K&P right out of his MBA from Harvard. "Great management teams can take even mediocre technologies and business plans and produce a winning investment."

Hank was not sure whether this was a backhanded way of saying his business plan was mediocre or a general statement of operating principle. His business plan was sitting in front of the partners and he had worked hard on it; all ninety-seven-pages. He always had a nagging feeling that this was somewhat pointless, since most venture capital firms said they spent less than twenty minutes in their initial review of a company. His consulting company, Made By Man, had done important projects in computer security for both large companies and the Defense Department. He was intimately familiar with the industry and knew many of the key players, as well as how to approach them. The business plan had felt more like a homework assignment rather than a useful document to assess risk and reward. Hank thought professors were behind the accepted format; they understood how to grade papers. An older entrepreneur had told him once that the best business plans were PowerPoint versions—living, breathing outlines.

"The management team consists of me as the CEO. I have a BS in electrical engineering and computer science from Colorado PolyTech."

"I've never heard of that school," Franklin interjected.

Hank ignored his comment and continued. "My experience includes four years working for the DOD Computer Security Threat Center and being the founder and CEO of Made By Man. Made by Man has grown from two people to eight people in six years, and our revenue is now $1.8 million a year. I'm its systems architect and chief bush-beater." Hank grinned and a few chuckles broke out around the table.

"Houdini's Chief Technical Officer is Warren Criss, who has over twenty years of experience in computer security." Warren's career had spanned being a pilot in the military, avionics, satellite antenna design, and finally, computer security. He loved figuring out simple solutions to problems that blew away industries. The browser came to mind. With Made by Man, Warren did all of the testing and building of prototype products for clients in the lab. Hank and Warren's clients asked for help with anything from designing smart mouse pads, haptic feedback systems in electronics, high-powered laser designs, to medical products, and others. "We plan to hire a sales and marketing manager upon receiving funding or receiving orders totaling $100K."

"Is that your entire management team?" asked the well-dressed James Holloway.

"Jeremy Winthrop, who many of you know, has agreed to serve as our CFO," Hank said, and looked encouragingly around the room. Jeremy had set up this meeting. He was currently biting a pencil and leaning back in his chair at the end of the table.

"Jeremy, are you working full-time in this position?" Holloway started to make notes.

"No. There isn't a need for me full-time at present," Winthrop acknowledged.

"So your management team consists of three people who have full-time jobs in some other business. Do I have that right?" Mike asked rhetorically, as he continued to write. Hank considered how to respond.

"Most tech startup companies start out as consulting companies and then decide to produce their own products," interjected John Smith. "Hell, Apple's management team consisted of a couple of twenty year-olds, one fresh out of an Indian Ashram and another who was an engineering dropout." Holloway looked a little incredulous but threw a bone Hank's way.

"Well, we would be able to help you fill out that management team, if we were to sign on," Mike gave a challenging look in Smith's direction.

"What about a patent?" fired Chris Branlo.

"We have three patent applications." The room was beginning to get warm. Hank wondered if the partners did that on purpose.

"Anything issued?"

"The first patent application we filed about two years ago, so we are hoping to hear back from the patent office anytime."

"You haven't heard from the patent office?" John Smith piped in. John's company had been built around a patent covering a groundbreaking technology found in almost every computer chip today.

"That's correct." Shit. The attorney had told him this was normal, but Smith seemed surprised.

"Kramer and Packard only look at companies with issued patents in their portfolios." Hank scanned the table to gauge the other partners' reactions.

"I will look into this as soon as I get back to the office."

"Why should I care about your technology? Why should the average person on the street care about Houdini? What is the 'so what'?" Chris Branlo seemed to be giving Hank a chance to get the momentum back.

"Computer security issues are not just about identity theft, or reclaiming lost data. They are a matter of life or death. Think about it. Our enemies can destroy our military, financial systems, hospitals, even our industrial base by taking over our computers." Hank had thought a lot about this when he was at the DOD. He noticed several people seemed to look up from their notes.

"You have our requirements in the packet in front of you. I won't take up any more of your time." Likely, K&P would not give him an immediate decision. He turned off the projector and the sharp smell of burning dust filled his nostrils.

Hank shut down the program and closed his laptop. Several of the partners worked their way to the head of the table to shake his hand. John Smith was last. "Houdini seems to be right on target. Don't worry about Franklin and Mike."

"Thanks." Hank shook his hand and noticed Smith's firm pat to his shoulder.

"Houdini reminds me of a young Synasptix. When we first invested in them, they were no bigger than Houdini. Three years later they went public with a market valuation of over a billion dollars."

"Wow," was all Hank could say. *Intelligent—you are so articulate.* There was an awkward pause.

"What I need from you is proof of sales in the neighborhood of one hundred thousand dollars in the next year, a technical explanation of your hashing system for some experts of ours down at Cal Tech, and an issued patent."

"Yes sir, I will get right on that." Hank felt a little bit giddy by the analogy to Synasptix.

On the flight back to Colorado, Jeremy was polishing off his second Seven and Seven. "I think that went pretty well. The old-line guys sure do love the technology but they are hung up on that patent. I didn't predict that. If you want to pull in the new guys, we're going to need to hire some management talent. I can help, if you'd like."

"It would be nice to take this to the moon." Hank pushed his chair back and sighed.

Jeremy turned toward him and leaned in a little too close. Hank could smell the whiskey on his breath. "I'm going to get rich this decade either way. Congress just passed the Truth in Accounting Act and it is going to make me and every other accountant a fortune."

"What is the Truth in Accounting Act?"

Jeremy took a sip from his drink. "Oh, it's one of those periodic updates to our securities laws that happen every time we have a crash in the stock market. It's designed to stop companies from playing games with their accounting statements."

"Will it work?"

"Probably not." Jeremy closed his eyes.

Hank was going to let Jeremy's cynical outlook fall within the noise compared to John Smith's comment about Houdini reminding him of Synasptix. He was bursting at the seams and had to tell someone. He decided to splurge and called Janine, his sister, using the airline phone. He heard the DTMF tones as he dialed his sister's number. As he waited, there was a small bump from the turbulence; then he heard a ring, then a second ring. On the fourth ring, he assumed she wouldn't pick up.

"Hello?" He heard Janine's voice, and perked up.

"Hey, what took you so long?" Hank chided.

"I didn't recognize the number on caller ID. I was about to let it go to voicemail but I had a feeling it was you. Well, how did it go?"

Hank told her about the meeting. "It was a little bit grueling; they fired questions at me so fast."

"Whiner. My little brother can handle a few tough questions. Quit stalling; how did it go?"

"Well, John Smith, one of the partners, pulled me aside and told me Houdini reminded him of Synasptix."

There was a pause and then Janine asked, "Is that good? Who the hell is Synasptix?"

"Synasptix went public within three years of receiving funding and raised over $1 billion."

He heard Janine take a deep breath. "Did you say a billion? I knew my little brother could do it. Woo-hoo! Exactly what did the partner say? What was the intonation of his voice?"

Janine always did this. It was as if she wanted him to be a human voice recorder. "Hey, I can't talk long right now. I'm on the airplane phone and it's costing me a fortune. But I wanted to ask you if you could meet me this weekend in Iowa at Iowa State. I've got a client who is doing an experimental heart procedure on a patient.

Since you're an ICU nurse, you can probably help explain some things that they'll be doing. I'll be watching; I won't be able to ask questions while they're doing the procedure."

"Well, first, congratulations, bro. It would be great to see one of your projects at work, so to speak. Also, fun to be back in Iowa—do you think you could find some time to drive around and see Grandpa's farm? I do have the weekend off. Let me see how I can deal with the kids and I'll let you know tomorrow. And Hank," Janine paused, "I love you."

"I love you too, sis," he whispered into the phone so Jeremy wouldn't hear and cradled the handset in its holder on the seat in front of him.

Hank leaned back in his chair a little but he was too excited to sleep. He thought about all the things he needed to accomplish when he got back to the office. This wasn't the drudgery of tasks associated with a nine-to-five job; this was the excitement of completing tasks that led to infinite possibilities—the company he would build, the exciting technologies he would get to work on and maybe that twin engine Piper Aztec he and Warren had been talking about buying. He closed his eyes. What would the Magellans or Lewis and Clarks of today look like? The frontier was no longer limited to borders, and the US was the greatest country in the world.

"Was that Hank?" Mark, Janine's husband, walked into the kitchen and hugged her from behind. Janine left the phone on the counter and squeezed his arms around her middle.

"He's all excited about his meeting with the VCs." Hank wasn't married or dating anyone seriously. A person needed someone to share their emotional life. Janine knew she was that person for Hank. They had always been close, but when their parents died in a car accident during Hank's senior year in college, they had become even closer. Janine was excited for Hank but didn't want to see him get his hopes up too high. She would be there for him if things didn't work out. Hank needed—well, he needed *someone*. He had only dated one girl seriously. It was when he was working for the DOD Computer Security Threat Center in California. He had abruptly left his post seven years earlier and started Made By Man with Warren. He had never told her why.

"He also wants me to meet him up in Iowa this weekend to help him with a client. What do you think?" She leaned back against her husband's chest.

Mark released her and she sat down at the kitchen table. Mark followed her example and took a seat facing her. "What I think is that it's too soon after the accident."

"Nonsense, the doctor said I was fine." Tristan and Jess ran into the room, giggling in their Disney-print pajamas.

Jess jumped into her dad's arms and a split second later Tristan jumped into Janine's lap. "OW!" Janine's face turned white.

"Tristan," Mark said a little sharper than he meant to. "Be careful; you hurt your mama." The ten-year-old boy's smile instantly vaporized and his eyes glittered with tears.

"Okay. Off to bed. Dad will tuck you in shortly." The kids somberly padded off to their bedrooms. Mark scowled at Janine. "That is not what the doctor said."

Chapter 2

Janine Rangar-Nelson grew up near Adel, Iowa, home to picturesque covered bridges, paved brick streets, sleepy rivers, and rich black soil. Both of her parents had been teachers and she and her brother were close to their grandparents, who ran a farm outside of town. Janine had always loved to read, and when she was a girl, her favorite book was *The Diary of Anne Frank*. She had been so profoundly moved by the young girl's chronicle of hiding from and then being killed by the Nazis during WWII, it had influenced her decision to choose a career focused on healing rather than destroying. As a child, she had subjected her tabby cat, Stripes, to numerous examinations, while she and her best friend Cammie played doctor.

Eventually she had become a nurse, and currently she worked in the ICU at Jewish and taught undergrad classes at Washington University in the heart of St. Louis. Every year, the new crop of earnest and excited students reminded her of herself fifteen years prior, drawn to a calling so much bigger than one person's decision to become a nurse. Whether in a hospital, doctor's office, field tent, or care facility, helping to heal the sick was the purpose. Teaching, however, invigorated the day-to-day job of nursing for Janine. Days filled with life and death, for sure, but also with endless and mind-numbing routines and paperwork that some days could distill down to something no more important than elevating throbbing feet.

She had driven up to Iowa State today to meet her brother, Hank, and observe a new procedure that was going to be performed on some brave heart patient. She was vaguely familiar with the campus, and as she pulled into a parking lot behind a large complex that faced a day-care center, she looked at the directions her brother gave her a second time.

"Hey, I thought you'd never get here!" Janine was startled by the muffled voice outside the driver's side window and looked up into her brother's smiling face. She smiled in response, opened the car door, and slid out of her seat.

"Hey, bro! So good to see you!" Hank gave her a bear hug. Janine winced. "Careful."

"I think there's time for a quick tour before the surgery. Let's go." Hank turned and stalked off across the parking lot. Janine watched her brother's tall, muscled frame take off. "Hey! Wait up!" She checked her blonde cropped and curled hairstyle in the rearview mirror, grabbed her purse, locked the car door, and jogged in Hank's wake. "Hank, why aren't we at the hospital? They do surgeries here?"

"Hmm? Oh, it's top-secret. We're keeping things under wraps. There's adequate facilities here to do what we need." Hank kept walking at a fast clip without turning around. Janine frowned but tried to keep up with his long strides. They entered a side door to a large grey building and Janine followed him down a long hallway bordered on both sides by doors announcing doctors' offices, storage rooms, lab this-or-that, and some unmarked, closed ones as well. They finally stopped in front of some sort of reception desk. Hank's strong voice boomed in the relatively silent hall. "How's it going, my man?"

Some guy in scrubs reached across the counter and shook Hank's hand enthusiastically. He had a scruffy goatee and looked grad-student age. They exchanged pleasantries and then Hank introduced Janine. As they continued down another hall, Hank introduced her to several other people, some with titles, some not, until finally Hank turned toward her. "I think we'd better head on over there. Ready?" They continued on, Hank's sneakers squeaking on the highly buffed institutional tile floor. Janine had no idea what 'over there' meant, but suddenly she saw there were windows into operating rooms on one side of the hall. Inside the second operating room people were milling about, and Hank looked at a chart hanging outside the door. "Excellent. Looks like we showed up just in time." He preceded her into a preparation room where gowns and masks were folded and shrink-wrapped in a bin. She scrubbed her hands and arms as directed, and put on a mask and a well-worn surgical gown that was a little too long. She looked over at Hank and saw his eyes crinkling at the corners. She knew he was grinning hugely behind that mask. They entered the operating room and stood at the edge.

Janine couldn't believe they were going to allow them into the actual surgery! She looked over at the patient and took in the surgical table, the rough straps that held the patient down, and the three people bent over it. The anesthesiologist quickly placed a mask over the patient as she let out a squeal. Once the patient was out, an IV was placed in her vein.

Janine noticed that her hands and fingers were cold. There was a slight breeze blowing up and through her gown. Someone, she assumed a technician, placed a number of sensors on the patient's body, turned on some electronic devices and then she heard sharp beats coming from the machines. The beats appeared to be perfectly rhythmic. She saw a green trace, which was the electrocardiogram. However, from her angle in the room, she couldn't make out the particulars. She turned toward Hank, and he seemed to sense her gaze. He gave her a perplexed look and she pointed to the sensors measuring the patient's heart, blood pressure, and blood oxygen.

There were two people next to the patient who appeared to be the surgeons, an anesthesiologist at the head of the patient, a couple of people who were apparently nurses, and a technician. One of the surgeons swabbed the patient's chest with a tan liquid and the room smelled of rubbing alcohol. No, that wasn't right; it smelled more like turpentine and formaldehyde mixed together. Unusual. The younger of the two surgeons took a scalpel and cut along the centerline of the patient's chest. Blood started to flow from the incision. Janine felt her own hot, moist breath against her face. Next, one of the surgeons picked up a clamp and placed it on the patient's chest. There was a sharp crack as the ribs were forced open. Janine felt her stomach come up into her throat. *Don't vomit; don't vomit.* That would really be something for an experienced nurse—not surgical, it was true, but nonetheless. The sharp crack momentarily transported her back to the instant of the car crash. Janine looked away as she placed a gloved hand on her stomach in comfort. She could hear the people in the room chuckling and talking. How could they be so detached? *Get a hold of yourself.* Her stomach settled down finally and she turned to watch the surgery.

Hank tapped her on the shoulder and they moved toward the patient's feet for a better view. She could see the purple-red mass that was the patient's heart beating. The patient was clearly a child or a little person. She thought this must be some sort of new open-heart surgery. One of the surgeons seemed to be poking the heart with a long needle. In open-heart surgery, they take a vein from the leg of the patient and use it to bypass a clot in one of the arteries of the heart. The left anterior descending coronary artery, or LAD, was often called the 'widow-maker,' because if it was clogged, you died very quickly. She thought she could make out the LAD on the patient's heart. The surgeon had a needle and was threading it below the LAD. He seemed to be tying a knot in the suture material. She could feel her heart thumping in her chest as she listened to the rhythmic breathing of the patient through the oxygen mask.

She half-wished she could move in closer. It appeared that if the surgeon were to just pull on the end of the suture material, the knot would tighten around the LAD, stopping the flow of blood and causing the patient to die very quickly. *That can't be right.* The surgeons seemed unconcerned and were discussing the patient's EKG. The EKG was putting out a steady, rhythmic beat. *Odd.* She then heard the surgery team counting down from ten. The surgeon was still holding the end of the suture material. She heard one, zero, and then the surgeon pulled on one end and she could see blood draining from the patient's LAD—*Oh God, what's happening?* Janine felt dizzy and everyone's form distorted momentarily. Hank grabbed her elbow. "Take it easy. Are you all right? Hey, you're the nurse."

She caught her breath and realized she was still hearing the rhythmic beating of the EKG machine—it hadn't skipped a beat. She could see the patient's heart beating; but how was that possible? The LAD was completely sealed off. The surgeons and two nurses were all patting each other on the back and cheering. It seemed more like the display of a football team than a surgery team. This was highly irregular. Janine turned toward Hank with a quizzical expression on her face.

Hank smiled broadly at his sister's pixie face all screwed up in a stern and questioning look. He swept his hand toward the gurney. "Janine Nelson, meet Wilbur the pig." Janine gave a wan smile and looked back at the patient. Hank lowered his voice and leaned in toward her. "You have just witnessed the first experimental surgery using the angiochannelizer technique. Our hardy patient here, Wilbur, has survived despite a complete blockage of his LAD. Of course, there is much more to do. Before they can test this procedure on people with weak hearts, they've got to automate the process. Failure to properly time things—" Janine looked back to Hank as he shrugged. "Well, it could result in death."

She punched his arm, hard.

Janine turned back to Wilbur even as Hank hooked her elbow and pulled her into the anteroom where the surgical staff was already cleaning up.

"Will Wilbur live?" Janine asked hopefully. Hank rubbed his arm where she had walloped him.

"No. He'll be dead within the month."

"But how do you—" Janine looked back toward Wilbur's EKG. The picture was strong.

Hank continued. "Wilbur's bacon. The FDA requires he be euthanized within thirty days. The old guy over there," whispered Hank, "that's Dr. Earl Cody, a retired cardiothoracic surgeon. Dr. Cody has spent years in this area developing new devices for open-heart surgery. He's like the Steve Jobs of surgical tools. He'd still be but, on his sixtieth birthday, he was working the ER when a crazed drug addict came in and started threatening people and slashing the air with a ten-inch bowie knife. As the guy slashed at one of the young ER nurses, Earl here rammed him with his shoulder. There was a fight and the addict's knife severed the tendons in Earl's right hand." Hank let the implications hang there between them. "Now he focuses full-time on his inventing career."

One of the nurses walked up to Hank. "Will Simon. You must be Hank's sister," he said, and stuck out his hand.

"Here's my big sis, Janine. Janine, Will is part of the company. We're partners in this little endeavor."

"Well, what did you think, Hank?" Will asked.

Janine interrupted, "I'm a little fuzzy on what just happened."

Will turned toward her. "Dr. Cody came to me with the problem of heart patients who died or needed additional surgery within six months of a stent, angioplasty, or bypass. He had a theory that arteries of the heart too small for any of these procedures were getting blocked and causing problems. Other people had tried to solve this by having the heart grow new arteries, which takes at least a month. Earl was looking for something with a more immediate result." Will smiled. He was tall and appeared to be in his early sixties. He removed his surgical cap and ruffled his dark hair, shot through with grey. "We worked on it for a while and then brought in Hank to help us out with some engineering issues." He spoke quickly and in elated tones, clearly excited about his subject and the success of the surgery.

"So this solves those problems?" Janine was interested.

"Yes, the angiochannelizer process provides immediate blood flow to the heart, as you saw when we tied off Wilbur's artery. It was amazing, don't you think?"

Janine felt a little overwhelmed. "I get how Hank can help Dr. Cody. What is your role—I mean, what's your background?"

"I'm an electrical engineer. Spent my life working in the aerospace industry. It's my job to define the procedure and build a machine to automate the process."

Hank took Janine's arm and looked at Will. "We need to tabulate the data and get out of here. You know they're charging us by the hour for this place."

The three founders and Janine met at a small bar and grill. They ordered barbeque and a pitcher of beer. Janine poured them all a glass of beer and proposed a toast, "To Wilbur," and Will, Earl, and Hank joined in. "To Wilbur!" They clinked glasses.

Will wiped his mouth. "I feel like I just aced a physics final in college." He took another big slug of beer. "Especially after our first surgery. How could those technicians not know that you shouldn't use blood from a euthanized pig for a transfusion?"

"True." Hank slapped Earl on the back. "I will never forget the look on Earl's face when the pig's heart stopped."

Earl winced, not with pain but at the uncomfortable memory of the event. "I should have checked on that before the surgery, but how could you anticipate such a boneheaded thing? I am so grateful you guys immediately made the connection between the transfusion and the pig's heart stopping."

Will looked at Earl. "What was amazing is that after we got the technician to pull out the transfusion, you were able to save the first Wilbur's life." With that, they toasted

EWE Technology, the name of their company, and a server showed up with their food.

Janine ate silently, watching avidly as the partners let go of the adrenaline which had surely been flowing heavily during the experiment. She looked at Hank, his face alive and happy. She didn't know half of what all he was involved with, but she was glad to have been here today and share in his success with yet another company. He was such a great catch for some intelligent, high-spirited woman. Why didn't he have someone to share all this success with by now? Janine wiped her fingers on a napkin and took a swig of her beer.

She took stock. She loved her husband deeply. She had two of the greatest kids anybody could want. She and Hank had a deep bond no one could break. Jessica and Tristan were close to their uncle; maybe in part because they didn't have grandparents. She felt a little sad being so close to where they grew up and thinking about her own great childhood and being close to her own grandma and grandpa. On the weekends during the winter, Grandpa would come into town and pick her up early in his beat-up Ford pickup. They would go off down the road as Hank watched from the living room window. At the local coffee shop, Grandpa would order her a hot cocoa while he drank coffee with the other farmers. They talked farm shop until spring and planting came around. Then they'd be working from before sunup to well past dark and not have much time to gossip like old hens. The day came when she was to stay with Grandma and Mom, and Grandpa would ride off to the café with Hank on Saturday morning. But it had been their special time together, and later morphed into pitchforking hay, learning to drive the tractor, and even scooping shit or dumping buckets of sop into the troughs. She'd been almost a teenager before she realized what she was doing was work. She looked up and caught Hank grinning at her. She knew he was looking forward to driving over to the old farm this afternoon, maybe more than she was.

Chapter 3

Hank opened the door of his rental and stepped out into crisp air and the faint smell of wood smoke. He heard Janine's car turn off onto the gravel road, tires crunching and churning through the gritty limestone, and then roar up the drive. The slap of a screen door turned his focus to the century-old farmhouse about fifty feet from the drive.

"Just in time, big guy!" Mark Nelson was sporting a huge grin and quickly moving toward Hank as Janine's car slid to a stop next to Hank's. "How'd everything go? Success?"

"Success. What's for dinner?" Hank slapped Mark on the back and gave him a quick hug. "Hey, is that flour all over your hands? Did you get any on my shirt?" He craned a look over his shoulder and wiped the residue away. Mark laughed.

"Will you have my famous chili or clam chowder?"

"Chili."

"Chowder!" Hank and Janine responded at the same time. Hank looked over at his sister as she alighted from the car. The soft dinging of the alarm abruptly ceased as she shut the door.

Mark brushed past Hank and pulled Janine into his arms gently. "Hey kiddo, tired?"

Janine gave a slight shake, blonde curls tumbling forward as she leaned into Mark's embrace. "Nope, nope, all good."

Hank wondered what that was about. He rounded the side of the car, popped the trunk and pulled out his duffle. "Where are the kids?" he asked, and walked quickly to the house.

He opened the screen door, strode purposefully through the kitchen and dumped his bag on the couch. His niece and nephew were engrossed in a game on the computer. Tristan turned at the sound of the screen door closing in the other room. His face brightened as he saw his uncle. "Uncle Hank! Uncle Hank! 'Bout time! We're hungry!"

Hank walked over to the kids and tousled Tristan's soft, board-straight mass of hair. He tugged on Jessica's thick ponytail of curls. "Hey!" Jess ducked her head into her shoulders, but otherwise remained glued to the screen.

"Homemade rolls! Mmm, they smell delicious. You're the best, honey!" Hank heard Janine exclaim in the kitchen, as he belatedly took in the aroma wafting through the main floor of the house. "I need a beer. Is the fridge stocked?" Hank asked the room in general and turned back to the kitchen. He crossed the room quickly and unlatched the handle of the ancient but reliable Crosley fridge, fondly remembered from his grandparents' days. He felt an icy blast as he reached in, grabbing two bottles of beer with one hand, a third with the other, and put his shoulder into closing the heavy door. "You're the best, honey," he mocked in a high falsetto.

Janine wrinkled her nose at Hank as he popped the caps off the beers with the old Coca-Cola bottle opener screwed into the wall above the trashcan. The caps plunked softly into the bin. As he crossed the room to Janine and Mark, he noticed the floor was gleaming wood...and new. "Hey! New floor. Gorgeous!" Hank then scanned the rest of the room and realized the counters were all some sort of interesting stone illuminated by understated under-cabinet lighting "New cabinets too." He handed the couple their beers and saw the pleased looks on their faces.

"We've been a little busy ourselves, Hank." Janine gestured to the old Viking stove in the corner.

"Wow. All cleaned up. And that's right! As it was, we would have smelled burnt rolls when we came in. You fixed it up!"

Mark beamed. "It wasn't that hard, just needed some TLC."

Hank took a swig of his beer and appreciated other new details in the kitchen. "Nice, guys."

"Hank, Janine has had some appointments." Janine looked at Mark, but he kept his gaze on Hank.

"Okay. What's up?" Hank said warily, and took another swig.

Janine gestured to the kitchen table under a bank of windows, overlooking the storm cellar. "It was just a checkup, you know, following the accident. Anyway, there are some concerns. We're set up—"

"Wait. What?" Hank interrupted. "I thought you were healing and everything was ship-shape?" He realized he didn't have the details, and by the look on Janine's face, she was being patient with him. "Jesus."

"We were a little taken aback as well. But the bruising on my torso is not healing well. As a precaution, I'm set up with a specialist early next week. No big deal. I'm just a little tired and these bruises," Janine covered her upper torso protectively with her hand and Hank winced.

"Damn, Janine. You didn't have to come to the experiment this weekend. I wondered why you looked so... Jesus!"

Janine smiled. "Wouldn't have missed it for the world. I'm fine, Hank. We're on top of this; please don't worry. Mark's more than I can handle on that score." She looked lovingly toward her husband of fifteen years. She abruptly stood and headed over to the living room.

"Hey kids, let's get washed up and eat before the rolls get cold and we have to throw them at Uncle Hank's head!" She grinned as she heard her kids rousing from the computer and strategizing for a potential attack.

The kids were settled in bed with their books and Hank felt the energy of the day, but the news about Janine nagged at him. A lot of good progress with EWE, and the possibilities for this technology to rock the medical community made him want to shout the way you would over a touchdown in the last seconds of the fourth quarter. Now he just wanted to take it easy and lazily unwind. He hoped Janine might join him on the porch but he could overhear Janine and Mark's low buzz of conversation in the next room. He decided to head downstairs and out to the porch. Hank grabbed his jacket, descended the stairs, ancient treads groaning and creaking with every footfall. He slipped out the back-door carefully, without letting the screen door bang. The night was clear, so he dragged an old rocker nestled in the corner of the large porch over to the stairs where he could rock and watch the stars. The night was still, only the occasional rustling of brittle leaves still left on the trees. He savored the quiet.

"Hey, can I play?" Janine's hushed voice startled him.

"God, do you always sneak up on people like that?" He hopped up and dragged the other rocker over to his and Janine sunk into it. They rocked companionably for some time, both contemplating the sky. "Shoot. We're just old fogies like Grandpa and Grandma."

"Hmmm." They continued to rock. "What's the number one thing you regret?" Janine's question hung in the air between them as they continued to rock their chairs slowly back and forth.

"I don't know. I don't like to think about stuff like that. Why don't you go first? What regrets could you possibly have, goodie two-shoes?"

She heard rather than saw his smile. "Lots of stuff. Not being able to say goodbye to Mom and Dad. Why I married Mark—" Hank stopped the chair on a forward rock. "What?"

Janine chuckled softly. "Nothing. More like a confession, I guess. I accepted his proposal, encouraged it even. But I didn't feel about him the way he felt about me. You were still in school; our grandparents were in their 80s. I needed to feel secure. Mark was older and already successful. He was ready to settle down, raise a family. But he also understood my need to have a career. I liked that he got the partner bit. I wasn't expected to do the entire childrearing. We'd be a team. He also doted on me. I needed that. Hell, we lost our parents in one moment, Hank. I missed them. I needed a lot of comfort, and you needed to escape."

"I can't imagine you, of all people, not completely sure."

"But then, we got down to our lives and one day it was just there. When Jess came along, well, there was just so much love and we had made this family. I remember looking at her when she was a baby and thinking, 'I'm determined to be at your wedding, little one.' Okay, your turn. I have always wanted to know why you don't talk much about your time in San Diego with the Department of Defense. Is it because the mission involved killing people?"

"No."

Janine pulled one leg up onto the chair, settling in for a good talk. "C'mon. What about their families?"

"What about them?" The utter clarity and innocence in his gaze was ruthless.

Janine shivered with the knowledge of it.

Chapter 4

"What the hell happened with the university?" Hank leaned back in his chair, rubbing the back of his neck.

It wasn't like Hank to snap at people. Warren put a check mark on his agenda, and dropped the pen onto his pad. "You know university types; they are always looking for donations. They wanted us to 'donate' ten percent of our time."

Hank frowned. "What did you tell them?"

His right leg was bouncing up and down on the ball of his foot. The habit was common for him, but when excited, nervous, or upset, he bounced faster; and right now, he was bouncing as fast as Warren had ever seen. Warren hesitated. "I told them that I would have to take it up with our management committee." He pushed his glasses further up the bridge of his nose.

"What do you think they'll do if we say no?" Hank's tone was confrontational. "I really don't want to walk away from this one. We could be a part of a revolution in remote medicine." Warren was fixated on Hank's bouncing leg. Normally, he thought Hank did this because the world just didn't move fast enough for him. It was as if Hank's mind was always three steps ahead of the rest of the world. But today something was clearly bothering him.

"We have a few more criteria than that for bonus work."

Warren searched Hank's face. "What the hell is bothering you?"

Hank slumped in his chair; his bobbing knee stilled abruptly. "I'm sorry. Janine is having complications from the car accident." Peggy poked her head into the small lab that did double duty as a conference room. "Hey guys, I've got Will Evans on the line wanting to talk with you."

"Great." Warren looked back at Hank. "Today EWE met with MedCon. Peggy, we'll just take the call in here. Thank you." Peggy popped back out as quickly as she had inserted herself. Warren leaned across the table and pushed a button on the conference speakerphone.

Warren waited for Hank to take the lead, but he said nothing. "Hi Will. I've got you on speaker. Hank is here with me, so don't say anything bad about him."

"Hey guys. Just wrapped up with MedCon. We're cooling our heels in the Boston Harbor Hotel while we wait for our flight back out."

"How's the chowder?" Warren asked. Hank didn't seem to be paying attention.

"Don't know yet. Just ordered it. Earl is here with me as well. They paid for our flights out and accommodations last night. Very VIP."

Warren leaned in. "A procedure that ensures no change in heart rate or EKG, what else could you ask for? My crystal ball says there's a few more of those paid trips in your future. MedCon is huge, right?"

"They dominate the worldwide stent market. That market brings in over a billion dollars a year. We are a natural fit." Will was talking so fast, he had run out of breath.

"That's awesome, Will." Warren noticed a slight grin on Hank's face. "So how'd it go?"

"We met with three principals. Zachary Switch, who is the head of the stents group. I was surprised to see how young he was. He started out in pharma sales out of college and he's now in charge of a group that's worth five billion a year. Hell, he doesn't look like he shaves his peach fuzz yet." Will chuckled at his own joke but he felt the years of the company trying to make it in his bones. "Then there was a senior doctor who asked most of the questions."

"What did he ask?" Hank interjected.

"Just a sec—I'll get to that. There was somebody else—I think it was head of marketing, right Earl?" There was a pause while Will conferred with Earl. "Yeah, somebody Johnson. He was mostly quiet. In charge of taking notes, I guess." Will chuckled again.

Will continued. "I thought we would spend some of the time on the costs and timelines associated with human trials and dealing with the FDA approval process. But they were savvy on how many we would need for our trials and what kinda cash we would need to get through FDA."

"What are those numbers; do you mind sharing?" Warren asked.

"Not at all. We need about three thousand people for the overall program, and the cost will be five million to implement and deal with the FDA."

Warren whistled low. "Not for just any sawbones, is it?"

Will chuckled yet again. "Nope. I imagine I'll be completely gray by the time we're through this, unless we sell out sooner. Anyway, we went through the procedure performed on Wilbur and the results. The doctor asked us about angiogenesis. Specifically, that there wasn't enough time for it to occur during the procedure and he wondered if the suture completely blocked the LAD."

"Wait a minute. What's angiogenesis?" Warren asked.

Will answered. "Angiogenesis is the process whereby the body creates new blood vessels when tissue is damaged."

"We explained that we are not relying on angiogenesis." Dr. Cody was now on the phone. "Angiogenesis relies on cauterizing the heart tissue next to the channels. My colleague at MedCon was not convinced that our procedure would not create heat due to the friction caused by punching the channels. Of course, in our case, the act of punching does not damage the surrounding tissue. Since no cauterization occurs, blood flows immediately to the heart."

Will took the phone back. "The good doctor got really interested at that point in the presentation and frequently leaned over to GQ head of stents to explain things, I guess. Made me a little nervous. What do you guys think about a company having the policy to never sign nondisclosures?"

Hank picked up his cup of tea, the smell permeating his nostrils as he took a sip—*damn, it went cold.* He felt wary. "Did they ask about patents?"

"Yeah. We told them we had one that hadn't yet issued." Will sounded confident. "Mr. Switch seemed concerned about whether it had been published yet. I told him I didn't think so. He seemed to be happy about that, I guess."

"The application is more important than any nondisclosure agreement, I'd guess. I've heard a lot of the big boys don't sign nondisclosures. They're big, they've got lots of irons in the fire, and they get sued—a lot." The phone was quiet for a few moments. "Will, what happened then?"

"They loved it! They want equity and they'll fund the trials! They want the exclusive right to market the technology!"

Hank looked up at Warren and they both grinned big and relaxed back in their chairs. "That's awesome, Will. Earl. What kind of funding for exclusivity?"

Will was laughing now. "Shit, that's all over the map. Anywhere from ten to a hundred million, that Switch guy was talking about. Had to get their venture people in on it—I don't know—I couldn't really listen after I heard a hundred million!"

Earl and Will ordered individual bottles of champagne on the flight home and toasted EWE. Dr. Earl Cody was in his seventies now and not in good health; in fact, he had already had open-heart surgery and had two stents implanted. He could benefit from the angiochannelizer. Earl had confided in Will that he hoped the procedure could be developed and tested on him before he died. He felt the bubbles of the champagne tickle his tongue, and after a couple of sips, he felt warm, cozy and a little tired. He leaned his seat back, closed his eyes and he thought of his wife, who had died a couple of years earlier. *Ruth, it's finally going to pay off. Remember how you scolded me for waking up in the middle of the night over and over again thinking about my patients who died a couple of months after open-heart surgery. There had to be something we were all missing that caused them to die. I was haunted by this. You would tell me life and death were ultimately in the hands of God but that seemed like giving up to me. As you soothed me to sleep, I knew deep down that this was within my power to solve.* Will noticed the semi-rhythmic breathing of Earl. He was finishing up an email to Hank. He wrote, "You know I sold Pandre on the idea of one more entrepreneurial venture four years ago and seventy thousand dollars ago. After our last startup, she was done." Pandre was Will's wife. "Sure, it seems like a lot of money but if you added in taxes and our lost wages, it was a good, but not a great return. It would have been an excellent return if the IRS hadn't stolen fifty percent. The IRS argued that the gain from the company should be considered ordinary income. If not that, then we had fraudulently declared the proceeds as dividends instead of income. After three years of arguing with the IRS— we had won on most points, but the amount we paid the lawyers ate up the difference. But today is truly a great day and I'm just looking forward. They say the deal will take three or four months to get cooking. I can wait that long, considering all the time we've put into everything. I just hope Earl can wait it out too. We'll call you tomorrow when we get organized and fill in the details. Thanks for all your help, Hank." Will got out of his email program and shut the laptop as the flight attendant asked over the intercom for all electronic devices to be turned off.

Will leaned back in his chair; the adrenaline of presenting the dream he had worked on for four years was beginning to wear off. He raised his champagne glass and gave a silent toast to Pandre for her support. She had found a good job in the medical industry after they sold their previous company. They had a couple of young kids and had hoped that the sale of their previous company would've fully funded their kids' college funds but it wasn't meant to be. Pandre had worked her ass off since then to support the kids and his new entrepreneurial venture. If MedCon came through, EWE was finally going to be their big payoff. He imagined visiting their kids on parents' weekend, walking the campus as the leaves were falling and discussing their classes in physics. He drained his glass and closed his eyes.

Chapter 5

"Director Morris! Director!" Stanford Morris slowed his gait and put his hand behind him, as if he was running a relay. His secretary was going to hand him a sheaf of useless reports and an itinerary for the meeting. He could hear her short legs pop against her skirt as she attempted to keep up.

"You sound out of breath, Lilly." Stanford looked over his shoulder quickly and noticed his secretary's efficient graying bun had let loose with a froth of tiny, rioting curls around her pinched and drawn face. She scurried closer in answer to his raised eyebrows, and stuffed another insidious document into his waiting hand, narrowly avoiding collision with his shoulder. He knew she would be mortified if that happened.

Lilly frowned and pointed to the last document he was holding. "Dr. Gorman from the NSF has already arrived.

He's wearing a bowtie, should be easy to spot." He nodded impatiently.

"What else?" he asked.

"Director, you asked for this meeting in order to show the NSF how far along the Patent and Trademark Office has come in increasing quality under your experienced tutelage."

"Just so." He nodded in affirmation.

"If we impress Dr. Gorman, we stand a greater chance of snagging Congress's collective ear. This will look good for the PTO, and if I may say so—for you, Director." Lily protruded her lower lip and blew some frizz off her forehead.

They reached a set of double doors, and he consciously increased his pace as he entered the conference room. He stopped abruptly and frowned slightly at the audiovisual goons who were still working on the projection system. *I do not have time for this.* "Lilly, why are they still in here?" Lilly followed his pointing finger to the head of the conference table and took off like a retriever earnestly wanting to please her trainer. Stanford Morris frowned at the papers still in his hand and unwillingly followed Lilly.

"This should have been completed an hour ago, this is an important meeting and you need to be gone!" Stanford tuned out the shrill voice of his secretary and turned to scan the human contents of the conference room. Usual suck-ups and suck-ups-in-training, he noted. Ah, there was that buttoned-up bitch, Tamara. He felt his groin uncomfortably tighten. *Easy, easy there stallion. The day is just beginning.* He turned back the other way, saw a pudgy man with a bowtie in the back of the room talking to Dan Reily and the papers in his hand fell like stones onto the table. *What the fuck is Reily doing talking to the head of the NSF?* He gazed in horror as Reily mauled Gorman's hand in a brutal shake.

He overheard Reily say, "Really? I thought all the MDs were over at NIH." Dan had a big stupid grin on his face as if he had one-upped someone. He had to break this up before Dan spoiled everything. He started to walk over but Tamara stepped in his way.

"Mr. Morris, since Dan Reily is here should we have him present the information on…" He looked over Tamara's shoulder and heard Reily say something about Fermat's Last Theorem. Gorman looked bored—great. Tamara leaned her head into his field of view. "So, should we have Dan present…?"

He cut her off. "NO," he said a little too loudly. Several people turned to look at him and Tamara looked horrified. "I'm sorry. Let's keep Dan out of this, shall we." He tried to step around her and heard Dr. Gorman saying, "I can't imagine why someone at the patent office would be interested in Fermat's Last Theorem," in a bored nasal voice. He felt a tap on his shoulder and turned to see his secretary.

"The audiovisual guys say it will..." But he tuned her out so he could hear whether Reily was upsetting Dr. Gorman. "Well, us bumpkins at the patent office," Reily was saying to Gorman. Definitely not a good sign. He broke free of his secretary and heard, "occasionally work on cutting-edge cryptography, which just so happens. . ."

He interrupted Dan as he held out his hand. "Deputy Director Gorman, I'm Stanford Morris, Director of the Patent Office." He purposely stood so that Gorman would have to turn away from Dan.

"It is so nice to meet you, Congressman Morris." He felt a stab of pain in his stomach. Every time someone reminded him of his short tenure in Congress, it amplified how far he had fallen. He had hoped and lobbied for an important position, like head of the EPA or the National Labor Relations Board, but the administration had given him the patent office instead. *Lemonade,* he reminded himself. "Likewise. I think we are about to get started. Let's sit over here," and he gestured Gorman to a seat near the front along the huge mahogany conference table.

He turned to Lilly and instinctively she caught his eye and he gave her a wrap-up gesture with his hand.

"Excuse me everyone." Lilly could command a room when she wanted to. Loud and decisive, just as he taught her. She'd be gone the day she tried out that tone with him, however.

Dan ambled over to the left side of the table and Steve followed slowly, clearly irritated that the remaining seat was by this Big Foot. "Joel, do you want to lead this morning?" Morris asked. The show needed to get on the road. Joel passed out the agenda. Stanford scanned it. Printed in italics at the top was: *Stanford Morris—Under Secretary of Commerce for Intellectual Property and Director of the United States Patent and Trademark Office.* Everyone knew where you stood in the pecking order when it was Congressman Morris; this sounded like some two-bit position from the Byzantine Empire. Joel laid out the agenda for the meeting and then introduced Tamara, who was to present the ongoing efforts to upgrade the training of PTO employees.

"This chart shows that the number of employees graduating from the Examiner College increased by ten percent in the last quarter. If you refer to the next chart, you will see that the quality of examination by graduates of the college is at the same level as patent examiners with three years of experience." Stanford looked over at Dr. Gorman to gage his reaction. Gorman caught his eye and nodded approvingly. *Shit, no one introduced Dr. Bowtie. The whole point of this meet and greet is to convince the NSF that the patent office's quality had improved. Their report to Congress last year on low patent quality damaged the PTO's reputation.*

Stanford rose from his chair. "Excuse me, I am so sorry, I forgot to introduce Dr. Steve Gorman, Deputy Director of the National Science Foundation. Steve, we are honored to have you attend our quarterly performance review." He felt his face heating; Reily always put him off his game.

"Thank you for inviting me. The NSF is aware of the important work that the patent office performs in applied sciences and for garage-shop inventors. Our interest is that the patent office continues its mission and that patents don't interfere with the work of fundamental science funded by the National Science Foundation." Stanford looked toward Reily and saw him screw up his face at the garage-shop remark.

Stanford gave Gorman an approving smile. *Mr. Ph.D. over there probably thinks all important scientific work is funded by the NSF or related agencies—that the PTO hands out patents with gold ribbons around them that have about as much meaning as the gold stars one's piano teacher hands out. Well there are always points to agree on.*

"Let's hear from Alan on our progress to ensure quality patents," Morris said. Gorman had seemed to appreciate the importance of the training at the Examiner College. Proving to the NSF that real changes had been made would only enhance his authority and possibly ingratiate an option here or there. Alan started, "Here, a number of charts show the quality of patents issued has improved across all technology groups at the PTO. Incorrect determinations of allowance..." Gorman was frowning. Alan's charts showed immense improvement at the PTO.

Gorman piped in. "It appears from your charts that you are only measuring Type I errors and ignoring Type II errors."

Type I, Type II errors —who cares? Stanford noticed an ironic smile on Dan Reily's face. As head of the 'appeals group' Reily was sure he was outside the normal chain of command at the PTO.

Alan was stammering and his face was turning red as he attempted to answer Gorman's question. Stanford looked at Gorman and saw he was not buying Alan's answer. He frowned. Alan was one of the brightest guys on the staff. There was an awkward silence and Reily piped in with a chuckle. "It appears that Dr. Gorman is not following your 'rejection equals quality' policy either."

He was always pulling shit like this. In quality review meetings, he would say, 'Why don't we just reject all patent applications, and then you will have 100% quality?' Now was not the right time.

Everyone in the room was looking at Dr. Gorman. "Please continue," Gorman allowed magnanimously.

"In the NSF report on patent quality last year," Alan held up a copy of the report, "the recommendations pointed to the problem of poor-quality patents being issued. Our quality programs were specifically designed to address this concern."

"You make some excellent points." Gorman smiled condescendingly, as though Alan was a particularly slow child.

Alan breathed a sigh of relief. "This chart shows how our examiners are faring when an inventor files an appeal. You can see—"

Gorman interrupted again. "This data seems to confirm that there is a problem with Type II errors."

Reily grinned that odious Cheshire cat smile, undercutting his authority in front of the NSF. *You don't become Under Secretary of Commerce for Intellectual Property and Director of the United States Patent and Trademark Office without understanding pecking order. This cock will be limping out of the barnyard, and soon.*

Unsure, Alan looked at Stanford. *Here we are, working our asses off to improve quality and Gorman is like a skipping record. Time to take control.* "We have a limited amount of time to get through this material, so let's move on." Stanford looked at Alan pointedly. Alan presented several more charts and wrapped up the meeting. The rest of the meeting was an annoying buzz. The wrap-up took forever.

Morris looked at his watch. It was an instinctive move he'd adopted while in college. He really had nothing on his calendar for later that afternoon, but it always served to cut things off and make it look like you had somewhere important to be. Leaving the room, he walked briskly to his large corner office. "Lilly, can you have Dan Reily meet with me immediately?" Not waiting for her reply, he walked into his office, closed the door and flopped down on the leather sofa, which flanked the wall perpendicular to his desk. A dull headache was beginning to form behind his eyes, and he massaged his temples, practicing some breathing exercises learned at a yoga class. Things began to calm down. Tamara entered his thoughts. She was not particularly beautiful, but there wasn't much selection at the patent office and he had an irrational desire to see the prissy bitch begging him to satisfy her. *She'd be on her knees in that tight blue suit she wears, with her blouse unbuttoned revealing those full breasts she's so stingy with. She'd crawl toward him with a seductive smile*—BUZZ. "Mr. Reily is here to see you." Lilly's shrill voice made him wince. *Danny Boy is prompt today, well, well.* Stanford reluctantly got up and moved to the chair behind his desk. "Show Mr. Reily in." He snapped the button on his phone.

Dan was a big man. It was widely known at the patent office that Dan had played football at a small Division I school and still managed to graduate in four years with honors in physics. He went on to get a master's degree in electrical engineering and graduate from Georgetown Law School using the education reimbursement available from the patent office. He was considered very bright but not very political. *No shit,* Stanford thought. Before Dan could sit down, Morris asked, "What was that all about in there?"

Dan smirked. "In statistics, a Type I error is the incorrect rejection—"

"That is not what I mean," he interrupted, frowning.

Dan casually sat down in Morris's guest chair, leaned back and pulled the other chair over with his right foot. Then he propped his right foot on the chair and waited.

The insolence of that gesture is appalling; and anyway, didn't his mother teach him to keep his feet off the furniture? Deciding to ignore the offensive gesture, Stanford continued. "We have a problem." He paused for about fifteen seconds, leaning back in his chair with his elbows resting on the armrests, and steepled his fingers together. When it was obvious Dan was not going to say anything, he leaned forward in his chair. "You obviously know how hard we are all working to increase the quality of patents being issued." Dan nodded noncommittally. "Our press release will show quality is up at least ten percent in the last quarter and up over thirty percent for the year. But the failure of the appeals group to uphold the decisions of the PTO makes us look like fools. Good thing Alan didn't point THAT out in the meeting, hmmm?"

"Mmm-hmm," Dan weighed in finally.

Stanford continued, "It looks bad when the appeals group is overturning our decisions more than fifty percent of the time." There was a pregnant pause as Dan failed to respond. "Again, what are we going to do about that?" Reily continued to be silent, so Stanford decided to prod. "Danny Boy?"

Dan pulled his foot down off the chair and leaned forward, resting his right hand on Stanford's desk. He would have Lilly polish that sweaty print off the minute Reily was out of his office. *Pig.* He looked pointedly at Reily's hand resting there.

"Well, perhaps your expectation that the allowance rates are too high is wrong. Actually, no perhaps about it—your quality policy is nonsense, which is why you looked like a fool in front of the NSF guy." Dan struck the desk for emphasis. "If you want my advice, you should quit intimidating the examiners into arbitrarily rejecting patent applications. Either way, my job is to determine if an invention deserves a patent under the law, not based on some arbitrary allowance rate. Your policy is killing the dreams of hundreds of thousands of entrepreneurs, keeping them from obtaining funding, denying inventors their property rights and due process, stifling employment and damaging the economy."

"You know, Dan, your raises and promotions all depend on my evaluation of your job performance." There was another long pause and Stanford said, "Well?"

"I'm sorry, I didn't hear a question. I might have heard a threat, and I don't respond well to threats. You're a political appointee, without the desire or the brains to understand the inventions being reviewed. You have no understanding of patent law. You seem to believe it is just as political and arbitrary as criminal law back in North Carolina." Dan stood, and his chair slid on the polished wood floor loudly. "WE don't have a problem; you do. I will not be part of a conspiracy to turn the patent office into a political ping-pong ball." Dan turned and strode purposefully out of the office, firmly shutting the door behind him.

Chapter 6

"Why are these doctor's offices in hospitals always so damned cold?" Janine looked at Mark for confirmation as he shrugged off his jacket and helped her slip her arms through the sleeves. She shuddered involuntarily. "Why didn't I wear pants today?"

Mark put his arm around her and stared expectantly at the receptionist behind the glass window. He absently wondered if it was bulletproof. "I told you to grab your coat as we headed out the door."

"I know you did. I was...distracted. I'm like Tristan. How much longer?" The last remark came out in a low whine. Mark chuckled lowly, the rumble soothing. Janine adjusted closer despite the sharp angles and cold metal of the armrest.

"Mrs. Nelson?" Janine started, rose quickly from her chair and moved forward to the waiting room door. "Right this way, please." Mark reluctantly followed.

"It appears that Janine has some sort of blood clotting disease but we're still doing tests. We have run a PT-INR and a PTT tests. They show Janine has a rare genetic disease that makes her prone to blood clots." The internist placed a folder in front of Janine. She scooted closer in her chair on the other side of the desk, opened the cover and leafed through a few pages of results.

Mark waited until she finished. "How is this treated? How does she get better?"

The doctor waited until Janine looked up. "This particular type of thrombocytosis is genetic. However, Mrs. Nelson, your condition has been exacerbated by the recent trauma to your sternum and upper torso when you had the accident.

"We have medications to thin the blood and reduce clotting. Many do well with this treatment. There is an oral medication as well as a shot you will take subcutaneously." The doctor waited a few moments for this information to sink in. "We will train you to properly administer the shots twice a day at first."

"I'm an ICU nurse," Janine said to the folder as she closed the cover and straightened the file.

The doctor nodded. "We'll map out a schedule for the treatment, but first, we'll do more testing including a CT and MRI to look more closely at the internal damage."

"How—" Mark cleared his throat. "Is this a risky condition? What are we worried about here?"

"Blood clots." Janine looked at Mark. "I have an increased chance of them occurring."

"Is there any chance you're pregnant? Should we first test for that?"

"No. I'm at the beginning of my cycle. I'm on birth control. I guess you'll want me off of that." She smiled wanly up into the doctor's face.

"Yes."

"What are the long-term risks here? What could happen?" Mark put his arm around Janine's shoulder, and was struck by how pale she looked.

The doctor began writing something on a prescription pad. "We worry about heart failure, stroke. You will need to be on the thinners probably for the rest of your life. There are some specialists I recommend you see. We need to get on this quickly. I've already made some arrangements…"

Janine felt a roaring in her ears. She could see Mark out of the corner of her eye, nodding and making notes on the folder. Suddenly, the roaring stopped.

"Thank you Dr. Eddy. We'll fill these here at the hospital and head over to the clinic." She looked at her watch and stood. Mark stayed seated, looking as though he wanted to ask more questions. "Mark. Honey, c'mon, let's go."

Stanford Morris stared at the door, strangling the shaft of his Green Innovation Initiative Award, personally presented to him by the President. He calmed a little and decided not to hurl the glass globe. He had had it up to here with two-bit know-it-alls telling him how to run his agency.

He tugged uncomfortably at his scratchy shirt collar. The cleaner had used too much starch again. His wife used to do that too. *I am surrounded by incompetents.* Stanford removed the fine linen handkerchief from the breast pocket of his suit coat and buffed the edge of his gleaming mahogany desk, recently marred by the blunt fingers of his *current* head of appeals.

He looked at his watch and saw the day was drawing to a close. Fortunately, the evening was just beginning and there was an opportunity to turn the day around. He had a dinner date with lovely Betty Jo Lurie. A savvy DC lobbyist, Betty Jo was a brunette bombshell with curves in all the right places and a razor-sharp legal mind. These days she didn't often sharpen it on judicial matters; she spent time getting everything she could for the pit bulls of big pharma. Curious why she was interested in the PTO, Stanford mused. She mostly wooed the senators and goons over at the FDA. No matter, he was looking forward to her honing in on him. He was the head of an important agency, was he not? And a former representative from the powerful state of North Carolina. Perhaps she knew something was in the wind to groom him for senator.

Stanford arrived at his upscale Georgian townhome, in the fashionable West End of DC. He tore off the offending shirt, discarded the rest of his clothing and turned on the shower. The hot water felt good. He leaned against a wall of the shower and let the water hit his head and roll down his back. He wondered if Betty was one of those women with a Brazilian wax. He imagined her beautiful naked body spread out on his bed. He heard the pipes clanking and felt a pulse of cold water that brought him out of his daydream.

Stanford toweled off quickly, and decided what to wear. They were going to Georgia Brown's, a low country Southern cuisine restaurant in the heart of DC. He always found it strange that even though the food was low country, the dress codes were not. He pulled out a thousand-dollar, dark blue, custom-made suit and a heavily starched white shirt but decided on a whim to wear a Jerry Garcia tie.

He hailed a taxi and arrived at the restaurant five minutes after eight. It was a glorious fall evening with just a slight nip in the air. The scent of garlic and butter wafted out the front door to greet him along with Betty Jo. She smiled slowly in greeting and hooked her arm around his elbow. Her warm body canted toward him just slightly and Stanford softened against the first warm human contact of the callous day. This seemed to be one of the gifts she had; no matter whether you showed up a half an hour early or an hour late she always seemed to arrive at exactly the same time. You never had to wait for her or feel she had been waiting for you. She was wearing a sleek gold silk charmeuse dress with a flippy hemline that played about her nice knees. She had on a navy blue worsted wool jacket. The maître d' held the door to the restaurant open for them as he asked, "Reservations?"

"Congressman Stanford Morris." The sound of Betty Jo's husky voice sent shockwaves through Stanford's torso and further down, he was surprised to feel. Even though she would be paying, or more correctly, her clients would be paying, he imagined she always made reservations in whomever's name was in her current sights. The maître d' escorted them to a booth at the back of the restaurant. Betty Jo took off her blazer, revealing spaghetti-thin shoulder straps and a low décolleté. Stanford had to think hard to keep his gaze on her face and not on those firm breasts she was offering up.

"Would you like some wine?" *Time to take charge.* Betty Jo gave her assent. "A chardonnay okay?" Stanford was prepared as the waiter came to their table.

"Sure, a chardonnay would be nice." *There was that husky voice again.* He ordered a Cakebread and they decided to start off the meal with fried green tomatoes. Stanford approved of Betty Jo's choice of blackened Salmon for an entrée and he ordered the low country shrimp and grits. She waited until the waiter moved on and then turned back to Stanford. "You are doing really excellent work at the patent office, Congressman. Has the appointment been fulfilling?" She smiled and lifted her right shoulder, pulling those twin beauties together. He ached to lick between them.

"Thank you. I doubt anyone's paying attention. World wars, economy in the tank—patents are in the noise." The waiter returned with their wine and all attention was on the small ritual of pouring. The waiter anchored the bottle of Cakebread in a silver ice bucket and moved on.

"That is not true," she offered conciliatorily. "Many of my clients have commented on your efforts to eliminate frivolous patents. This will rein in the trolls down the line." She lifted her glass in a semi-mock salute and her large, luscious mouth took a small sip. Stanford paused slightly before enjoying his own first sip. The Cakebread was excellent.

Trolls were companies that didn't produce any products, and Stanford always had to hear the large corporations bemoan their existence, while they fought off infringement suits. Whether or not the companies infringed was not his concern. He liked influential multi-nationals happy with him. "Most of my days are spent listening to people complaining about poor-quality patents issuing and, on the other hand, arrogant patent attorneys complaining we didn't grant some dumbass invention a patent for their pinhead inventors. On top of that, today I was treated to the NSF complaining that we weren't following their recommendations to improve quality."

"Well, Stanford, you know better than most that public service can be a burden. Those of us in the trenches really appreciate your self-sacrifice for the good of the country. Do you run, Congressman? You have the physique of a marathoner." The waiter arrived with the tomatoes, and Stanford served Betty Jo a few slices and took a few for himself. He cut off a portion with his fork. It was cooked perfectly, and Stanford enjoyed the tart flavors filling his mouth. They somehow even tasted 'green.' "Why are we having dinner together, Ms. Lurie?" *Let's get to the point already.*

Betty Jo finished her own bite and tucked into the point. "A client of mine has become aware of a situation," she paused infinitesimally and then continued. "Apparently, one of those hideous little mythical creatures, pretending to be a small startup, is trying to patent some important technology. If they succeed, this technology could end up in court for years. This will delay it becoming available to the public and our partner will waste valuable resources in litigation. That money would be much better spent on developing and deploying the technology."

"This is exactly the situation my reforms are supposed to prevent. However, PTO resources are limited." He gave her a 'what-can you-do' shrug and took a long pull of wine, carefully setting the glass back down on the table and adjusting it a little right of his plate.

"My client was wondering if you might look into this issue personally." He could tell she read his reticence. "For the good of the technology, of course, and getting it out to those who need it." She pressed on, "When you run for Senate, this client would be in a position to provide significant resources for your campaign through their political action committee."

"And who is this client of yours?" *Let's just see how important.*

"They prefer to remain anonymous at this time." Betty Jo smiled warmly. Stanford had no doubt that Betty Jo was going to earn her paycheck this week. There were reasons she was one of the top lobbyists in Washington. Regardless of where the night would lead, he was enjoying himself right now, and besides that, he would enjoy thwarting the efforts of a patent troll even more. "I'm listening."

Betty Jo leaned forward, those beautiful breasts just brushing her plate. "The patent was filed by a front company called EWE Technology and we want you to delay their sham application until another application under assignment to AltruMedical has issued."

"You know that I can't just delay an application."

"Of course, Congressman, but you could suggest that EWE's patent be pulled for special review as part of a random quality check, couldn't you?"

"Let's get to the point, Ms. Lurie."

"Please, Congressman."

"Why should I stick my neck out, Betty Jo?" The waiter brought their entrées. He poured another glass of the chardonnay for Betty Jo and then one for himself. They started to eat and Stanford watched Betty Jo close her bright red painted lips over a forkful of soft, pink salmon. She certainly had a way of dressing that pushed the limits of overt sexuality without completely crossing the line into crass. The dark red lipstick was a perfect example of this.

They ate together in companionable silence for a time while Betty Jo casted around for the hook. "I love your Garcia tie. Are you a huge Deadhead?"

Stanford was going to play at biting awhile before he let her reel him in. "Yeah, I followed them around in college for a few summers. I sold tie-dyed t-shirts to pay my way."

"Such a rule-breaker! Do you ever let that naughty side out with all the weight you carry on your shoulders watching over us little people?" He felt her hand slide up his thigh under the table. A slight bulge was beginning in his trousers and he fought for control of his facial features. He blinked his eyes slowly a couple of times and asked, "Would you like to have dessert at my place?"

Her hand was now on his upper thigh and danger-ously close to his erection. "Does that mean that we have a deal?" He was the surprised fish flopping around in the bottom of the boat.

"Lawson? Stanford Morris here. I need some informa-tion on a possible investment opportunity." Gale Lawson was head of a venture capital fund out of North Carolina. He had helped steer the state insurance venture money Gale's way when he was a state legislator. "I've got my eye on a little up-and-coming medical equipment company, AltruMedical. Heard of it?"

"Nice to talk with you, Stanford. AltruMedical? Give me a few here and I'll see what I can find out. Had the boys and girls do some reports recently on high-tech medical equipment—ah, here it is." Lawson was silent for a few moments on the other end of the line. Stanford heard typing on a keyboard. Lawson continued, "The funder is Irish Star Ventures out of Boston. They have received a rather large grant from the National Science Foundation. I think you'll be interested to know that Senator Fowl from Massachusetts is the second largest backer. There's the link to the NSF. Must be a fatted calf." Stanford absorbed this information. Fowl had become rich in Washington and it wasn't because of his salary. His investment record ranked with Warren Buffet's. It was rumored that he was worth over $100 million, although his congressional disclosures only showed him being worth a third of that amount.

"Any way to stow on the ship without being caught?" Stanford felt his heart racing. He knew Gale Lawson was well-connected politically. "Will do, Stanford. It'll be the usual management fee arrangement, and maybe a new little fund to add to your portfolio. Want me to send the papers over?"

"Why aren't they already here?" Stanford chuckled and stretched his limbs amongst the silk sheets covering his bed. He carefully placed his cell on the bedside table, crossed his arms behind his head and stared at the violent tangle of sheets. Lovely Ms. Lurie had taken herself off early this morning, before he even awoke. They had been up most of the night enjoying rowdy bed sport and he was pleasantly sore and tired—like he always felt after a good workout.

Stanford had already worked out how he would handle Betty Jo's little request. He would speak to the examiner's supervisor in charge of EWE's application. While the supervisor would be suitably flustered at a private meeting with the head of the Patent and Trademark Office, he would slip in his request. He would point out that his group's allowance rate was higher than other groups and this was a strong indication of sloppy work. Stanford would be patient and understanding while the supervisor would stutter excuses and finally quiet, looking suitably chagrined. Pointing seemingly at random to EWE's application on a list, Stanford would indicate this one should be pulled for a thorough review, effectively pulling EWE's application out of the standard queue. He would also mention in an off-hand way that AltruMedical's technology was an example of the sort of pioneering technology that should obtain a patent. The sooner it was approved, the sooner lives would be saved. Altru would receive a patent and EWE would be stuck in a bureaucratic black hole. He chuckled again, this time to himself. Today was going to be a good day.

Chapter 7

"Don't tell me you went skiing?" Warren noticed Hank's distinctive sunburn—the mark of a skier.

Hank grinned. "Of course I went skiing. I told you I was going up to Silverton."

Silverton was the closest thing to heli-skiing you could get at ten percent of the cost. It offered only expert skiing; over four hundred inches a year with no groomers or clear-cut runs. Hank had been talking about skiing Silverton for over a year.

"Yeah but what about the blizzard? The San Juans were supposed to receive over three feet of snow last weekend."

"Yeah, I'd guess that was about right." Hank pulled up a chair.

"I guess your Scout can make it through anything." Warren knew better than to refer to Hank's vintage International Scout as a Jeep. Silverton was at 9,305 feet and could only be reached by passing through a narrow mountain pass with thousand-foot drop offs. Only an insane person would drive those roads in a blizzard. "Well, I guess you're alive—dumbass. How was it?"

Hank cracked his shit-eating grin. "It was fucking awesome. Champagne powder up to your knees, no tracks, picture perfect—sparkled like diamonds. Ah...the guide wasn't too bad looking either."

"Your guide was a woman? What did she look like?" Warren jabbed Hank in the ribs. Hank rarely talked about women. His wife had tried to set Hank up but he would have none of it. Hank said nothing, just continued to smile.

Warren thought about pushing, but decided to change the subject. "How's Janine doing?"

"Good news there too." Hank leaned back in his chair. "The blood thinners seem to be working."

"That is great to hear." Warren headed to his office.

Hank went to find a datasheet on an optoelectronic microwave oscillator chip he was working on. He found it buried under an IEEE Spectrum magazine. Picking it up, he strode back to the lab bench. At the bottom of the datasheet, he saw the device had a number of patents. He remembered he had promised Will that he would check on the EWE patent application. Having the patent issue was critical for EWE to obtain additional funding, just as it was for Houdini. He called EWE's patent attorney, David Stevens.

"Hello, David Stevens."

"David, it's Hank. You're in early. You're not going to charge me overtime for this call, are you?"

David chuckled. "You're such a pain in the ass; I should charge you triple time. How can I help you?"

"EWE just gave a pitch to MedCon the other day—"

David interrupted. "That's great. How did it go?"

"It went pretty well." Hank didn't want to brag, but he shared a familiarity with David, so was comfortable opening up. "They talked about funding us to the tune of ten million. Nothing on the dotted line yet, but—"

"Really? Awesome. Those guys dominate the stents market. It's great to have a strategic partner in this funding environment."

"Yeah, but we got some pointed questions about our patents," Hank paused to see if David would jump in, "and they were surprised that we had not heard back from the patent office. When do you expect to hear from them?"

"In your area of technology it will probably be another two or three years before we hear something," David explained.

That was deflating news. This was the same shit he had heard about Houdini's patent application. "What? We filed for the patent a year ago. Is there something we can do?"

"Yeah, you can tell your congressmen to quit stealing your patent fees to fund their pet projects."

Hank noted a bit of disgust and perhaps sarcasm in David's voice. "What? How will that help?"

"When you write out a check for a patent application it goes into the general treasury for the United States government. Congress then appropriates back the money to the patent office. In their infinite wisdom, Congress over the last decade has decided to divert over $850 million to other programs." David paused to let that sink in.

"That's bullshit… It's just plain stealing." Hank rubbed his neck. This was going to lock EWE into MedCon for all of their funding. Options were critical for a startup.

"Yes, it is." David was having more of these conversations since Congress passed the America Innovates Act. It made his job a lot less fun.

"Isn't there anything we can do to speed things up?"

David had heard this question a lot too. His answers varied from 'no' to a sarcastic: 'turn sixty-five.' Apparently, there was a fast-track program for seniors. "Make sure you get that funding from MedCon."

"Thanks, keep me informed if anything comes up." Three to five years; it just didn't make any sense. In the three to five years it took to get your patent examined, the whole world could change; competitors could drive you out of business. *How was this possible?*

Hank heard the signature long-stride footfalls of Warren coming across the lab, which jarred him out of his daydream. Warren pulled up a chair, turned and straddled it. "What's happening with K&P?"

Warren loomed over Hank with his over six-and-a-half foot frame and lived for his morning coffee, which he set down on the lab bench. "I ran into a bump. David says we won't hear on the patent for at least a couple of years. He just told me the same thing about the EWE patent application."

"You're kidding."

"Nope." Hank gave Warren an ironic smile, which stung his sunburned face.

Warren stared out the window; the swirling snow danced and brushed against the glass.

"I have a meeting with a friend of mine at USA Bank next month in San Francisco. If we get that account, we could blow projections out of the water," Hank said hopefully.

"Need my help on anything with that?" Sales was really Hank's domain. Hank had dreamed up Houdini and Warren was happy to go along with it. After all, it would lead to interesting engineering projects.

"I think I have things under control."

Warren grabbed his coffee and unfolded himself from the chair.

Arriving for the meeting with the head of computer security at USA Bank ten minutes early, Hank was surprised that he felt a little anxious. Yuri was a good friend and he was looking forward to seeing him. If he could just get the internal IT department of the bank to install Houdini's system, it would mean an initial sale of around ten million and at least a million a year in service contracts. If the bank adopted Houdini on its entire network, it could mean five to ten million a year in recurring revenue. Houdini would have VCs lining up to fund them. *No big deal. No wonder my hands feel a little sweaty.*

The headquarters were located in a standard glass highrise in downtown San Francisco. The lobby had a polished marble floor and soared three stories, with a large reception counter situated between the entrance and a bank of elevators, gateways to hundreds of offices located above and below. This was not a retail location and everyone had to pass through turnstiles that were only unlocked by an employee badge reader or by a guard if you had a guest pass and were escorted by an employee. Hank approached the reception desk and heard his rubber-soled wingtips squeak with every step. A nice looking woman in her late twenties in a highly tailored Tahari business suit, who appeared to be the receptionist, said, "Can I help you?"

"Yes, I have an appointment with Yuri Mishkin. I'm Hank Rangar," Hank handed her his business card from Houdini Security.

She glanced at the card, cocked her head when she saw he was a CEO. Hank replied, "Rangar with an 'A' not an 'E'," and smiled. She dialed someone, and after a moment of back and forth, said, "He will be right down to escort you, Mr. Rangar with an 'A'." She returned his smile with one of her own, and looked him over boldly. As she returned his business card, Hank had to tug it, briefly, before it released from her fingers. *Little minx.*

Yuri and Hank had met when they were in the DOD Computer Security Threat Center, almost a decade prior. They were close professional friends. Hank was far too busy to have time to make non-business friends, with the exception of the people he played tennis with. He picked up a Wall Street Journal, one of many copies arranged on low coffee tables surrounded by modern, sleek, black sofas in the center of the lobby. He imagined Houdini's initial public offering or IPO being splashed across the front page of the Journal. He felt his phone vibrate. It was Mark's number. "Mark. What's up?"

"Hank." There was pause. "Janine's in the hospital."

"What?" Hank started to pace.

"She'd been feeling weak for a couple of days. The silly girl ignored that she was hemorrhaging. Thought she was just having a bad period."

Hank could hear the strain in Mark's voice. "Is she okay?"

"She's lost a lot of blood. They think it's under control, but they have to take her off the blood thinners."

Hank stopped pacing. "But the blood thinners are critical for preventing blood clots. Right?"

"Yeah, but they have to stop the bleeding first. I'll call back when we know more. We'll keep you in the loop."

The phone showed the call had been terminated. He sat down again and put his head in his hands.

"Hank, it's great to see you." He looked up into the smiling face of his friend. Yuri was in his early thirties, with a swimmer's build, prominent nose, and dark, snapping eyes that rarely missed much. They shook hands and patted each other on the back.

Even if Yuri was his friend, he was on a sales call. He had to compartmentalize. "How ya' doing, you SOB? Based on your digs here, you seem to be living the rough life—but do you ever get any sun?" Hank laughed.

"Don't let the man in front of the curtain fool you. Our offices are standard Dilbert; although I have graduated to my own cubicle next to the window, which means I sweat like a pig on sunny days and freeze on cloudy cool days. The entrepreneurial life seems to be suiting you, though. What other working slob can afford to have a raccoon tan in February?" Yuri pulled Hank toward the elevator and punched the button indicating the 21st floor. They took the elevator up and exited, walking down a wide hall to a small conference room decorated with the standard issue whiteboard on one wall and long conference table.

Hank pulled out his computer and brought up his standard Houdini PowerPoint presentation. "Houdini Security is unique in the distributed nature of its computer network security system. The technology will provide a time-stamped state of every computer on the network. Houdini's software will provide a one hundred fifty percent return-on-investment to USA Bank in the first year after implementation." Yuri did not ask any questions during the presentation—very unusual. He had seemed almost uninterested in the presentation. Hank wondered if his preoccupation with his sister had affected his pitch.

Yuri scratched his head—clearly uncomfortable. "Hank, have you heard of a company called Thurston Network Security Software?"

"No, someone competitive with Houdini? What do they offer?" Hank was sure that Yuri had not understood the real capabilities of their product and he could clearly delineate Houdini's advantages once he understood what Thurston was selling. Yuri showed him the sales literature. As Hank read through the glossy, it felt like someone had slugged him in the gut for the second time that day; it knocked the breath out of him. The literature looked like someone had rewritten Houdini's. It even discussed Houdini's new hashing system. Yuri was staring intently at him as he read. "Yuri, I don't know what to say. It looks like they are describing our product."

"Based on what you told me earlier, I thought it sounded similar. Our Chief Information Officer was approached by Thurston and he thought it was a great concept. So he charged me with the task of investigating it. We have been running tests on a small network here and I can tell you that their software is just not up to our standards or the standards we had at the DOD. The software is riddled with bugs. The architecture is not well designed; it crashes frequently, and slows down the whole network."

Hank took a moment to process this new development. Until he could research Thurston software, his appeal might fall on deaf ears. "That would be some great marketing data. Can you provide us with the results of your testing?" He needed time to absorb what he had just learned.

"Sure, what do you say we go get a beer?" Yuri looked quickly at his watch and was clearly relieved to end the uncomfortable situation.

An hour and two microbrews later, Hank was still distracted. The image of Janine lying in a hospital bed haunted him and he wanted to call Mark for more information. When he was able to force this from his mind, he remembered his conversation with David Stevens, his patent attorney, about Houdini's patent application being published. Thurston could have easily reverse-engineered Houdini's product with that information.

"I really admire your entrepreneurial spirit. Taking those sorts of risks scares the hell out of me." Yuri took a swig of his beer. "I've decided on a different path to early retirement."

Hank wasn't looking for early retirement; if anything, he wanted to be able to spend more time working on projects that interested him—creating new inventions, building businesses and spending less time on administrative drudgery.

"Real estate is booming in Silicon Valley. I've invested in a couple of apartment buildings. At the present appreciation rate, I should have a million in equity by the end of the decade." Yuri caught their server with a wave of his hand and ordered them another round. "It really helps with the tax bill too."

Hank was a little disturbed by the turn the conversation had taken. When they had worked together, Yuri had been passionate about computer security, its importance to commerce, and national defense. "I hope it works out for you."

"Hank, this is not the decade for technology startups. This is the decade of housing and real estate. Banks are practically giving away money." Hank frowned.

Yuri noted Hank's frown. He liked Hank; the last thing he wanted to do was upset him. Not eating lunch had turned out to be a bad idea; the beer was getting to him. He clapped Hank on the back. "You're different. Who else could have taken down the Iranian nuclear program single-handedly? I'm sure Houdini will be one of the shining exceptions."

The loudspeaker announced the final boarding for Denver. "Mark, any news on Janine?" Hank pressed the phone to one ear while covering the other.

"They're planning on releasing her from the hospital tomorrow. They're doing a number of tests to determine whether she had an adverse reaction to the blood thinners."

"I'm relieved she's getting out, but the lack of answers here really bugs me."

"You and me both, brother."

On the flight back to Colorado, Hank started making plans to reverse engineer Thurston's software and sue them for patent infringement as a way to distract his mind from Janine's plight. Clearly, he had to focus on sales in the near term and use Houdini's success in the market to obtain funding. *This goddamn Thurston has already screwed up my chances with USA Bank.* He felt dirty, upset, and confused. Robbery victims, he had read, often felt this way. Knowing that didn't provide any comfort. He sighed and looked out the window. It was sunset and the plane seemed to be flying into a black abyss. Galileo had said that theft of one's invention was worse than murder, because it stole a man's reputation.

Hank pulled out the complementary airline magazine and began to flip through it. There was an article on skiing the back bowls of Copper Mountain. It showed a picture of a perfect powder day and someone jumping off a snow precipice into Copper Bowl, one of Hank's favorites. Copper was the friendliest ski resort in Colorado, in his opinion, and he was hoping he could get up there several more times before the season was over. Another article entitled "The Death of Venture Capital" by Christine Patel caught his attention. The author stated that the amount of money flowing into venture capital had declined by 80% since the passage of the Truth in Accounting Act. The law made it almost impossible for new companies to be listed on stock exchanges because of the prohibitive cost of complying with the law. Adobe, Home Depot, and Cisco were just a few well-known companies that would not have been able to go public and obtain the capital necessary to grow if this law had been in effect when they were startups, according to the article. The author predicted that half of venture capital funding in the US would be gone within the next three years. *Great, just great.* He looked back to the blurb about the author, which had a picture. She appeared younger than he was, and was a stunning beauty of Indian descent.

When he returned to Colorado, he would check out more of her articles.

Hank woke up early but refreshed. He always faced reality head on. He started reviewing Houdini's situation in his head. He was already working sixty to eighty-hour weeks to keep Made By Man, Houdini, and EWE running, putting out fires and keeping spinning plates in the air. He needed Houdini or EWE to take off so he could focus on it and get more help to run Made By Man. They had hired one sales guy and a programmer/support person for Houdini, but this more than ate up their profits. He had already tried to raise capital from Colorado VCs. They gave him a warm reception but no one had any money for new investments at this time. Now he had to deal with this new competitor eating into his market. Like most entrepreneurs, he was a perpetual optimist—and had a better product. Yuri confirmed this. Perhaps Thurston's presence would just expand market awareness. Houdini would take advantage of that to expand faster. He grabbed a protein bar and his keys and headed out the door.

Heading up the pass and passing slow curve-takers, Hank thought about the new feature he'd been working on that would provide Houdini a killer distinction. This time, he would not make the mistake of filing for a patent on it. They would bury it deep in the code and keep it a trade secret, only explaining the benefits to the public. All data over the Internet had a unique signature, sort of like a fingerprint. This signature would normally be considered meaningless noise by the computer and by electrical engineers. However, it could be used to trace the origin of the data. This would allow Houdini to identify computers of hackers and provide information on how to disable them. They would bury Thurston.

Chapter 8

It was late on Friday as Hank grabbed a beer from the Made by Man refrigerator. Hank looked up at Warren and held up his beer. "Want one?"

"Sure. I've done some digging into Thurston."

Hank handed Warren a beer, sat down and opened his beer. "And?"

Warren pushed up his glasses. "They have Google and Yahoo ads that pop up whenever someone types in Houdini."

Hank leaned into the table. "That can't be legal." Hank took a slug of his beer.

"They have several print ads running and appear to have three full-time sales people. They also have an article in this month's SC Magazine." Hank could tell that Warren was distressed by what he had found out.

Warren slapped the article on the table between them. "This looks like we wrote it. Bottom line—they are much better funded than we are."

"Where the hell did these guys come from?" Hank was genuinely perplexed.

"They first show up about three months after our patent application was published. Their software appears to have been written by a group out of India. They seem well funded but I was unable to track down the source." Warren rubbed his temples and pushed back on his wheeled chair, which slid several feet across the buffed concrete floor.

"We will just have to match their advertising and hire a PR firm to get some of our own articles out in the press. We should probably hire another inside sales person also." Hank rifled through the material on the table.

"That will cost us $50K to $80K and we don't have that sort of money," Warren said as he twirled around in his chair, staring at the ceiling.

Hank absorbed the news. "We can take it out of my salary from Made by Man until we get some investors. I'll consider it a loan to Houdini so it doesn't alter our ownership positions."

"Investors don't like to see loans from founders on the books."

"We'll deal with that when we get an investor. Right now, we have to make sure we don't get buried by Thurston or there will be nothing for them to complain about."

They both sat at the table staring down at the Thurston article and finished their beers. The workroom was velvet black. Only the desk lamps illuminated the table between them. Neither of them wanted the other to see the expression on their face. Hank cleared his throat.

"It's late. Go home to your beautiful wife and kids."

Hank decided to check emails before he headed home to Manitou Springs, just down the pass from Woodland Park, where Made By Man was located. He leaned back in his chair and thought if Houdini's patent would just issue, they could go after Thurston. *Clearly, our technology was stolen. What the hell was Congress thinking when they starting publishing patent applications for the world to see? Well, I will just have to work harder.* Janine would not have approved of his decision to 'just work harder.' She had been after him for years to slow down and date more. She often reminded him that she wanted to be an aunt—it was unfair; he was an uncle twice over.

His cell phone roused him from musing. At this time on a Friday night, it was probably a sales call. He looked at the caller ID and saw it was his sister. Despite the setback with the blood thinners, he needed to stay upbeat. "Hey Janine, what's happening?" But the voice he heard was not his sister's.

"Hank, Janine has had a heart attack." Mark's voice was breaking up.

"What… Are you kidding?"

"It happened this afternoon and the ambulance took her to Jewish Hospital. She's stable, but the doctor said there was some damage to her heart."

Hank could hear Mark's intake of breath. "God, Hank how is this possible? A healthy woman in her thirties?"

"Is this because they took her off the blood thinners?" Hank's question was accusatory.

"They had to take her off the blood thinners. She almost bled to death."

Hank was up and pacing. "What's the answer?"

"The doctors aren't sure. There are other blood thinners they were looking at and there is the possibility of stents or bypass surgery. I really don't know."

This had all started when she was in the car accident. The guy was an illegal alien without insurance. "I'll get the first flight out."

Hank slowly opened the heavy hospital door and peered into the darkened room. He allowed his eyes to adjust to the low light, then entered quietly. His sister was tucked in neatly on the bed and the headboard was raised. Tubes were connected to her nose and wires came up from either side of the bed and hugged her chest and arms. Machines blinked and soft alarms beeped for attention. He looked back out the door behind him to see if a nurse was nearby. There was a male nurse efficiently checking items off a chart and talking to someone. Clearly, the alarms were merely signals that all was hooked up and working. He walked up to the bed and looked down into the intelligent bright blue eyes he knew so well. She was going to argue with him.

"Hank," Janine started up, her voice strong even though her body looked small and defeated. "We haven't seen you in months! What the hell have you been doing? Companies should not come before family. Jess and Tris miss you terribly!" Her scolding was stopped by a racking cough that had her clutch her side beneath her left breast.

Hank's hand shot out and closed around her arm lightly. "Hey," he said softly. "Let's take it easy, here, okay? Take a breath. Do you want some water?" He looked at the table attached to the hospital bed and grabbed a plastic jug filled with ice water. He helped her take a hold of the handle of the water jug and carefully brought the attached straw to her mouth. She sipped weakly, and her head dropped back to the pillow. He furrowed his brow and looked at her, considering. "Do you want me to call someone?" he asked. Janine shook her head in the negative twice; her short blonde bangs fell into her eyes. Hank pushed her bangs off her forehead and lingered there, feeling for warmth.

"You feel cool; and here I thought you were sick." He cracked a bright white-toothed smile and cocked his head to one side. "You know, there are simpler ways to get me into St. Louis for a visit." She gave him a watery smile in return and took a few deep breaths. She placed her right hand under her right hip and tried to lever herself higher against the head of the bed. Hank reached out immediately and helped her accomplish it.

Her eyes turned back to him, snapping with renewed scolding. "I'm serious; you're all I have left of my family." She settled into a smile and reached out for his hand.

He reached forward, clasped her hand and squeezed. "Um, I don't think I need to remind you that Mark, Jess, and Tris might not agree with you on this—"

"You know what I'm talking about," she sharply inter-jected. She looked around him toward the door. "Did you bring a girlfriend?"

Hank slowly shook his head. "NO? Maybe a boyfriend?"

"All right." Hank's tone told her they would not con-tinue with this discussion. "What's next?" Hank decided to change the subject.

Janine sighed. "More tests and then some more and probably more after that. I'm sick of being wheeled around every square inch of this place to have them poke, prod, enclose and humiliate me by pulling down this sad excuse of a nightgown to expose my chest for yet another test."

"I'm so sorry—"

Janine's hand shot up surprisingly fast, her palm toward Hank. "Gotta do what the good doc says, just a little cranky right now."

Hank looked around the room. "The digs gotta be nicer here than ICU, you have to admit."

Janine laughed, then coughed again. Hank reached for the water jug and Janine waved him off. "No, I'm fine. Now that was funny. See, if I miss you enough to laugh at your lame attempts, we know it's gotta be bad."

Hank's brow lowered again. "Bad?—It's looking up from here, right Jan?"

Janine was silent but she looked at him intensely. They didn't speak for some time because there wasn't anything to say. Hank realized that his own heart hurt. He wanted to clutch at it and knead the feeling away. But he just kept staring into his sister's eyes and hoped she knew how he felt. They did this for a while and then Janine turned her face away toward the window and asked Hank to raise the blinds. Grateful for the job, Hank rounded the base of Janine's bed and adjusted the chains that maneuvered the blinds open. The snick, snick of the pull was loud in the room.

"Janine, how we doin' here?" A big bear of a male nurse entered the room and completely controlled everything with his swift body movements, simultaneously grasping the IV bag to check its flow and grasping her wrist with his other hand. He then lifted a beefy and hairy arm, consulted his watch for a minute, and lowered Janine's hand back to her side. He pulled the plugs of the stethoscope, hanging loosely on his chest, up to his ears and unapologetically slipped the cold silver orb beneath her nightgown and listened. He then raised her up and listened to her back. Janine squirmed and frowned but said nothing. "Well, everything sounds good. Those tests woke you up today, didn't they?" He smiled warmly at Janine but she gave Hank a withering look.

"Mark here, really pisses me off." Mark the nurse let out a booming laugh. "I bet all the Marks in your life do that, sweetie. Here, let me tuck you in." He began to smooth her sheets and tuck the sheet and blankets tightly in against her side. She shook her head back and forth while looking at Hank. "He's mummifying me—that's his real goal."

Mark, the nurse, laughed again. "Honey, have you ordered dinner yet? I hear it's lasagna."

"Mmmm, sounds good. I'm hungry." Hank slapped and then rubbed his hands together.

"Yeah, well, at least I'm not cooking tonight." Janine sighed again and tried to move her legs back and forth against the tight tucking of the blankets. "Good God, Mark—I never tucked my babies in this tight."

The nurse didn't appear to hear as he whooshed back out of the room on to the next.

Hank pulled a chair over and, sitting down so they were at the same level, he slowly ran his hand up and down her arm and felt the hot tears well up. *Don't cry, don't cry*, he kept the mantra going, scared that he would lose and she might cry too.

"OH stop; I'm healthy as a horse. I'll be outta here in no time. I've got kids to pack off to school and tennis and

God knows what else in all of a day. No time for this kind of foolishness."

The tears pooled in his eyes and he felt the hot tracks they made down his cheeks and his nose burned. He sniffed loudly and patted her hand. "Janine, I will always be here for them. No, hear this. You'll be fine but I need you to know I will always be significant in Mark, Jess, and Tristan's lives."

Janine returned the gesture, patting Hank's hand in return. "Silly man, I know that. Tell me something I don't know. Got anything in that head of yours that's interesting—no, distracting?"

Hank smiled and told Janine about a video game he'd brought for the kids. "A client of ours developed this game that connects an electronic keyboard to the computer."

Janine frowned. "All I need is Tristan addicted to a video game."

Hank grinned. "This client is a professor of music at Polytech. This is a real teaching tool for students, not just a game." The software connected to a server and let others add new music, while protecting copyrights. It allowed teachers to set up competitions between their students and others. "I played with it. It was a blast. Made me want to start up piano lessons again."

"Like you ever enjoyed that. I actually went to my lessons." Janine reached for her water and took several long drinks. Hank felt awkward, sad, and scared. He was grateful for the distraction of a loud rap at the door and they both turned their heads to see a petite, forty-something woman in a nice peach dress with a longish white coat come into the room. "Good evening, Janine."

Hank noted the stethoscope around her neck and wondered if this was Janine's cardiologist.

"Hello, Dr. Dearing. This is my brother, Hank. Hank, Dr. Dearing, my cardiologist and my colleague. I work with her in the ICU."

Hank nodded and reached out to shake her hand. Dr. Dearing shook hands with him and immediately turned her attention to Janine. She stood at the foot of the bed and leafed through the charts while asking Janine basic questions about how she was feeling and what tests had been completed that day.

Hank had some questions of his own, so he decided to jump right in. "Doctor, I don't understand. Janine has always been athletic. How could she have had a heart attack? Is this related to her hypercoagulable disease?"

"Most likely. It appears she had a clot in one of the smaller arteries near the left anterior descending artery. Sometimes these are just freak occurrences where some tissue breaks off and blocks an artery; but most likely it's the disease." Dr. Dearing turned a few more pages of Janine's chart and made some notes.

Hank waited until she finished. "How is this treated? How does she get better?"

There was click as the door opened and Mark slipped into the room. Dr. Dearing turned toward Mark. "Hi Mark. We were just discussing treatment options. As you know, Janine had an adverse reaction to the first blood thinner drugs we tried. We are doing tests to determine why that occurred and if she might respond better to other drugs."

"How long will that take? I mean, she could have another blood clot at any time. Right?" Hank looked at the doctor, who nodded her assent.

"Other options include stents and bypass surgery. For some reason Janine seems at higher risk for clots lodging in the arteries of her heart."

Hank's mind immediately jumped to the angiochannelizer EWE was developing. "There's this technology—a company I am part of is developing that is designed to deal with clots in the small arteries of the heart. It might be ideal for this."

Dr. Dearing was frowning. But before she could say anything, Mark jumped in. "Janine is not a pig, Hank. Your technology hasn't even been tested on humans yet. No, we are definitely sticking with tried and true treatments."

The doctor seemed a little confused by the conversation. "As I was saying, stents and bypass surgery are potential options. The concern with bypass surgery is that Janine didn't react well to the last set of blood thinner drugs. Stents don't have this limitation, but recent research shows that many people with heart disease have blockages in arteries too small for stents."

Mark looked at his watch. "I put your reading glasses on the stand. I've got to pick up the kids, but I'll be back this evening." He gave Janine a peck on the cheek.

They watched Mark walk out of the room. Hank turned to Janine. "You saw the angiochannelizer. You know it works."

"I don't think we should jump to experimental procedures." Dr. Dearing looked directly at Janine earnestly.

Janine sighed, "Hank, let me think about it; don't bother Dr. Dearing with stuff I already know. Anything else, Doctor?"

Dr. Dearing consulted the charts once more. "Hmm, I think we are going to increase your medication to get the heartbeat a little more regular, but other than that, most likely you won't see me tonight. But I will be back in the morning. Sound good?"

"Yes, thanks doc," Janine said cavalierly. Hank looked down into Janine's face. She seemed very pale and was withdrawing. He felt helpless.

Janine's dinner had come in the meantime, and after she picked at 'okay' lasagna, green beans, and drank a carton of milk, Hank opened a Jell-O cup and ate it in three bites. He then pulled her table off to the side. "Hey, remember when that asshole was going to gun down the muskrat I had been feeding? You know, it got caught in the sewer drain after a storm that one summer? That's how mad I am this happened to you." Hank grinned.

Janine returned his grin and laughed. "You have always been so stubborn and righteous." She shook her head slowly side to side. "Dad had to pull you back from going after our neighbor."

Hank laughed. "I can still see that asshole, riding in circles on his golf cart, steering with one hand and cradling a shotgun with his other arm. He was yelling at his buddies as if it was some sort of foxhound hunt. I wanted to kill him. I think I might have."

"Yeah, Dad saved you from a murder charge." Janine cocked her head to the side and said lowly, "Nose to spite the face, dear brother." She pointed a finger right at his nose, "Nose to spite the face."

Hank felt himself stiffen under Janine's consideration and adjusted himself in the uncomfortable chair. "You were a perfect child specimen."

Janine barked out a laugh. "I was always good at exceeding expectations." She sobered. "Hank, I want you to know something. I haven't any regrets. I have accomplished what was most important to me. I have a great family; my kids will be good people. I couldn't dare ask for more than that. I think it's weird that we just visited the farm, and I am grateful to have seen it one more time." Hank straightened and opened his mouth to protest.

"NO, Hank, I mean it. I am happy there's nothing I will regret—well, maybe grandkids. And," she paused briefly, getting her voice under control. "I wish my kids had known Mom and Dad." Her eyes sparkled with unshed tears. "Definitely being an aunt. Get the fuck busy, brother. Literally."

Jess and Tristan stuck on Hank like glue as they meandered through the walkways of the St. Louis Zoo. They had finished viewing the large land tortoises; one was a gift to the zoo from President Jefferson and unbelievably going strong, if not slow. The kids were still clearly shaken by their mom's condition and Hank found himself carrying on with constant conversation, keeping the twelve- and ten-year-old distracted. They had come to a large pond and were enjoying watching a mother hippopotamus swim with her young baby, named 'Little John.'

"Ever hear the story of Robin Hood?" Hank asked. Tristan piped up for the first time that entire afternoon. "Isn't he the guy with the longbow who stole from the rich and gave to the poor? Longbows are cool; I saw a movie about it."

Hank led the kids to a bench next to the pond and they sat down on either side of him, Jess leaning into his shoulder. "You know, that's what everyone remembers about the legend of Robin of Loxley but it's not really true. Do you want to know the real story?" Jess and Tristan both nodded their heads.

"There was this big war in another land, and they called it the Crusades. Robin was a knight fighting in this war for his country, and when he returned home, he found his father had died and their lands had been seized by the king. The people were starving because the king was taxing everyone who lived there and all the surrounding villages very steeply. When they ran out of gold to give the king, the king took their livestock and finally their harvested grain—even their seed corn."

Jess furrowed her brow. "What's seed corn?"

"Seed corn is what the farmers held back from every good harvest to plant the next year."

"What did Robin do?" Tristan fidgeted in his seat, expecting some good action.

"Robin banded together with other landholders, including someone called Little John, like this fella here," Hank nodded in the direction of the pond behind them, "who had lost their land or their harvests to the king, and they began to plan how they were going to survive. They decided the king would have to pay for his force and theft against the people; and so they began to organize ambushes to attack the king's guards when they came to take the people's property."

"Yeah! They used their longbows, right?" Tristan enthusiastically joined in.

"They used longbows, and clubs, and just clever tactics to catch the guards unaware. But what was really important—they returned the people's property to them so they could live. Eventually, the evil king was deposed and the people had control over their own lives again."

Jess looked into his eyes. "That story is different from how we learned it. I always thought that the rich people were just stingy and wouldn't help the poor people, so Robin Hood decided to make things fair."

Hank sighed. "Just because someone is stingy—does that justify stealing? Is it fair when someone does work to earn money and that money is taken from them to give to someone who hasn't worked to earn it? People are generally kind and helpful to their neighbors. They don't need a king or government to tell them what is fair. And what if they disagree? The king can take their earnings away, because he will use force—"

"What do you mean, force?" Tristan sat up on the bench and seemed intent on Hank's answer.

"If you don't pay your taxes, the government will eventually take the money from you or put you in jail." They all sat in silence for a few moments and then Tristan jumped off the bench.

"Tigers next, Uncle Hank!"

"To the tigers then." Hank stood and Tristan clung to his hand as they walked around the pond to enter the big cat house.

It was late in the evening and the children were tucked into bed, reading. Hank and Mark sat in Mark and Janine's kitchen. There was a massive farmhouse-style oak table anchoring one wall of the cheerful room. Janine's home reminded him of his grandparents' farmhouse, but where that structure had been a two-story Victorian, this house was a sprawling ranch, set back from the narrow wind-ing road in the St. Louis suburb of St. Charles. The white clapboard shingles and bright green shutters were comple-mented by large flowerbeds: red roses and lavender rioted with yellow yarrow and orange zinnias. Oregano, cilantro and basil scented the air. Janine loved to garden, and she was quite proud of the view from the road.

Mark stood next to the counter, watching the coffee pot percolate. Hank folded and refolded a cloth napkin at the large farmhouse table. They were quiet for a time and then Hank cleared his throat. "I've got a client who is doing research on damaged hearts."

"I know that Hank. It was just an experiment."

"Let me talk with her."

"You don't know that this would change anything. Too much has happened—the damage—we can't go back to where it was before."

"No, we have to go forward. There's a possibility; this company is doing work on a procedure that would be help-ful for Janine. It's worth exploring at least and...and, well, I won't just sit around without exploring all of our options."

"Her," Mark responded quietly.

"What?"

"*Her* options. This is my wife's life. WE will be vigilantly looking at all options available to her. Everything her cardiologist recommends, we'll look at."

It was after midnight and Hank lay in his bed, his arms behind his head, wide-awake. His thoughts drifted and he recalled a camping trip with the family one fall in Utah. The air was crisp but the sun was hot. He and Janine had scrambled up some boulders a ways from the campsite and were hotly negotiating what to play. They settled on their standard 'Indians,' and as Janine explored a ways ahead in a dry creek bed, Hank continued to scramble upward to check out the view. He continued up to the ridgeline and looked out over an expansive vista. He could hear Janine singing softly in the distance and the ping of small rocks as they hit the canyon walls of the creek bed and echoed off the other canyon wall. The orange rocks glowed in the noon sun and Hank looked at the expanse of blue sky and made a mental list of all the things his plane would have. It would be able to skim on top of the water and go under water. It could encase itself in a force field that would deflect weapons. The autopilot would recognize his voice and he could walk around his plane telling it where to fly and the plane would follow his instructions. He had a smaller plane inside this one he could fly out the back and go exploring while his big jet would just hover in the sky waiting—"HANK!" His name echoed several times off the walls below him.

"Hunt a deer and bring it to me to make for dinner!"

Hank grimaced, cupped his hands around his mouth and called down to her, "I'm goin' to set a snare for a rabbit. I'm bringing a dead rabbit and you're gonna skin it!" He grinned.

All was quiet, then, "Not a rabbit again! They're too cuuute—"

Hank called down again. "What did you say?"

"I said, NO RABBIT! I won't pretend to eat something cute and furry and that's that!"

"Some Indian you'd make—you're gonna starve and DIE." *Girls.* Hank pondered their uselessness as he picked his way along the edge of the wall. Maybe a jetpack. Yeah, something he'd strap on his back and take off. He'd fly real low and catch the rabbit or a bird; yeah, he'd fly as fast as a bird—no, faster—and just reach out and grab it. He'd feel its little heart beating fast against his hand—

Hank started and was disoriented for a second. He ran his hands over his face and through his hair. He must have dozed off. He turned on his side and made a mental list of what he needed to do tomorrow, including contacting EWE Technology. They were doing some pretty amazing stuff and he thought he'd overheard Warren discussing with them something about human trials. Maybe, just maybe. He suddenly felt very sleepy, exhaustion winning out. He fell into a deep, dreamless sleep.

Chapter 9

"Damn it, Joe, I spent over a month on that story." Christine Patel slammed the papers on his desk and continued her pacing.

"I know; I know. But the publisher thinks it's too risky." Joe held up his palms in a gesture of surrender.

As her boss and editor of *The Financial Reporter*, Christine knew she should be more respectful to Joe, but this was idiocy! "You're the one who keeps telling us to dig deeper, reach for more." She put her hands on her hips and gave her best death stare. After ten seconds of holding her gaze, he looked away.

"You're right, of course." He looked back at her just in time to see her stomp down her heel like a high-spirited horse. "I mean it IS a great story, but attacking a senator—he's a powerful senator, and he brings a lot of money into Connecticut."

"By manipulating the FDA approval process." She finished his thought. "So we are only against corruption when it doesn't benefit local corporations, like MedCon?" She could not believe what she was hearing. Her boss was usually reasonable. This was too good a story to give up on that easily; there had to be a way.

Joe fidgeted in his chair. "Well no. But people have to believe in their government. We can't have anarchy." He knew it was a weak argument and he could tell by the way she pushed one hip out—and what a beautiful hip it was—that she wasn't buying it either. However, it was what the publisher had told him when he had raised these same issues. Some days being a boss implementing corporate policy sucked.

"If *The Financial Reporter* does not have the guts to publish it, then I'll quit and take it across the street."

He could see her nostrils flare slightly and her flat belly expel air under her form-fitting dress. He should have been offended by her threat, but he didn't buy his own argument. Besides, he had been begging for a story just like this—a multinational company, MedCon, manipulating the FDA and legislative process with the help of a powerful, bought and paid for senator. Unfortunately, his job was to protect the company's interests and implement its policies. "I am sure that you're aware that the company owns the copyright to that work and you have a non-compete clause." He sighed, again. The last thing he wanted was to be was a bully, especially to Christine.

She could tell Joe was uncomfortable. He had been a great boss and she hated making him uncomfortable, but... "You know I was making ten times as much when I was a bond trader. If I am not allowed to report news—break stories—what's the point?"

She was one of the rare ones. She had that fire in the belly it took to wade through hours of research to find the needle in the haystack. She didn't have to work here in the pit, as the reporters referred to the main newsroom. He knew he could not keep her because she needed the money.

"Christine, sit down already." Joe saw her hesitate. "Please." She slouched into the heavily polished French Baroque guest chair. He tasted the acrid flavor of this morning's cigarette. He needed to quit one of these days. "I will promise to fight for this." He hesitated and looked her in the eyes. "If you promise you won't leave."

She looked out the window. It had started to rain, and the emotional exhaustion of the fight was wearing her down. She hated rain in the city. "That sounds good, but my side of the promise is tangible, observable, and your side is not. I need a promise that this paper will not waste my time again."

"Yeah, me too." Joe started to laugh, not the laughter of joy but resignation. She joined in his laughter, which released the tension a little. When they stopped laughing, the spatter of rain against the window could be heard. "You know it wasn't my decision. Can I buy you lunch?" She heard the 'to make up for it,' but it wasn't said aloud.

They took a cab to Jimmy's Bar and Grill, a local dive that reporters could afford. She was hit with the smell of fried food mixed with beer as they entered. She was cold and her legs felt wet from the rain splattering her pantyhose. She heard the click of her high heels on the wood floor, which made her feel conspicuously out of place as Joe led her to a booth. It was a dark wood, high-backed booth with hard flat surfaces that felt more like a torture device than a place to relax. She placed her purse and coat next to her in the booth and tried not to look her boss in the eyes.

"A couple of black and tans," Christine heard Joe order. "How about a couple of shots of Jameson, too." She thought about objecting but she had contradicted her boss enough for one day. She settled for giving him a questioning look. "Have you ever had a black and tan?" He didn't wait for her to answer. "It's Bass Ale on the bottom and Guinness floating on top—it's awesome." He was looking about the bar.

The server brought over well-worn menus and they reviewed them in silence for a while. An Irish jig filled the bar as more patrons entered from the rain. The server brought over the drinks. Christine was determined not to have the shot of whiskey. She had work to do and this would make the afternoon drag on interminably. Joe grabbed his shot glass and raised it. He was waiting expectantly for her. The smoky, caramelized smell was inviting. It would be rude not to join in—you never moved up if you were always seen as an outsider and she was a woman. *What the hell*. She raised her glass. "To the press," and they clinked glasses. She felt the whiskey burn and then warm her.

"Did you ever have a story killed—one you knew was good—one you knew the world should know about?" She sure was an earnest kid.

Joe gave her a wry smile and then the server showed up. "Are you ready?"

Joe turned toward the server. "I'm ready. Christine?"

"I was debating between the steak and kidney pie and—"

Joe interrupted her. "Steak and kidney pie definitely. Make it two." Joe grabbed her menu and handed it to the server. He took a sip of his beer and she decided to join him. "I hate New York in the rain, don't you?"

She thought he was trying to change the subject. She stared at him but he refused to look at her. "Did you?"

He took another drink of beer. "Did I what?"

She reached across the booth and slapped his arm. "Did you ever have a story killed?"

He looked at her for a long time. His normally penetrating eyes seemed sad. "Of course, it happened to me all the time. It happens to every reporter." She gave him a frown. "Okay, okay. Nothing like your story. No companies trying to corner the market in drug-eluting stents by paying off a senator and manipulating the legislative process to destroy a competitor. But there was a story back when I worked for the *Times* in Richmond." He took another big drink of his black and tan. Christine decided to join him. She had always thought good beer smelled like liquid bread—and this was good beer. Joe's cell phone went off and he looked to Christine for her okay. She immediately nodded "yes" and Joe stood up, walking toward the front of the bar. Christine surveyed the interior of the pub and appreciated the gleaming oak bar. It probably was from Ireland or Scotland and had to be a century old.

Joe had been gone for quite a while and Christine was curious what the heck was happening over at the office. Finally, he came back to their booth just as their server, who had a silver pin piercing her nose and purple hair, showed up with their order. Joe turned toward the server and made a circle in the air with his index finger. "Another round." They ate in companionable silence for a while.

"What was the story?" she goaded him between mouthfuls of flaky crust, an awesome beef gravy and succulent pieces of meat.

Joe took a bite and chewed, considering what to tell her. "Well, this was years ago. It was about some land deal." He took another bite and seemed to be contemplating. She decided to join him. The rich taste of the gravy and steak fortified her but the heat made her take another slug of beer to cool her tongue.

She prepared to take another bite and noticed Joe staring off in space. She twirled her fork so she didn't have to say "AND" aloud.

"There was this farm on the edge of the town that was zoned residential. The farmer tried to get it rezoned but after he died and the farm was sold in foreclosure it was rezoned and the new owners made a mint." He turned his attention to the television over the bar. She finished her beer and contemplated. *What the hell was he talking about?*

The server showed up with the next round of drinks. Joe immediately picked up the shot glass. "To the land of the free." She didn't need another. She grabbed her glass, tapped it to his and threw back the Jameson. It didn't burn as much this time. She followed it up with a slug of beer.

She leaned into the table. "Are you going to tell me about the story or not?"

"Ah, yeah, well everyone knew Johnny Ashe, the farmer, was disabled and didn't have any kids to work the farm. The property taxes were high because the land had been rezoned to residential but it was next to the airport and no developer would buy it. No farmer would buy it because it had been rezoned residential but everyone knew it was worth a fortune if it could be rezoned commercial." He scraped his spoon along the bottom of the ramekin. "Well, I found out that several members of the zoning board were part of the corporation that bought the land, and one was a major shareholder of the bank that held Mr. Ashe's mortgage." He leaned back and folded his arms across his chest.

"Okay, but why wouldn't they publish it?"

He took a big breath. "I was never given an answer. Years later, when I had moved on, I was reading some publishing news about the *Times* being sold. Apparently, that banker owned a piece of the paper. You see, Christine, no matter what it is, remember that someone owns it."

Chapter 10

"Hank?" Janine's voice sounded a little shaky. "Dr. Dearing and Mark are here with me. We're on speakerphone. I'm going to let Dr. Dearing explain what we've found." Hank shut the door to the conference room and turned up the volume on the phone. He remained standing.

"Hello Hank, Michelle Dearing. It's good to talk with you again. First, I want to thank you for getting me in touch with EWE Technologies. Based on my discussions with Dr. Cody about his procedure and the possibility of Janine as a candidate, we completed a four-dimensional Doppler ultrasound scan of Janine's heart. As I told Janine and Mark, think of it as a CAT scan, except that it provides a time picture—a video. Does that make sense?"

Hank noted Dr. Dearing's explanation left out the Doppler effect, which is how RADAR determines the speed of an airplane. "Go on."

"Using this we can see that Janine has blockage in some of the small arteries of the heart."

Hank jumped in. "That is exactly the issue the angio-channelizer is designed to solve."

Janine cut him off. "Hank, let Dr. Dearing finish."

He stood up and starting pacing. They still needed money to get the ball rolling. Why did everything take so long? The technology was sound. The industry would completely change. So many people would be helped. His own damned sister, for chrissakes. MedCon had not returned calls to either Will or Earl in over a month. He leaned heavily against a bookcase filled with electronic component catalogs and software manuals. Not one a how-to about bringing new medical technologies to market. He wanted to throw every book to the floor.

Dr. Dearing continued, "As you know, these vessels are much too small for bypass surgery and stents. Normally, we use blood thinners and clot-busting drugs for people with hypercoagulable diseases." There was a long pause. Hank felt his heart beating fast.

"However, these drugs are always dangerous for pre-menopausal women. There is a risk of uncontrollable internal hemorrhaging, as in Janine's case." Hank took a deep breath and ran his fingers through his hair. "Do you have any questions, Hank?"

They must have heard him breathing heavily, he realized. "Please continue."

"Janine appears to have an allergic reaction to these types of drugs. People like Janine exhibit a non-linear reaction and their body's response has a tendency to become more pronounced over time."

"Meaning?" Hank asked impatiently.

"Meaning, bypass surgery and stents are off the table." Dr. Dearing paused for this to sink in.

Hank's mind was racing. If Janine took the drugs, she would most likely die of internal bleeding. If she did nothing, she would die, sooner than later, of a heart attack. This made the EWE procedure all the more important. *What kind of timeline were they looking at?* He heard the sharp sound of wood against some surface. A door was closed somewhere in the lab.

"Bottom line is that our normal tools for dealing with hypercoagulable diseases will not work for Janine." Hank could hear shuffling papers. "I have reviewed Dr. Cody and EWE's technology. I have spent several hours discussing the technology and protocols with the doctor by phone and by email. I am reluctant to suggest experimental treatments."

How long? How long?

"But in this case, it's our best option. Dr. Cody's history of groundbreaking work in this area only reinforces my opinion."

"How long do we have?" Hank surprised himself with the loudness of his voice.

"I will admit we are in uncharted territory, but generally these hypercoagulable diseases accelerate over time."

"Janine?" He needed to hear how she was taking all of this.

"Yeah?" Her voice was wobbly. He had to stay strong now.

"I'll get with Earl and Will, and we're going to move this right along. All of our resources at Made By Man, every VC—well, whatever it takes. We'll get this trial set up—" His voice betrayed him and faltered.

"Hank. I trust you. I know you'll move the earth and stars. If it was good enough for Wilbur, I'm happy to be the next volunteer for science." She laughed shakily.

"That's my sis. You always wanted to be part of the cure." He kept his voice even and squeezed his trembling free hand between his thighs. *That's MY sis.*

The conference room was still. Hank's limbs felt like lead. He was surprised to find time slowing in these moments, in the here and now, while time was racing ahead for Janine in St. Louis. He listened and heard familiar sounds on the other side of the conference room door. A couple of the engineers were excitedly arguing over the best way to do some process or another. Hank let the air expel from his lungs, and he tried to ground himself in this place, his business, the place where ideas met action and action produced processes and products that people used in San Francisco and Singapore—even St. Louis. He leaned over and punched in Will's number. First action, get permission from the team to call funding sources. Second action, get that patent issued.

Warren looked up, startled, as Hank smacked a brochure on his desk. "We have to pay the final installment for the booth today."

There was a security conference in Arlington next month and Warren knew Hank wanted Houdini represented there. But more importantly, Hank was on a rampage and he wanted to tell off some legislators and government officials. This was not going to be good for business. Warren took off his glasses and started cleaning them with a microfiber lens cloth. "Houdini doesn't have the money."

"I thought we were supposed to get paid by Xenix this week?"

"Yeah, but it's only Monday." Warren's dark eyes stared at him.

"We'll lose our deposit if we don't pay today." Hank paused. It wasn't Warren's fault Houdini didn't have the money for the symposium. He had already given up his Made By Man salary to fund Houdini, but they had to go to the conference if they hoped to move Houdini forward. "I'll pay for it and Houdini can pay me back when the Xenix check comes in."

Warren gave him a concerned look. "How you going to do that?"

"Don't worry about it." Hank got up and took the brochure with him. Warren leaned back in his chair and stared at the door. Once Hank made up his mind, there was no changing it. The deal with his sister was a bad one. He'd give Hank some room there, but funds were another story, especially if they came from their core operation.

When Hank got to the conference room, he punched a line on the conference telephone and was met by a dial tone. He pulled out his wallet, removing his Visa card. He never ran a balance on his credit cards, except when he had started Made By Man, and he didn't like doing it now. When he hung up, he looked out the window. The wind was howling, dark clouds were moving up the mountain, and sleet started popping on the window.

His feet were killing him after running the eight by five booth for two days at the conference. He couldn't afford a carpet floor for the booth, so he made do with the bare essentials. There was a fair amount of traffic and a lot of good leads. He was bone tired. He hated big cities in the first place. He hated big city airports even more. He remembered pulling into the airport and feeling the frustration of cars jockeying for position to get into the terminal. The logjam of cars reminded him of the patent office. Nothing could get through. He had blasted on the horn futilely. It was so unlike him. Never before had so much shit stood in his way.

He had a 10 a.m. appointment with Congressman Burnett and a 3p.m. appointment with Stanford Morris. To get an appointment Hank had to threaten Congressman Bill Burnett with letters to the editor explaining his unwillingness to meet with constituents. But this finally worked and he got his appointment with Burnett and the director of the patent office. Congressional representatives intervened with federal bureaucracies on the behalf of their constituents all of the time, playing hero to voters back home. By God, it was time they started serving this constituent.

Hank didn't know it, but Burnett had to remind Morris of the help he had given him in supporting his cowboy poetry festival in western North Carolina while he was in Congress in order to get him to agree to meet with Hank. At $700,000 per year in taxpayer money, Burnett felt it a steal for his help with this constituent and Morris's support of the Truth in Accounting Act.

Hank arrived for his meeting with the congressman ten minutes early. He was dressed in his Brooks Brothers suit, which he reserved for weddings and pitches to investors. Burnett's staff asked him to take a seat and offered him a cup of coffee, which he politely declined. The chair was an old wooden one that reminded him of the chairs in the principal's office in elementary school. He read the *New York Times* while he waited. An article reported that Congress had just approved a 'National Dress Up Your Pet Day.' His butt was beginning to hurt; he looked at his watch. 10:15 a.m. Their appointment was at 10 a.m. "Mr. Rangar, Congressman Burnett can see you now," the severe-looking young secretary said. He shook the congressman's hand and noticed the office was dominated by a huge, dark, highly-polished desk that looked like it had never seen any paper.

"How can I help you, Mr. Rangar?" Burnett was dressed in an expensive suit that reminded Hank of a mortician. He was in his mid-forties with brown hair that looked like he had just come from the barber. Hank noticed the strong scent of cologne.

Hank got right to the point. "The main reason I am here is because my sister, Janine, is likely to die if she does not get an experimental procedure that is being held up by the patent office. This company, EWE Tech, has developed the angiochannelizer and it is her best hope for living, but they cannot get funding because the patent office takes forever to issue patents." Congressman Burnett leaned back, folded his hands like he was praying, and pressed his index fingers to his thin lips. "Secondarily, I am here because the Truth in Accounting law and our dysfunctional patent system are destroying innovation in the US." Hank took a breath.

Burnett leaned forward and looked him in the eye. "I am so sorry to hear about your sister. I know that many people have concerns about the patent system and we in Congress are working hard to address these concerns. We understand the importance of a strong patent system that balances all the stakeholders' interests. Unfortunately, the issues are quite complex and I admit that I am not an expert. But I can assure you that the opinions of average citizens like yourself are very important to those of us in Congress." Hank bristled at the 'average citizens' comment and raised his hand to interject but Burnett didn't seem to notice. "The Truth in Accounting law was a critical piece of legislation for restoring investor confidence in the accounting statements of companies and to prevent fraud. I consider it one of my most important legislative achievements."

Hank did not understand how people like Burnett were able to string together words as if they were saying something without forming a coherent thought. He didn't know where to start to respond to this nonsense. "Excuse me, Congressman, but do you realize that the TIA law is killing off the venture capital industry and funding for technology startup companies?" Hank wanted to add, 'How could you consider that an achievement?'

Burnett smiled. "I think you are mistaken, Mr. Rangar. The top accounting firms in the country just did a study showing that the TIA has resulted in increased investor confidence and created over 100,000 accounting and related jobs."

Hank noticed that he had not really answered the question; he was not going to let him off the hook that easily. "Accounting jobs are not part of the venture capital industry or part of the technology startup industry they fund. Are you aware the damage the TIA has done to these industries?" Hank leaned in to emphasize his point.

The congressman stared at him with a blank face for at least fifteen seconds. "I think creating 100,000 jobs is quite an accomplishment, don't you?"

Hank could not believe what he was hearing, "Compliance jobs—jobs whose only reason for existing is to comply with government regulations—do not add to the wealth of the country, or to the average person in the US. Those jobs came at the expense of the jobs of Americans who produce real goods and services that people want." Hank could feel his face getting flushed.

The congressman stared back. "I guess we will have to agree to disagree."

Great, I only have a limited amount of time and debating the merits of TIA is not why I am here. "Congressman Burnett, I think we have gotten off track. My sister is going to die if EWE Tech cannot obtain funding quickly for human trials. They have investors lined up to fund them if they receive a patent. I need your help to get the patent office to accelerate this case."

"My hopes and prayers are with your sister. I am sure that the patent office is doing their best," Burnett said with his best empathetic expression.

"I am not interested in your empathy, hopes, or prayers, Congressman."

Congressman Burnett was shocked. This line always worked. Whether people were religious or not, offering to pray for someone's loved one was taken as genuine sympathy and indicated good intentions.

"Only the procedure using the angiochannelizer will save her life." Hank felt as if he was explaining basic algebra to a fifth grader.

Congressman Burnett took off his suit jacket and placed it carefully over the back of his brown leather chair, loosened his cuffs, rolled up his sleeves, looked Hank directly in the eye and said softly, "What do you want me to do, Hank?"

"I need you to intervene with the patent office bureaucrats and get the EWE patent issued."

"Mr. Rangar, I have to deal with many important legislative matters here and I don't have the authority or time to intervene in one company's patent."

Hank realized that he had reached an impasse. "Sure, Congressman Burnett; you are much too busy passing National Dress Up Your Pet Day to take time out of your busy schedule to make sure that the patent office does its job and saves my sister's life. After all, it's not as if protecting the rights of inventors is part of your constitutional duty. Oops, actually it is part of the Constitution, but the serious business of placating pet owners is a truly important legislative matter." Hank slapped the *New York Times* on Congressman Burnett's desk and left. The paper was folded to the article about National Dress Up Your Pet Day.

Congressman Burnett was amazed at this display. How could anyone fault him? He always took all the stakeholders into account in his calculations about what course was for the greater good.

Hank purchased a hot dog from a vendor outside the patent office building. Once again, he was early for his appointment, so he decided to explore, hoping it would wash away the negative feeling of this morning. The building was a brick and glass cathedral that screamed 'expensive government building.' The main entrance was a multistory atrium with marble floors, which probably cost a fortune and provided little value except to impress visitors. Despite this, Hank felt a reverence. In these walls were Edison's patents on the electric light bulb and the phonograph, Tesla's patent on alternating current, and the patent on the transistor that won Bradeen, Brattian, and Shockley the Nobel Prize in Physics.

Visitors were only allowed in the atrium and the public search facilities. Hank spent a little time familiarizing himself with the search computers. When it was 2:45 p.m., he went up to the reception desk and told the receptionist he had an appointment with Director Stanford Morris. The receptionist was a well-dressed, thirtyish, overweight woman who exuded boredom. She lazily took Hank's business card, handed him a visitor badge that said he needed an escort and told him to sign in to the visitors' register. "When you have signed in you can take a seat. Someone will be with you shortly," she said with a slight Southern drawl.

Twenty-five minutes later an officious woman in her late thirties or early forties with brown hair in a bun approached him. "Mr. Rangar?"

"Yes." Hank stood up and reached out to shake her hand.

"I'm Tamara Byron." She shook his hand and gave him her card. "Right this way, Mr. Rangar." She turned on her heel and headed for the elevators.

She took Hank to a large conference room on the top floor with a wall of windows that Hank suspected would have had an excellent view, but the blinds were drawn. This made Hank feel a little claustrophobic. That and his suit made him feel a little like a caged, chained animal. He was introduced to a number of people and Tamara told him that Director Morris would be along shortly. "While we're waiting, Director Morris asked that we provide you an update on the patent office's performance and account-ability report." Hank was a bit perplexed by this but decided to go with the flow.

The lights were turned off and Tamara started the presentation. Just as she got started, Stanford Morris entered the room, looked around, spotted an unfamiliar face and correctly assumed it was Hank. "Mr. Rangar, I just wanted to say hi. I'm Stanford Morris and when my team is done with the presentation I will pick you up and we can talk." Morris gave a quick wave and was out the door. Hank wondered how long this presentation would take.

Tamara picked up the presentation, which Hank sus-pected was a puff piece about the patent office. After wading through the patent office's efforts to improve its recruitment, the presentation moved on to the office's quality systems. Hank was not really interested and thought it an odd presentation for a visitor. However, his mind quickly noticed that the office was only measuring Type I errors and their system was only designed to correct these. Hank raised his hand and said, "You only seem to be measuring and testing for patent applications that were incorrectly issued. Do you have data on incorrectly rejected patent applications?" Tamara looked slightly perturbed.

"The applicant always has the right to appeal the office's decision, so these errors are self-correcting," she snapped, and turned to pick up where she left off.

As long as he was stuck in this presentation, he was not going to let her off that easily. "But the delay and cost of filing appeals increases the cost to the inventor and the patent office. It now takes over three years for most patents to be examined and issued. As a result, many startups are unjustly starved of capital and go out of business waiting on the patent office. Type II errors have real-world implications to startups like mine."

Ms. Bryon pursed her lips and put her hands on her hips. "It is not the concern of the patent office whether a couple of little startups do or do not receive funding. The patent office is not a source of funds for startups and there are a myriad of reasons why a startup might not receive funding. For you to suggest that it is the fault of this office is without any factual basis and frankly, impolite."

Hank thought her reply was both impolite and failed to address his question. "Perhaps, but this office doesn't seem to understand the basics of quality control nor how its decisions affect its customers and even more appallingly, it does not seem to care."

She looked at him with undisguised scorn. "We deal with inventions from the most prestigious universities in the world, the biggest companies, and the most prominent government research laboratories. None of these celebrated institutions are concerned with Type II errors. Whether some little inventor receives a patent or not is unlikely to have any earth-shattering implications." Ms. Byron clicked on to the next slide.

Hank would have enjoyed toying with this buttoned-up bitch if she and the patent office were not destroying real companies and lives. Janine might die because of ignorant, arrogant bureaucrats like her. "You seem to believe that the Wright brothers, Alexander Graham Bell, or even Chester Carlson, inventor of the photocopier, were unimportant inventors, since none worked at any of the celebrated institutions you mentioned. In my case, my sister will die if she cannot get the experimental surgery developed by EWE Technology. But of course, EWE Technology is not a 'celebrated' institution, so according to you my sister's death will not have any 'earth-shattering' consequences." He heard a gasp from a man in a dark suit to his left.

There was an awkward silence and Tamara attempted to continue with the presentation.

"I think I have heard more than enough of the patent office's deceptive self-promotion. Please tell Mr. Morris that the presentation is over and I wish to speak to him."

Tamara started to object but saw the determination on Hank's face. The other patent office employees filed out of the conference room and she followed. Tamara was not looking forward to explaining what had happened. It was her job to sell the public on the great job the patent office was doing. Director Morris was not going to be at all happy about how the meeting had gone. He tended to shoot the messenger. Perhaps if she did not tell him, Director Morris would eventually return to the conference room and Rangar would be the messenger. Besides, by not telling Morris, Rangar would be left waiting in the conference room. The thought of that arrogant bastard having to cool his heels suddenly brought delight to her.

Hank waited for about five minutes and then walked down the hall and found Stanford Morris's secretary, or executive assistant, as they preferred to be called today. She wore a grey business suit, and had a schoolmarmish sort of look. He walked briskly up to her and just as he was about to speak, she said, "Where is your escort? You're not allowed to roam the halls without an escort!" she said in a squeaky voice.

"Miss, tell Mr. Morris that Hank Rangar is here to see him."

"But where is your escort? How did you get here?" she asked.

Hank said authoritatively, "That is unimportant. Please let Mr. Morris know I am here." Hank had learned that the best way to deal with schoolteachers, and others who thrive on authority instead of reason, was to give them what they wanted.

The secretary slowly picked up the phone and with a slight sneer said, "Mr. Morris, a Hank Rangar is here to see you," and then she turned away from Hank, covered her mouth and conspiratorially said, "He doesn't have an escort."

"Please show him in," Stanford replied. He had expected the presentation to take longer. Oh well. He hated dealing with constituents. They didn't understand how things worked in Washington and seemed to have some sort of perverse idea that he worked for them personally. Luckily, being the director of the patent office had relieved him of that unpleasant task—the only good thing about not being a congressman.

Stanford sat behind a massive mahogany desk, its surface marred only by a sleek black computer monitor. He stood up and told Hank to take a seat on the other side of the desk. Hank noticed that Morris had a small table for meetings next to the window but had chosen to stay behind his desk. "How can I help you, Mr. Rangar?"

Hank explained his sister's medical condition and that only if she received the procedure using EWE's technology would she survive. When Hank mentioned EWE, he noticed a slight flush in Morris's face and Morris shifted his weight in his seat.

There was an awkward silence and then Stanford replied, "You have my sympathy and prayers for your sister. You do not happen to be the attorney of record for EWE?" he asked without any emotion.

"No," Hank said.

"Well, I am not allowed to discuss individual patent cases with anyone but the attorney of record. It's the law," Morris said this as if he were explaining to a child.

How could he sit there so callously? Janine's life is a stake, and this pencil-necked, arrogant bureaucrat is worried about a legal technicality. He thought about jumping over the desk and snapping this guy's neck, but said calmly, "So you are just going to sit there and let my sister die?"

Stanford noticed Hank's powerful arms grinding his hands together. He wondered whether this Rangar guy was unstable. He pressed himself into the back of his chair. "The patent office is doing the best we can. We can hardly be held responsible for your sister's death. Unless you have something else you wish to discuss, this meeting is over."

You can't dismiss me like I am just some serf. "Can you explain why the patent office is only concerned with Type I errors?"

Stanford closed his eyes. *Another fucking person asking about Type I and Type II errors.* He still didn't know the difference. "Mr. Rangar, you just left the room with the experts on this issue. Did you ask them?" he asked in a sickly sweet voice.

"I did and the answer I received was bureaucratic nonsense."

Stanford's patience was at an end. He stood up and said, "I am sorry I could not be of more help, Mr. Rangar. My executive assistant will be happy to escort you out."

As Lilly entered the office, Hank stood. "You are killing people, much more clearly than cigarette companies or a bartender who served a customer too many drinks. How can you live with yourself?"

The goddamn patent office is run by a bunch of arrogant, incompetent bureaucrats who either don't know or don't seem to care about the real-life consequences of their actions. He entered the dark stairwell of the subway entrance and descended below the street. Hank was tired, and frankly, felt the place left him with a bad smell. He headed back to his hotel room to take a long, hot shower.

Chapter 11

Hank sprang into action. Action relieved the anxiety—raising funds for EWE was the only way to save Janine's life. There just was no way of knowing how much time was left. He pulled Made By Man's secretary in on contacting VCs and angel investors. Peggy White was in her early fifties, a little plump but extremely efficient. She was a bulldog when given a task like this.

She had made up a list of potential funding sources. Hank divided the list and they started calling. Getting past call screeners, human and machine, slowed down the process. When they did break through, most VCs said their funds were fully invested. Angels appeared to be more promising, so they focused on them exclusively. They stayed on the phone most of the day, hunting down decision-makers and leaving contact information. Hank got hold of one angel, a Mr. Conklyn, and started explaining the opportunity that EWE presented. As Hank was explaining the technology, Conklyn interrupted him. "Are you from AltruMedical?"

"No, I am calling you on behalf of EWE Technology." Hank was a little surprised by the question.

"Oh, well I'm not interested," Conklyn responded and hung up. Hank was perplexed by the abruptness with which the call ended.

Warren Criss entered the lab and closed the doors. "How's it going?" It was around 5:30 p.m.

"I've solicited more people in the last couple of weeks than most prostitutes, and with a lot less success. I think I feel more abused too. What's happening?"

"Houdini is bleeding cash." Warren pulled up a chair and sat down. When Hank didn't say anything, he continued. "You don't have enough time to spend on either Made by Man or Houdini. Made by Man will be fine even in this poor economy, but we have to make changes to Houdini."

"What sort of changes are you thinking about?" Hank put his call list aside and faced Warren. He knew that this was difficult for him.

"Well, we have some loyal customers and some steady cash flow even with Thurston screwing up the market.

But without capital, we just don't have the marketing and sales muscle to grow as fast as our projections." Warren fidgeted in his chair.

"You know that without a patent we can't get any investment capital right now. And the idiots in Washington just keep making it harder to raise capital—hell, it's easier to gamble a $100K in Vegas than it is to invest in a startup." Hank stood up and walked to the windows, which overlooked Pikes Peak and the surrounding mountains. A heavy, wet spring snow was blanketing the landscape. He felt cold, and for the first time in a long time, he didn't know what to do next. Warren followed Hank's gaze and they stayed there together, silent, staring at the snow.

Warren hated bringing up this subject, with all the things Hank had on his mind. If it had been one of his daughters in this position, he would run over anyone in his way. "Yeah, I heard that the whole Washington trip turned out to be a cluster-f."

"Enough talk about what we can't do; what can we do?" Hank turned back to his partner, his gaze intense.

"I think we need to let one of the outside sales guys go until we can get sales up to 1.2 million."

Hank's shoulders drooped. Hank was good at growing companies, not preserving them. "I'm sorry. I've been sort of checked out. You know I trust you completely; if that's what we need to do then you have my support."

They had been partners—technically co-owners—for years. They had different styles, but each knew that they would always do what was right for the company. Besides, Warren was the person closest to the situation and was in a better position to make these sorts of operational decisions.

"All right, we'll do it." Warren slapped his palm down on the desk with finality. "I'm for home. Hank, you should go home as well."

"I just have to finish up some expense reports and get some information together for our tax accountants," he said. On his drive home, he thought of all the time and effort they spent on government compliance issues. Here he was at the office past eleven, doing government compliance bullshit. There was nothing productive in any of that besides making his accountant wealthier. All that money—billions companies spent every year on just the IRS compliance, and he'd read in a business magazine that altogether it was over six billion man-hours a year. Add in SEC, EPA, FTC and state versions of all of these; just imagine the costs both in dollars and hours. What a waste. What a total waste.

Hank drove an International Harvester Scout II that he had restored. People often mistook Scouts for old Jeeps. The Scout II had an offset differential that provided higher ground clearance than the center differential design of Jeeps. Hank had rebuilt the 345 V-8 and had restored the interior. The body of the Scout was a canary yellow with black covering the cargo area, just like it looked off the factory floor. It was a great off-roading vehicle but Hank rarely found the time for that anymore. As he pulled into his garage, he caught the faint smell of campfire, which made him smile. The night was cold and damp. Someone had a wood fire burning.

He entered the foyer, dropped his keys on a small table next to the door, crossing the living room and opened the door to his bedroom. He pulled off his jacket as he sat on the bed and toed off his loafers as he fell back. He was so tired he thought he would sleep in his clothes tonight.

I need to tell Warren tomorrow about the changes I want to make to the interface of the Houdini software. I need to meet with Peggy to see if she had any luck talking with the VCs.

His mind was racing, so he decided to get a glass of water and take off his jeans and shirt. He wondered why it was that his mind always did this when he felt so tired from a long day at work. He forced himself to think about taking his Scout to Lake City and fly-fishing the Lake Fork of the Gunnison River. His favorite spot required him to hike up the river a half mile. The aspens higher up the mountain were just beginning to turn, producing blindingly bright patches of yellow, occasionally outlined in a soft red. He could feel the breeze and sun on his face competing to cool and heat him. The sun was sparkling on the water. It was a perfect early fall day. The huge bolder up ahead in the river was his favorite spot. It formed a perfect seam on either side of it. It was a dry fly day. He tied the fly onto his leader and formed a couple of giant Ss in his line. The fly landed a little past the seam. No matter, how could you complain, the tranquil sound of the river bubbling along, the intense smell of the pinesap wafting past your nose. Another giant S and perfect, pull in line, a little more, BAM—set the hook, beautiful—keep tension but not too much; give her room to run. Musical notes, what the—*it's my damn phone. I never take my cell phone fly-fishing.*

Hank woke up a little disoriented and looked at who was calling him at this time of night. He had finally fallen asleep and it was such a good dream. It was a 314 area code. He quickly answered, "Hello."

"Hank, it's Mark."

Hank knew it couldn't be good news at this hour of the night.

"Hank, are you there?"

"Yeah." Hank sat up in bed and ran his fingers through his hair.

"They think Janine has had another heart attack. She was feeling weak and having some problems breathing."

There was some crackling on the line and Hank overheard Jess talking to Mark. "Is Momma gonna be all right?" There were some sniffles.

"I hope so, dear." There was a loud clank as the phone hit the floor, followed by some scratching noises. "Jess, I'm talking to Uncle Hank on the phone. I can't hold you right now." This was followed by what sounded like both kids crying. Mark tried to comfort them. "Sorry about that. It's very hard on the kids. She's in stable condition in the ICU. Dr. Dearing did pull me aside and ask me when EWE's procedure would be ready for human trials."

"I don't know. I'm working as hard as I can. How much time do I have?" Hank could feel himself getting flushed.

"Uh, well, you remember Dr. Dearing said things would accelerate."

Hank quickly did the math. "Give my sis a hug and tell her to stay strong. Ah…and call me with any updates." Hank overhead Tristan. "I want to talk to Uncle Hank."

"Hey buddy, are your being strong for your dad?"

"Uncle Hank." There was a pause.

"Yeah."

"I miss you."

Hank could hear some sniffles. "I miss you too." Hank searched his mind for something comforting to say.

"Uncle Hank, do you remember the time you took us to the zoo and told us the story of Robin Hood?"

"Of course I do." Hank could hear Mark in the background.

"Uncle Hank has to go now. Give me the phone."

"Can you come over tomorrow and play Uncle Hank?"

"I would love to, but I have to work."

There was a pause as Mark got Tristan to hand the phone back to him. "I'll keep you updated. Bye."

Hank heard the connection drop and said goodbye into the ether.

The alarm clock displayed 4:00 a.m., but Hank had yet to fall asleep. Frustrated, he threw off the covers and jumped into the shower. The hot water quickly steamed up the room. He tried to scrub away the pain, to no avail, so he turned his mind to the problem at hand. He needed to know exactly how much money EWE needed to perform the angiochannelizer procedure on Janine. Will had been looking into these numbers. He toweled off and felt the cold air rush in as he opened the door, causing goose bumps to form. The cold of the floor bit his toes as he headed into the bedroom. He threw on some jeans, a t-shirt and a fleece pullover. A pair of blended wool socks brought instant relief to his toes. It was 4:37 a.m., but Will was an hour ahead.

"Hank?" a groggy voice said.

"Yeah. I need to know the absolute minimum amount necessary for a single procedure."

Will thought this was an odd question. "Ah, well you know we are looking for a five-million-dollar investment."

"Yeah I know that, but what I am interested in is what would it take to jump through the Food and Drug Administration's hoops to perform a single human surgery with the angiochannelizer." Hank noticed his knee was bouncing up and down at a rapid rate.

"What good would that do us? We need a sample size of at least three thousand to get approval from the FDA to bring the technology to market."

"Damn it. Janine is back in the hospital. She needs the surgery now!"

"I'm sorry. I didn't know." Will thought about it. "We need a premarket approval from the FDA and I think those costs are about $200K."

Hank quickly did the calculation. His house was worth somewhere around $350K and because of the life insurance he had received from his parent's death he owned it free and clear. "I could get that."

Will could hear the enthusiasm in Hank's voice. "But we also need to pay the consultants to write the premarket approval plan for us. I think that is about $200k also. Plus, we need the money to pay the hospital and the doctor to perform the surgery."

Hank started writing down numbers on a pad. "I am pretty sure that Janine's doctor and the hospital where she works would be willing to donate that part. If I could get you $400k, then we could get the approval process rolling?"

Will didn't like being closed without more time to think about it. "I think that's about right, but I'll have to double check and get back to you."

I think I can wing that. I will have to meet with my banker. "How long from the time I get you the money until we get approval?"

"Hank, I'm not an expert on that but I believe the consultants told us it would be around a month, if we didn't run into any snags with the FDA."

"All right. Call the consultants and tell them to put us in the queue. I'll try to get you an answer by today." Hank hung up without saying goodbye.

When the doors to the Rocky National Bank opened at 8 a.m., Hank was waiting outside the door. He walked straight into his banker's office. "Darren, I need a mortgage on my house as fast as I can."

Darren stood up and pushed up his glasses with his index finger. "It's nice to see you too Hank." They shook hands and Hank explained the situation with Janine. They discussed a number of options: a ninety percent loan to value on the house would probably bring in $320K and a loan against Hank's interest in Made by Man would bring in another $70K.

$390K, still ten grand short. Well, I can take that from savings or a credit card. "How fast can we fund the loan?"

"I'll push this through. I would say three to four business days."

By that evening Hank had the loans in process and Will had confirmed everything with the consultants. Mark confirmed that Janine was stable and out of the ICU. Mark had found Dr. Dearing and she thought it would be no problem donating her time and the hospital charges for Janine. When Hank told Janine that night, she tried to ask some probing questions but Hank was able to deflect her. It was late, Hank opened a beer and the aroma of baking bread filled his nose. He plopped into his favorite chair and felt it envelop him. *Finally, something seems to be working right.*

Chapter 12

The offices of *The Financial Reporter* in New York City occupied the second and third floors of an old bank building on East 52ⁿᵈ. The pre-WWII elevators still worked in the building and were quite charming to admire if you didn't have an eminent deadline or the editor had called you in yesterday. When the elevators brought you to the second floor, you were in a large open newsroom or the 'pit' as the employees called it. The pit was separated into cubicles accomplished by five-foot tall interlocking carpeted dividers—soundproof they were not. Where once old landline black rotary-dialed phones rang incessantly during the trading day, now there were incessant cell phone vibrating alerts and callers hunched over the soft glow of their laptops speaking softly to those on the other side of the virtual line.

If you worked in the pit, you knew how to traverse the warren of quixotic cubicles to get to your own five by five space. However, if you were visiting the *Financial Reporter*, you would not have a clue where to check in. There was no reception area, so to speak, nor anyone who seemed to be in charge of directing outsiders to the appropriate place within the news organization. After all, nowadays, most communicated to the newsroom by phone, email, or tweet; and anyone in the physical needing help was just damned annoying.

Christine Patel was having this feeling as she looked over toward the elevator and saw a visitor disembark. Her cubicle was closest to the elevator and, therefore, she was the de facto welcoming committee. She suspected her male colleagues had something to do with this; as she looked to the right and left, she noted studiously engrossed poses over laptops. She sighed, and plastering a bright welcoming smile on her face, she offered assistance. Luckily, the visitor was meeting one of the other reporters for lunch and was happily dispatched across the room.

Christine watched as the female visitor strode along the outside of the pit to her destination, her heels clicking sharply against the travertine marble floor. All along the outside of the pit were offices framed up by large glass windows. These windows could be privatized by blinds, but rarely did any of the senior staff choose to do so. There was nothing so effective a motivator as watching your fellow reporter get reamed a new one in pantomime behind one of those office windows; and as Christine appreciated currently, all was quiet on the western side. This might be due to the new editor *FR* had secured. Christine liked him immensely compared to that last blowhard.

The third floor was occupied by the publisher, assistant publisher, and several conference rooms, where the board met and the tone and direction of the *Reporter* were set by people who never worked in a pit in their life but did understand bottom lines. The third floor had a reception desk; it was rather large and occupied by fierce gatekeepers who were not prone to smiling. Since she had just recently handed over her current assignment dealing with the success of a startup that sold out for millions and would possibly change a portion of the health care industry and since an old guard senator was up to his eyeballs in that merger, she possibly was going to make the front page for the foreseeable future. She decided to take a break. Peeling a banana at her desk, she took a bite and sighed her pleasure audibly.

"Jesus, Patel—a man's gotta work over here! Is Jenson under your desk and up your skirt or something?"

Christine screwed up her dark features into disgust. "You are such an idiot, Manch. I am enjoying my breakfast."

Sometimes it was all she could do to suffer these slovenly idiots who took assignments and applied ten percent of themselves to the job. Although she hadn't graduated from a fancy Eastern university, her small Midwestern college experience had been a good one and she excelled in her graduate studies in finance. She couldn't shake her passion for journalism, however, and after a few years on Wall Street working the floor, she graduated to this pit. Her stories had been picked up by other media outlets before but her co-workers seemed irritated by her enthusiasm and disdainful of her positions on big business, especially here in New York. Manch would always end their meetings with, "OH, and Christine, don't bite the hand that feeds you." All the guys would laugh and the women would share nods of solidarity against the sophomoric behavior.

"Got a bar over there for me? Didn't eat breakfast, I'm starved and can't leave for lunch. Got a big deadline this afternoon." Manch was going to continue to be annoying. She grasped her shoulder-length dark hair with one hand and tugged it to the back of her neck as she looked down at her computer screen. The boring assignment that had to be completed was still glaring back at her. She was tasked to a follow-up article about the medical startup community and drew a blank. She took another bite of banana and then another.

"It's a banana, not a bar," Christine said between bites. "It is nature's perfect snack and you don't even have to pay for the packaging." She chuckled lightly.

"Well, Polyester Ann, no wonder you get all the puff pieces with a prim little attitude like that."

That did it. She flung the banana peel up over the divider.

"Hey!" Manch shot to his feet and glared over the partition at her. Palms up and out she gestured toward her computer as if to say 'I'm workin' here,' and furiously began typing on the keyboard. Manch picked up the peel and flung it into a trash receptacle outside his cubicle. He slammed down into his desk chair and Christine cringed at the squeak of the chair wheels as he pushed himself closer to his desk. "Bitch!" he softly but viciously retorted.

Christine ignored Manch and checked the comments section of her latest article online. She scrolled through the usual peanut gallery accusing her of bashing the senator with no proof—ha! Farther down, she responded to a request for information on contacting the senator's office in DC. She already knew how many comments were not included due to the inappropriate naming of parts of her anatomy or references to her as a female dog. Manch was buddies with the online editor who monitored the comments, and he kept a tally when she'd make the front page. She glanced up to see Joe walk by the cubicles and he caught her eye, gesturing toward his office. Grateful for a break, she followed him.

Joe Benson shut the door behind him as they entered his office.

"Things have changed." He looked at her steadily.

"What's changed? Today's article has gotten click-throughs in the five figures. You've got the damage on that scum to run tomorrow for another maybe six figures in looks. I said I'd soften it on the company." Christine screwed up her face.

"Look. The senator's office has contacted the paper. I'm getting leaned on from upstairs. We're backing off."

"Are you kidding me? I am this close to proving he used his influence in an insider trading deal! He got those grants for them! He—"

"Christine. Look, we ran with it. It's out there. Let the rest of the media pick up on it. Do you see my cell phone constantly ringing from the major networks? We're done. Moving on." He crossed behind his desk and sat. Christine took some deep breaths for control.

"Blumenthal does not know what he's passing up. Corruption like this goes on every day, no one seems to care. I've got this asshole digging his own grave and you guys refuse to nail him in the coffin! Bunch of spineless—"

"That's enough. We're done here, Ms. Patel." Joe bent to some task on his laptop.

Christine hesitated, weighing whether to leave the office or try a different approach. "Joe, this is some great dirt. It's going to stick…" Joe held up his hand to silence her. Why the hell did he think that would stop her from making the point? She screwed her eyebrows inward as he turned his laptop toward her.

"Look at this." She leaned in and started reading off the screen.

I don't care for lying reporters.

This city doesn't need your kind.

Go back to whatever country you came from and we'll forget a little curry cunt like you ever existed.

"The moderators pulled it and sent it to me an hour ago. I've been upstairs, and this plays into the decision. I don't have the budget or manpower to deal with Fowl's kooky base. He has been in the Senate a long time. Lots of companies and constituents would be in an uproar if anything goes bad for the senator." At first, Christine found herself a little excited she was creating enemies, but she had to admit the racial anatomy slur made her uneasy. She looked up and saw Joe reading her expression.

"Christine, we take this carefully. We develop the whole story."

"What more do you want? Pictures with the CEO? Who cares about that?"

"This paper is not going to be accused of witch hunts. I know it's not as exciting, but come at this from the other end. Let's see who approached whom, get back-stories on all perceived players here, not just the senator. In the meantime, I've got to get legal in on this. Christine, it's probably nothing, but be careful."

The subway was surprisingly empty for Thursday evening. It made her feel colder. There was one filthy old guy asleep at the back, a thick knit cap pulled low over his forehead. The stench of smoke and alcohol seemed to roll along the floor and assault her nostrils. He opened one glassy eye. It rotated in its socket and stared at her. A college-aged woman with short brown hair was intently listening to music on her iPod. But that was it. The train pulled into the next stop and the doors slid open with a whish. No one got off. The platform was an empty cavern. She started unzipping her pack and heard something scrape against the doors. She looked up and saw a gangbanger in a hooded sweatshirt slide through the doors sideways just before they closed. She could feel her heart racing and closed her eyes for a moment. This was ridiculous! The one online comment had made her jumpy all afternoon. Things like this happened to every reporter. It was a public venue and anyone could surf the Net and be a blowhard with some crazy username. She watched the man work his way back toward the old guy. He slid in a seat, pulled a brown paper bag out of his coat and took a slug. Christine took out her notebook. Catching up on emails would keep her imagination from running wild.

Luckily, the street lights were all working as Christine left the station behind on the way to her apartment building. It was a short two blocks and her stride was brisker than normal. She took the elevator up to her apartment. Her apartment enjoyed the view of a small park nestled between the buildings. She raised the key again to open her door and realized it was slightly ajar. Icy fear filled her veins and she stepped back. Careful not to let her keys jangle, she regripped them like she had been taught in a self-defense class, and slowly backed away. Her neighbor across the hall was a bodybuilder. Unfortunately, he wasn't around much in the evenings. She turned and rapped softly on his door. No answer. She expelled her breath in silent frustration and looked back at her door. It still was ajar and the hallway remained quiet. She softly padded back, leaned forward and peered around the door. Dark and quiet. She pushed the door open with her foot and simultaneously flicked on the overhead light. The bright room slammed into focus. Her things were everywhere: the floor, her couch. A chair was overturned, shelves were knocked over and drawers were open or upturned on the floor. She took a few moments to let the implications sink in. The door to her bedroom was closed. She stared at the closed door and debated whether to cross the ransacked mess and open it. White-hot anger replaced her fear. Keeping the keys ready, she used her other hand to fish the phone out of her bag. Using her thumb, she dialed 911.

"Ms. Patel, it looks like they picked the lock. We'll need an inventory of anything taken. But when they are brazen like that in the day or early evening, walking right out of your building with electronics or what not, that's pretty unusual. See anything obvious they took?"

Christine remained staring at the mirror above her headboard. They would have had to crawl onto her bed to write that. She looked away and around the room.

"I don't have much jewelry. My laptop was with me. The TV is still here..." Christine trailed off.

"We'll go through this in stages, miss. We need to complete the search for fingerprints. I'll use my pen here to help us check things out. Let's start with your jewelry. Where do you keep it?" She noticed that he was pointedly not looking at the mirror and trying to divert her attention away from it as well. She headed to the bathroom. "In here, Officer."

Officer Nowak flicked on the bathroom light with his pen. The harsh yellow light blanketed the small white room. Christine took in the shredded shower curtain and spilled shampoo and body wash, their soft tones of amber and white mixing into yellow and seeping toward the drain. She stepped into the room, Officer Nowak too close behind her. The small bureau opposite the sink was lying on its side, jewelry, cosmetics, and hair appliances covered the floor. She slowly bent down and sifted through the wreckage of her morning routine to examine what remained of her jewelry. All the gold was missing.

Maybe it was worth no more than three or four hundred. She wasn't sure. Her silver and costume stuff were scattered across the floor, untouched most likely.

"Ms. Patel, are you missing anything?" Christine nodded her head slowly and stood up straight.

"Yeah, some gold jewelry. It's not worth that much. I don't see anything else obvious."

"Captain! Could you come back in here please?" One of the officers appeared in the doorway to the bedroom. Officer Nowak backed out of the bathroom and Christine debated whether to follow him.

She reluctantly took up behind him and stopped when she reached the doorjamb. She looked around the door and spotted the officers crouched low over one of her dresser drawers. A pair of her panties were draped over Officer Nowak's pen and she felt bile come into her throat as she realized they were in tatters.

"All of them, the whole drawer." The officer whispered the last part to Captain Nowak. Christine hugged herself and walked back into the living room. She sat on the couch, her legs together, and continued hugging her arms close. She felt cold now, the anger turning back to fear. She struggled for control of her physical self, for control over what had happened to her. The violation of her property and home was combating the self-assurance and wellbeing she took for granted. She concentrated on the fact that New Yorkers were robbed daily; nothing special here. Just her turn, that was all.

"Ms. Patel, do you have somewhere else to stay tonight?" Christine stood from the couch and began righting the overturned chair and picking up books and replacing them on the shelf.

"Are you gentlemen done in here? I need to pick this mess up." She continued to ignore Captain Nowak and bent to retrieve a folder, scooping flown papers together and straightening them. Order. That was key here. Getting everything back the way it had been. A shower curtain and underwear were easy to replace. She glanced sharply to the sofa table behind the couch and spotted the overturned picture frames. She ran back to the couch and grabbed the closest one. Its glass frame was untouched and the picture of her brother and mom and dad felt comforting. She continued to pick up the pictures one by one. Fine. Untouched. The last picture she overturned was her favorite of herself with her college roommates. The glass was broken and a knife or some sharp object had obliterated her smiling and happy face. Her roommates were untouched. She held it against her chest and felt the tears spilling down her face. She closed her eyes hard and tried to blink them back with no success.

"Ms. Patel, I need you to pay attention to me now. This is no ordinary break-in. We got us here a brazen attack and it looks personal. We take these kinds seriously and I need you to see, whoever did this, they might come back. Do you have any thoughts on who this might be? Jilted boyfriend, jealous ex-girlfriend?" Christine shook her head and dropped her chin to her chest. She heard the sound of broken glass crunching into the picture and lightened her grip. She glanced up and through the cloud of tears, she stared at the neat block letters marching across her mirror.

NO MORE LIES CUNT

Chapter 13

The loans had funded in four days. Janine was in stable condition and they were planning to release her from the hospital tomorrow. Mark wasn't happy about this, but the new system was to push patients out of the hospital as quickly as possible. Dr. Dearing had confirmed that the hospital would donate their fees.

The stack of loan papers seemed to be endless. Darren had stepped out to get a notary public. The conference table was ten feet of polished cherry. Hank could see his reflection in it. He had put on his suit for the occasion and he wondered who this guy in a suit was, looking back at him. There was a faint smell of lemon wax. He pulled out his cell phone and started checking emails.

Hank heard footsteps and saw a very smartly dressed, redheaded woman following Darren into the conference room.

"Ms. Johnson, this is Mr. Hank Rangar." Hank stood and shook her hand, which was surprisingly firm. "Ms. Johnson is a notary."

They all sat down and Ms. Johnson pulled out a black book. "Can I see your driver's license, Mr. Rangar?" Hank pulled out his wallet and handed it over. Ms. Johnson started meticulously writing down information in her black book. Hank felt something vibrating against his leg and an instant later "We Will Rock You" started playing from his phone. It sounded so loud. "I'm sorry." Both Ms. Johnson and Darren looked at him with questioning faces. "Just let me turn this darn thing off." He started to hit the cancel call button, when he saw it was Mark. *Mark probably wondered if he had signed the papers for the loans.* He hit the answer call button. "Mark, I can't talk right now. I'm signing the papers for the loan and then—"

"Hank, shut up… She's dead." Hank saw the reflection of his shock in Darren and Ms. Johnson's faces. Hank didn't know what to say. "Well, brain dead. She went into cardiogenic shock in the middle of the night. She's on life support."

Hank stood up immediately and the room started spinning. He slumped back into his chair. He could hear Mark trying to control his voice. "We thought you would want to say goodbye to her."

"Yes." He hung up and turned to Darren, tears streaming down his face. "I'm sorry. I no longer require the loans." With that, he left the conference room and started walking south on Tejon Street. *There was no reason for her to die. The technology was there to save her.* He kicked a stoplight pole at the intersection. People were looking at him, but he couldn't be bothered with that. *They wouldn't give us a patent, they put obstacles in the way of our funding effort, then they needed a half a million dollars so that they would let us use the technology we had invented, developed and funded. What did the government do except put roadblocks in the way of saving Janine's life? A reckless driver is responsible for the deaths he causes, what about the government?*

Hank could not remember driving to the office; his feet seemed to move without any conscious thought. He was the only one left in his family; he wanted to talk to someone, but Janine was gone. He felt so alone in the world.

He pushed open the door to the lab, headed to his bench, pulled out the standard blue padded office chair on wheels and flopped down. *One step at a time, one step at a time, he told himself.* He picked up a pen and started to make a list of the things that needed to be done: 1) pack bag, 2) review updates of Houdini software, 3) go over new Made by Man projects.

His block printed letters were bold and dark on the white pad. *What's next? I needed to check the EWE microcode—damn.* He slammed down his fist. *It could have saved her. I know it. Those weasels didn't care... Don't think about it; don't think about it; don't think about it.*

They were guiltier of her death than some bartender who served a guy one too many drinks, guiltier than a surgeon who left a sponge behind when he sewed up a patient, more than the cigarette manufacturer, or the vaccine manufacture, or the airplane company. They knew—I told them—they didn't give a shit. They were too busy playing politics. How come people in government are immune to any sort of incompetent action but the liability of private people just keeps expanding? How does that make any sense? Don't think about it; don't think—

"Hank," he heard Peggy's voice over the speaker on the phone.

He slammed the talk button with his hand. "WHAT."

"You don't have to take my head off," Peggy said, genuinely hurt.

"I'm sorry, Peggy." He felt miserable. Peggy was a great employee. How could he have snapped at her?

"I know you're sad; no apol—"

"I'm not sad; I am MAD. They killed her, Peggy, and they are going to get away with it."

Peggy was not sure what to say. *What did he mean they killed her—who killed Janine?* "Hank, Will is on the phone for you."

"Thanks, put him through." Nothing felt real. He had once had a conversation with his college roommate about what a nightmare was. His roommate had said it was just something that was frightening. He had argued that it was when things didn't make sense, when reason and logic don't apply, when the laws of physics no longer apply—that's a nightmare. His roommate was a political science major and told Hank to free up his mind. All these rules of physics were just limiting his thinking. Einstein had proven Newton wrong and everything was relative. It always amazed Hank that people who could not pass algebra-level physics could lecture him on what the Theory of Relativity meant. Hank tried to explain that Newton was completely correct within certain conditions and the Theory of Relativity did not make everything relative. That people's minds in the Dark Ages were not burdened with Newtonian rules of physics; the result was constant fear. They thought that the sun might not rise tomorrow, or that their ship might suddenly sink, or that the sky might fall, or they might fall off the sides of the Earth. Understanding physics and science is what freed the mind; it did not enslave it. He sealed and addressed two death announcements and stacked them neatly in front of them.

"Hank, HANK?" Peggy White said as she walked up to him.

"Ah, yeah?" Hank tried to focus on Peggy.

Hank's neck muscles seemed to strain. "You seem awful angry. It's a normal part of grieving, but perhaps you should take the day off."

Hank tried to talk calmly. "Peggy, they killed her. It's not part of the grieving process; it is a rational response to someone who has stolen something from you."

Peggy decided to let that drop. "Did you ever pick up the call from Will?"

Hank picked up the phone, dialed Will's number, and when Will answered, he told him that Janine had died.

"I heard. I'm so sorry. I just know that we could have helped her, if only we had been funded." Will wasn't sure what to say. Hank had both a personal and professional interest in EWE, and the news wasn't good on either front.

"Every time I think of Congressman Burnett's or Director Morris's smug faces. I didn't need prayers. They killed her Will, just as surely as the 9/11 terrorists killed the people in the World Trade Center."

Will was a little overwhelmed by Hank's anger and not looking forward to sharing his news.

"And the delay in getting the angiochannelizer on line will likely kill more than the three thousand people killed in 9/11." Hank paused. "I think I am going to send them news of her death." Hank's mind drifted to this thought.

Will didn't know what to say.

"How are things going at EWE?"

Will could answer this. "It's not looking good. Did you see the news article about AltruMedical?"

"No, why?" Hank remembered the odd call with an angel who had asked him if he was with AltruMedical.

"Well they just sold out to MedCon for $245 million, and from what we can tell, their technology is very similar to ours."

"How similar?" Hank was trying to wrap his head around this.

"We thought that if they were close enough, they might be infringing our patent. We looked to see if they had published any papers or filed any patent applications.

It turned out that they had filed a patent after ours, a month after we talked to MedCon, and it already issued. Coincidental, don't you think? We don't know what happened, but it stinks."

"I don't believe in coincidences." Hank wasn't sure how this fit in but it added to his surreal feelings.

"I know. Earl is beyond consolation. This AltruMedical news means it will be almost impossible for us to raise capital." Will's voice was low with defeat.

"Well you should be able to sue MedCon once your patent issues, right?" Hank pleaded for some justice in the world.

Will sighed. He felt so depressed; he felt as low now as he had been high after the MedCon meeting. He felt betrayed and defeated, and guilty—here he was talking with a guy who had lost his sister, not just his business. Wearily, he said, "In theory, but we are running out of money. And our attorney says that it costs about a million to bring a patent suit to trial. Even if we get the patent, we don't have the money for a lawsuit."

Chapter 14

When Hank was at the patent office, he had seen their security was built around a single point of access to the main computer systems. The advantage of this was that it was easy to monitor all computer communications coming into and out of the office. However, the downside was that once someone had broken through this firewall the rest of the network was as open to scrutiny as a stripper. This single point of access was typical of the way bureaucrats thought about security. For instance, the Denver airport was built with a single point through which all passengers had to go in order to access their planes. This was convenient for the bureaucrats but not for the passengers and gave the bureaucrats a false sense of security. This was the exact opposite of how Houdini's software worked and how the Internet worked. Houdini's software made every computing device part of the security system. No one point had nearly the horsepower of a centralized system but working together it was more robust. AltruMedical had somehow stolen Dr. Cody's invention. Hank was determined to figure out how.

He had written some primitive code to analyze the noise associated with the bits of a computer message. He used this to analyze the email from Morris's office for his appointment. This analysis gave him a good idea of what was necessary to get into the PTO's network as Morris from a remote site. It was just a matter of building a program to test for minor variations he had not yet worked out. He also placed a coupled of phishing programs on routers through which the office's communications would flow. Between both of these, he was able in a couple of days to access the entirety of the PTO network.

Getting into a computer system was only twenty percent of the battle, unless you just wanted to be a voyeur. Hank was not interested in just reading Morris's emails; he was looking for very specific information related to AltruMedical and EWE Technology. A simple scanning algorithm that used his hashing technique analyzed all of Morris's emails, Word documents, PDFs, etc. to determine if they were about this issue. He also looked up the examiners in charge of these patents and their superiors. He did the same analysis of their correspondence. It turned out that the patent office used Internet telephones. Because of this, he was also able to analyze their voicemails and some of their live conversations.

While his program was gathering and crunching this data, he researched the public information on these companies. In 2000, the US had decided to publish all applications. This meant that once a case was public, you could go on the website and see all of the correspondence. He looked up EWE's application and saw that it took three years before it was assigned to an examiner. Then there was a document about an interview. Hank already knew about this. This was the interview that made EWE believe their patent would issue shortly. Then there were some indecipherable entries a couple of months after EWE went to see MedCon. These were the last entries.

Next, he looked at the file for AltruMedical. It showed that AltruMedical had filed a patent about a month after EWE went to see MedCon. The application was immediately assigned to an examiner and issued within a year. This occurred at a time when most patents took over three years to issue—suspicious but no smoking gun.

He dug into news articles about AltruMedical. There were a number of stories on the acquisition by MedCon. He opened one of the articles; it read: "All-American Success Story. The meteoric rise of AltruMedical proves that the American dream is alive and well, even in this down economy. A brilliant inventor with a dream creates a device that will revolutionize the field of cardiac surgery. Investors with foresight and courage, in this case Irish Star Ventures, provide the capital to move the invention from the laboratory to clinical trials. This is a uniquely American story, from Thomas Edison's light bulb and General Electric; to Chester Carlson, inventor of the photocopier, and Xerox; to Robert Noyce, inventor of the microchip, and Intel."

Hank felt like puking. The better analogy would have been the story of how RCA and David Sarnoff stole the invention of FM radio from Edwin Armstrong. How crony capitalism enriches established companies with political connections at the expense of inventors, startups, and the income of ordinary people.

The article quoted Zachary Switch, VP in charge of the stents group for MedCon, explaining how AltruMedical's technology would be an important part of the suite of products and services MedCon provided to the cardiac market. This was the same guy EWE had told about their technology. There was no way this guy didn't remember EWE. *I suppose it is possible that MedCon might have acquired Altru instead of EWE if they were farther along in the development process. This seems unlikely since they filed a patent much later than EWE; however, EWE had become stalled in their development because of a lack of funds.*

The byline on the article said it was written by a Christine Patel. The name was familiar to Hank. Oh yeah, she was the reporter who wrote the excellent article on the death of venture capital. He had read several articles by her and they had all been good. This was disappointing—it was almost as if the author needed the narrative to be true—it tried too hard. Then it hit him—MedCon had no intention to develop the angiochannelizer technology. They were going to deep-six the technology. Hank had never felt so certain of anything in his whole life, but he couldn't nail down why. He had heard the conspiracy theories that the oil companies had bought out a carburetor invention that would allow cars to get one hundred miles to the gallon and other nonsense. Hank had even calmly pointed out the physics of why this would not work. But Hank was seeing more and more examples of large companies buying startups for their technology and then incorporating some of it into their existing products and letting the competitive or revolutionary parts of the technology die. Hank knew EWE's technology threatened MedCon's stent market. He decided to work out the numbers, pulled up a search engine and looked up MedCon's SEC filings. The stent market was worth over a billion dollars a year to MedCon last year. *That's serious money.* Hank felt confident that over time the angiochannelizer would eliminate the market for stents. He and Will had estimated that the angiochannelizer might be worth three hundred million per year to MedCon on the high side. Not exactly a good trade for MedCon.

It was late. Hank stretched and walked across the lab to the refrigerator for a Mountain Dew—the patron saint of programmers. He noticed it was snowing outside, not the pretty sort of large dry flakes Colorado was famous for, but the heavy, wet, ill-formed clumps that happened when the sky couldn't make up its mind whether it was going to snow or rain.

The article was frustrating but it had given him some leads. He found the incorporation papers for AltruMedical online. It showed that the company had been formed after the EWE pitch to MedCon. One more coincidence? He found some obscure press releases that AltruMedical had received a substantial NIH grant several months after they were incorporated and a couple of NSF grants almost immediately after incorporating. This seemed odd to him but he had never dealt in the world of government science grants. He had always had the feeling it was an inside game.

He decided he needed some help from a professional to chase down some of the financial details of the MedCon acquisition. He wondered if he could tempt Christine Patel to dig into this story. Perhaps an email? He noticed that her byline provided an email. But she couldn't know who sent the email, so he hacked into *The Financial Reporter*'s email server and made it look like she had sent the email to herself.

From: C.Patel@TFR.com
To: C.Patel@TFR.com
Cc:
Subject: All-American Success Story?

Dear Ms. Patel,

Things are not always as they appear. Have you ever heard of Dr. Earl Cody? How will

AltruMedical's technology affect MedCon's revenue?

I hate to be presumptuous, but I think a better analogy than Edison and GE might be RCA and Edwin Armstrong.

You must be wondering why I passed this information on to you. All I can say is I only like offering this to a very select few.

After he sent the email, he called it a night.

It was bright, sunny, and cold the next morning. Hank took a hot shower, fogging up the mirror, threw on some jeans and a sweater, headed to the kitchen and made himself some hot chocolate. The spoon clinked on the side of the coffee cup and the rich smell of chocolate made him anxious to take a sip. He sat at his glass and steel kitchen table, sipping his hot chocolate as his portable computer fired up. He pulled up his filtering program and saw it had found an email from the supervisor in charge of EWE's application complaining that Director Morris had come to see him. According to the email, Morris bitched at him about the allowance rate of his group and made him pull the EWE case and put it through some special review process. The examiner in charge of the case was pissed. He had spent a lot of time on the case and was going to lose production counts. *Whatever that means*, thought Hank. The email went on to explain that Morris told him the AltruMedical application was the sort of technology that was truly innovative.

Hank took another sip of his hot chocolate, leaned back in his chair and stared out at the sunbeams filtering through the ponderosa pines. Hank remembered how Morris had looked uncomfortable when he mentioned EWE. Why the hell would the director of the patent office be getting involved in individual patents, considering he made it crystal clear he did not do that? There had to be something more to this puzzle. You would think he considered it below his station in life to dig into the details of an invention. He looked up; the clock said 8:30. The Made by Man staff meeting was at 9:00; he'd better hurry. He closed his computer, grabbed his coat and keys and headed out the door.

Traffic was light; he knew the curves up the pass like the back of his hand, which freed up his mind. *Why would Morris have taken this extraordinary action? Was it just a coincidence?* Hank was not a big believer in multiple coincidences all aligning. *If Morris somehow made some money or got some other favor, this whole thing might make sense. But AltruMedical was a private company—no money to be made trading in their stock.* He put it out of his mind as he pulled into the parking lot.

The staff meeting lasted longer than usual. When it was over, Hank answered emails that had been piling up for several days. He leaned back and rubbed his eyes.

"Want to go to Carlos Miguel's for lunch?" Warren's tall frame filled the doorway.

Hank ordered the huevos rancheros even though it was lunch. Carlos had great green chili that you could only find in Colorado and New Mexico and theirs had large pieces of pork in it. The dish started with a fried tortilla, then a layer of refried beans, melted cheddar cheese and the two eggs over easy smothered in green chili. Warren had the chili rellenos. "We are making great progress on the haptic feedback system for the remote surgery project. Once we solved the negative feedback issues everything else has been falling into place." Warren took a large bite of the chili rellenos.

Hank attacked his own dish with equal gusto. "That's great. That could provide some nice residual work and royalties in the future." Hank looked up. "Hey, I wanted to run something past you."

"Shoot," Warren said between mouthfuls.

"I have been doing some snooping on the patent office's network and found some odd things."

Warren choked on his rellenos, carefully set his fork next to his plate and leaned in toward Hank. "You're hacking into a government agency's network! Jesus, I hope you are using a proxy website. You could get us into shitload of trouble."

Hank felt a little insulted. "Of course. Who do you think you're talking to? I have a semi-random set of proxies that change for every query. Besides, they use a single point firewall system that can't track you once you're inside the network." Hank lowered his voice. "Now, are you willing to help me with something or not?"

Warren leaned back in the booth, rolled his shoulders, brought his forefinger and thumb up to the bridge of his nose and pinched. "Go ahead."

"Well, here is what I found out. AltruMedical, the company with the technology like EWE's, sold out to MedCon. That's public knowledge. AltruMedical filed a patent application almost immediately after EWE talked to MedCon. AltruMedical's application sails through the patent office and issues in less than a year. EWE's application is in limbo for three years and then it gets sidelined in some quality review process, where it is still stuck."

"Yeah, what do you expect from a government bureaucracy?" Warren didn't see the point.

"Sure, but it appears that Morris interfered in both applications."

Warren frowned. "How do you know that Morris was involved?"

"I found this email from the supervisor of the group in charge of EWE's and AltruMedical's applications and he complains about Morris interfering in them."

"That's weird, but it could just be a coincidence." *Hacking into a government agency's computer system—it just wasn't rational.*

Hank hated it when Warren played devil's advocate. "Is it just a coincidence that AltruMedical files a month after EWE gives a pitch to MedCon, that AltruMedical is bought out by MedCon a year later, that Morris gets involved in both cases when he says he never gets involved in individual cases?" Hank was exasperated.

"I understand you're upset about Janine's death—" Hank started to speak but Warren held up his hand. "Let me finish. If I didn't know you, I would ask: Why would the head of the patent office do that?"

That was exactly what Hank wanted Warren's help with. "Well, the obvious answer would be money. But it could be a favor, or a grudge, or it could just be coincidence, I guess." There was a long pause while Warren pondered the information Hank gave him. "I think we can rule out coincidence, don't you?" Hank raised his eyebrows, challenging Warren to disagree with him.

"Yeah, and…?"

Hank interrupted Warren, "And a grudge does not fit the facts."

"True," Warren conceded.

"So that leaves a favor or money," Hank punctuated the point with his finger on the tabletop, "but how do I find out which and how do I get the details?"

"If I was getting money or doing a favor I wouldn't use my government email, would you?"

Hank took a long swig of iced tea and thought on it. "That's a good point. I'll just have to take a peek at Morris's personal emails."

Warren started to object but Hank stood up and made it clear that he didn't want to hear it.

When Hank got back from lunch, he went about trying to find every email account that Stanford Morris used. Most people access all of their email accounts from their laptop. He found one of Morris's personal email accounts from his work computer. From there he was able to hack into the server and looked for his other accounts. This process was repeated for each email he discovered. Then he hacked into Morris's laptop and his computer in his house in North Carolina. From there, Hank used his filtering and acquisition program to analyze all of Morris's email correspondence from his two computers.

While he was waiting for his program to acquire and analyze this data, his voyeur side overtook him and he decided to look into Morris's bank accounts. Most of it was pretty dull, but Hank was bored and he kept flipping through the data. Then he saw a transfer into Morris's bank account of $200,000 about a month ago. Shortly thereafter, there was a check to a Porsche dealer in Asheville, North Carolina for $167,549. Hank wondered how a government bureaucrat could possibly afford such an expensive car. He decided to follow the $200K transfer back. He found that the money came from a venture capital fund. It turned out the fund had invested in AltruMedical. *BINGO. Morris intervened in the EWE and AltruMedical patents in order to line his own pockets. The sleazebag made over five million dollars on the deal and killed my sister in the process. Hanging would be too nice for this shithead.*

Hank couldn't think straight, so he decided to take a bike ride. He drove up to Rampart Reservoir out of Woodland Park and took off on the mountain biking loop around the lake. There was some snow on the ground; the air was crisp but the sun was warm. He pedaled furiously, alternatively thinking about his sister and how to kill Morris. Even though it was only forty degrees out, Hank was sweating copiously and there was the faint smell of pine trees. He was oblivious to the scenery of Pike's Peak framed behind the reservoir. As the exercise began to work out the adrenaline in his system, he became calmer. He would confront Morris. If Morris did not make things right, he would go to the press. Janine might be dead, but there were thousands of other lives that hung in the balance.

He pulled up to his Scout II and heard the crunch of the bikes tires on the gravel come to a stop. As he stood up, the cool air raced down his sweat-drenched back, chilling him slightly. He undid the rubber straps on his trailer hitch bike rack and felt stinging in his right eye. He stopped and wiped his forehead with his bikers' glove; it was rough against his skin and smelled of leather soaked in human effort—effort that was the common lot of people less than one hundred-fifty years ago. He realized it was new technologies that had changed the world from an end-less physical toil, where the average lifespan was forty years, to a world in which people engaged in physical exercise for recreation and the average lifespan was eighty. It was not just medical technologies that had made this possible but the internal combustion engine, oil drilling, refining, computers, and yes, even security software. Without ever-increasing levels of technology, the average human's life was the same as his grandfather's, whose life was the same as his grandfather's, whose life was the same as his grandfather's, and so on. Now the US government appeared to be out to stop the progression of humankind. His business, Houdini, was slowly being destroyed by Washington and the government had killed his sister. *Is there a target on my back? Not likely; it's more likely that this is a systematic issue of an arrogant government run amok.*

I was so busy building my businesses, thrilled to solve new problems, that I hadn't noticed that our government had gotten out of control. Without new technologies, we have death by a thousand cuts, and when we free people to pursue new technologies, we have life by leaps and bounds.

Chapter 15

Nice hotels were a treat, especially if comped by one's employer. But two weeks? This visit was wearing thin. The police detectives assigned to her break-in were courteous but disinterested and there appeared to be no connection to the article they could see. Joe was being overly cautious, but it was time to get her life back. Christine showered, changed, and debated how to spend the rest of her evening. She had met some friends for dinner who were solicitous about her situation, but she was tired of feeling victim-y and so probably wasn't great company. She had just repacked her suitcase in anticipation of checking out in the morning and moving back into her apartment. She grabbed the remote and fished for something on the TV to watch. Nothing seemed very interesting, so she settled on a cable business station and leaned back against the headboard of the firm hotel bed. It was actually a nice mattress, the maids did a good job, and if she thought about it, she ate out most every night as it was. The place had a decent gym, so she didn't have to get up early like she did at home and jog the seven city blocks to the place she had a membership at. She sighed and slid her laptop over next to her on the bed and decided to check emails.

"All-American Success Story?" The subject line of the newest email had her full attention. C. Patel was the sender. Feeling bored one minute and then having a fight or flight feeling abruptly in the next was a unique sensation. One week had passed without incident; what the hell was this? Was this going to be one of those messages that fried her computer with a virus? Right now, it would hardly rate on the Richter scale. She clicked on the message after a brief pause and opened it. Scanning it quickly she took in the name of Earl Cody and realized the sender had read her article. "I hate to be presumptuous, but I think a better analogy than Edison and GE might be RCA and Edwin Armstrong." Edwin Armstrong? Who the hell was that? No threats. That was good. No way to reply, either, but since the sender had taken the time to read her article, she decided to bite.

She searched Edwin Armstrong and RCA on her laptop. So this Armstrong guy had invented FM modulation. Interesting. Apparently, the head of RCA had not been happy about this. All of RCA radios in 1933 were running AM frequencies. Production centered on making models cheaply, not worrying about improving the sound quality. Armstrong worked for RCA, but they parted company after RCA refused to license the technology. He enjoyed success and began competing. They offered him one million to sign over all of his patents and walk away. He refused. Eventually, after the military in WWII used FM technology for its communications, RCA brought in the government. Apparently, the first televisions had a channel one, run on 44-50MHz. After RCA and their government buddies got through, FM requirements were raised to 80MHz—obsoleting all of Armstrong's products. He sued RCA for patent infringement and, after several years of litigation, killed himself. Wow. That was just sad and wrong. Christine pulled up her article and quickly reread. She then went back to the email message. *Who is, or was, Earl Cody, anyway?*

The purpose of her article had been to focus on the commercial success of Altru and in doing so, run into Senator Fowl. Joe had asked her to look into the other principals, but so far, having covered MedCon, nothing was more interesting than this Switch guy's relationship to Fowl.

A search on Earl Cody showed a painter of some renown, a genealogy chart showing an early western settler, and one Dr. Earl Cody, surgeon. There were several papers authored by Dr. Cody. They all discussed technology similar or at least in the space of Altru. Was there a relationship?

Christine opened another search window and, scanning the principals of the corporation, didn't see Dr. Cody come up. Since she had just read about the Armstrong dude, she searched for some patent assignment or licensing deals between Altru and Cody. After searching for a better part of an hour, she saw no connection between Iowa State and Dr. Cody to Altru. The only thing she came up with was a small LLC called EWE Technologies. Their website featured Dr. Cody's papers, a discussion and pictures regarding what looked to be testing of this procedure on pigs, and a statement that they were going for a first round of funding. The only other information she got from the clearly stale site was contact stuff. She already had interviewed the head of Altru; time to dig a little deeper. She picked up her phone and dialed a home number listed in the White Pages for Dr. Cody. She didn't get a response. So she left a message.

Christine then checked out the EWE Technology website and decided to phone the cell of the other partner, William Devon. After the third ring, someone picked up. "Hey."

"Oh, hi. I'm Christine Patel and I'm, interested in getting in touch with Dr. Cody, Mr. Devon." She grimaced. That sounded professional.

"Regarding what exactly?" The guy sounded a little suspicious. Better disarm him.

"I work for *The Financial Reporter*. I'm calling from New York, and I have a couple questions about the merger. Have you heard of AltruMedical?"

"Christ!" Christine waited but Mr. Devon wasn't offering anything else. She decided to forge ahead.

"I thought that since Dr. Cody worked in a similar technological space—"

"Never mind that," Mr. Devon interrupted, though he sounded more resigned than combative, Christine thought.

He continued, "Look, now is not the greatest time to bring up those sleazebags with Earl. He's kinda incapacitated and talking to you isn't going to make things any better. I'm his partner; if you have questions, I can probably answer them. But let's get one thing straight. Dr. Cody is in a *technological field* all on his own. Those assholes over there at MedCon and Altru are thieves. We're not in that field, if you take my meaning, Ms. Patel." Mr. Devon was clearly upset but this was getting interesting.

"Christine. And you're, William. Bill?"

"Will. Nice to meet you Christine. Don't get too many calls lately. I'm getting all rusty, you know?" Will laughed. "Sorry for the abruptness. Losing your company, well, it saps your patience and manners."

"I've heard people say having their own company is like having a kid."

"Yeah. It's like giving birth in a wagon train and burying your baby along the trail. That's what it feels like."

"So, what happened?" Christine grabbed a pencil and steno pad on her desk and leaned back in her chair.

"We were in negotiations with MedCon for Dr. Cody's system. Huge potential. We thought they'd want first crack. But, see, this Altru comes outta nowhere and lands a patent. There's no history to show they had the research before us, and somehow we're all of a sudden screwed."

Christine stopped writing and considered Will's last remarks. "In my line of work, when you need to find something out, you follow the money."

Will laughed. "Well, honey, the trail's gone cold if you're talkin' to me." Christine's laugh joined Will's and she felt the tension drain a bit out of the conversation.

"I am going to dig around in the financial stuff that's public and I'll let you guys know if I come up with anything. If we start to build a timeline here," Christine paused, "if your company decides to pursue things against MedCon, well, maybe I can help a little." She really did feel bad for these guys if that's what had happened, but so far the story was hers to tell. And there was a story here, she was sure of it. *Make sure you cover all the bases.*

"Will, are you and Dr. Cody aware of any trials starting on Altru's technology?"

"I have no idea. Been too busy here breaking apart the tent show. There's money enough in the buyout for that to happen sooner or later. But I haven't read anything, and we look, every day.

Christine felt excitement coursing through her veins. "What if MedCon didn't want the stents market to take a hit? What would the advantages be if they just sat on things over there?"

"They've paid a hell of a lot of money for a seat cushion, then. I don't know, Christine. Earl and I, we don't think like that. Saving lives—and I mean thousands a year—kinda hard to sit on. We had already signed up doctors for the trials. These people don't have lots of procedural options available once they're on the table and their heart is being played with. Know what I mean?"

"I'm getting the picture, Will. It might be good, for the sake of my article, if I could interview some possible participants. If trials are not eminent, how do these people feel about that? We can drum up some interest that way. Might you be willing to give me a couple of names?"

"Due to medical privacy laws, I can't help you there. But maybe I can do one better, Christine. You should talk with Hank Rangar. He's worked on some engineering issues and trials we did on animals. He understands the technology and what we lost to those sons of bitches. And his sister had a heart condition. Let me get you his number."

Because the card had a handwritten address, Congressman Burnett's staff passed it along to him without opening it. Burnett had all his mail forwarded to his office so that his staff could help him screen the unimportant and to answer routine correspondence. Burnett was daydreaming about the two-week ski trip he and his family would be taking in Aspen at Christmas. A contractor he had helped secure some highway funds was allowing him to stay in his 10,000square-foot full log cabin on the Roaring Fork River. Burnett only skied the blue cruisers, and three or four hours of skiing wore him out, but he loved to ogle the ski bunnies at the après ski at the bottom of the slopes. Aspen was great because only the right sort of people had the money to get to Aspen in the winter. You didn't have to put up with families brown bagging it and their screaming brats. The ski bunnies were beautiful and rich or were beautiful and trying to marry rich.

He flipped through his mail and saw the handwritten address on the card. He decided to open it first. There was a printed card on quality stock. He wondered if it was an invitation to a party. One of the great perks of being a congressman was getting invitations to events from people all over the world. Burnett tried to make as many of these parties as he could. There were always beautiful and sophisticated women. He opened the card and it was a death announcement with a handwritten note inside. "In loving memory of Janine Rangar Nelson" and underneath were the date, time, and place of her funeral. He panicked a little when he realized it was past the date of the funeral. He racked his brain; who was Janine Nelson? But he didn't remember. He unfolded the handwritten note. "Since you had so much to do with her death, I thought you would want to see the end product of your efforts. Constituent, Hank Rangar." Burnett could feel his blood boiling. He yelled out, "That fucking arrogant prick; who the hell does he think he is!" A staffer poked their head into his office with an expectant and perplexed look.

PTO Director Morris was at his apartment in DC, having his second Maker's Mark on the rocks as he flipped through his mail. A nice card with a handwritten address caught his attention. He opened it and a handwritten note fell out. "Since you had so much to do with her death, I thought you would want to see the end product of your efforts. Hank Rangar." Morris stood up abruptly, spilling his drink on his new silk tie, and threw the glass toward the brick fireplace. Instead, the glass exploded against an expensive Waterford crystal vase that his wife had gotten him last Christmas.

Chapter 16

Christine tried to get comfortable in one of the rows of built-in seating at her gate in the JFK airport. Opening her computer, she found a Wi-Fi signal and started reviewing what she had found. Irish Star Ventures was a well-known venture capital firm in Boston. What was unusual was that this particular fund was formed about the time Altru was founded. She did some digging in the Massachusetts Secretary of State's website and the Massachusetts Securities Division's records and found that the investors in this fund included Senator Fowl, Mr. Zachary Switch, some other names and a late investor in the fund after it closed. The late investor was a small venture capital fund out of North Carolina. Investing in a venture fund was sort of like investing in a Certificate of Deposit at a bank. You had to agree not to withdraw your money for a period of time, usually ten years. Banks issue many CDs and a venture capital company like Irish Star Ventures might have many funds they were managing at any given time. Because of this setup, it was extremely rare to let an investor into a fund that was already closed.

Senator Fowl's presence on the list of investors was interesting. Christine leaned forward in the chair and pulled up the homepage for the NSF. From there, she selected a listing of new grant recipients and looked for dates. The funding from the NSF came on the heels of the Irish Star Ventures investment in AltruMedical. It usually took at least six months from submitting a proposal to the NSF or NIH to receive funding. This was clearly fast-tracked. She then went to the NIH site and was able to confirm two similar grants awarded to Altru for further research that were funded less than six months after Altru's formation. In total, a little over ten million dollars in grants were awarded to Altru, and they were all fast-tracked. It wasn't absolute proof that Senator Fowl had used his influence to get grants, but it was a smoking gun. She thought a Freedom of Information Act request to NSF and NIH would resolve this issue. She typed one up and sent it off right there in the airport while it was on her mind.

Another interesting name on the list of investors was one Mr. Zachary Switch, current VP of Stents at MedCon—the same MedCon that had bought out Altru. Christine wondered if Mr. Switch had disclosed his interest in Altru to the MedCon board. She stretched and looked up and saw her flight was delayed. *Standard operating procedure for O'Hare,* she thought.

That was quite a ride for Altru. An initial investment of a million, and then matching the grants with another ten before selling out to MedCon, and Senator Fowl had himself a nice little profit. So did all the principals of Irish Star. Altru's CEO, Dr. Myron Salthwaite, was fresh out of Mass General, just getting wet in entrepreneurial mud for the first time. Everyone else rounding out the main team seemed to come from other startups, nothing interesting there. The voice came over the loudspeaker, announcing the boarding for her flight. She'd let the information settle while she figured out her next move. Clearly, she needed to vet Senator Fowl's participation with Altru. There were all those grants, and with no real research to their name, how did they secure that kind of funding in such a short timeframe? You would have to have some pretty high-up connections for that to happen. But that kind of corruption was commonplace in Washington and was just part of the overall noise. So what, Fowl was lining his pockets with grant money, perfectly legal for senators to invest in companies that the government funds. But Zachary Switch that was a different tale; did he violate his Non-Disclosure Agreement with EWE Technology? Did he violate his duty to MedCon, under the Corporate Opportunity Doctrine?

It was fairly common for employees to spin off their own startups and to be bought out by their former company. But Switch never quit working for MedCon and Altru had almost no time for R&D before they started winning grants. And where was MedCon headed? AltruMedical had no human trials planned, whereas, EWE was ready to start. You didn't just see a publicity blitz and overnight funding wrapped up neatly in a buyout, all in under a year. And what about all those people who could benefit from the procedure in the first place? MedCon definitely had the money and backing, but in all of their press releases, there wasn't a peep about building the acquisition. This was looking like crony capitalism run amuck, and could be her bluebird. Hearing her row called, she put her computer into her bag, fished out her ticket and got in line for the flight.

It was late in the day and Dr. Steve Gorman, Deputy Director of the NSF, was tidying up his desk when his computer chimed, telling him he had a new email. The email was about a FOIA request. Dr. Gorman asked that all FOIA requests be run past him first. He opened the attachment with the email and saw that a reporter from *The Financial Reporter* named Christine Patel was asking about a grant that had been awarded to AltruMedical. Gorman remembered this grant well. Senator Fowl's office had demanded that it be fast-tracked or the NSF's funding would suffer in the next budget cycle. Gorman decided it would be wise to let Fowl know. He would not perjure himself for Fowl or to protect the NSF but he could give Fowl a heads-up. He sent an email to Fowl detailing the FOIA request.

"Ms. Patel?"

Christine rose from the 1950s modern Eames chair in the apparent waiting room. Although, looking around, everything seemed more like a chic living room or salon. There wasn't a lot of furniture, but what was there was clearly carefully chosen for the large space. It was grouped together intimately and across the middle of the space. The only things against the walls were large cactus in smooth blue-gray clay pots. The cactus strained toward the long bank of windows situated along one side of the room, stretching from floor to ceiling. The ceiling was low, but due to the design of the room, not smothering, and sort of antithetical to the Colorado esthetic of large ceilings and jutted prow windows. *Those Coloradans can be bigger than life, just like the Texans,* Christine wryly thought as she rose from her seat. She ran fingers through her soft black hair, pushing it behind her ear, and firmly grasped Rangar's hand in greeting. "Ms. Patel." His voice sounded rich, like strong black coffee.

"Christine." She had a firm grip on his hand. Her dark hair was below her shoulders and looked unbelievably soft. "Hank. Nice to meet you."

"Hello, Hank." She gave him an open smile, reached for her computer bag and looked beyond him to the large opaque glass doors clearly designed to control inquisitive visitors' entrance into Made By Man.

"If you don't mind, let's make this a walk and talk—" Stunned over his initial reaction to meeting Christine Patel, he abruptly turned without giving her a chance to answer and strode toward the opaque doors.

Christine noticed that as he neared the doors, they silently slid open, revealing a corridor bathed in sunlight. "Fine with me, but is there somewhere I can drop this?" She lifted her laptop bag.

"Sure, sorry. You can leave your computer over here." The opaque doors snicked closed and they walked down the hall. Christine looked through large windows on either side into what appeared to be some sort of lab setup. Every several feet a solar tube flooded their path with natural light.

"Wow. I didn't realize how big this place was from the front." Hank didn't look much over thirty, and this was a big operation.

"Made By Man employs eight engineers and scientists. We are sort of a skunk works for new products our clients are developing—we need large workspaces to accomplish that most of the time. Besides, the cost of rent in Woodland Park is a lot less than in Manhattan." Hank stopped and pushed a door inward, stepping aside to allow Christine to enter. She moved past him into what appeared to be a comfortable office: large mahogany desk, old world maps lining one wall, and a large flat screen on the opposite wall. She walked toward the screen and noticed it was displaying a world map with what looked like flight plans arcing between the continents. Every ten seconds or so the display changed, updating new paths. "This is interesting."

"Yeah, this is my partner's office. He's a pilot. You can leave your laptop over here." Christine walked over to the chair Hank had indicated and carefully set her bag on the seat.

"The style in here is quite a bit different from the reception area."

"My partner and I have different tastes. I don't maintain an office here; I tend to move between labs and administrate on a smart device. So, he gets to have his sanctuary and I dictate the front." He flashed a smile. His teeth were the white of an iceberg against a cold sapphire sea.

"Where's your partner now?" Christine looked down from that dazzling smile and folded her hands primly below her waist.

"We'll run into him somewhere along the line. Ready?" She was clearly nervous. Could she tell he was interested? Was he coming on too strong? Ever since, well, he just couldn't school his emotions into not alarming people. He needed to regain some control here.

"Let's walk."

"Let me pull out my notepad." Christine unzipped a side pocket of her bag, grateful for the task.

She had a firm derriere clad in beige pants, and he caught a whiff of some musky perfume as she slid past him into the hall. He opened the office door for Christine and felt the irony of behaving politely, in a way which also gave him a discrete way to check out a woman's ass. "On the phone you said that you wanted to talk to me about Made By Man and EWE. What exactly are you interested in?"

"As I told you on the phone, I'm doing some investigative research regarding MedCon's acquisition of AltruMedical, and in the course of that research I came across your former clients at EWE Technologies. In speaking with Will Devon, he explained how everything was on track for starting human trials." She registered Hank's nod.

She continued. "All of a sudden Altru comes out of the blue and disrupts everything. My own investigation has led me to some...inconsistencies, hmmm, improprieties with Altru-MedCon's merger, and I was hoping you could corroborate some of the things Will told me." Christine looked squarely at Hank.

"Also, I understand your sister is ill and was to be part of the first trial." Really, she was hoping to put a human-interest stamp on the piece. Hank's expression changed from interested to unreadable at the mention of his sister. Christine felt nervous that he might end the interview. Some people felt reporters were just above lawyers or used-car salesmen, especially when they delved into people's personal lives. Hank Rangar stared at her for few seconds and seemed about to formulate some words, but nothing happened.

"Ms. Patel." *We're back to last names now—not a good sign.* She would have to explain to her boss why she had wasted all that money on a plane ticket to Colorado.

"My sister is dead." His voice cracked and he turned away.

She was sorry, and shocked, and she needed to make sure she was not kicked out of this interview. Before she knew what she was doing, her hand was on his shoulder.

"I am so sorry. I didn't know." He glanced down at her hand and Christine pulled it back as if she had just touched a hot burner.

"They fucking killed her." He whispered this and his stare was fierce. She flinched involuntarily. She was shocked by his words and the sudden change in mood. Questions began to formulate.

"Whoa, I mean what…circumstances?" Christine's voice trailed off as she watched Hank's mood change just as suddenly again.

"Made by Man helped EWE with some of the embedded code to control the angiochannelizer. Because of my sister, I also tried to help EWE secure financing. Unfortunately, I was unsuccessful." He had already given her enough of the trail to connect most of the dots. Was it possible she already knew about Morris?

"Will told me that they had undertaken animal trials with pigs." She was writing something on that notepad. Hank watched her bite the end of the pencil. Adorable. Who used yellow pencils out of grade school?

"Yes. The results were better than could be expected. It showed that a pig could live without the major artery providing any blood to the heart," Hank explained. Christine asked about the timelines when EWE undertook their research and how he came to work with them. She tread lightly and Hank explained, "The principal developer, Dr. Earl Cody, knew most everyone involved in that field of research. He had published on it, and consulted with top heart specialists all around the world. No one had heard of AltruMedical or their lead scientist as being in this sphere of research."

Christine wanted to ask more questions about Hank's sister. "Married, kids?"

"Ah, me? No." Hank looked down into Christine's warm brown eyes, a little bemused at the question. Realization dawned.

"Oh, you mean Janine? Yes. Mark and my niece and nephew are in St. Louis. It's been hard."

"I am very sorry," Christine repeated. This was clearly too sensitive an area but she needed to ask one more question. "Don't you think it is odd that AltruMedical gets these huge grants from the NIH and NSF, is bought out by MedCon, but no human trials are forthcoming?"

"Yes, I do." The words were spit through Hank's clenched jaw.

Christine decided she had pushed him a little too far. Time to change tactics. "What project is that?" she asked, pointing to a guy holding something that looked like a glove made of chain mail. Hank started walking over to the man and Christine followed.

"Warren." The man with the glove looked up and Hank said, "I would like you to meet Ms. Christine Patel, from *The Financial Reporter.*"

Warren was blown away by the Persian beauty who stood before him. He stood up and started to move his right hand out to shake Christine's hand, forgetting it was in the haptic feedback glove. The robotic hand behind the glass window almost slugged a technician. The wires connected to the glove pulled some instruments along the bench making a horrible 'nails on a chalkboard' sound, before Warren realized he had the glove on. His face blushed as he pulled off the glove. "Very nice to meet you, Ms. Patel."

"It's nice to meet you. Please, call me Christine." She glanced warily at the glove.

Hank noticed her glance and gestured toward the lab. "If you didn't kill Collin there, or destroy the glove's connections, could you show Christine what you are working on?"

Warren fiddled with the instruments and determined nothing was damaged. "This is a haptic feedback glove we are working on for the University of Colorado Medical School. A simple version of haptic feedback is the controller for video games that vibrate. Are you familiar with these?"

Christine was not some video game nerd, but her younger brother had gotten her to play Grand Theft Auto, so she was familiar with controllers that vibrated based on the action happening in the game. "Yes, I am somewhat familiar with that idea."

"Well, this is like an advanced version of that. It's designed to give a surgeon enough sensory feedback to perform surgery while being thousands of miles from the patient." Warren went on to explain the problems Made by Man was solving and how it would revolutionize medicine. "Doctors United is very interested in this technology and has provided some of the financial support for the research. Imagine what they could accomplish if their doctors could treat patients from anywhere? Imagine the money that could be saved, the number of patients that could be seen." Christine could not believe that this little company in Colorado was working on such important technology. Warren proceeded to demonstrate the glove.

Christine was dumbfounded and all she could manage to say was, "WOW, that's amazing." She felt a little stupid that she didn't have something more insightful to say, but she felt like a kid at the Museum of Science and Industry in Chicago.

Warren then said, "You know the funny thing about this project, is that it would be illegal for a surgeon in Colorado to treat a patient in Alaska with this."

"What... Why is that?" Christine was genuinely perplexed.

"Our medical licensing laws don't allow a doctor licensed in Colorado to treat a patient in Alaska. The laws are specific to each state." He offered an ironic smile.

Christine turned from watching Warren and swung her gaze to Hank. "Do you work exclusively in medical technologies?"

"No, we work on a variety of things, from computer security, to medical, to aerospace." Hank gave Christine a warm smile. Hank was tired of talking about business but he didn't want this beautiful reporter leaving. He considered his chances. No one spoke as Christine jotted down some notes on her pad. He estimated her height to be about six inches shorter than his own six foot one inch frame. Her long hair fell forward, blocking her vision, so she swept it behind her ear again. He imagined what that silky black mane would feel like if he were to draw his fingers through it. He picked up a subtle scent of lemon and something a little muskier—maybe amber—and wondered if it was her shampoo or some perfume she wore. The scent was clean and crisp, much like her manner, but also there was that undertone of something a little darker, which intrigued him. Was this polished reporter just as she appeared? Or was the woman more complex? She startled him out of his daydream.

"...This all began with looking into the financials. You know this was just supposed to be a success story in an exciting new area of technology. I set out to tell a happy tale of a startup gone through the roof. But the background didn't add up. Frankly, there are more questions than answers surrounding this acquisition." Christine held the pad against her chest as if to protect what she had written.

Hank was wondering just how much she was going to show her hand. She clearly had uncovered something—maybe more than he knew himself. Perhaps relaxing the conversation might help. And he was interested in getting to know more about this bright, beautiful reporter. He decided to chance it.

"Do you have plans this evening? I was thinking we could continue this discussion over dinner—"

"Oh, I'm sorry, but I'm otherwise engaged with my suite at the Residence Inn," Christine stammered.

"Well, then, home cooked wouldn't persuade you to reconsider?" Hank asked. Christine realized that she didn't have anything to do tonight and dinner might be a perfect chance to find out what Rangar was hiding.

"Reconsidered. I'd love to," she said.

Chapter 17

She knew enough. After all, he'd dumped some of it in her lap. Hank had been surprised that after she had talked to EWE, Will had sent her right back to him. It also surprised him that he felt a strong attraction to her. Tipping her off was a means to a completely different end. His attraction for her could cloud the ultimate goal of finding out everything Christine had already pieced together. Did she suspect that EWE's patent had been derailed at the highest levels of government, or did she just suspect those thieves at Altru? He recalled her intelligent, dark chocolate eyes searching his face for some answers. He might be willing to give her a few but he hoped she might know even more than he did. They settled on 7 p.m. for dinner and he worried a bit that she might get lost—Manitou streets were narrow and winding, and frankly confusing as they carved out the bottom of Pikes Peak.

He let himself into his updated Victorian and threw the keys on a small table next to the door. He carried his two bags of groceries over to the kitchen bar and set them down. Walking through the main area of the house, he switched on a few lamps. He stopped for a moment and looked around his neat, orderly, sparsely furnished living room. Would Christine learn anything about the man who lived here? He startled himself with a laugh. He hadn't had many long-term relationships in the past. He preferred to date casually while he was married, in a sense, to his businesses. His goal had always been to really grow a business that would see him set for life, then consider finding someone special and settling down to start a family. He was a little surprised that so soon after Janine's death and in the middle of this fucked-up situation his guard would come down and he would feel this attraction so strongly. He walked over to a long table and, opening his laptop, flicked a few keys and Miles Davis filled the room.

Dinner would be scallops sautéed in garlic butter and salad to start. Bachelors were not normally known for their cooking skills, but Hank was another story. He pulled out each item from the shopping bags and set it on the counter. Arranging everything before him, he reached for the bottle of chardonnay, went over to the sink parallel to the bar and opened a drawer. Pulling out a corkscrew, he pulled the cork, reached above the sink to a cabinet and drew out two wine glasses. Pouring a half glass for himself, he sipped and savored the buttery flavor. *I hope she is not a damn teetotaler. Do Buddhists drink alcohol?* He rarely thought about people's religion and he had no idea if Christine was Buddhist, Anglican, or an atheist.

He unwrapped the scallops, washing and patting them dry; he placed them on a platter and slid the platter and the wine into the fridge. He washed and tore up a head of romaine into a salad bowl and slid it into the fridge as well. He checked the time and decided to take a shower. After shaving, he changed into a white silk Hawaiian-style shirt, slid on his favorite Levis, and checked himself in the mirror. He slipped his feet into an old pair of Ferragamo leather loafers. He ran his fingers through his still-damp hair and gave his head a quick shake. Glancing at the bedside clock, he saw it was 6:30, still half an hour before she would show up.

Just in case, he collected his discarded clothes on the bed and floor, smoothed the coverlet on the bed, and imagined Christine lying across it, her gorgeous hair spread out around her naked, supple body. Well that was a bit premature, since it was a first dinner date, but this exotic-looking reporter was headed back to the East Coast soon and he'd have to make some serious inroads. Once again, he startled himself with a laugh. Where were these thoughts coming from? Missing Janine must be fucking with his head and making him think uncharacteristically. Either that or he was doing all his thinking with his dick.

Back in the kitchen, he set a pot of water on to boil with a generous pour of olive oil and pulled out a cutting board and set it next to the stove, chopped a shallot and crushed a couple cloves of garlic. He loved the smell of fresh garlic. He halved a large lemon and scored the flesh before squeezing the halves into a small bowl. He chopped some fresh thyme and set it aside.

There was a strong knock at the door; wiping his hands on a towel he had thrown over his shoulder, he went to answer it. When he opened the door, he looked down into Christine's intense dark eyes and smiled his welcome. She looked gorgeous in a dark blue-black silk sleeveless sheath, a perfect partner to her blue-black shoulder-length hair pulled up and away from her face in a soft chignon at her nape. She flashed him a bright smile and then moved around him into the living room.

"Impressive—modern and understated inside. Is that the kind of guy you are, Rangar?"

"Hello, and yes, even though it's a crazy little Victorian, I'm not into lacy curtains and doilies lying around."

"Doilies?" Christine's musical laugh teased his ears and inflamed his lust.

He joined her laughter and surprised himself again. "Would you like some wine? I just uncorked a chard."

"Mmm, thanks, I could use a drink after the day I've had. Hectic and less productive than I'd hoped."

Thank goodness she's not a teetotaler. "Was I that bad?"

Christine quirked a smile and gave him a rueful, considering look. "Well, that depends—are you a good cook or is it going to be take-out?"

Hank returned her smile and bowing slightly, he gestured with his arm toward the kitchen. "If you'll take a seat at the bar, hopefully, I can impress you."

"Sounds divine. I had some computer issues and wasted hours trying to get onboard with the *FT* servers." Christine moved to a bar stool and situated herself. "What can I do to help?"

"You can sit there for a minute and enjoy your wine," he brushed her fingers as he handed over a glass of chardonnay, "and when you're ready I'll have you slice this ciabatta."

"Happy to help. I'm good with knives."

Hank paused infinitesimally before turning back to her and sliding the loaf and a wooden board in front of her. "Then you'll be pleased to know I keep mine sharp."

She barked out a deep-throated laugh that finished on a sigh. *She seems to be enjoying herself*, Hank thought. He selected a serrated bread knife and passed it to her hilt first.

"Nice laugh." She blushed a little and he decided to save her. "I'm going to get started here. Like scallops?"

"Mmmm." She dropped her bag as her cell phone vibrated. It startled her and she felt herself flush. "I'd better turn it off so I'm not thinking about work all night."

"Good plan. I want you to concentrate on my stellar cooking."

Christine fished the cell out of her bag and glanced at the display. It was a text from one of her colleagues asking to go out for a drink. She sighed with relief, quickly responded she was out of town on assignment and turned off the phone.

Hank lit the gas fire beneath a large stainless skillet and pulling out some butter from the fridge; he cut away a couple tablespoons from the soft yellow bar on the plate and scraped it off into the skillet. As it sizzled, he added the shallots and garlic.

Christine sipped her wine and wondered how best to get his guard down and reveal what he knew about the Altru deal. She was certain that he knew more than he admitted to knowing during the interview this afternoon, and she was determined to get him to open up. She considered the best tack to take and settled on a direct approach.

"So, Hank, what are you not telling me about the EWE deal?" Hank paused slightly while working over the skillet.

"What makes you ask that? I answered all your questions." Hank added lemon and capers and a rich, tangy aroma filled the room. He turned toward her with a slight frown marring his strong brow.

Christine lightly massaged her neck and looked down, a little embarrassed. "I agree. It's just that..." she paused, considering, as he turned back to the stove and dumped the fettuccine into a shallow ceramic bowl and tossed it with the sauce. She decided to push a little farther. He'd either open up or he wouldn't—yet. She felt her cheeks heat and hoped he wouldn't notice. "Here's the thing. I might not have asked the right questions, perhaps."

Hank was intently adding large pale scallops to the skillet, working them around in the pan so they wouldn't stick. After a couple of moments, he used the spoons to flip the scallops and watched for them to turn opaque. He lifted a large pepper grinder on the stove and turned the handle a couple of times over the seafood. He removed the pan from the flame. He turned back toward Christine and wiped his hands on the towel over his shoulder.

"Since you're the reporter, aren't you supposed to be good at the question thing?"

"Touché, Mr. Rangar. I'd like to take another stab at it, if I may."

Hank returned to the bar with two large white plates, napkins, and silverware. Christine arranged their makeshift table while Hank brought the salad, fettuccine, and finally the skillet. Christine helped herself to the pasta and Hank gently picked up some scallops and placed them next to the pasta on her plate. He gestured with his spoons for her to portion him some pasta and when she had done this, he served himself a few of the scallops. He discarded the skillet back to the stove, grabbed the wine and butter and rounded the bar to Christine's side. She had already twirled a fork of the fragrant pasta and gave a low moan as she closed her eyes and savored the flavors. Hank's eyes sparkled with amusement as he watched her ravenously take a large forkful of scallop. Chuckling to himself, he turned his attention to his own plate and twirled off a bite of pasta. "Let's stab at this for a little while and when we're fortified, I promise I will answer whatever you ask truthfully."

They ate in companionable silence for a time and Christine polished off her wine. She stabbed some salad and started back up.

"Will is pretty suspicious that someone at MedCon stole their idea. That maybe MedCon and Altru were in bed together from the beginning. What do you think?"

"I'd say there's lots of bad to go around in the big, multi-national world." Hank stabbed several bites of salad and chewed while watching Christine intently.

She lowered her fork to her plate and sighed appreciatively.

"I am stuffed. Wonderful dinner, but my glass is empty." She bent closer to Hank and placed her right hand gently on his left knee. Apparently, the subject was changing.

"Another chard or something rich and red?" Hank stood and rounded the bar. He crouched and opened the door to the wine cooler.

"Got any shiraz in there?" Christine twirled her empty glass.

"As a matter of fact, I do. How about an Australian '06 Groom?"

"Don't know it." She pushed back her stool and stood. "Wouldn't it have been interesting to know what an ancient syrah tasted like?"

"Hmm, you know the history. Shiraz, the city in Persia—a long ways away from the Aussies." He uncorked the bottle and pulled out two large bowled stems and a crystal decanter. He decanted the bottle and Christine came around the end of the bar with the salad bowl and their napkins. He put his hands against hers and then gently tugged the salad bowl from her grasp. "Wanna move to the living room?" He cocked his head toward a lean beige suede couch in the living room. She turned slowly and walked into the living room, curling herself into a corner of the sofa and kicked off her stiletto pumps. For the first time he noticed the sleek lines of the pumps and then the startling red soles. Siren. He chuckled low.

She massaged one black stocking-clad foot with her hand. "Long day, but definitely looking to be a nice finish."

"Definitely," he murmured as he handed her a shiraz-filled glass and moved over to his laptop. Balancing his wine in his left hand, he tapped some keys with his right and then a Juan Carlos Jobim ballad filled the room.

He came back around the couch and slid next to her, making sure there was only about an inch of space between them. Enough to make their bodies hum with wanting to touch. She leaned back and closed her eyes, humming the tune. "Quiet chords from your guitar." Hank watched her silently as she softly sang the lyrics. As she lapsed back into a hum, he replaced her hand on her foot with both of his and continued the massage. "Oh, that's heavenly." She leaned back and unfolded her long slender legs into his lap and he continued to knead the balls of her feet for a while and then stroked up her calves. "You're in the wrong line of work, invention guy."

"Perhaps I only like offering this to a very select few."

Christine stiffened momentarily and looked into Hank's eyes. Hank removed his hand from her foot and looked back, questioning. What the hell? Where had she heard that? She relaxed a little and nudged his hand with her foot. *Think.* The anonymous email. She watched Hank as he focused all his attention on kneading her feet. Was she getting used here? Was he the perv who had ransacked her house? *Damn, he is so good-looking. Pull it together, Christine.*

"Well then, my pleasure to be selected." She rolled her shoulders and sank back further into the cushions.

That creep was someone in the city doing Fowl's dirty work to make her cower. But…she contemplated the likelihood that Hank was her deep throat. A laugh escaped.

"What's so funny?" Hank had now moved the massage to her ankles. His hands were gentle and warm. Christine admired Hank's shoulder and arm muscles flexing as his fingers made small circles there. He cupped first one heel and then the other. Finally, he applied both hands to the balls of her feet; first the right and now the left. *I can't even remember what had me so worked up a minute ago.*

"Are you maneuvering for a big tip?" She was purring. Hank slowly lowered her legs back to the polished old pine floors.

"Tip? No tips accepted here." Hank smiled. His eyes crinkled in the corners. She was a sucker for that.

Christine smiled back and wondered if her eyes crinkled in the corners. She didn't know. "Today you said, 'They killed her.' Hank, what did you mean? MedCon? How?" She sipped her shiraz and rolled the liquid around her mouth before swallowing.

Hank watched her while he tasted his own pour. They were silent for a time, both sipping and enjoying the rich wine warming their insides and relaxing into an intimate place.

"I may know some things about the merger you might not know."

Christine took another sip from her glass and carefully set it on the simple wood table next to the couch. *Okay, here it comes.* She looked at him and added, "I want to tell the public the truth here. If it is a success, I want readers to root for Altru." She paused. "If it isn't right, if people were hurt—" Hank looked at her pointedly. "...

if, if people were hurt and betrayed, it is my job to point that out to the readers, and—" she held her hand up to hold him off a bit, "for justice to be done." She looked in Hank's eyes intently and waited.

"What if it involved people pretty high up in this country? ...Who," his voice faltered a bit but then resolved, and Hank continued. "Would not want any of this to come out?" He raised his eyebrows and cocked his head, clearly sizing her up. "Are you game?"

Christine slowly smiled and leaned into Hank. Barely whispering, she examined his mouth and said, "It's my day job." And then she crushed her lips against his, while Hank pulled her tightly into his chest. She responded hungrily and for a while, they fought tongues and hands as they maneuvered each other's heads this way and that, seeking closeness and some way to take the edge off their mutual lust and frustration with the world. Between teeth gnashing Christine asked, "Hank?"

"Yes?" They were breathing harder and having a struggle talking.

"I will, yes, oh this is good." Christine turned closer toward Hank and straddled his lap. He gently kissed her jawline and nipped at the underside of her ear as his hands stroked up the outside of her thighs, hitching her dress up with each pass. He stopped for a moment as he realized her stockings only went thigh-high. He growled low in his throat and moved his hands up her back to the nape of her neck. Tonguing her mouth ferociously, he moved his fingers to the zipper at the top of the back of her dress and slowly slid it open. His hand slipped under the open fabric and he gently smoothed circles between and around her shoulder blades.

"Would you like some exercise?" His other hand pulled the dress up past her thighs. Christine lifted and the dress pulled up over her very fine ass as she returned each of his kisses with scorching ones of her own. She slowly raised both of her arms above her head bringing her chest close to his face. "Race ya," she whispered into the top of his silky hair, as he pulled the dress over her head left it to flutter behind the couch.

Hank awoke to the sound of the shower and someone humming Jobim. He smiled and hitched himself up, resting against the headboard. He ran his hands over his face and through his sandy brown hair. He looked around the room and noticed one long black stocking slung over the end of the bed. Leaning forward, he snatched it toward him and fingered the fine silk between his fingers. "Want me to make some coffee?" He threw this remark over the back of his shoulder toward the master bath.

"God, I'd love it but I haven't time." He heard the shower turn off. "I've got to get farther on this thing before my editor pulls it. Got a blow dryer?"

"Left cabinet." Hank looked once more at the stocking in his hand and bunching it up he inserted his fingers inside and examined the sheerness and stretch. He then flung his legs over the side of the bed and walked across the room to the closet. He opened the walk-in and grabbed a t-shirt, running shorts and briefs, slid the stocking underneath some folded sweatshirts on a low shelf and reached down for his trail hikers.

"Good morning sleepy head," Christine spoke to the mirror as she continued blow-drying her hair, seeing Hank come up behind her, a broad grin breaking across his face, those little crinkles in the corners of his eyes. She turned off the dryer and considered the mirror as his arms came around her midriff and he kissed the side of her neck. She angled her head farther to the side, giving him freer access. He continued to caress her neck softly with his breath and squeezed her back into him. "We both have deadlines." His disappointed tone made her smile and she clasped her hands to his hands around her waist. "Well, work before pleasure," she sighed and squeezed his hands. "I wanted to tell you that it's okay if you don't want to tell me everything you know. I'm going to figure it out sooner than later." Hank bit her earlobe softly and released her.

"It's not that I don't trust you," Hank smiled apologetically. "It's just that I've made up my mind on a few things and I'm acting on my own. I don't need a team. No one can bring my sister back, but there are lots of people who can benefit from that technology. The inventors at EWE deserve some reward for what they accomplished." He thought she had tensed in his arms but she now was leaning back against his chest. *She trusts me.*

"I need some leverage if this is going to work out, and sharing with you some of what I know too soon might take the leverage out of the equation." Hank gave her a squeeze and loosened his hold. Turning, he walked out of the bathroom calling back across his shoulder, "Can you stay another day? I sure would like to see you sooner than later."

Christine thought about everything he said and then considered his last question. "I think I could arrange a little time for you, Rangar. What I'd really love to do is take a hike on this famous mountain."

"It's a date. One o'clock, and we'll start from here, okay?" Hank walked through the bedroom, out through the living room to the front door and opened it. He stretched for a moment in the doorway, first pulling his right foot up against the back of his thigh and then his left. He closed the door with a soft snick, bounding down the front porch stairs and jogging slowly up the steep street to the mountain road behind his house. Christine walked to the bedroom doorway and stared at the front door. She had the sudden realization that his impulsiveness of the night before, though uncharacteristic, just might lead her somewhere very interesting. Just because Hank Rangar wasn't talking—well, that didn't mean she wouldn't find leverage of her own.

Chapter 18

Hank and Christine eased up the street behind Hank's house, falling into an easy pace. They climbed the narrow, tightly curved road, lengthening their stride, and Christine noticed her thighs burning slightly from the incline. The road abruptly ended in a small parking area about one half mile from his house. A trailhead began at this point, and they began rocky switchbacks, dodging back and forth to avoid large rocks and exposed roots hazarding the trail.

After about twenty minutes, they stopped, drank some water and looked down over Manitou Springs. The sun was hitting the trail up here because of the rise from the tight pass below and both of them lifted their face to it instinctively, appreciating its warmth as the trail turned back into the mountainside. Now it plunged into mostly shade. Christine shivered in response to the coolness of the altitude. The trail was on the inside of a scree field and a tight aspen grove sharply rising to the right of the trail.

A stream forged a narrow passage up through this area and cascaded over large boulders down the mountainside. Little falls loudly rushed into quieter deeper pools framed up by blue columbine and white mountain lily. The trail was slightly damp in the shade from a recent shower, which had made one of its usual afternoon visits.

Christine breathed in the earthy loam and sharp pine scent from the tall, thin ponderosas between the stands of the aspen. She reached forward for Hank's hand instinctively and Hank firmly nestled hers in his own. She felt a little shy but Hank seemed to react positively, so she was going to enjoy the little intimacy. The mountain air was thin but clean smelling. There was only the occasional scamper of a small squirrel or startled rabbit or bird to mar the utterly peaceful mountain afternoon. Occasionally, they saw bikers or trail runners, but as they progressed up the mountain, it was just an occasional hiker.

The trail narrowed and was now easier to hike. An unseen rock, root, or deadfall on the trail, would pop up now and then, but they were nimble, avoiding tripping. Hank liked the challenge of unforeseen obstacles and kept their pace brisk. They began a steep downhill for a while and they carefully picked their way through the tight angles of the momentary plunge, listening to each other's breathing become louder with their increased exertion. He was enjoying the small freedom from everything else— Janine, Earl, and Will, that asshole Morris, those crooks at Altru. At the bottom, the creek crossed the trail and

Hank looked back at Christine. Tightening his grip on her hand, he hopped back and forth on semi-submerged boulders, Christine pulled closely behind.

Hank paused for a moment to make sure Christine had her balance and when she smiled encouragingly, he turned back and they maneuvered the rest of the way across. As she stepped on the last boulder, her right foot slipped off. She felt the icy creek water drench through the mesh of her trail runner. "Damn!" Hank hauled her out of the creek and up against his chest. He felt warm and smelled male, so she inhaled appreciatively. *Cold foot, sure,* but clean soap and the musky smell of a new lover made it worth the slip. "Are you okay?" Hank asked, looking with concern at her foot. "Yeah, I'm fine. My pride is a little stung, but let's keep going." He turned his attention to her face, looking into her eyes and then at her mouth. She was sure he was going to kiss her. She felt herself soften, as he tightened his hold. *What are you waiting for? Me?* He smiled slowly and released her.

Hank turned back to the trail and she guessed they were headed on. Soon, the annoying squishing Christine was feeling with every footfall dissipated and she once more was drawn into the afternoon idle. The trail cut through a narrow pass, and the sun was behind the mountain. She shivered again as the breeze cooled the fine sheen of sweat on her arms and across her back. Hank increased their pace upward, and they began naturally breathing in a controlled rhythm. *In through the nostrils, out through the mouth*—Christine concentrated, feeling a slight burn as she continued the upward climb.

"Wow," she said between breaths, "I guess I have a healthy regard for rarified air." Hank stopped and turned to look into her face, mentally assessing her ability to hike farther.

"Let's just pause right here and get our breathing normal. Here, take a swig of water." Hank pulled Christine's water bottle from the pack on his back and she reached for it gratefully. She took a few small drinks and began to feel her breathing calm.

The trail stopped at the top of a pretty falls and Hank looked forward to sharing the view with Christine. They were now two thirds of the way to the turnaround. He suddenly heard the sharp pings and soft thuds of scree dislodging and tumbling off to their left. He turned that direction, expecting to see a runner on the other trail or possibly some interesting wildlife he should point out. It would be fun to give her a little jolt, seeing a cougar or bear, which was fairly common on this trail.

They then heard a distant rumble and Hank attributed it to the tram that pulled tourists to the top of Pikes Peak. But the rumble grew steadily louder and they both realized the sound was more distinct. It was like a large animal or several crashing down the mountainside on their right. They looked at one another and then up the trail but did not see anything. The crashing noises became louder.

"Hank, what's going on?!" Christine was visibly shaken and she stared ahead, above the trail. There was no obvious answer to the noise. Just then, Hank turned and realized large aspens were snapping like twigs against a medium-sized boulder, bouncing down, helter skelter, its path changing direction with each bounce. He grabbed Christine's arm and they moved back and then forward, recognizing with horror the erratic direction change of the boulder pitching down the mountain could not be anticipated. Hank almost felt an irrational urge to charge up toward it.

The boulder was now less than twenty feet away. They stood frozen as it landed on the trail about three feet in front of them and then sprang back into the air with huge force and hit the creek, splashing the trail and the both of them.

It was completely still. Hank grabbed Christine and held her tightly against him. He looked up the mountainside. Wide paths of aspens all the way to the top of the ridge were pushed over like sticks. *Shit!* He could feel Christine's heart frantically beating against his chest and he brushed his lips across her temple.

"It's fine; it's fine," he soothed. They turned their gaze toward the creek, where they thought the boulder landed.

At first, Hank couldn't even figure out which one it was. All the boulders in the creek bed looked spilled haphazardly, as if they'd been there a millennium. Suddenly, their narrow escape from death hit full force. They both started shuddering uncontrollably, sweat chilling their skin.

"Hank, what's up there?" Christine's concerned tone pulled him from his thoughts. He looked up at the top of the ridge and maybe he was hearing things—he wasn't sure—but it sounded distinctly like the click of gears and a bike tire skidding on the trail above. He released Christine and took off in a run. *Had some asshole carelessly started this whole thing?*

He cut the switchbacks and crested the ridge, breathing heavily. Churning through loose dirt and rocks, he stumbled up the steep terrain. He used his knees to steady himself as improbable handholds left him fisting clods of dirt and grass. Sunlight flooded the area farther up the trail.

He couldn't see through the glare. Many trails interconnected up here. If someone had been ahead, the likelihood of Hank seeing them now was low. He continued the climb up, but now his lungs were burning. He suddenly felt exhausted, and he bent over, placed his hands on his knees and concentrated on breathing. In all his years living and playing hard in Colorado high country, he had never experienced rock avalanches. Sure, they happened with some frequency—usually along the highways cut into mountainsides forming manmade passes. And of course, he had a healthy respect for avalanches on the mountains in winter. *Fucking close call.*

He turned and picked his way carefully back down the trail. Slower and with less confidence than when the hike began, Hank's breathing returned to normal. He found Christine crouched at the base of a large ponderosa pine, arms wrapped tightly around her middle, her chin resting on her knees. She started as he slipped on the trail, small rocks pinging and skittering in front of her.

"It's okay; we're okay." He kneeled and held her, stroking her hair and murmuring soothing sounds against her forehead. She was shaking badly.

After several moments, Christine broke their hold. "Shit, nothing like that has ever happened to me before. Was someone up there or is this just Wild America?" She debated whether to tell him about her apartment.

Hank laughed in relief. "I can assure you, the only thing I considered ordering up was a soak in my hot tub, no suit required." He flashed a broad smile, and a small dimple appeared in his chin.

Okay, not man-made. Which was worse? She wanted out of here, now. "Well, thank you for that. I might need a stiff drink, as well." She should tell him. He deserved to know everything about slimy Fowl. Of course, he was still holding back on his own information. She turned down the trail and began to jog lightly, picking her way around roots and rocks. Occasionally she rubbed her arms, reliving what had just happened.

Above, a man in a dark hooded sweatshirt and jeans watched the runner bend over and then examine her arm. He roughly grabbed a mountain bike by a handle and the seat, which was leaning against a pine. Slamming it in position, he mounted and pushed off down the other side of the mountain.

Chapter 19

It was only 3:30 p.m. but the sun was already behind the mountain. He poured himself a glass of chardonnay from the bottle he and Christine had opened the other night and sat down in his leather sofa, missing her. There was a candle on the coffee table; Janine had given it to him a couple of years ago for Christmas. He had forgotten it until now. Lighting the candle, he remembered how it had snowed that year and he had built Tristan and Jess a snowman, and Janine found an old scarf and hat for the snowman. She would never be there for another Christmas or Thanksgiving, or for Tristan and Jess' graduation. Morris's indifferent voice saying he wasn't responsible came to him and he punched the couch.

His mind turned to the task of exacting justice. He had already decided to confront Morris. He could hand over his profits from Altru to EWE or Hank would go to the press—Christine. The image of the boulder racing down the mountain toward them popped into his mind.

Hank turned his mind to question of how best to approach Morris. Morris would not willingly meet him. Besides, he thought an unexpected meeting would have a bigger impact on him. Hank used Morris's cell phones to track his location over time. He created a program that plotted Morris's location versus time. By placing the cursor on the trace it showed the time, location, and speed of travel.

Pulling up the program on his computer, it was clear that Morris traveled a lot. The three locations he spent the most time were his apartment in Washington DC, his office, and his house in North Carolina. Hank first thought about confronting him at his apartment. This would be a private spot and it would be difficult for Morris to call the police. But he decided it would be more intimidating if he showed up at his office unannounced.

He took a sip of his chardonnay—it had a rich buttery flavor, with a slight astringent aftertaste—and realized he would need a patent office employee badge. He had never created a fake ID, not even to get into bars before he was twenty-one. He had been far too busy with his IT business and college. The first step was to find a template. From the patent office's computers he found an example of how the employee badge looked. The badge stated that the person was an 'EMPLOYEE' in sixteen-point, New York font. The word was printed in red. Below this, it said United States Patent and Trademark Office in blue. Above this was the employee's picture with the Patent and Trademark's seal in gold over the picture. He took his digital passport picture and cropped it to the correct size. The next day, Hank bought a generic white magnetic card and created the badge in Adobe. Then he printed the badge using a sublimation printer at work. He looked at his handiwork. *Not bad for my first time creating a fake ID.* Peggy White walked past him as he was admiring his handiwork. She frowned at him, so he slid the badge into his pocket.

He grabbed a Mountain Dew and turned to the problem of how to populate the data on the magnetic strip. Without that, he would never get through the employee turnstiles. He hacked into the computers at the patent office and found the data stored on the badge's magnetic stripe. Made by Man had a magnetic stripe encoder from a project they had done for the DOD. He waited until everyone had gone home for the day and populated his forged card with Morris's information. This would provide him unlimited access inside the building—perfect.

Once in DC, Hank took the Metro to King Street Station. At that time of day, there were very few fellow travelers. He got off the Metro and walked through the tunnel under Duke Street. The tunnel was cool and every sound echoed softly. He walked up the stairs. There was a glimpse of light at the top. Halfway up he began to smell the outside air instead of the dank smell of the tunnel. He no longer felt the reverberation of every sound. As he came out onto the street, it felt like he had emerged from the land of zombies to the land of the living.

The day was dreary and humidity cut through Hank's clothes. He shivered slightly. With time to kill, he strolled leisurely, which was hard for Hank. Purposeless activity was foreign to his nature –it made him uncomfortable, like moldy bread or fungus in the shower. It required effort to consciously force himself to walk slower and gaze at the shops. He saw a little coffee shop café and went in. The place was decorated with overstuffed couches and chairs arranged in little groups. The floor was tiled with expensive blue and green slate with streaks of gold. The place was about half full. He approached the counter, where a sullen, twenty-something woman asked him what she could get for him. Hank was not a coffee drinker, so he ordered a hot chocolate. The woman smiled condescendingly and said, "That'll be four dollars and fifty cents."

Hank found an empty overstuffed seat as far away from any of the other patrons as possible. He checked the location of Morris using his smartphone. Based on his earlier research Morris tended to work late on Wednesdays. Hank was hoping this pattern would continue. The phone showed Morris in the northeast corner of the building. So far so good. If Morris did not work late today, Hank would have to spend the night in DC. Without a reservation, it would cost him a fortune. Hank checked the stock market and found it was down slightly and reviewed the latest business news but nothing caught his interest. He over-heard a conversation between a couple. The man asked, "Is the patent office still putting the NO in innovation?"

His companion laughed, tossing her hair back, "What do you care? You make more money off of each case if you have to argue them for your clients."

The man smiled conspiratorially and whispered, "Whatever you do, don't tell anyone."

Hank felt sick. The cynical nature of the remark was beyond his comprehension. He turned away and forced himself to concentrate on his phone, trying to create a cone of silence to block out the pestilence that surround him. Hank checked the time. It was about 4:30. He sent a message to the patent office's security system that showed Morris leaving through the turn-stiles. Hank got up, left the coffee shop and walked to the patent office. He was dressed in a conservative blue business suit. Not his best color, according to his mom, but it blended perfectly in DC. When he entered the patent office, he walked briskly over to the turnstiles. His shoes squeaked on the marble floor. He headed to a turnstile farthest from the guards. He pulled out his employee badge and scanned it through the card reader. His heart skipped a beat as it took a second for the light to turn green and unlock the turnstile. He tried not to make eye contact with anyone as he headed to the elevators.

Once he reached the top floor, he headed for the bathroom. He had looked up the floor plan, so he knew exactly where to go. He entered the bathroom without seeing anyone. His heart was racing, and he tugged at his collar. The bathroom had the same expensive slate that was in the coffee shop. In fact, the whole bathroom seemed designed to impress, like an overly expensive hotel. He headed for a stall. The door creaked as he entered. Hank closed the door and latched it. He planned to hang out here until most of the office cleared out. Opening his phone, he checked on Morris's location. It appeared that Morris was in his office. Hank started searching the Web on his phone. The door to the bathroom opened and a couple of guys entered. They were talking about their plans for the weekend. One of the guys opened the stall next his. It was unlikely that a lot of strangers ended up in this bathroom and Hank began to worry this guy next to him would try to start up a conversation. Hank made some noises like he was doing his business. After an eternity, the guy got up and left the stall. When he left the bathroom, Hank let out a sigh of relief. The guy was gone, but not the stench he left behind.

At 5:30, Hank disabled Morris's office phone using his Android. He plugged in a small directional microphone. Punching in a URL, Hank set up the phone to record. He then exited the bathroom. Walking down the hall, he noticed that the administrative staff had all left for the day, which was good. He spotted Morris's office, opened the door and walked in silently. Morris did not notice him until he was standing in front of his desk.

"What the hell are you doing here?" Morris demanded as he stood up from his chair. His face went immediately red with anger.

"You killed my sister."

Morris's face changed from anger to fear. He reached for the phone to call security but when he lifted the handset, there was no dial tone. The line was dead.

Hank laughed and nodded toward the phone. "I made sure that we wouldn't be disturbed while we had our little chat."

Morris couldn't fathom how Rangar had gotten past security, let alone how he was able to cut off his telephone. He looked nervously toward the door.

"You interfered with EWE's patent application, which kept them from receiving funding. As a result, my sister died. I believe I sent you a death announcement." Morris was slowly realizing what he had in Mr. Hank Rangar.

He grabbed his chair handles so tightly his knuckles turned white and quickly tried to assess if Rangar had a weapon. "I told you I don't get involved in individual patent cases and I don't see how I can be held responsible for the death of your sister or anyone else you claim I killed. Why would I possibly want to do that?"

Hank noticed Morris looking toward the door, assessing his chances of escaping. "If you don't get involved in individual cases, why is there an email from the group supervisor stating you told him to put the EWE case in a quality review black hole?"

How the hell does he know that? Morris could feel a drop of sweat roll down the back of his neck. "Even if I did somehow sideline EWE's patent case, it was for the greater good. EWE was never going to be able to develop the technology. AltruMedical had the funding and the talent to make it happen."

Hank slammed the desk with his hand. Morris hunkered as if there were incoming mortars.

"Greater good? Your job is not to decide what the greater good is. You swore an oath to uphold the Constitution, which includes protecting the rights of inventors."

"Mr. Rangar, you are mistaken; the Constitution does not say anything about protecting the rights of inventors." *This guy broke into my office to give me a lecture on the Constitution?*

"Article 1, Section 8, Clause 8 specifically states that Congress will secure 'the exclusive rights' of inventors. You didn't uphold the Constitution as you swore to; you decided to play puppet master." *This guy was a US congressman and he hasn't even read the Constitution.*

"I took all the stakeholders into account and did what I thought was best for everyone. Surely you can't fault me for that?" Morris was beginning to relax. Rangar was clearly a madman but he didn't seem to have a weapon, and the conversation had changed from killing people to an academic debate.

"Perhaps you are confused about the purpose of government. We all have certain unalienable rights and 'to secure these rights, governments are instituted among men, deriving their just powers from the consent of the governed,'" Hank quoted.

"What sort of clap-trap nonsense are you spouting, Rangar?" Morris had no idea what this guy was talking about.

"It's called the Declaration of Independence; perhaps you've heard of it. Nowhere does it say anything about the greater good or stakeholders or government officials playing puppet master." Hank spat with disgust.

In a hostage situation, the longer it went on and the more the victim could humanize himself by talking to his captors the more likely he was to survive. Rangar was obviously crazy, talking about 'unalienable rights' and ignoring the greater good. *Just keep talking; just keep talking.* "I don't possibly see how such a system could work. Who would tell the people what was right and what was wrong? Are you suggesting that government officials not pursue the greater good?"

"Hitler, Stalin, Moa and every other two-bit dictator said they were pursuing the greater good. Those three killed over a hundred million people, all in the pursuit of 'the greater good.' You killed my sister and thousands of other people who may have benefitted from that technology in pursuit of the greater good. You have destroyed the hopes, dreams, and business of the founders and inventors at EWE."

Morris studied his face; he didn't like it that this mad man was talking about killing again.

Hank leaned across the desk, "The Declaration of Independence states that when people are faced with a despotic government, it is their duty to throw it off. I would like to throw you off a cliff, but instead I am going to allow you to resign, admit your guilt, and disgorge your profits."

This guy is an idiot. Doesn't he know government officials have immunity for their actions? "Why would I resign, Rangar? You have no proof. Even if you did, the worst

I could be accused of was bureaucratic bungling," Morris scoffed.

"That might be true, except that you invested in AltruMedical and you made five million dollars off that investment." Hank grinned, wryly.

"What makes you think that?" *How the hell does this guy know about that?*

"About a month ago, there was a five million dollar transfer from a North Carolina venture fund to your Scottrade account." Morris began to squirm in his chair. "That venture fund's only investment was in AltruMedical, which is rather suspicious given that most venture funds invest in multiple companies. This will be damning to you if it comes out in the press."

"How the hell—that is a pure fabrication of your deranged imagination."

Hank decided to embellish his narrative so that Morris would be under no delusion that he was just guessing. "About a month ago there was a 200K transfer into your personal banking account in Asheville. You then wrote a check to a Porsche dealer in Asheville, North Carolina for $167,549.00 for a new Porsche 911 Turbo S."

He broke into my bank accounts—that's against the law. Morris had not been a prosecutor in North Carolina for nothing and he knew judges and juries were sick and tired of identity thieves. Morris took a breath. "Whatever. You clearly broke multiple laws to find out that information and you will go to jail if you ever reveal it to anyone."

"Perhaps, but the journalist I have in mind will never reveal their source. Besides, once the story takes off, no one will be interested in some computer engineer who leaked this information to a reporter. Their only interest will be why the director of the patent office killed the man's sister for his own personal profit."

"What gives you the right to ruin my life?" Morris's neck veins started to bulge and perspiration glistened on his forehead.

"Just doing my patriotic duty." Rangar gave a malicious chuckle.

Morris felt a chill up his spine. Rangar did not appear to be stable. He decided to play along. "What exactly do you want me to do?"

"Resign as director of the patent office, never hold another public office, and give EWE Tech's founders the five million you made off of your AltruMedical investment. If you do this, I will never release the information I have. You have two weeks or I go to the press."

"But—but, if I turn over the five million dollars, I will still have to pay taxes on the gain and I will have no way to do so. It will bankrupt me," Morris complained.

"Yeah, and that exact situation happened to a lot of technology entrepreneurs with their stock options and I didn't see you sponsoring legislation to correct it. Actions have consequences, Mr. Morris. That's the deal; take it or leave it." With that, Hank turned abruptly and walked out of the office.

Chapter 20

Christine Patel was sitting at her desk mulling over the last paragraph of her story on the MedCon acquisition of AltruMedical. She had to walk a fine line. She was accusing the powerful Senator Fowl of manipulating NIH funding to benefit a company in which he was an investor. She wanted to be hard-hitting, but if she was too sensational, her boss would make her rewrite it. He was rightly concerned about being sued for libel and always reminded her that in the US you can sue anybody for anything. That doesn't mean you will win, but it is an expensive endeavor for a newspaper to defend itself against.

She was pleased with the article; it was honest and stuck to the facts. A Pulitzer Prize could be in the cards. She had been dreaming about that since her second year in college as a journalism major. Reading over what she had written, she stretched and thought, *Not bad, not bad at all.* She sent the article over to her editor and decided to take an early lunch.

Joe Benson had recently taken the job as editor of the *Financial Reporter* and was told that the paper needed to increase revenues or face layoffs. It involved a substantial pay raise; it was a career advancement from his editorial oversight position at the *Washingtonian*. Despite this, he had found the position less interesting. Where was the drama in reporting the earnings of companies and their stock prices? Occasionally a CEO would get fired or there was an accounting scandal, but these didn't compare to the drama of backroom deals being made on legislation that would affect the whole country, or the sex scandals that would ruin a congressman's career.

He checked his emails and found one from Christine. She was one of his brightest, and definitely his best-looking reporter. The story she had been chasing on AltruMedical and Senator Fowl had drama, backroom deals, and even the death of an innocent woman. This story had the potential to be award-winning. *The Financial Reporter* was a conservative paper, so he had told Christine to be careful about her conclusions—let the facts speak for themselves. This story was potentially explosive. To be sure he was not burned by it, he had kept the publisher informed of this story from the beginning. Back at his old paper, they would have run this without vetting. The headlines would have screamed about murder, backroom deals, and graft. Follow-up editorials would have kept the story alive. He read the headline "The Altru-MedCon Merger: A Case Study in Regulatory Capture." It sounded more like an academic journal than a newspaper. Despite this, Joe was

254

sure it would set off a firestorm with all the political rags, like his old paper, wanting to jump on the bandwagon.

The email contained the final draft of her article. He got up out of his leather chair, walked across his Manhattan office overlooking the city and closed the door. He was looking forward to reading it. When he got to the final paragraph, he read it carefully.

> Senator Fowl used his position in the US Senate to steer NIH grants to AltruMedical, a company in which he had invested. This was a conflict of interest and a breach of the trust the voters placed in him. But more importantly, these crony capitalist arrangements undermine the initiative of our inventors and entrepreneurs and may have cost Janine Nelson her life. When entrepreneurs and investors believe that the game is rigged, they are reluctant to invest in new technologies; inventors have a hard time funding their inventions, causing them to seek some other means for supporting themselves and their families. When that happens, we are all worse off. The development and deployment of new technologies is the only way to increase our standard of living and quality of life. Where would we be today if Edison's inventive efforts had been thwarted by this sort of crony capitalism? How long would it have taken for the phonograph to be invented or a practical electric light bulb or the motion picture? We are

all poorer because of these inside deals; they steal our initiative, our creativity, and our self-esteem.

Upon finishing, he jumped up from his chair, thrust his fist in the air and yelled "YES." His secretary turned her head and gave him a concerned look through the office window. He waved and smiled at her. She frowned and turned back to her computer screen. He realized that a story that got him this pumped up might mean trouble. He sent Christine's article over to the publisher of the paper who had hired him.

It was not widely known that Senator Fowl was an investor in several newspapers in his home state. He had found it prudent to take anonymous stakes in papers as a way to ensure favorable coverage. This strategy had been useful in making sure that his involvement with several white supremacist organizations in his early years was not reported. As his wealth and influence had grown while serving in the Senate, he decided to expand this strategy to some national newspapers, including *The Financial Reporter*. Only the publisher was aware of his involvement.

Fowl was at lunch with the beautiful Betty Jo Lurie. She was a lobbyist and she had helped him submarine the EWE patent and make him a small fortune from the Altru-MedCon merger. Betty was flirting with him—which he loved, but as an octogenarian they both realized that it was all for show—when his Blackberry buzzed at him. He would have ignored it, but his staff had set his Blackberry up with different tones based on the importance of the call or message and this tone meant it was urgent. His eyes were failing him so he needed Betty to read the message. He trusted her completely, not because she was trustworthy but because their mutual interests were so intertwined she would be a fool to stab him in the back. Fowl passed the phone to Betty and asked for her help.

"Your wish is my command," Betty said coquettishly. She started to read the message. "It's from some guy at *The Financial Reporter.* He has a story he wants you to read immediately." Senator Fowl waved his hand for her to go ahead. Betty started to read "The Altru-MedCon Merger: A Case Study in Regulatory Capture," by Christine Patel. . . ." As she read, she could see the veins in Senator Fowl's temple bulge. Luckily, the article did not say anything about her role in convincing Stanford Morris to submarine the patent—in fact, the author did not seem to know anything about this. Betty loved to see powerful people squirm. Upon finishing the article, she looked intently at the senator. "It's very well written, don't you think?"

"I think Miss Patel doesn't know her place. I have some business to attend to, will you please excuse me." Betty knew not to push the senator further. Besides, she had plenty of reading to do and clients to see. "Thanks for lunch, Senator," she said, although she had paid.

Christine Patel had a little bounce in her step on the way home. Her editor had told her that the article was excellent but he needed to run it past the publisher. She was daydreaming about winning that Pulitzer Prize as she opened the door to her apartment. Just as she stepped into her dark apartment, someone grabbed her and put a rag over her mouth. She tried to scream and thrash but she felt dizzy and everything went black.

While holding onto the drooping body of Christine Patel, the man softly closed the door and locked it. Then he picked her up in a fireman's carry, walked across the room, and laid her on the couch carefully. He had gloves on, a tight fitting nylon shirt, a hairnet and nylon stockings under his jeans. This was all designed not to leave any hair or skin particles for the police to find. He knew the police would not look too hard if the incident looked like an accident.

Christine had leased this apartment because it had a great claw-foot bathtub in the newly tiled bathroom. She had often enjoyed relaxing by candlelight in the tub or reading the latest novel. The intruder had noticed the bathtub and decided it was the perfect accidental death. Drowning in a bathtub was more common than drowning in a pool, and this sort of bathtub made it perfect. He stood up walked around the couch into the bathroom, put the rubber plug into the drain and turned on the water. While the bathtub was designed to look like an old-claw foot tub, federal regulations required that the faucet be a single handle faucet with an anti-scalding feature. Because of this, he set it for the hottest temperature.

He went back to the couch and started to undress Christine. As a professional killer, he generally didn't think about his victims at all but she was quite attractive. He unbuttoned her blouse, pulled off her shoes, her panty hose, her skirt, and then had to lift her hips to get her thong underwear off. He didn't want anything to tear. He was a little worried she might wake up. People reacted differently to chloroform. He placed the chloroform-soaked rag in his pants pocket, lifted her up to a sitting position and removed her bra. She appeared to still be out cold. He set her head down against the shoulder of the couch and her body started to slouch onto the floor. He grabbed her by the hips and put them securely on the couch.

He headed back to the bathroom. He didn't want the tub to overflow—it would alert the downstairs neighbors if water came running out of the ceiling. The tub was about half full and he pulled off his right glove and put his index finger in the water to test the temperature. If it was too hot, it would scald the body. This would tip the police off that it was not an accidental drowning. Ideally, he wanted the temperature between 102 and 105 degrees Fahrenheit. The water felt a little warm, so he turned the faucet a little to the right. He found some sandalwood-scented bubble bath and added it to the water. The smell immediately permeated the room. He thought it was a nice smell, and if the body started to rot, it would mask it for a while. When the water was about two thirds up the side, he turned off the water. He headed back to the couch and watched her breathing for a minute. It was rhythmic, indicating she was unlikely to wake up imminently. He crossed the room to where Christine had a bar cart. She was clearly a vodka drinker; she had a bottle of Stoli Elit that was almost full, a bottle of Grey Goose that was about half empty, and a couple of bottles of Skyy, both of which had less than a quarter left. As long as you are going out, you might as well go out in style. He opened the Stoli Elit.

In order to make this look like an accident he needed her to wake up long enough to drink the vodka, not aspirate it. He kneeled down next to her naked body and gently tapped her face until she began to wake up. He grabbed her chin with his left hand and forced his index and thumb finger over her cheeks and between her teeth. This would keep her from spitting out the vodka. She was groggy and did not put up much of a fight. He carefully filled her mouth with Stoli Elit vodka; in her dazed state, she first started to aspirate the vodka but then swallowed it. She started to squirm but the chloroform made her actions sluggish and weak, despite the fact that she was in excellent shape. He poured another mouthful of vodka into her and repeated it until two thirds of the bottle was gone. He could no longer tell whether the chloroform or the alcohol was making her groggy. He put the Stoli Elit vodka on the wood floor out of the way and picked her up.

He carried her into the bathroom and placed her gently into the tub full of bubbles, feet first. He gently eased her torso into the tub but despite this some of the water spilled onto the floor. He checked and it was not enough water to leak into the ceiling below. He put his hand on her head and held it under water. She struggled weakly at first and then fought with surprising strength a minute later. She clearly had a strong will to live, but it was only a matter of time. At about a minute in a half, he noticed a bunch of bubbles that indicated she had aspirated some water into her lungs, and her body convulsed for about fifteen seconds. A minute later, he noticed another bunch of bubbles and he thought this indicated that her body had given up. Despite this, he held her head under water for another couple of minutes. When he was sure that she was dead, he got up, went to the living room and picked up her clothes. He was not sure whether she was fastidious or sloppy but from the state of her apartment, she looked fairly fastidious, so he folded her clothes onto the edge of her bed. He then got the Stoli Elit vodka bottle and laid it on its side next to the bathtub. Next, he placed a waterproof dildo he had brought with him on the floor on the other side of the tub. He thought about lighting the candles she had around the tub but did not want to risk the chance of a fire. The longer it took to discover the body the better. With that, he got up and cleaned the surfaces where his hair could have fallen out, picked up the chloroform rag and left.

Hank was struggling with a particularly difficult control system problem. There were race conditions, which forced him to program in assembly code instead of a high-level language like C++. It was tedious. He walked to the window to clear his mind; the metallic odor of solder invaded his nostrils as he headed out of the lab. It was early. The shadows from Pikes Peak stretched forever. He saw the ridge where he and Christine had hiked. He remembered her firm buttocks as she hiked, her smiling face, the sweat on her flush face. Then he thought of her naked body in his bed. *Damn, I am like some lovesick teenager. I've got work to do.* He resolved to think about the race condition and how to solve it. Pacing, he focused on the structure of the problem. He pulled back the layers of the problem but it was no use, his mind drifted to Christine's beautiful breasts, the smell of her perfume on the nape of her neck, the way her body of reacted to his. *Perhaps if I call her that will clear my head.* It was two hours later in New York. He checked his watch; that meant it was 11:00am. He called her cell phone—no answer, so he called her office. She didn't pick up. He punched zero to get the receptionist. A raspy voice told him Christine was not in.

"Is she on assignment?"

"Excuse me, who is this?"

Hank thought about how he could get this gatekeeper to provide him more information, "I have some time-sensitive information for Ms. Patel."

"That doesn't tell me who you are, Mr.?"

Hank heard the implied question. He knew the AltruMedical story was more than routine. "Rangar. This is important; it is about the MedCon acquisition of Altru. Now could you tell me how I can reach Ms. Patel?" It was more a command than a question.

"Ah, Mr. Rangar, Christine did not show up for work today. I have no idea how to reach her."

"What do you mean she didn't show up to work today? Was she expected?"

"I don't know how I could have been clearer. Goodbye." He heard the click on the line; it was so final.

Joe Benson looked up at the clock and saw that it was 11:30 a.m. Christine was a very punctual person and had never been late for work without calling in first. It was not uncommon for other reporters to be late and at Christine's level, they were not required to report in, especially if they were on assignment. However, she was not on assignment and it was contrary to her nature. He told himself to relax. She probably got stuck on the subway or celebrated a little too much. He started working on some stories for tomorrow's paper. He started to read, "GE's earnings did not meet expectations…" but his mind started to wander. He just couldn't concentrate. "This is silly; I just need to get some air."

He headed out of his office and asked his secretary if there were any messages for him—perhaps Christine had called and his secretary had decided he was busy and screened her call.

"No, there are no messages for you," his secretary said.

"I'm going to take a walk. I need to clear my head. A ha, if Christine shows up, call me on my cell phone," and he held up his cell phone. He blushed slightly. *Why I am so nervous—why I am I so worried about her? Do I have a crush on her?* He thought about it but that was absurd. He was happily married and almost twice Christine's age. What he felt was more like a very protective father whose daughter had failed to show up from her first date at curfew time. He took the elevator down to the street and started walking. The fresh air felt good. He loved the rhythm of the streets, the hustle of the people in New York. He walked about five blocks and his mind was clearing when he looked up to where the World Trade Towers should be and felt a little dizzy; he felt he could see himself looking at the missing towers, as if he was not part of the world around him, when his phone rang. "Yes?"—it was his secretary and she was telling him that he was late for his daily meeting with the layout team. He told her he would be there as soon as possible and to get started without him. His secretary was about to hang up when he asked, "Has Christine shown up?"

"No, should I call her?"

He thought about it and decided it was no longer irrational to begin to worry about her. "Yes, please?"

It was 1:30 p.m. when the meeting was over and there was still no sign of Christine. Joe resolved to head over to Christine's apartment. He called up personnel and told them he needed the address. He hailed a taxi and headed to Christine's. When he reached her apartment, he exited the taxi, heard his shoes slapping the sidewalk, entered the lobby and noticed the faint smell of Pine-Sol. He explained to the guard behind the desk that he was Christine Patel's boss and was worried she had not showed up for work. The guard looked to be in his early sixties had dark, dull eyes, he slowly picked up the phone and called Christine's apartment. Joe tapped his fingers on the counter, while he waited. The guard hung up. "Sorry, she's not home."

"I'll go up and knock on her door." Joe headed for the elevator in a fast clip.

"Hey, you," the guard started to chase Joe but his chair slid back and he almost fell. He held onto his cap as he scrambled across the tile floor to the elevators and slid his hand into the elevator's doors just before they closed. He bent over and grabbed his side with his right hand. "You are not allowed to enter this building unless I have specific authorization from a tenant."

"Look, you can escort me, but I am going to check on her."

The elevator stopped and Joe exited with the guard following close behind. Joe knocked on Christine's door: nothing looked out of place but no one answered the door either.

Something about Joe's demeanor convinced the guard that he was better off not fighting this guy. The guard knocked again and they waited another couple of minutes and knocked again. No answer. The guard pulled out a set of keys and said, "You'll have to wait here." The guard unlocked the door and entered Christine's apartment. It smelled slightly of sandalwood and was dark. The curtains were closed and nothing looked out of place. The guard walked cautiously into the apartment calling out, "Ms. Patel... Ms. Patel, are you here?" But there was no answer. He checked out the kitchen but this was silly since he could see most of the kitchen from the door; then he headed into the bedroom. Clothes were neatly folded on the edge of a made bed. This was not the scene of a crime, he thought to himself. He called out again, "Ms. Patel?" He was feeling relieved but knew he needed to check the bathroom or this guy would not be satisfied. He entered the bathroom and saw her in the bathtub. What the . . . ? "Ms. Patel . . . MS. PATEL!" he shouted but there was no reaction. *Shit, damn . . . Okay, don't touch anything. Call the police.*

As the guard was on the phone, Joe shouted, "Hey, what's going on?" The guard was slightly irritated at the interruption but he finished his conversation and hung up.

Joe saw the look on the guard's face and he felt like someone had knocked the wind out of him.

When police showed up the guard was irritated by the delay. "About time you guys showed up." They ignored him. The taller of the two, who had salt and pepper gray hair, asked where the body was. The guard led them in. When they came out five minutes later, they asked Joe to stick around until the detectives showed up. Joe rubbed his forehead and pushed his hair back. "Sure, I'll stick around." They roped off the apartment and called the detectives. Joe slid down the side of the wall into a crouching position. I need to call her parents. *Oh Jesus, how am I going to explain this to them.*

The detectives didn't show up for another fifteen minutes. One detective was overweight and wore glasses. The other detective was taller and balding. The overweight detective questioned Joe and the guard while the balding detective scoured the apartment. Joe explained that he didn't know much about her personal life but he told them about the story she was working on about AltruMedical and Senator Fowl. When he mentioned Senator Fowl, the detectives looked at each other for a second and then they told Joe if they needed anything more, they would contact him.

They found Christine's cell phone next to her bed. As part of their normal investigation, they checked the recent calls and came across Hank's name and number. The taller detective called Hank. It was standard procedure to follow up with anyone that the victim had been in contact with recently. "Mr. Rangar."

Hank was in the Made by Man labs when his phone rang, "Yes."

The detective explained who he was and told Hank he was calling about a Ms. Christine Patel. Hank slumped in a chair.

The detective explained matter-of-factly that she had been found in her bathtub, dead. Hank's head spun. *What? That can't be; I just saw her.*

"Sir, did you know Ms. Patel?"

Did I know her? She can't be gone.

A gravelly voice interrupted Hank's thoughts. "Mr. Rangar, are you still there?"

"Ah, yeah, I know her."

The officer continued by asking what they had done together, where he was last night, etc. Hank felt uncomfortable with the interrogation and decided to be honest but not volunteer anything. The detective asked if he knew anyone who would want to hurt her. *Better be careful how I answer this question.* He explained that he did not know

Christine that well but the story she had interviewed him about was likely to upset some important people. "Do you think she was murdered?" he asked the detective. But what he thought was, *Of course they fucking murdered her. First, they murdered Janine and now they've murdered Christine.*

"It looks like it was an accidental drowning but it's part of our standard procedure not to rule out anything at this stage. I don't have any further questions at this time. We will let you know what we find." The detective hung up the phone.

Hank punched a wall in the lab. His hand hurt, and he sat down in a chair. *There is no way Christine drowned. She was my only contact in the press. Without her, my threat to expose Morris will be a much more difficult proposition. Is it possible Morris had her killed? I didn't tell Christine about Morris or Morris about Christine. No way she could have found out about Morris's involvement, at least the way I found out about it.*

That made it highly unlikely that Morris had been behind Christine's death. However, he was sure someone had killed her because of the AltruMedical story. Perhaps someone at MedCon or one of their political cronies? These people were so arrogant that they thought the law did not apply to them. His recent experience taught him that they protected each other too, no matter what their political affiliation. Even the police could not be trusted, because they were ultimately political animals as well.

She had just started her career. Her talent could have taken her anywhere, but they couldn't allow that. And I had barely gotten to know her, but we already had something special. She was so bright and beautiful. They have stolen her from me. I am not going to let them get away with this—those fuckers are going to pay.

Chapter 21

Stanford Morris entered the Metro station. Long ghost-like shadows played on the walls. Footfalls in the distance reminded him of the cadence of *The Raven*. It took forever for his train to arrive. Its brakes squealed like a banshee. He entered the train and found a seat. *When is this goddamn train going to get going?* He stood; the train jerked and his shoulder slammed into the solid, unforgiving silver hand pole. He was irritated. Millions of people who had picked their nose, consumptively coughed in their hands, urinated or defecated and not washed their hands put their hand on that pole. He could feel the germs on his suit coat. The train decelerated erratically. Stanford instinctively reached out for the pole and grabbed with his hand. *Damn.* He quickly pulled his hand away and looked at it as if it were glowing green with unseen germs. He wiped his hand on his pants, which just served to spread the germs and the green glow in his mind. He sat down in frustration. At this time of night, the Metro stopped at every bump along the line and it took twice as long to get home. It provided plenty of time for the adrenaline to wear off. Getting off the Metro was a chore. The fucking patent office job should have come with a chauffeur, Stanford thought. *Why am I forced to take the subway like some stupid twenty-year-old intern?* The steps he heard echoing were his own. The escalator was broken so he had to walk up the stairs. Each step required concentrated effort and with each step, he imagined another way to kill Hank Rangar.

It was a dark night with no moon as he slogged the three blocks to his apartment. There were people walking on the street but he didn't notice them. *What kind of world is it that a peasant like Hank Rangar could assault me in my own office? This douche bag, crazy inventor is not going to ruin my career.* He reached his apartment building and did not notice it when the doorman said, "Good evening, Mr. Morris." He had an apartment in DC and his house in North Carolina. His wife hated DC so she spent most of her time down South tending her elaborate flowerbeds. She had called his cell phone several times but he did not feel like talking tonight. He fumbled for keys, unlocked the door to his third-floor apartment and poured himself a large tumbler of Maker's Mark and took a big slug. The warm burn reinvigorated him. I'll teach Rangar to fuck with me. I am not going to just kill him; I going to wipe him off the face of the Earth. I not only want him dead, I want anything he has touched to be contagious. I want people to curse his name when they think of him.

Morris settled on a two-prong approach to obliterating Rangar. First, eliminate the man himself; second, destroy everything he had built. Roland Hawthorne was perfect for the first, a former Green Beret who had been one of the first soldiers on the ground in Afghanistan after 9/11. Hawthorne was the CEO of The Sam Adams Financial Group out of North Carolina, which was one of the many new private companies that the CIA and DOD hired to handle issues that were too hot for them politically. This had been one of the growth industries in the last decade. Morris met Hawthorne while in Congress. Hawthorne was known as something of a mercenary, and Morris was sure he would know best how to affect Rangar's demise. Stanford got up and poured himself another Maker's Mark.

He had been briefed on Hawthorne's background once. Hawthorne had been a colonel in the Green Berets and was instrumental in planning and executing the war against the Taliban and Al-Qaeda. President Bush had been under a lot of pressure to respond to the 9/11 attacks and asked the regular Army how long before they could be in position. The conventional forces in the Army said it would take a minimum of nine months. This was a politically unacceptable answer for George W. Bush. Morris shuddered at the thought.

Bush asked his generals if there was another solution. The Special Forces piped in that they could be in Afghanistan in two weeks. Roland Hawthorne was put in charge of developing the operation and he suggested a low profile action that would back an alliance formed by Hamid Karzai. Hawthorne didn't just plan the operation; he was part of the ground team. The result was better than anyone could have expected—the Taliban was defeated before the end of 2001, making President Bush look like a genius. *Exactly the sort of take-charge guy I need in this situation,* Stanford thought, taking another pull of the caramel liquid that smelled of slightly burnt sugar and oak.

The success of the operation looked certain to propel Hawthorne to a 'one star,' until some irregularities in his interrogation techniques sidelined his career. It was rumored that when the standard interrogation techniques failed with a particular prisoner, Roland had shot off his pinkie and threatened to shoot him in the gonads next. The prisoner sang like a bird after that, which supposedly allowed them to stop a car bombing attack. Hawthorne was given the chance to retire with full pay or face a court martial. Morris felt a little giddy thinking the same fate might befall Hank Rangar.

Morris decided to also put a pox on everything Rangar ever touched by unleashing the IRS. The Supreme Court had it right when they said the power to tax was the power to destroy. Morris would use the IRS to inflict a plague on anything and anyone associated with Rangar.

John Farmer was a political appointee to the Treasury Department, but everyone knew him as Prince John and he was perfect for the second prong. It was widely known in DC that he was the guy to talk to when you wanted the IRS to investigate a political opponent. This technique was widely used against churches and nonprofit groups that one political party or the other thought were getting too vocal. Stanford would give him a call in the morning. He stood up, stretched, and decided to go to bed.

Morris arrived a little later than usual for work the next day. The Maker's Mark and the adrenaline from last night made him feel drained. As he got off the elevator, he felt a little anxious. Walking down the hall to his office, he expected Rangar to jump out from behind one of the cubicles. "Good morning Mr. Morris," Lilly, his administrative assistant, said, causing Stanford to jump a little.

"We'll see, Lilly, we will see." He entered his office and closed the door. Stanford walked around his desk and slumped in his chair. He turned on his computer and looked out the window as he waited for it to boot up. He looked up Farmer's cell phone number and called him. There was no answer, so he left a message. Then he looked up Roland Hawthorne's cell phone number. He decided to call Roland on his cell phone. That would emphasize how important the call was. Stanford dialed the number.

Roland Hawthorne felt his phone vibrate. He looked at the caller ID and saw it was Congressman Morris. This could mean business. "Congressman Morris, how can I help you?"

"Roland, how the hell are you?" Morris said trying to sound like this was a casual conversation.

Hawthorne knew that when congressional representatives, even former congressional representatives, were acting casual it meant that they needed some sort of personal service. While these were not as lucrative for The Sam Adams Financial Group, they were necessary to grease the wheels for the more profitable projects. "Kicking ass and taking names. In other words same ol' same ol.' How about you?"

"I was wondering if I could take you out for lunch today?"

Hawthorne thought, *If Morris wants to meet today it must be really important.* "Well, it just so happens that I am in DC; where do you want to meet?"

"How about Charlie Palmer's at one o'clock? I feel like a steak."

Charlie Palmer's was one of the most expensive restaurants in DC. Hawthorne thought it was overpriced and overrated, but it was a signal of how important this meeting was to Morris. "Sounds good; I'll see you there."

Morris had a hard time concentrating that morning. He rehearsed in his head exactly how to tell Hawthorne that he wanted Rangar killed. Having never done this before, he was unsure how to go about it. He was sure that it was important not to state his intentions directly. However, he could not afford to be misunderstood either. If Rangar leaked that he had manipulated the patent system and made a fortune by investing in AltruMedical, his career would be over and he would probably spend twenty years in prison. Morris was not sure which was more terrifying. Rangar had given him two weeks before he would go to the press, so Stanford had to make sure he was dead long before then.

If this thing exploded and Senator Fowl's role became public because of me, more than my reputation might be at stake. He shivered.

He left early for his lunch meeting. His stomach was in knots and he was not sure whether he could eat anything. He arrived fifteen minutes early.

"Do you have a reservation?" the maître d asked.

"Yes, Morris."

"It will be just a few minutes until your table is ready. Would you like to take a seat in the bar?"

Stanford was torn but he hated hanging out in the waiting area of a restaurant. So he headed for the bar. As his stomach roiled, his mind raced. What if someone found out that he was trying to hire a hit man? What if

Hawthorne is working with the FBI? He pulled out the bar stool and sat down.

"Can I get you a wine or a Blood Mary, sir?" the bartender asked.

Stanford thought about it and decided a nice merlot might settle his stomach and his nerves. "Yes, a glass of your house merlot." He twisted on his bar stool and saw Betty Jo Lurie entering the restaurant with the senior senator from North Carolina. Ms. Lurie had gotten him into this fix. She had asked him to sideline the EWE patent application. On the other hand, she had been the reason he now had a Porsche 911 Turbo S. Just then, the bartender brought him his merlot. He took a larger swallow of wine than was polite. He realized he was thirsty. Roland Hawthorne walked into the restaurant. Stanford picked up his glass, headed to the maître d and waved at Hawthorne. Hawthorne acknowledged him with a smile.

"Good to see you Roland." Stanford extended his hand.

Roland grabbed his hand. "It's nice to see you too, Congressman Morris." Secretly, Hawthorne felt uncomfortable about the overt meeting. Not because he was worried about being seen with Congressman Morris but because his Special Forces training taught him to blend in and to not do anything that called attention to himself. Hawthorne was five foot ten inches, had graying brown hair, and the build of a fifty-year-old man who ran marathons or did Iron Man competitions. He had a tan face that was otherwise unremarkable. He was dressed in a business suit that looked like the suits worn by every other bureaucrat in DC. Hawthorne's eyes quickly scanned the restaurant. He noticed the senator from North Carolina.

The maître d' came up to them saying, "Table for two," and led them to the back of the restaurant, handing them two menus. They sat down on opposite sides of the table. Hawthorne knew that it was his job to put Morris at ease, but he liked seeing people squirm.

Stanford was not sure what to say and he began to feel uncomfortable. Sports were always a safe topic, so he said, "How about those Panthers?"

Keeping up with sports teams, Roland knew, was important to schmoozing with clients. This meant he always read the latest news in the morning. Personally, he found them only marginally interesting. "Well they are still in the playoff picture and anything can happen once you get into the playoffs."

The server came over and efficiently took their orders. "Their quarterback is a good front runner but if they are down he panics," Stanford added. Hawthorne thought, *Just like you pencil-necked metrosexual politicians.* He purposely didn't say anything for a while. He could see Morris begin to fidget. He thought, *Okay, enough fun, let's earn some money.* "What concern can I help you with?"

Morris played with his wedding ring. "I do have an urgent issue. A Mr. Hank Rangar from Colorado has given me a project that has to be completed within the next two weeks."

"I see. So you need us to complete a background check before then. Is that right?" Background checks were a standard part of his industry, and so they could be used to hide a multitude of sins.

Morris was grateful that Roland was making this easy. "Yes, we need the termination date for the project as soon as possible. See, Mr. Rangar has . . ."

Hawthorne interrupted him. "Mr. Morris we have a policy at The Sam Adams Financial Group—we work on a need-to-know basis only." The idiot was about to justify why he wanted this guy dead. Hawthorne could care less. He just wanted to make sure they got paid.

The server walked up with their orders. They started eating and Hawthorne asked, "Did H.R. serve in the military?"

Stanford finished his bite of steak. "No. I think his background is engineering. His company is in Colorado somewhere." His stomach was beginning to settle.

Roland paused while he thought of what he should charge for the job of killing Hank Rangar. He wasn't military, so that should make things easier. In fact, he would probably subcontract out the work. "I think we can help you with that. We will need ten grand for expenses."

Morris almost choked on his bite of steak and his face began to turn red. "I'm sure you remember the ten million dollar inter-service training program I steered your way."

Roland knew that congressmen got so used to everyone else paying for them that they felt they shouldn't have to pay for anything. He was ready for this sort of objection. "Yes, Congressman Morris, I certainly do and I'm sure you remember our generous contribution to your campaign and super PAC in your last election." It was standing policy at The Sam Adams Financial Group that all employees were required to contribute to designated campaigns.

Morris relented. "Okay. How would you like payment?"

"We accept cash or gold. Many of our clients prefer to pay in gold." His non-government clients preferred to pay in gold, because the IRS required every cash transaction over ten thousand dollars to be reported. The ostensible purpose for this rule was to inhibit drug transactions and transactions like this one. However, the real reason for it was to prevent capital flight. The government, through the Federal Reserve, was flooding the market with new money, which they handed out to their friends. This debasing of the currency always resulted in the wealthy people trying to get their money outside of the country. However, this would defeat the government's purpose of stealing its citizens' wealth, so they put in reporting rules like this one. They also made it almost impossible for US citizens to have bank accounts outside of the US.

Stanford thought it was outrageous that he was being charged for this service, but it was a small fee compared to the five million dollars he had made off AltruMedical. He decided to relax and thought about driving his new Porsche 911 Turbo S in the mountain roads of North Carolina. "I will get your expenses today. And I can expect the job to be completed when?"

"We should be able wrap this up in three to four business days." Morris's eyebrows rose in slight surprise; he didn't think people in Roland's line of work were concerned about 'business days.'

They finished their lunch and on the way out Stanford's eyes met Betty Jo Lurie's across the lively crowd. She cocked her head and smiled broadly, as the senator leaned across the table and whispered something in her ear. Hawthorne made a quick exit and Stanford checked his phone. He noticed that he had a call from John Farmer. Stanford called him back. On the third ring Farmer answered, "Stanford, to what do I owe the pleasure?"

"Prince John my liege, you know I always enjoy your company but I am calling about an individual who needs to be reminded of their civic duty."

"Does this individual have a name?"

"Yes, his name is Hank Rangar. He lives in Colorado somewhere. He is also a major shareholder in a couple of companies—Made By Man and Houdini Security."

"The best way to initiate this is for you to file an anonymous tip. Then let me know when you have done that and I will make sure that the tip is followed up on aggressively."

As he ended his call with Farmer, he saw Betty Jo Lurie's nice ass leaving the restaurant. That had turned out to be an expensive fuck. He was disappointed in himself for not getting more out of the deal. Yes, he had indeed been a naughty boy. He wondered if Tamara would enact a suitable punishment. He would have a sleepless but satisfying night and, within three to four business days, start with a clean slate.

Chapter 22

Roland Hawthorne had just picked up a new project from an important client. It was one of those small projects that you really didn't make any money on but you did it because it was good marketing. In this case, his company would be lucky to cover their expenses and time.

The Sam Adams Financial Group was not a financial company at all. The name was meant as a diversion. The company provided services for the CIA, the military, foreign governments, and occasionally private clients. The present project fell into the last category. The core of the company was made up of ex-Special Services types—Green Berets, Navy Seals, Delta Force guys.

Hawthorne leaned back in his leather chair and yawned. He always felt a little tired when he ate too much for lunch. Adding a side helping of pandering to politicians didn't help. He decided not to fight it. As he nodded off, he thought of how far he and the group had come. Sam Adams was founded by John Smithson, who had been as unremarkable as his name. The group had gotten its start during the first Afghanistan war, transporting shoulder-launched surface-to-air missiles from Pakistan to the Mujahidin.

From there, the company had provided various logistics services to the CIA and the military in Columbia, Grenada, Guatemala, Panama, Saudi Arabia, Iraq and other hot spots around the world. When he joined Sam, the company was in decline. His reputation in the Special Forces community turned things around. The only limitation on Sam's growth was Smithson's reluctance to take on contracts that were more proactive than security and logistics operations. Smithson was past the age of retirement, but try as he might, Roland could not convince him to retire. When he had minor stroke, Roland saw his chance to act. Roland arranged and paid for a three-week trip to Acapulco, where Smithson fell to his death on one of the famous cliffs. Sam had grown by leaps and bounds since then. Roland had a smile on his face as he drifted off.

He woke and rubbed his eyes. Light was streaming into his office and dust could be seen floating in the air. His mind wandered back to the job of eliminating a Hank Rangar, not the sort of project Smithson would have allowed Sam to undertake. He didn't know who Rangar was and he didn't care, except for what was necessary to carry out this task. He called up one of his research assistants in North Carolina. "Find out if a Hank Rangar ever had any military training, if he ever served in the police, and whether he has a concealed-carry permit." Ten minutes later his assistant called back and told him Rangar had worked as a civilian for the military in computer security but all the other answers turned out negative. Rangar lived in a town outside of Colorado Springs, called Manitou Springs. This meant Rangar should be a relatively easy target. All of Hawthorne's field operators were busy, so he would have to subcontract out this job.

The economy was in the toilet, and the military had been downsized, so there were a number of low-skill groups that would happily perform this task. He had been given ten thousand in gold, and he figured he could contract this out for about five thousand. He contacted Stan Weiss using an electronic dead-drop. Electronic dead-drops worked sort of like physical dead drops, except jobs or instructions were posted in encrypted form on semi-random servers. Markers, like the old chalk line on a mailbox, were often embedded in pictures on websites, blogs, or even Facebook. This made them virtually impossible to detect.

Stan Weiss was a business acquaintance in Colorado Springs. His business was similar to Sam's, but on a lower skill level. Roland explained that it needed to look like an accident or at least a random mugging, and he needed the job completed in the next two days.

As Hawthorne waited for the dead-drop to be posted, he turned his mind to other issues. Did Morris hire him personally, or was he acting on behalf of someone else, such as a foreign government? Did the CIA hire him to cover their tracks? Had this Rangar character gotten on the wrong side of some foreign government? Perhaps he had killed someone and fled to the United States or perhaps he embezzled funds from them. Whatever, this Rangar character clearly had what was coming to him. Honest, everyday people did not end up with contracts on their head.

Stan Weiss knew some ex-soldiers who were hurting financially that would take on the job for two thousand dollars. He asked fifty-five hundred. He headed to a strip bar on the east side of Colorado Springs. He hired extras with enough regularity that he was fairly well known by the former soldiers who were willing to be hired muscle and looking for a little cash on the side. It was the middle of the afternoon when Stan entered the strip club, but there were already a smattering of customers. He found a booth against the wall that gave him a view of the entrance and the bathrooms. Stan preferred this strip joint, because he could get a beer. However, this meant that the dancers were not allowed to be totally nude. 'What a man wouldn't do for a beer.' A pretty young girl, who looked like she rarely saw the light of day, asked if he wanted a drink. He ordered a Coors and let his eyes adjust to the low light of the bar. He recognized the girl doing the pole dance. She was athletic, but her dances were more gymnastic routines than sexual.

His server brought him his beer. He gave her a ten-dollar bill. She carefully counted out her change, while letting him admire her half-clad body. "Is there anything else I can do for you?" she held out the waistband of her skintight shorts. This was a sign that Stan was supposed to tip her. He placed two dollars against her hipbone; she snapped her waistband, securing the bills. "Thanks, cutie." Stan was under no illusion that she thought he was attractive. He was thirty pounds overweight and teenage acne had left his face pock-marked. He sipped his beer, listened to the music, and glanced at the dancers while he waited. His mind drifted. *I wonder if this Rangar character is some sort of environmental wacko or property rights freak that's screwing up a politician's real estate deal? Or perhaps he just embezzled from a business—legal or otherwise. Well, whatever he did, the dumbass certainly had what was coming to him. Average Joes did not get whacked.*

He finished his beer and noticed a couple of guys enter the club. These guys reeked of ex-soldiers hard up for money. Stan found it was very important to be able to read people when hiring extras. They didn't sit down immediately and their eyes didn't fixate on the semi-nude dancer on stage. The server approached them to take their order and they waved her off. They stood in the entrance while their eyes adjusted to the low light of the club. Scanning the bar, they saw Stan sitting at a table against the wall, walked over to him and pulled out a couple of chairs. Now they pretended to be interested in the strip show. Stan recognized them. He didn't know their real names but he was sure that he could find them again if he had to. "You guys looking for some work?" The taller of the pair said in a slight Southern accent, "It all depends on the type of work and what it pays." Stan slipped a piece of paper over to the taller guy. It had Hank Rangar's name and his address on it. Stan explained, "This guy needs to go on a permanent vacation, but it's his own decision—you understand."

"Yeah, we understand. But this is going to cost you more than just walking around money," the taller of the two said.

Stan stared at the two former soldiers until they started to fidget in their chairs and looked at each other nervously. "His vacation needs to start in the next day or two, and I can give you a grand up front and a grand upon completion." Both guys nodded their head in assent and Stan pulled out ten one hundred dollar bills and gave them to the taller guy. "You get the other half upon completion of the job," and Stan waved the back of his hand at them.

When the soldiers got in their pickup truck, the taller one, Jim, said, "Damn, now that is easy money, Billy."

"You got that right Jim. How are we going to make it look like an accident?"

"How about a house fire? We make it look like the gas line broke and our friend buys the farm," Jim said. Jim and Billy had created an ingenious little device that pierced a gas line by remote control and provided a little spark to start a fire. The resulting fire destroyed all evidence. They went to Billy's house, picked up some equipment and dressed like a couple hikers, the standard uniform of Colorado. Then they drove over to the address given by the guy in the bar. Billy asked, "What do you think this Rangar guy did?"

Jim was irritated. "Don't waste your time thinking about that too much; what he did was give us a chance to earn two grand for a couple of hours of work."

"I suppose you're right. No one is going to spend that money to kill someone who's kept their nose clean."

This Rangar character lived on a road that bordered the National Forest on Spruce Trail Street in Manitou Springs. Manitou was an eclectic mountain town out-side of Colorado Springs. The houses on this street were built around 1900. They were probably vacation homes originally. It turned out that Rangar's house was on the mountain side of the road, easily twenty feet above the street-level. It had a driveway on the left side of the house but no garage. The house was a rambling wood structure with a porch on the front that had been enclosed to pro-vide additional space. The house was painted a soft yellow and it looked like it would burn like last year's firewood.

Behind the house was a forest of ponderosa pines so typical for that elevation in Colorado.

Jim and Billy drove past the house and turned right on Trestle Trail; from there, they headed for the parking lot of The Incline. The Incline was the remnants of a cog railroad that took people to the top of Pikes Peak. It was frequented by fitness nuts. Going up The Incline was like doing a Stairmaster on steroids. No one would notice their pickup truck in the parking lot while they scouted out the area behind Rangar's house. They parked and started hiking. It took three quarters of an hour of picking their way through scree, cactus, and pines for Jim and Billy to get to a spot about one hundred yards up the mountain from Rangar's house. The backside of the property revealed a propane tank and a flat gravel spot on the right side of the house. The house had old shake shingles. It was late afternoon.

Jim said, "Let's wait awhile and see if anyone is home." They found an old log to hide behind; it smelled of dry rot. Jim pulled a pair of binoculars out of Billy's backpack. Jim scanned Rangar's house and the neighbors' for any signs of activity. After fifteen minutes he was satisfied no one was home. They slowly crept toward the structure in a crouched position, found where the propane line entered under the floor and Jim noticed a door that accessed the crawl space. He pulled it open and attached his gas-line piercing device on the pipe under the house. This was going to be easier than he had originally planned.

The fact that the gas line was accessible from under the house would allow the propane to build up before they started the fire. This would cause an explosion that would probably kill Rangar even before the fire or smoke got to him. Jim placed the latch back in place and they crept up the mountain away from the property to Billy's pickup truck. They decided they'd come back after dark and finish the job.

Chapter 23

Hank Rangar was taking target practice with the Colt Detective Special he had just purchased. He had asked the advice of his friend Warren Criss about which pistol he should carry for protection. Warren's first advice was to get a revolver. As he explained it, "Cover your ass; leave no brass." Hank was a little confused by this statement. Revolvers held the 'brass' cartridge in the chambers of the cylinder after the bullet was fired. This was important because brass cartridges could be used by the police to trace the gun that fired a bullet, sort of like a fingerprint. The trade with a revolver was that the chamber was not completely sealed like a 9mm semiautomatic pistol. This meant that some of the energy was lost when firing a bullet, so it required slightly higher cartridges to get the same firepower. However, Warren assured him that the .38 Detective Special had more than enough firepower. In addition, Warren suggested using hollow point bullets because they essentially disintegrated when they hit the target. This made it very difficult to tell anything about the gun from the bullet, if it was ever found.

The gun was a double action, short-barreled revolver often known as a snubbie or a belly gun because it could easily be concealed in your clothes. It weighed only twenty-one ounces and its total length was just under seven inches. Colt quit producing the Detective Special in 1995 and Hank's was an earlier model but it was in mint condition. Hank had experience hunting with rifles and shotguns on his grandparent's farm in Iowa but had never fired a pistol. He fired a number of shots and got used to the action of the revolver; it had almost no recoil. Hank enjoyed the smell of the spent gunpowder.

He had threatened the livelihood and reputation of some powerful people. They might react in a violent manner. It was a wise precaution to be prepared for this eventuality. The revolver was just part of Hank's plan to be prepared. If these people turned violent, it was unlikely that they would be stopped by one unsuccessful attempt to divert him from his course.

If attacked, Hank had resolved he would go on the offensive. Stealth would be a necessary part of his offensive. *How do you become invisible in this digital age? These people could probably get at his banking transactions and other digital transactions. As a result, he could not use his credit cards, ATM card, or even withdraw cash at the bank.* Because of this, he pulled out several thousand dollars and put thirty-five hundred dollars of the cash in a fire safe at his office and twenty-five hundred dollars of the cash in his fire safe at home. He also decided to carry thirteen hundred in cash in his wallet.

He would no longer be able to use his cell phone if he wanted to disappear. The GPS receiver in phones could be used to track your exact location. Even without the GPS signal, your general location could be tracked. He bought a prepaid mobile and put it in his backpack with his gun in case he needed it. Even your car's navigation could be used to track you, but Hank owned an International Harvester Scout II; it didn't have a navigation system.

Warren looked at him with his jet black eyes. "How does it feel?"

"It was an excellent choice, thanks. Take a look at my last grouping. Considering I've shot less than one hundred rounds with it, I think that's pretty good."

"Not bad, for a coder," Warren teased. "How about we get some lunch?"

"I feel like barbeque; how about Front Range?"

"Sounds good."

While they waited for their food, Warren asked, "So how did the trip to DC go?"

"I think I got their attention, which is why I need the Colt." Warren thought Hank was overly paranoid. When he thought of the director of the patent office, whom he had never seen, he saw nerd with a pocket protector. What was he going to do, stab Hank with a mechanical pencil?

"Speaking of which, thanks for your help with the night vision cameras." Hank had gotten interested in night vision cameras to spy on the wildlife behind his house. He had looked at putting in some off-the-shelf cameras in his backyard but he didn't like it that they used infrared flashlights. Some animals, including snakes, butterflies, and most importantly ticks, were sensitive to this light. Ticks were actually attracted. As a result, Hank and Warren had decided to use image intensifier technology. This worked by converting light into electrons, which are then accelerated, multiplied, and converted back to photons. No infrared flashlight for the ticks or others to spot. They put a fisheye lens on the image intensifier to increase its field of view. Special software was used to convert the fisheye images into standard images. This allowed the camera to cover almost a one hundred and eighty degree field of view. The camera used software to only record images when there was movement, which saved disk space and more importantly meant Hank did not have to wade through hours of video where nothing happened.

Hank had placed a couple of the modified cameras in the trees behind his backyard. The cameras recorded bobcats, mountain lions, porcupines, bears, and tons of deer.

Hank remembered one time a camera had caught a mountain lion attacking a deer. This had been a great source of entertainment for Hank. When Hank had told his sister Janine about this, she was horrified. He complained she was being overly sensitive, that this was natural. She countered that if he had made her an aunt, he would understand that death and violence were not entertainment. He still had not understood her point and laughed.

"What's so funny?"

"Oh, one time our cameras caught a mountain lion killing a deer and Janine was horrified." Hank smiled sadly.

Warren put down his fork. "Well those new cameras we put around your house and the office will probably catch more of those events."

They finished lunch and headed back to the office. Hank worked on some end-of-the-quarter accounting that he had been putting off. He didn't leave the office until around six o'clock. Being a bachelor, he decided he didn't feel like making dinner that night, so he stopped at one of his favorite bar and grills in Manitou. As he was waiting for his food, he flipped though emails on his smartphone.

He had set up the cameras to send alerts to his cell phone when they recorded anything. He noticed that he had a slightly larger number of alerts than usual. This made him curious; besides, what else did he have to do while he waited for his food? He opened one email that was from three o'clock that afternoon. The camera covered the street in front of his house. This usually meant it was just a car driving past. In this case, it was a pickup truck. It was one he didn't recognize. His street did not have a lot of traffic, but it wasn't unusual for a car he didn't know to drive past his house. The next email was from 4:33 and it just showed his neighbor. Other camera shots appeared to have occurred because a bird flew past or a tree branch was blowing in the wind. But one image showed a couple of people walking behind his house around 4:39. They had on hiking clothes and one guy was wearing a day-pack. People would occasionally hike in the forest behind his house but—he felt a pat on his back and jumped slightly. "How the hell you doing, Rangar?" He turned and saw Rick, a neighbor friend who was also a bachelor. Occasionally, they met up for dinner or some beers at one of the local bars in Manitou.

"I've been preoccupied lately. Work has kept me busy and, well, my sister just died."

"Geez, I am sorry, man. Is there anything I can do?" Rick looked stunned. How do you respond to that?

"No, I just didn't feel like cooking tonight. The company feels good." Hank gestured at the crowd.

"Join us for the game."

"Which game?"

"Colorado is playing UCLA. If Colorado wins they'll be in the driver seat for the conference championship." Hank hesitated for a second. He wasn't really interested in the game but he had nothing pressing at home. He needed to keep his wits about him but one beer couldn't hurt. Being able to relax was important to making sound decisions.

"Only if you're buying," Hank equivocated.

Jim and Billy were having a beer and going over their plans at Jim's. "Let's take the night vision goggles." Jim extended his hand. "I'll put them in my pack." They each grabbed their Berretta M9 semiautomatic pistols and put an additional clip in their backpack. The Berretta M9 was the official pistol of the US Army, and as a result, there were a lot of them floating around. It was a 9mm pistol with a fifteen-round magazine.

The idea was to make it look like Rangar died in a house fire, but if he somehow got out of the house it would look like a robbery gone wrong. "Don't forgot the remote control." Jim grabbed it and an extra nine-volt battery. They put on gloves, donned skullcaps, and finished their beers. At 9:07, they piled into Jim's pickup truck. The tension of the hunt caused Jim's adrenaline to kick in, and he was doing sixty in a forty-five zone when they saw a cop car coming the other way. "Cop! Slow down, dumbass,"

Billy punched him in the shoulder. Jim tapped on the brakes and was down to forty-five when the cop passed. Suddenly, they heard sirens and Jim saw the cop car's lights come on. "Damn!"

"Don't fucking panic—what's the cop doing?"

"He's continuing in the same direction. He's not after us." Jim's hands began to shake a little. Billy turned around to verify the cop was not following them. Jim pulled off on Manitou Avenue and decided to drive five miles per hour under the speed limit. *I have to be careful because cops often pull over people driving too slow also, assuming the driver is drunk.*

Hank left the bar and started walking to his Scout to head home. He had enjoyed the game. The air was crisp and he stopped to zip up his jacket. He saw a pickup driving up Manitou Avenue. It looked a little bit like the pickup he had seen in the emails from his night vision camera. He took a close look at the truck and noticed the silhouettes of two people in the cab. He involuntary shuddered. *Get a grip, Rangar. There are hundreds of pickup trucks like that one in this town.* But he just couldn't shake the uneasy feeling.

Jim and Billy noticed a guy stepping out of a bar. The guy stopped and stared at them. "What the fuck is that guy staring at?"

"How the fuck should I know" Jim responded. Jim turned left on Ruxton Avenue and headed up the mountain to park where they had earlier in the afternoon. They noticed a gate across the entrance of the parking lot. "Damn, I didn't know they closed at night."

"Maybe we can just park in front of the gate. There's plenty of room." Billy gestured to the space in front of the gate.

"Dumbass, if anything goes wrong we don't want them noticing my pickup here." With that, he continued up the road and found a U-turn. There were several cars on the road because of a restaurant up this way, which made Jim nervous. As he headed back down the mountain on Ruxton, he noticed a road on the left and headed up North Pilot Knob Ave. It was an old residential street with houses built around the 1900s. It was a fairly dark street and he found a place to park.

"So we're going to leave the pickup here?" Billy whined. "How is this any better than in front of the gate of The Incline parking lot?"

"Well, we're not illegally parked at least, and we don't have to walk as far." Jim opened his door and looked around.

Billy felt exposed here. "I don't like it."

"Shut the fuck up and get your pack," Jim growled. It took a minute for their eyes to adjust to the moonless night. The air was crisp and they could see their breaths against the brilliant stars. Jim pointed to an opening between two of the houses that lead to the National Forest behind Rangar's house. Their feet crunched on the frost-encased grass no matter how softly they stepped. Billy was sure the whole world could hear them. Once they reached the ponderosa forest, things were a little better unless one of them accidentally stepped on a dry twig. They were so focused on not making any noise that they didn't notice they walked past a couple of the night vision cameras that Hank and Warren had mounted. The cameras took short videos of them as they passed within the field of view. This triggered alerts that were sent within a couple of minutes to Hank's cell phone. When they were about two hundred yards away from their destination a four-wheel drive vehicle pulled up next to the right side of the house. The headlights of the vehicle briefly moved past them and Jim and Billy froze. The human eye was designed to detect movement, and they had learned in the Army that the best way to avoid being seen in these circumstances was to freeze. They saw someone get out of the vehicle, unlock the door, go inside and turn on the lights.

Several moments passed. Billy whispered, "Do you think he saw us?"

"No way. He didn't hesitate at all. Let's get in position. When the dipshit gets in bed, I'll set off the explosion.

You take the left side of the house and I'll take the right side of the house. If he tries to leave, kill him." With that, Jim and Billy moved out and took positions about fifty yards away from the house.

Rangar turned off the Scout and grabbed his backpack, which had his Colt Detective Special, his prepaid cell phone, some extra rounds, some gloves and a stocking cap. He pulled out his keys and opened the door. His phone beeped, letting him know he had an email. This bothered him a little but it wasn't uncommon for him to receive emails at all times of the day. He turned on the lights, placed his keys on the rack next to the door, and headed to his study, which was really a second bedroom on the street side of the house. He had chosen this bedroom as his study because at night a street light lit up the room, and he slept better in perfect darkness. He turned on the light, sat down to his computer with his backpack slung over his shoulder, and started to review his emails. While he had been at the bar, he had received over twenty emails. A couple were for services that would catapult Houdini's website to the top of the search engines. He ignored these and found three emails that were alerts from his night vision cameras. He clicked on the first one and saw a couple of guys in camouflage walking past the camera. The hair on the back of his neck stood up. He checked the time of the video and it was twelve minutes ago.

He pulled up the software that controlled the night vision cameras and noticed that one of them indicated that it was tracking an event right now. The camera showed a guy crouched near a tree. The guy looked like a ghost. He didn't seem to be moving. Hank thought about how they had made Christine's death look like an accident. He pulled out the Colt Detective Special from his backpack. The camera showed the person in the same position. The guy's hands came up to his face as if he were warming them by blowing on them. He didn't seem to be in any hurry.

Hank's study functioned as his guest bedroom also. He had a futon couch on the wall of the room that ran along the hallway. His sister had not approved of the futon and told him he needed a more inviting room for guests. "It needs a women's touch," she explained. The door to the room opened in, and was on the interior corner. Hank determined that if he situated himself on the couch, then someone entering would not see him until they had fully opened the door. This would allow him to see any intruders before they could see him. He picked up the computer while holding his pistol, turned off the light and sat down on the futon facing the door. His backpack was still slung over one shoulder. He wanted his eyes to adjust to the low light conditions so that the guy outside his house was not able to see him more easily than Hank could see his attacker. He thought about the light he had left on in the kitchen and decided that leaving it on might screw up his attacker's night vision. There was no reason to risk going out and turning if off. He could feel his heart pounding in his chest as if he had run a hundred meter sprint.

Billy noticed the light go on in a room at the far end of the house from where the scumbag had entered. He assumed that it was his bedroom. Five minutes later he saw the light turn off. He pulled up his walkie-talkie and pressed the button. "Jim, he just turned off a light in the bedroom on this side of the house, do you see him moving around?"

Jim held the walkie-talkie to his mouth. "I don't see him yet." They hoped this guy would fall asleep and then they could set off the gas explosion. That way the guy would be caught off guard, hopefully unconscious, and die in the fire. The last thing they wanted to do was shoot him.

Hank looked at the computer and noticed the guy hold his hand up to his face. But still there was no sign he was moving. He could hear himself breathing. It sounded so loud but he knew that was an illusion of the quiet and his adrenaline. Hank began to think of all the ways they could make his death look like an accident. They could make it look like he'd drowned, like Christine. The thought of what they did to her made him sick. *Concentrate, if you want to live.*

I know that an intruder is outside my house; I have a gun; I am in position to see him before he sees me. I could grab my deer rifle from the garage, walk down the street a couple hundred yards and cut back into the forest and pick this guy off. The garage was at the street level, which was twenty feet below the house, so it didn't appear to be attached. A long, old hidden stairway that felt like a cave led from the house to his garage, which is why he often parked next to his house rather than in his garage. He thought that would be fairly easy and was getting excited by the plan. But if he shot the guy, then it would be clear his attacker had not succeeded and it would make it more difficult for him to get at Morris. He was sure Morris was behind this attack, and once he escaped, it would be his turn to go on the offensive.

A car accident was a good way to make it appear someone had not been murdered. But he doubted the guy outside his house was going to hang around all night long. Hank was beginning to feel a little antsy. Hank noticed the guy fidgeted every once in a while but he had not moved from his original position. It had been over twenty minutes since he had gotten home and Hank was getting impatient for something to happen.

Jim pushed the button on the walkie-talkie and hoarsely whispered into the mic. "Billy, I haven't seen him; do you figure he's asleep?"

"I haven't seen him moving around either. I am colder than a witch's tit in a brass bra. I say we blow this thing. How about you?"

"Let's do it. He'll probably die from the explosion. Once this is done let's get a beer and look at some titties."

Jim found the remote in his backpack and oriented it in his hand. The button on the left would activate the device to pierce the gas line, while the one on the right would cause a spark. He wanted to let the gas build up for a minute or so before he ignited it. The more gas that escaped, the bigger the explosion. It was a calm night so the wind would not disperse the gas. He pressed the left button.

Hank looked across the room now that his eyes were used to the dark and saw the endothermic fire extinguisher. This fire extinguisher worked by removing the heat from a fire instead of depriving it of oxygen. Damn, a house fire would be perfect way to kill someone and make it look like an accident. He heard a hissing noise and wondered where it was coming from. The sound seemed to be below him; he lay down and put his ear to the floor. He glanced at his computer; the guy still had not moved. The best way to make a house fire look accidental was a gas leak, he realized.

The gas had formed an invisible pool of death under Rangar's house. Jim pushed the left button. Hank felt the house move and was thrown into the air and slammed back to the floor with the futon on top of him. He saw stars and his ears were ringing. There was dust in his nostrils and it took a while before he could gather his wits about him. *I can hear fire engulfing the house, and a water line in the bathroom is broken.* The water was running on the floor, or what was left of it. He scrambled on his belly out from under the futon. His backpack strap caught on the arm. He yanked on the backpack and pain shot up his left shoulder. Damn, that hurt. He grabbed his pistol on the floor in front of him and the exothermic fire extinguisher and sprayed it all over his body and his backpack.

The best thing would be for that guy out there to think I died in this fire. To do that, I need to stay inside the house as long as possible. I can exit down the staircase through my garage. The exothermic goo will protect me from the heat. Hank decided to slowly crawl into the hall, find a towel, get it wet and put it over his head. *I don't want to open the bedroom door too quickly and alert my attacker to the fact that I am alive.* He slowly opened the door and was hit by a wave of heat and a loud roar. He felt burning in his chest and was concerned he had scorched his lungs; this was another way people could die in a fire. Crawling into the hall, he poked his head into the bathroom. There was water everywhere, and he found a towel, pushed it around in the water and put it over his head. *I'll stay in the hall next to the bathroom as long as I can.*

Billy was so excited by the fireworks display, he pushed the talk button "Shit, that was one hell of an explosion. I think it singed my eyebrows off. Look at that fire go."

"Keep your eyes open. We want to make sure he's dead." Jim felt there was no way someone could have lived through that explosion.

Hank was amazed at how well the exothermic goo was working; he hardly felt the heat except around his eyes where he could not apply it. The roof fell in on the kitchen and pushed a wall of embers and smoke over Hank. He held his breath and waited for the embers to singe his body. After a minute, the smoke cleared a little and no embers singed him. *I've played possum long enough.* He crawled down the stairs until he was halfway and stood up. The air felt moist and it soothed his nostrils. When he got to the garage, he could hear the sirens of fire engines. He used the wet towel to remove the goo and a dirty rag to dry off.

He took off his backpack, put on an old work jacket he kept in the garage, pulled a stocking cap out of the backpack, put it over his head and slung the backpack with his pistol and his prepaid telephone over his shoulder. Slowly opening the side door to the garage, he peeked out. Neighbors were coming out of their homes to look at the fire, but there was no one on the sidewalk next to his garage. He exited, shut the door and walked to the back of a group of onlookers. In the confusion of the fire trucks pulling up to the house, he started heading toward downtown Manitou Springs. His plan was to find a motel and hide out until morning.

Chapter 24

Hank opened his prepaid cell phone. "Warren. Shit. Could you pick me up at the Buffalo Lodge in Old Colorado City?"

"Who the hell is this?" There was a pause. "Hank?"

"Yeah. Now could you pick me up?"

Warren heard the exhaustion in Hank's voice. "Why are you calling me on this number, and why are you at the Buffalo Lodge—and come to think of it, where the hell is the Buffalo Lodge?"

"It's on El Paso in Old Colorado City. Can you pick me up on West Colorado in a half an hour?"

"Yeah, but what the hell are you doing there?" Warren was totally confused. What number was this? It wasn't Hank's cell, home phone, or work. Why was Hank calling him from Old Colorado City so early in the morning? This was so unlike the regimented Hank he knew.

"It's a long story. I'll explain when you pick me up," and with that Hank hung up.

The Buffalo Lodge was one of the old motels in the Manitou area. During the winter, they looked run-down and you were sure they were going to fold. But once spring came around they spruced up, and in the summer they were packed with tourists. Their gaudy neon lights screamed old-fashioned family tourist vacation.

Warren pulled up exactly a half an hour later in his maroon Ford Explorer. Hank climbed into the passenger seat. Warren stared at him. "Okay, where to?"

Hank only knew where he didn't want to go. "We can't go to the office; I don't want anyone to know I'm alive."

"What the hell are you talking about? Why would anyone think you're not alive, Hank?"

Hank had hardly slept the night before and the question irritated him. "My house burnt to the ground last night. An assassin made it look like the gas line broke and I was supposed to die. I want him and Morris to think they succeeded." He leaned his head back on the chair.

Warren turned onto Highway 24 and headed toward his house in Divide. Who could possibly want to kill Hank? He was the most straightforward, hardworking, and decent guy in the world. Warren had met plenty of sleazebags in the Navy and in the aircraft business. "I think you're letting your imagination run away with you."

Hank was always impatient with people who couldn't connect the dots, especially when he was tired. "Warren, they murdered Christine over the MedCon story, didn't they?"

"The police never said she was murdered, and even if she was, you don't know who killed her or why." This wasn't making sense; Warren felt like someone who'd accidentally stepped out of a plane while skydiving.

Hank gritted his teeth. "I know that Morris was willing to kill my sister in order to profit from his investment in AltruMedical. I know he stole EWE's technology, which could have saved my sister's life. I know that Senator Fowl steered massive NIH grants to AltruMedical. I know that Senator Fowl and Congressman Morris made a small fortune when MedCon bought out AltruMedical. I know that Christine was going to write about Fowl steering NIH grants to Altru and his investment in Altru when she died under suspicious circumstances. I know that I threatened to expose Morris's malfeasance to the press just a few days ago. I know that an assassin started my house on fire by faking a gas explosion. I think the evidence is pretty overwhelming." With each point Hank slapped his hand on the dashboard. When he finished he took a deep breath. "And with Christine's death I no longer have a source in the press to expose Morris." Hank's shoulders slumped. *Warren is one of my best friends. He knows all about the Altru-MedCon merger, Janine and Christine's deaths. He is one of the smartest people I know, but here I am having to explain this to him.*

Warren was trying to figure out how to calm his friend down as he took another hairpin turn up Ute Pass to his house. "Hank, how do you know that someone set your house on fire? Your house was pretty old. Isn't it possible that it just caught fire?"

"Goddamn it Warren, I have the fucking assassin on tape. Our infrared cameras caught a couple of guys walking around my house yesterday afternoon. At first I just thought it was a couple of hikers. But when I got home last night, I checked the cameras and there was a man about fifty yards southwest of my house. I watched him for thirty minutes until there was the explosion and fire. I escaped through the garage, walked down to the Buffalo Lodge and spent the night. So NO it is not possible that my house just caught on fire." He didn't say 'fucking asshole,' but they both heard it.

Warren couldn't understand why his friend was browbeating him. He decided Hank was just tired. If he had the whole thing recorded, that was great. "Why didn't you tell me that you had this stored on the server? Let's call the police."

Hank wondered whether his partner was a moron or was just playing devil's advocate, which Hank felt many people did to avoid the logical conclusions of the situation. Hank rolled his eyes at Warren. "And how will that help me get Morris?" Hank had an indignant look on his face. "It's unlikely that he hired these goons directly, and even if he did they will probably be dead long before they can point the finger at Morris. I'm not interested in a couple of hirelings being sent to jail; I want Morris to pay for his crimes. I want him dead, just like Janine is dead."

Warren braked for a stoplight in Manitou. He was scared; he had been in battle where people were trying to kill him, and it was the last thing he wanted to be involved in again. "Jesus, this is beginning to sound like a LeCarre novel. You never mentioned killing Morris. I thought you were going to the press."

Hank could not believe his normally logically partner was acting like a college student arguing the military should be abolished because it kills people. "Are you fucking listening! Christine is dead. These guys are willing to kill anyone who gets in their way. Besides that, I don't have any contacts in the press now. If I try to cultivate another contact, it will take time, and I'll be dead before anyone believes me. Besides, it's clear that the political elite will protect each other to the end. They aren't interested in exposing the dirty ways in which they get rich or how they kill people." Hank pulled his stocking cap lower and slunk down in the seat to avoid being recognized by anyone at the stoplight and because he wasn't interested in Warren's equivocating. If Warren wasn't willing to help him, then he would just have to do this all on his own. He crossed his arms and closed his eyes.

The light turned green and Warren accelerated. He was thinking about what Hank said. Hank was his business partner. In some ways, he was closer to Hank than to his wife. He didn't want to see him throw his life away. It was impossible to believe that here in the United State of America, this was happening. It's not like they were in Venezuela or something. He would happily blow away every corrupt official in that cesspool. The sharp, hard, honest lines of Pikes Peak, which he had always loved, seemed out of place.

Warren's stomach gurgled; the coffee on an empty stomach was beginning to burn in his stomach. He had a couple of daughters starting college soon, and he needed all the money he could get. They were making good money, but the cost of college just kept going up. He could run the day-to-day operations for a while but Hank was critical to pulling in new business. Without Hank, his income would suffer and it would be painful paying for college. Why is this shit happening to me now?

"Are Carolyn or your girls likely to be home?" This startled Warren from his thoughts.

"No, not at this time. Why do you ask?" Hank frowned at him. Warren didn't miss the dumb-shit look Hank gave him. He turned onto the dirt road that led to his property. There were drifts of snow on the side of the road and Pikes Peak was framed up in the rearview mirror. The town of Divide, where Warren lived, was at ten thousand feet and looked pretty barren from Highway 24, but Warren had thirty-five acres in a small valley and about half of it was covered in aspen trees and pines. He had a small pond at the back of the property, and an old horse barn on the edge of the trees about one hundred yards from the pond. Warren's girls, Samantha and Kate, had been after him to get a couple of horses. Warren pulled into the driveway and parked in the garage. As they were getting out of the car, his cell phone rang.

"It's the office; do you want me to answer it?" Warren waved the phone at Hank.

"Yeah, no problem. But remember you haven't seen me. You have no idea where I am. Act surprised if anyone asks about me."

"Aren't you being a bit overly paranoid?" Warren answered the phone. "Hello."

"Warren?" It was Peggy White from Made By Man, but her voice was somehow different.

"Yeah, Peggy, what's happening?" he said in his best awe-shucks manner.

Agitated, Peggy asked, "Have you been listening to the news? I think Hank's house burned down last night."

Hank caught just a little of the conversation. He knew it was Peggy. He thought he heard something about a house, which he assumed meant his house.

Warren was a terrible actor and worse liar. He tried to sound surprised. "Why would you say that, Peggy?" Hank grimaced at the horrible acting.

"The news is talking about a gas explosion and house fire in Manitou Springs on Spruce Trail. They showed a picture of the street and I could swear it was Hank's house. The news said the police were uncertain whether anyone was in the house at the time and they called here looking for Hank."

"What? You're kidding."

"No, I am not kidding. I'm scared, Warren. First, that woman who came here to interview Hank is killed, and now Hank's house burns down. I've been trying to call him but his phone immediately goes to voicemail. Have you heard from him?"

Warren looked over at Hank and said carefully, "No. I'm sure there has been some sort of mistake, Peggy. Don't worry about it."

"DON'T patronize me. I am not a child." Warren blushed. "And that's not all. Fifteen minutes ago a couple of guys showed up at the office. They were IRS agents, demanding to see Hank. I told them that he wasn't in and I couldn't reach him by phone. Then they asked to talk to you. I told them you weren't in; they started talking about how Made By Man and Houdini owed a lot of money in back taxes and how they would hate to see me get caught up in this matter."

"No fucking way!" Warren had never cussed around Peggy White. How the hell could Hank Rangar, one of the most normal—well not normal, he was an extraordinary engineer, but the most danger-ous thing Hank did was ski extreme terrain, he didn't even sleep around as far as Warren knew—have the police and IRS call for him? Hank was the opposite of nefarious; the antonym in the dictionary for nefarious could be a picture of Hank Rangar. *Even worse, what is going to happen to our businesses? Am I going to have to find another job? Carolyn will kill me if I can't pay for the girls' college.*

"Yes way—what are you, twelve years old? What am I supposed to do?"

There was a long pause while Warren thought and Hank stared at him. "Peggy, why don't you take the day off and let's close the office to the public. Tell the other employees to go home also. Don't answer any calls from reporters. Let me sort this thing out and see if I can find Hank. I'll let you know how to proceed tomorrow." Warren clipped the phone closed.

"You won't believe it." He looked to Hank.

"What?"

"The police called for you, and a couple of IRS agents came by this morning." Warren screwed up his face.

"Makes sense."

"What do you mean it makes sense?" Warren could not understand why Hank said that. It was as if he had said the sun revolves around the Earth and Hank had said, 'Of course.'

They got out of the car and headed to Warren's office, which was on the back side, lower level of the house and had a view that looked out over his pond. Pikes Peak anchored the left side of the view.

Hank thought Warren was acting like people hit by a tornado or wild fire. It took a while to comprehend that their world had been turned totally upside down. This was normal, but made him less useful. "I told you Morris and his types in the government would stop at nothing. They believe they are above the law, and worse, they believe their actions are morally justified. Morris told me straight out that he thought he had done humanity a service by helping AltruMedical to steal EWE's patent. He felt sure that Janine's death was justified because more people would be saved in the long run. And the profit he made on the deal—well, that was for the sacrifice he had made by being in public service."

They sat down in a couple of conference chairs in the office and leaned back. Warren turned to Hank. "Okay, I agree Morris has certainly targeted you but it's not worth it to risk your life to kill that scumbag. Why risk ending up in jail for the rest of your life? Hide out in Canada or Central America or Europe for a couple of years and let this whole thing blow over. Hell, you deserve a vacation."

Hank's face boiled with anger. "What if everyone took that attitude? Was Hitler not a scumbag? What about King George and the British Army? If the minutemen had taken that attitude, we would still be a colony of England. If everyone took that attitude, the tyrants and mass murderers would win, Warren."

Warren was taken aback by Hank's anger and recoiled physically. "That may be true, but what are you going to accomplish by killing Morris? You can't bring back Janine, and you're not going to succeed in a one-man revolution."

"True, but I will know that justice has been done and perhaps the story will serve as a warning to other government officials who are happy to murder and steal from us."

Warren understood Hank's arguments, but people didn't just start killing other people unless they had cracked psychologically. "I know you and Janine were close but I didn't think you had lost it."

"I haven't fucking lost it, Warren. Morris is a mass murderer and he needs to pay for his crimes. My course of action is logical."

Warren thought Hank's arguments made sense, but he couldn't comprehend a world where this was true. "Are you going to go around killing every corrupt government official? Hank, it's just not practical." Warren laughed nervously.

"Morris is not just another corrupt government official. He killed Janine, and when I gave him the chance to turn himself in, he tried to kill me. I didn't pick this fight. I have a right to self-defense, and the government clearly is not going to enforce that right, is it?"

Warren sat there for a long time thinking of how he could convince Hank to choose another path. Hank was imminently logical and his plans always followed. He could be incredibly pigheaded that way. He could either distance himself from Hank, or help him. "All right, what's your plan? Are you just going walk up to Morris on the street and put a bullet in his head?"

Hank ignored Warren's sarcasm. "I think I've come up with a pretty good plan to make it look like an accident. I can create an EMP pulse that will knock out the micro-controllers in his car and cause it to go careening off the side of a mountain."

"Sounds great, but how do you know Morris will be driving fast enough? And how do you know where he will be and when he will be there?"

"I did some hacking into Morris's accounts, remember. I know that he bought a Porsche 911 Turbo S, and by tracking his cell phone GPS and the GPS in his Porsche I know he likes to take it on drives along the Blue Ridge Parkway in North Carolina. Every single time he is home in Asheville for the weekend, he takes the Porsche out for a spin, and from the GPS data, I know he likes to drive fast. There is a perfect hairpin turn on the parkway for his car to lose its brakes."

Warren was stunned. He knew that Hank had the ability to find this information, but he just didn't realize that Hank's thought process had gone this far. "Well, you're going to need to create an EMP pulse that doesn't leave any traces. Military EMP generators use a broadband microwave signal, but they're expensive and not very portable." Warren scrunched up his face.

"True, but I thought we could create the pulse using a sort of Jacob's Ladder configuration with Leyden jars."

Warren started scribbling down some drawings; he decided to throw himself into the engineering. Hank leaned in and they began talking about R-squared losses, the breakdown voltage of air, centrifugal forces, the static coefficient of friction, drawing out scenarios and scribbling down equations. They were enjoying themselves, and Hank felt some of the tension of the last couple of days dissipating.

Chapter 25

Roland Hawthorne monitored the news from Colorado Springs for what he hoped was a job completed cleanly. When he heard about a house fire in Manitou Springs, he suspected that this might be Rangar's. A local AM radio station was reporting the police didn't know if anyone was in the house at the time. This made Hawthorne nervous, but it wasn't unusual for there to be a delay in finding a body in fire. The embers were probably still hot and the structure was not safe, both slowing down the investigation. He decided to turn his attention to other assignments.

Stan Weiss was also monitoring the news. He had heard about the fire, and was pleased with how quick the guys he had hired acted. The lack of a body seemed a detail that would be checked off soon. Around 2:00 p.m., he decided to head back to the strip joint. The two ex-soldiers would probably be looking for their other grand. He paid promptly to avoid complications and misunderstandings.

The hinges on his old Ford F150 pickup truck squeaked as he opened the door. A chime nagged at him as he turned the key, reminding him to put on his seat belt. *The damn government's going to mandate how we have to wipe our ass at this rate.* He drove over to the strip joint, listening to the local AM talk/news station. They were still reporting on the house fire in Manitou. The police spokesperson said the owner-occupant of the house could not be reached. Stan worried about this like a tongue probing an achy tooth.

When he pulled up to the strip joint, he could hear the music pulsing out into the parking lot. Some rap thing. Stan grimaced. *Fucking bullshit music. This is why America's turning into a shit heap.* He opened the truck door, wincing at the screeching grind of the hinges, and hopped down. He anticipated the much-needed long, cold draw of the first beer inside as he walked through the door and adjusted his eyesight to the dim interior. The dank smell of wood and stale beer assailed his nostrils as he made his way to a table far from the stage. A tired-looking server who was painfully skinny and probably younger than she looked came up to Stan, swathed the table with a wet, rank smelling rag. "What'll it be?" He ordered a Fat Tire and she moved slowly off toward the bar. Stan turned his attention to the stage as a plump but pretty blonde gyrated along the pole. He had spent too much time in strip bars and rarely paid attention to the show, but the dark interior suited his office appointment needs. The patrons and workers were like a canary in a coalmine, instantly warning of police presence, and he didn't like any surprises. A chair scraped and Stan realized he hadn't been paying attention. His hand went to the gun under his jacket as he quickly turned toward the noise with deadpan face. If it was a police officer, he didn't want to appear jumpy; however, if it was someone else out to do him harm he had to be prepared. He looked up into his independent contractors' smug faces. They knew he was unhappy being caught off guard. It was a practical joke to them but could have cost all of them their freedom and maybe their lives. The taller ex-soldier turned toward Stan. "Did you see the news?"

Stan leaned back in his chair, removing his hand from the pistol, let his heart rate settle down and accepted a beer from the server. She looked expectantly at the two soldiers. They refused to make eye contact with her. The taller guy ordered them a couple of beers, waving his hand for the server to leave. Stan waited a moment. "Yes, I did. I really appreciate your promptness—ah, however, it concerns me we do not have actual proof of job completion." Stan opened his arms, palms upward in a gesture that said 'What are you going to do about this?'

The taller guy leaned in toward Stan. "The target definitely died in that fire. We saw him enter the house and covered the exits. No one could live through that fire." He punctuated the last statement with a blunt finger beating the sticky wood table.

Stan picked up his beer and took a long draw, appreciating the cold tang against his lips and the frothy swish down his throat. He arched his back and cleared his throat. "The client isn't going to like it." He rested his right hand on the revolver strapped to his waist underneath his jacket and leaned forward, speaking softly. Jim and Billy leaned in to hear. "Here's what I can do for you. I can give you six hundred now and the rest when it has been confirmed."

Jim looked at Billy. Stan watched as they appeared to be calculating how to play the situation. Stan's finger curled toward the trigger. Billy gave Jim a slight shrug and a sigh. Jim turned his piercing gaze back to Stan. "No problem. The police will find the body. But we expect to be paid the rest as soon as they do." Jim pointed his fat finger at Stan. "Are we clear?"

Stan was amused at the show of bravado but relieved that there wasn't going to be any altercation. "Sure. I wish I could pay you everything now and be done with it." He loosened his grip on the pistol and grabbed his money clip. He counted out six crisp one hundred dollar bills and pushed them toward Jim. They stood up abruptly and moved closer to the stage. Stan left a twenty on the table and headed out to his truck.

When Stan got home, he decided he couldn't procrastinate any longer. He sent a message using the electronic dead-drop to Roland Hawthorne putting the best spin he could on the situation. The message played up how fast he had moved and the complete destruction of the house. Hawthorne had not authorized him to use any subcontractors, so he fudged on this point. He thought Hawthorne certainly knew that he was not going to carry out the job himself, but he may have thought Stan would at least use someone in his direct organization. Hawthorne probably didn't know that Stan's organization consisted of three people—'me, myself, and I.' He could feel the sweat flowing under his arms and yet his fingers were a little cold. Hawthorne was a dangerous man.

Hawthorne picked up the electronic dead-drop message immediately. Maybe he had another twenty-four to forty-eight hours before Morris would start breathing down his neck. As he read the message, he became convinced that Stan Weiss was trying too hard to reassure him. He might have to become more involved in this one. *Damn.* He sent Stan a reply, asking to be kept informed and reassuring him the police would find Rangar's body shortly. People did stupid things when they panicked.

Hawthorne decided to get his computer expert involved. Nat Rice had worked at the NSA until he was caught diverting money from banks that were getting zero-percent loans from the Federal Reserve Bank and then loaning the money back to Uncle Sam for 2.4 percent interest. Nat had skimmed the accounts of the banks and had a couple million dollars in a Cayman Islands bank account by the time he was caught. Hawthorne admired Nat's creativity and moral reasoning. The program was legalized counterfeiting. The NSA privately agreed the security breach wouldn't look good, so they accepted Nat's resignation and hid the money in a black account. Neither the banks nor the Feds were the wiser.

A couple of months later, Hawthorne appeared at his apartment and offered him a job. Despite having to wade through two months of pizza boxes and Mountain Dew cans, Hawthorne was pleased to add Rice to his arsenal. The master's in computer science from MIT notwithstanding, he marveled at Rice's skills. The Sam Adams Financial Group needed some electronic surveillance capabilities and a friend had alerted him to Nat's recent unemployment.

Nat was allowed to work out of his condo in South Florida. SAM paid for his computers, his Internet access and any miscellaneous expenses he had. Nat set his own hours. He had been a great addition. He tracked people's electronic signatures, their cell phone usage, their Internet usage, the GPS in their phones and in their cars, their credit cards and bank transactions—in short, he was a font of information. However, he didn't really fit in with the ex-Special Forces guys, so his remaining in Florida was fine by Hawthorne. Hawthorne dialed his cell and waited until Rice answered. "What's up?"

Hawthorne thought about how much he was willing to divulge and decided to keep it on a need-to-know basis. "I need information on a first name Hotel Alpha November Kilo, last name Romeo Alpha November Golf Alpha Romeo from Manitou Springs, Colorado. Current whereabouts, phone, credit card activity, recent travel within the last twenty-four hours."

"Sure, no problem."

"All right, I'll send along what info we currently have." Nat grunted an assent and hung up his encrypted cell.

He went back to playing World of Warcraft online. He was a level sixty. He didn't appreciate being interrupted for what seemed like a run-of-the-mill background check and was irritated when almost immediately an email came from Hawthorne. The file was five pages long but Nat only needed the social security number and a name to find bank accounts, cell phones, credit cards and even a car's GPS information. He jumped out of WoW and started digging for this information. He found the target's cell phones, home phone, credit cards, debit card, and email accounts, but nothing came up for a car GPS system. He started searching to see if there had been any activity. Because this was a routine request, he had automated the process. It took his bots about an hour to locate the information, and the results showed no transactions in the last twenty-four hours. There had been fairly regular activity before that, including numerous calls from his cell phone. He double-checked for business cell phones, emails, etc.—nothing.

Hawthorne made an airline reservation to Colorado Springs. There might be a mess, and he liked things squeaky clean. He felt antsy and decided to take some target practice. The nearest range was fifteen minutes away; he was looking forward to firing his trusty SIG Sauer P226. His was the 9mm model with the Tritium night sights. Target practice relaxed Hawthorne and allowed his mind to free up. This was his best mode for solving problems. He unloaded the first magazine and was changing it out to a new one when his cell phone rang. He was reluctant to answer it but saw it was Rice. Nat informed him of the inactivity. Hawthorne told him to keep checking hourly and hung up. This news was consistent with Rangar having died in the fire. He inserted another magazine and went back to his target practice.

Hank and Warren had spent the rest of the day creating and testing his homemade EMP device in the barn. When Carolyn and the girls came home in the afternoon, Warren put off their curiosity by explaining he was working on a prototype for a client. They had learned not to ask about these projects or they would get a boring lecture on physics or electronics. When Hank felt the design was perfected, he carefully packed up the device. It was late and Warren hurled a sleeping bag at Hank and paused for a moment. "There's a space heater in the house. I should get it."

"No, that will just draw attention. I'll be fine. After last night, this seems five-star. Nothing will keep me awake."

Warren looked around the barn, imagining where Hank might bed down. "The hay bales up in the loft might make a decent surface. You'll be poked but at least not on the ground." They climbed up the ladder to tug at bales and lined three up in a row, creating a makeshift bed. "I'll sleep like a baby, really." Warren nodded, climbed down and walked silently to the front of the barn. He turned and readied himself to say something, thought better of it and slipped out, prodding and pulling the door closed. Then it was still.

Blinking in the semi-darkness, now that the door had shut on the dusk to dawn light outside the barn, Hank found he couldn't move. The cool air of the autumn night seemed to come in under the door and between cracks in the walls in a stealthy flow. He pulled the zipper of his fleece up to his chin, blew on his hands and turned toward the sleeping bag. *Might as well crawl in.*

He had that feeling of falling, then hitting the ground, and either he was dead, or no, just conscious. At first, he felt such impenetrable velvet blackness, he wasn't sure if he was right side up or down or just suspended in some way. His eyes began to adjust to the darkness and he realized where he was—in Warren's barn. *Shit! It's fucking freezing in here.* He turned from his back to his side and pulled his knees up to his chest. He reworked the cinches at his head so only his nose was outside the bag. Hank shivered uncontrollably. He moved around, trying to get some sensation back in his toes, fingers, and nose. *Hell. Six months*

335

ago, if anyone would have told me that I would walk away from a bright future with two successful businesses and clients who were changing the world, and work with everything I have to destroy one man, I would have looked at them like a madman.

Most of the people in Hank's life didn't understand why anyone would take such risks to build their own business. *Better to concentrate on becoming an expert in their field, letting some other administrative hacks deal with the numbers and business decisions. How could you accomplish anything, if you were always changing your hat do be in charge of this or that and not your main career?* He knew early in his teens that he was different this way and had taken the potshots tossed to him about not being a 'good team player' with good humor. These comments were true, and a major motivator behind taking this route.

Of course, he thrived on competition, but always felt an affinity with others, even competitors, who were building their own dream. As he started gaining success, the jokes turned from good-natured ribbing to pointed questions. It was against his grain to be a corporate button-up in a tiny cubicle working for others. His friends began to resent his flexible schedule and his ability to take time off. When he made bold decisions, Janine in particular would seem overly concerned for him. She would ask questions about biting off more than he could chew, or that his risks would swallow him up one day and he would have nothing. Perhaps their chiding and concerns were absolutely correct. He was wide-awake in the middle of the night in someone else's barn, freezing his balls off, with only the cash he had in his pack. Maybe he had gambled it all away on the hope Morris would do the right thing and regret his thievery.

It seemed somewhat ironic that the same friends who were concerned he was becoming cold and calculating in building businesses mighr lambast him for trusting someone whom he gave a second chance to make things right. Now Houdini would be history. Warren would have to find another partner for Made By Man or sell out. When would he see Tris and Jess again? Suddenly, a vision of Christine loomed in front of him, her eyes soft and her face taut with spiraling passion. He felt her heartbeat against his chest as she moved on him slowly, taking him in deeply and moaning low. He squeezed his eyes shut and tried to hold the image. He willed himself to make it brighter, sharper. He was stirred by the physical memories of holding and caressing her and was beginning to feel his arousal dull the ache in his chest he hadn't been able shake since he had heard of her murder. The need to avenge made his chest tighten even more and he worked himself in the sleeping bag to slake something, anything. An easing for just a little while was all he needed.

Hawthorne slept poorly, finally deciding to get up at 4:30 a.m. He checked the Web for any information on Rangar. The police and media were still reporting that no one had died in the fire; however, they could not find the owner of the house—not a good sign. He checked in with Rice and found out there was no new info. This was a good sign. He felt like skipping his flight and going back to bed. *I am getting way too old for this shit,* he thought, but a good commander prepared for the worst and hoped for the best. He grabbed a small bag packed the night before and his TSA-approved gun case with his SIG Sauer P226. He took a taxi to the airport.

As he stepped out of the taxi at Reagan International, he could smell the aviation fuel fumes rolling off the roof down to the departure ramp. It brought back fond memories of his early days in Special Forces. He went in to the airline counter and declared that he had a firearm. A fiftyish plump female airline reservation agent looked up over reading glasses, "Oh, just a minute, let me get an agent to assist you. Please wait over here." After a small delay, a young, dark-haired man dressed in the uniform of his carrier briskly walked toward Hawthorne. Hawthorne unconsciously stiffened as the attendant went through the process of having him sign the card stating that the gun was unloaded. *In what world can this pencil-necked loser determine what I can do?* Hawthorne carefully placed the gun in its zippered case, handed it over to the attendant, accepted the receipt and headed to his gate. *Flying as a civilian is a pain.*

His flight had a stop in Atlanta. He didn't arrive in Colorado Springs until 1:30 that afternoon. He checked in with Rice—no news on Rangar. *So far, so good.* His plane had arrived a few minutes early, and retrieving his firearm was quickly done in this small airport. He headed toward the rental counter, selected Avis for a car, and after signing the paperwork for an upgraded SUV, he walked out of the terminal and headed toward the Avis lot to pick up his car. They had given him a Jeep Liberty in one of those bright green colors, like nature on crack. Hawthorne unlocked the vehicle, threw his backpack in the backseat and carefully set his gun case in the passenger seat on the other side of the car's console. He started the engine, and was wryly reminded of starting a small lawnmower. Cheap-ass small cars were all you could get anymore at these rental places. He felt a minute's regret for not having his Mercedes E63 AMG, a sedate sedan exterior with an engine that could kick everyone's ass. He looked across the wide expanse of open space owned by the airport and then toward Pikes Peak majestically piercing the deep blue, clear sky. *Gorgeous.* He imagined what it would feel like giving the Mercedes her reins on the winding mountain highways empty of the choking traffic of DC.

Turning on the GPS, he plugged in Rangar's address. As he headed out of the airport, the view of Pikes Peak filled his windshield. He turned onto the Martin Luther bypass, turned right onto Interstate 25 and got off on the Highway 24 exit. Once the light turned green, he turned left, heading up Ute Pass.

In the morning, Warren brought Hank a bagel for breakfast after Carolyn took the girls to school. Warren was a little nervous about the extent that Hank wanted him involved in his project. He opened the door and hesitated. *What else will Hank ask me to do? If I'm thrown in jail as an accessory to murder, Carolyn will lose the house, there won't be money to send the girls to college.* His mind flashed to Carolyn standing on the exit ramp of I-25 and Cimarron with a "Will Work for Food" sign in a ragged coat. He shook his head. "So now what?"

"I need to get out of here as soon as possible. I've already put you and your family in more danger than I had any intention to." Hank paused and looked into Warren's eyes, "Thanks." Warren took a deep breath. *I should have known.*

"If you could drop me off at the Ramblin' Express bus station in Divide that would be great." Ramblin' Express was a free bus service that took gamblers from Colorado Springs up the mountain to Cripple Creek. It also allowed the revelers to imbibe a little more freely while gambling, which loosened up their purse strings.

"Sure, but where are you going? What are you going to do?"

Hank grabbed his backpack, heading for Warren's SUV. "I think it would be better if we kept that on a need-to-know basis." Warren immediately understood his logic but it wasn't very satisfying.

Warren clicked on his key fob and the Ford made an unlatching sound. Hank got in and started to eat his bagel as Warren drove him the seven miles to the bus stop. Warren waited for Hank to finish his bagel. "How am I going to get in touch with you? I mean, what about the University project? We have to deliver it in five weeks."

"I don't think it would be wise for us to be in contact at all until I have eliminated Morris. When that is done, I will let you know. I guess we will have to take it one step at a time."

Warren saw that look in Hank's eyes. *This is what is going to happen.* Warren wondered if there had ever been anyone faced with Hank's determination winning with their own. He doubted it.

Hank didn't have to wait long for the bus to show up. He was surprised at the number of passengers at that time of day. He found a seat and felt the warm air blowing on his boots. The rocking motion of the bus heading down Ute Pass put him to sleep. He woke as the bus stopped at the corner of 27th Street and Highway 24 in Colorado Springs. He rubbed his eyes, grabbed his backpack, and headed for a bike path that followed Highway 24. As he hiked, he could feel a slight wetness under his armpits forming despite the crisp fall temperature. The leaves were turning yellow and Hank imagined he was hiking up one of his favorite trails near Salida. The bike path passed along the north side of Highway 24 at 13th Street and Hank was pulled out of his daydream by the cars passing on his right. He felt some-one was staring at him—it made him realize that he had no idea what his killers looked like. *Has my disappearing trick convinced them I died in the fire? Has it convinced the police or are they still looking for me? How vigorous will their search be?* He had no definitive answers but figured that his pursuers would probably assume he had died until it was clear no one had died in the fire. The path quickly veered away from the highway and he was headed to America the Beautiful Park, which had a large green lawn and featured a modern art statue that functioned as a fountain. This cleared his mind and allowed him to relax again.

Hawthorne drove past 13th Street on Highway 24 toward Hank's razed house. Hawthorne got a glance of a bum with backpack walking along a path on the side of the road. *These damn bums are multiplying like rabbits in this economy.* He took the exit to Hank's house. As he drove up Spruce Trail Street, his GPS indicated that the house was just up the way on the left. He slowed, rolled down the window, and the acrid smell of a house fire filled his nose. He could see the police crime tape as he looked up the hill but there was nothing left of the structure. It brought a smile to his face as he surveyed the damage. A gun sight high up on a tree was pointed at him. A chill ran down his spine; he slouched down in his seat and had the urge to gun the car. He imagined an RPG streaming at his Hummer. Just as he was about to stomp on the accelerator he remembered he was in Colorado, not Afghanistan. He looked at the sight in his slouched state and realized it was some sort of camera. That was better than being shot at but he didn't need anyone taking his picture either. He rolled up the window and accelerated past the charred remains of Rangar's house. Once past, he noticed some of the houses on the hill had street-level garages. He headed to Stan Wiess's 'office.'

Hank entered the bus station on Weber Street, scanning for cops or killers—no police and no one seemed to be paying him any attention. He located the ticket counter, where an obese man in his late thirties was waiting patiently to serve the next customer. He had checked online that you could pay with cash and without an ID but the information was ambiguous at best—it didn't say they required an ID or that they wouldn't take cash. He looked at the departure screen. He rejected several destinations and settled on El Paso. If someone was following, it would look like he was trying to get out of the country; that misdirection might be useful. He walked up to the counter and noticed a camera. He tried to avoid looking in the direction of the camera. "A ticket to El Paso, please."

"That'll be fifty-five dollars."

Hank held his breath as he handed over three crisp twenty-dollar bills.

The clerk took the cash, printed out a ticket, and gave him the ticket and a five-dollar bill without even looking at him. *Excellent.* He took the only available seat in the station, next to a swarthy guy who looked like he had not had a bath in a week. Unfortunately for Hank, he smelled like it also. Hank fidgeted. Normally, he checked his email, text messages, blog or industry forums every five minutes. Just as he thought he couldn't stand it anymore, a bus pulled into the parking lot and he heard the whoosh of the air brakes. He knew this was his bus, grabbed his ticket, stood up and put on his backpack.

Once he was on board the bus, he scanned the people getting on board to see if anyone was paying attention to him. *So far, so good.* He pulled out his computer and checked the news—the house fire was under investigation, the owner could not be located, and no one had been found at the site, according to the article. The fire had been thirty-six hours ago and the idea that he had died in the fire was beginning to wear thin, he could tell from the tone of the article.

It was time to create a diversion. He hacked into his own cell phone account and made it look like he had called his brother-in-law, Mark Nelson's house, but got an answering machine and then called Mark's office shortly thereafter and had a short conversation with Mark. The calls appeared to originate from I-70 near Kansas City. *That should keep them guessing.* He looked out the window across the empty plains of eastern Colorado. Having planted this diversion, Hank packed away his computer and realized just how tired he was. He fell asleep instantly.

Nat Rice was microwaving leftover pizza when his computer issued a nagging noise that an alert had triggered. "Yeah, yeah, yeah." He pulled his pizza out of the microwave and slapped it on the counter. Happily engrossed in WoW, he was frustrated by the interruption. He pulled up a window showing the alerts he had set. *Damn*, the computer showed a couple of calls from this Rangar guy on his cell phone. He did some quick research and realized the call had been to his brother-in-law in St. Louis. With some more digging, he found the call had originated from a cell tower outside Kansas City. He dialed Roland's cell phone number and waited for the connection.

Hawthorne was driving south on I-25, "Nat, give me some good news."

"Boss, I think that is exactly what I have for you. Rangar made a couple of calls on his cell phone fifteen minutes ago."

"Son of a bitch, he's alive?" Hawthorne was excited by the news but had mixed feelings. If Rangar was alive, then Hawthorne had a lot of unfinished business, but at least he had certainty.

"Well either he's alive or someone used his cell phone to call his brother-in-law in St. Louis. From what I can tell, he tried to get a hold of his brother-in-law at home but got an answering machine. Then he called him at his office and had a short conversation. The call was a little over a minute."

"You think he's headed to his brother-in-law's to hide out?"

"I can't say for sure. The calls were placed in the vicinity of KC. But normally someone who has covered up their electronic tracks for over a day is contacting someone for help." Nat had assisted field agents track numerous targets based on their electronic signature while at the NSA. He knew that it was dangerous to draw too many conclusions.

"Well that's almost on a straight path to St. Louis. All right, I will clean up some business here and head there. Let me know if you find out anything else. Oh, by the way, when I was driving past Rangar's house I saw a camera. It scared the shit out of me—DAMN," Hawthorne swerved to avoid a semitrailer. He pulled onto the shoulder of the I-25 and stopped the car.

"Boss? Boss? Are you okay?" Nat was ambivalent about his boss personally but he liked this job. He was well paid with little oversight or bureaucratic hassles.

"Yeah, I'm fine." Hawthorne sighed at his own stupidity.

"Camera? What sort of camera?" Nat was perplexed.

"It was weird; I first thought it was a gun sight—a night vision gun sight. That's why it scared the shit out of me. Can you check on cameras? I mean, why a camera would be on a residential street? In a tree?"

Nat paused. "In my old job we often tapped into security cameras. I can check on it and see what I find." Hawthorne thanked him and hung up. So Rangar was alive after all, and clearly smart enough to worry about leaving an electronic trail. Unfortunately, he would have to clean things up in Colorado Springs before heading to St. Louis. When operations failed, people started talking, and this wasn't Columbia where he could pay off the police with a high-priced hooker—at least not yet.

Stan Weiss was in his 'office,' which meant he was sitting on the couch watching TV in his little house outside of Fountain, Colorado. Stan was a little surprised by Hawthorne's unexpected visit. "Ah, hi. Ah, Mr. Hawthorne?"

"Stan, we got a little problem. I just got a call from my IT guy and Rangar's alive."

Stan stood up. "How does he know? My guys assured me they watched his house burn to the ground." Stan's heart was thumping. His face was flushed. This was dangerous territory, and he was uncertain how to react.

"He hacked Rangar's phone records, and Rangar just placed a phone call to his brother-in-law in St. Louis. I need you to eliminate those guys, while I take care of Rangar. Can you handle that?"

"Yes, sir. No problem. I... I just wish I knew how he got out of the house." Hawthorne thought this was irrelevant, when the image of street-level garages came to him.

Hawthorne ran his hand over his head. "If I had to bet, I'd say that Rangar escaped out through his garage. The garage is twenty feet below the house and doesn't appear to be connected. I'll bet there's a passageway from the house to the garage."

Hawthorne got into his car and drove to the airport. The next flight to St. Louis left in forty-five minutes. Colorado Springs had a small airport, so he thought he could make that flight even with the necessity of checking in his SIG Sauer P226. As he waited in the TSA line, his tapped nervously at his thigh and listened to the hum of the HVAC system. He looked at his watch. He had twenty minutes until his flight took off. *Why does TSA have to be so slow? It's all for show anyway—they're completely useless. If Congress spent that money on Special Forces to hunt down the terrorists, we wouldn't need the goddamn TSA.* When he got to his gate, they were calling for final boarding of the flight to St. Louis as his cell phone rang. He looked at the caller ID and it was Stanford Morris. "Congressman

Morris, how can I help you sir?" *I hope this blowhard doesn't talk too long.*

"I saw on the news that there was a house fire in Manitou Springs. I hope everything is okay there?" The muffled sound of a flight being announced could be heard over the line.

"No, it's tragic. The house burnt to the ground." Hawthorne hated deceiving his clients, but Rangar would be dead shortly.

Morris was not sophisticated in these matters. "Let's keep in touch."

Hawthorne boarded his flight.

Nat starting looking into the camera near Rangar's house. He didn't find anything, so he decided to check out more on Rangar's profile, starting by reading the complete file sent by Hawthorne. *What the hell? This dweeb was part of the DOD Computer Security Threat Center. 'Hank Rangar'* he thought, *'Hank Rangar'—what's familiar about that name?* Nat suddenly realized what it was. He knew of a Henry Rangar who had worked at the DOD Computer Security Threat Center a decade or so ago. He was famous at the NSA. During the first Iranian nuclear weapons program crisis he had figured out a way to infect the nuclear centrifuges used to separate out weapons grade uranium. A virus he created took control of the computer-operated motors that drove the cylindrical rotor. It timed the motors in such a way as to create harmonics the caused centrifuges to fail catastrophically with parts flying everywhere, which killed at least seventeen Iranian nuclear scientists and technicians—*awesome*.

The really hard part had been inserting the virus. Originally, the DOD had thought it was necessary to use some Special Forces guys to penetrate the lab holding the centrifuges, but Rangar figured out a method of broadcasting the virus from an ordinary server inside Iran. The virus then hijacked the DSP chips in the control system of the centrifuges to test for the distinctive noise spectrum associated with gas centrifuges used for nuclear fuel separation. This allowed the virus to spread without causing any damage until it found the correct target. *It worked so well that it took out a nuclear processing site we didn't even know about.*

He should have figured this out sooner, but generally his work involved numbers—he had a social—so why even look at the spelling of the name? Man, this was clearly a fail. He worried if Hawthorne would kick his ass when he found out about this. He contemplated how to spin it. Nat grabbed a Mountain Dew and played WoW to clear his head; when he died, he decided it was time to contact Hawthorne. Nat picked up his cell phone and tried to call Hawthorne but it immediately went to voicemail. *Damn, he must be in the air.* Nat tried to call Hawthorne every ten minutes.

When Hawthorne's plane landed at St. Louis, he turned on his Android and saw that Nat had tried to call him five times in a row. He called Nat. "What's up?"

"Why didn't you tell me you were chasing Henry Rangar?" Blaming the other guy for your mistake was a time-honored way to shift blame.

"Henry—Hank, that's a common nickname. So what?" Hawthorne was tired and his IT guy was playing word games.

"True, but why can't the guy spell his last name right?"

"What's this all about?"

"He's famous at NSA. When he was at the DOD Computer Security Threat Center he took down the Iranian nuclear weapons program singlehandedly." Nat shared the story.

Hawthorne thought about this. "Killing those Iranians was a violation of Executive Order 12733. Caused all holy hell, I bet. No wonder he no longer works there. Okay, that's interesting and it explains why he didn't leave a big electronic trail. But clearly he made a mistake and called his brother-in-law."

Nat was exasperated. "You don't get it. He didn't make a mistake. He sent us on a wild goose chase. He doesn't make those kinds of mistakes."

Hawthorne could hear the intensity in Nat's voice but was puzzled—well, irritated really. "Do you think this guy is dangerous?"

"He singlehandedly took down the Iranian nuclear weapons program. He killed seventeen people without firing a shot, without risking a single American life. Have any of the Neanderthals you've hired ever killed seventeen people at one time? Without firing a shot? Damn straight he's dangerous."

Hawthorne contemplated what Nat had told him.

"Boss, are you there?"

Hawthorne had forgotten about Nat. "Yeah, well, what's the plan?"

"Ah, well we can assume that Rangar knows that we're tracking his electronic activity. We also can assume that he wanted us to see the cell phone call. He's trying to throw us off his path." Nat was at a loss what else to do.

If electronic tracing was useless to find this Rangar guy, they would have to use old-fashioned investigative boots on the street. "I'm heading back to Colorado Springs to see if I can find out anything. In the meantime, think about what you would do in his position." Hawthorne hung up.

Nat mulled this over—how could you travel about the US without being detected? He turned on the oven and pulled out a pizza. He began to worry that Rangar might find out he was pinging his accounts and trace it back to him. He decided to stop all electronic surveillance until he had this figured out. He took a bite of his pizza—how to fall off the world electronically? *First, you would have to avoid airports and trains. You could travel by car, but only if it didn't have a built-in GPS unit. You could travel using an old car or a motorcycle, but it would have to be one that was not registered to you. Buses allow you to buy tickets with cash and without any identification—bingo.* Nat was excited. It was easy to look up bus schedules.

When Hawthorne's plane landed in Colorado Springs, he immediately checked his cell phone and saw more calls from Nat. Hawthorne hit the symbol to return the call.

"Hey boss, I think I've figured it out."

"Okay, hit me with your brilliant idea." The flight attendant announced that the passengers could use their cell phones over the intercom.

"I'll bet my bottom dollar Rangar got on a bus."

"Why?"

"Well, you don't need an ID to buy a bus ticket and you can pay with cash."

Hawthorne wasn't sure about this idea. "As good a place as any to start. Did you get me an address?" Nat gave him the address of the Greyhound bus station.

Hawthorne picked up his gun case and headed to rent a car. It was dark, moonless, and the air was brisk, biting his cheeks. Colorado reminded him of Afghanistan; even the slight smell of sage in the air was similar. He drove over to the Greyhound bus station on Weber. He walked up to the ticket counter and asked the clerk if he had seen anyone meeting Rangar's description. The clerk was a heavyset man with a tattoo of Chinese symbols on the side of his neck. He seemed reluctant to talk, so Hawthorne folded over a twenty-dollar bill and slid it across the counter to the clerk. "Hey, I'm not sure it was him but this guy seemed out of place here. He was wearing clothes like most of the people and had a backpack but he didn't seem to fit in—had a damned nice-looking computer. Anyway, he bought a ticket for El Paso. It pulled out about six hours ago."

Hawthorne folded up over another twenty-dollar bill. "Thanks." *El Paso? Leaving the country until this all blew over would be a logical choice.*

Hawthorne called up Nat and had him check on flights to El Paso. The quickest flight to El Paso was out of Denver. Nat bought him a ticket and Hawthorne got in the car and started driving to DIA. This damn job was turning into a major cluster fuck and he had taken it on to stay in the good graces of a guy who couldn't even steer any significant money or influence his way currently.

Hawthorne's flight landed approximately forty minutes before Rangar's bus was supposed to arrive. He rented another car and headed over to the bus station. El Paso looked like a dust bowl. He could feel the grit on his lips and it was bitter. He reached the station just as a bus pulled up. He jumped out of the car, full of energy even though he had been up the last twenty hours. Not wanting to look out of place, he grabbed his ball cap from the dashboard, pulled it on low over his forehead and unzipped his jacket. He sauntered inside and checked that the arriving bus had originated from Colorado Springs. He found a spot outside, away from the lights, and watched the people get out of the bus.

As he waited, he heard the crickets chirp and a sweat bead roll down his spine onto his SIG Sauer P226, which was in the waistband of his pants. Half the bus had unloaded and no one looked like Rangar. While the weak economy had increased the quality of the people riding the buses, these people all looked tired and long on their luck. Hawthorne was tired and he wanted this whole thing to be over. He started thinking about how he would kill Rangar. He could shoot him as he got off the bus, but that would be too public. He would probably go the bathroom after getting off the bus. He could sneak up behind him, twist his head and break his neck instantly. If he put his arms around him like an old buddy telling him he shouldn't have had the last drink and helped him into a stall, no one would probably pay any attention.

Thinking of how to kill Rangar brightened his mood a little. But it was short-lived—it appeared that the last person had gotten off the bus. Hawthorne held his breath and then he saw the legs of another passenger in the doorway. The guy was wearing those zip-out hiking pants, he looked to be over six feet tall and was carrying a backpack. *This has to be him,* Hawthorne thought. The guy staggered out of the bus. He was at least six foot three but probably didn't weigh more than one hundred and forty pounds. His cheeks were sunken and he looked like a meth addict on his last leg. Hawthorne was frustrated but there was no time to indulge his feelings. He quickly cornered a female passenger from the Colorado Springs bus but found out nothing. The next guy remembered Rangar being on the bus because 'he didn't fit in' but couldn't remember when he got off the bus. Hawthorne then found the driver. The driver seemed reluctant to talk, as if he was violating some ethical duty. But forty dollars seemed to assuage his conscience. The driver remembered Rangar and said he had gotten off back in Albuquerque.

It was 2:13 in the morning and Hawthorne knew he would never get a flight to Albuquerque before six or seven in the morning. Once there he would have to rent another car, putting him at the bus station around ten or later. He sighed, pulled off his cap and rubbed his arm across his face. He would just have to drive to Albuquerque. Hawthorne stopped at the local 7-Eleven, where English appeared to be a second language. He got a large coffee to keep himself awake and headed up I-25 to Albuquerque. The coffee smelled acrid and tasted like it was left on the warmer too long, but that would just help keep him awake.

The bus ride from Albuquerque was boring. The land was featureless and dark, with only a rare dusk to dawn light to break the tedium. The smell of disinfectant, stale cigarettes and the dry air that left him too hot one minute and too cold the next added to his sour mood.

He tried to concentrate on how he could find out who Morris had hired to kill him. Unfortunately, this brought up images of him being shot in the back and dying in a ditch or Warren's house burning as the girls screamed for help. He shook his head side to side to rid himself of the images. If he couldn't figure out how to find his killers, the next best choice was to create another diversion.

This diversion involved him using his ATM card in San Francisco. The account transfer was bogus and he transferred his money to another bank account. He had all future inquiries into his bank accounts, debit cards, cell phone, etc. rerouted to a spoofing server. The server was designed to show random activity throughout the world that increased exponentially over time.

When Hawthorne arrived in Albuquerque, he found out that Rangar had likely taken a bus to Chicago. Rangar could get off at any stop along the way, and Hawthorne realized he wasn't making any progress; he needed some sleep and to regroup. He checked into a Motel 6.

When Hawthorne woke up, he called Pete Raithbone, an old friend from the FBI. Pete had been in paratrooper training with Hawthorne until he cracked a vertebra in his back, which ended his Special Forces career. His back eventually healed up and he became a field agent in the FBI. Hawthorne and Raithbone stayed friends, and since Hawthorne had joined the Sam Adams Financial Group, they had been able to help each other out professionally again. Hawthorne explained he had a sensitive matter to discuss, which is why he'd called Raithbone on the secure line. "Pete, I need a little help in tracking down a guy." Hawthorne then explained the situation. Raithbone checked on this Rangar character using the FBI computers while Hawthorne was talking.

"It looks like the IRS is also looking into this guy. I think the FBI would be interested in interviewing him as a 'person of interest' in our arson investigation. His IRS problems give him motive for the house fire. I can send out a request to bring him in for questioning." Hawthorne asked Raithbone to keep him informed, thanked him and hung up.

It was early morning when Hank got off the bus in St. Louis. He had to figure out his next step. The bus had excellent Internet service and Hank had used it to check in on Morris. Hank saw Morris was planning on heading to North Carolina for the weekend, which meant Hank had to be in western North Carolina by Friday night. He knew someone was hunting him and they were working for Morris but he didn't know who they were. Perhaps Morris's records would give him a clue. He reviewed Morris's telephone calls and calendar but the only unusual activity was a meeting with someone from the Sam Adams Financial Group and a couple of calls to a telephone number registered to them. Hank figured Morris had met with his financial advisor—a fee-for-service guy, because Morris appeared to have all his money in a Scottrade account.

He looked up at the schedule board and saw the next bus to Atlanta would leave in an hour. He bought a ticket and found a seat. The bus station had the intoxicating aroma of sweat and urine mixed together. The old fluorescent lights buzzed and Hank had problems concentrating on his computer.

Morris's computer records had not been much help. He decided to check Morris's bank accounts. There he saw a couple of unusually large cash withdrawals within a couple of hours of each other. Together, the two withdrawals added up to just under ten thousand dollars. Morris was no idiot; any cash withdrawal of ten thousand or more was reported to the IRS instantly. Hank figured the money was used to hire the guys who burned down his house.

A squeak alerted him to slow steady footsteps on his right. The footsteps stopped and Hank's heart rate jumped. He slowly looked to his right; he saw polished black shoes, blue pants and the uniform of an overweight police officer with his right hand on his billy club. He was staring at Hank with an ironic smile; he raised both his eyebrows and then started walking again. The PA screeched, a speaker announced it was time to board his bus. He was starting to close his computer, when he received an alert from his electronic snooping system—the FBI was looking for him in connection with the fire that burned down his house. His heart skipped a beat. *Shit.* He boarded the bus and found a seat. This was certainly going to make things a bit more complicated. He had to find a way to throw the police and FBI off the trail, but it had to be subtle. He thought about trying to infect their computer system, causing it to crash but that was complicated and not subtle. He thought about trying to change his appearance.

He stared at the description of himself. They had taken his picture from the Houdini website. In the written description below it stated he was about six foot two inches and weighed about one hundred seventy pounds. Below that, it listed distinguishing marks, tattoos, scars, etc. There was nothing next to this entry. *What if the description of my appearance changed,* Hank mused. This would be subtle and not too complicated. He found that any FBI agent could provide updated information on a case. This allowed agents to quickly and freely share information. All he had to do was hack into the FBI system and add a distinguishing mark. He decided his right arm was badly scarred and had discolored skin. He entered this into the FBI system.

George Washington Carver Smith had been a police officer for over thirty years. He didn't believe in newfangled DNA evidence, fluorescent lights, etc. He believed in old-fashioned police work, keeping your eyes and your ears open, noticing anything unusual. The new guys on the force were so busy learning about blood spatter patterns or playing Rainbow Six that they missed the easy things. He knew it was these observation techniques that solved most crimes and more importantly prevented crimes. His beat included the bus station in downtown St. Louis. He normally returned to the police station about an hour before his shift was over to fill out reports and check on any new crimes or suspects that he might have seen. When he got back about midday, he saw the FBI was looking for a guy in a possible arson case. The picture somehow looked familiar.

Then he remembered seeing the guy who looked out of place in the bus station. George reported a possible sighting of Hank Rangar at the St. Louis bus station that morning.

Hawthorne's cell phone rang and Raithbone told him a police officer thought he spotted Rangar at the St. Louis bus station. Hawthorne asked him if the St. Louis Police Department was likely to follow up on this lead. Not likely, Raithbone explained the sighting had been several hours ago and this case was not a priority for them but he would send out a couple of FBI guys to check on it. Hawthorne hung up and found the next flight to St. Louis from Albuquerque, which in this day and age of hubs meant he first had to fly to Dallas and then to St. Louis. *Damn, by the time I get to St. Louis I will be eight hours behind Rangar.*

Hank's bus stopped in Nashville, where he was planning to change buses. There was a police officer to his left as he entered the bus station. *Don't worry; he probably hasn't even seen the FBI report on you.* Hank headed to the bathroom at the back left side of the station—the police officer followed him. Hank felt like a cornered rate. *Think, damn it, think. My gun is my backpack; I could head for a stall and get it out. No, no that won't work, shooting a police officer in a public place. Besides he probably has on a bulletproof vest.* A number of men were entering at about the same time. *Perhaps he could get lost in the crowd somehow.* Hank found an open urinal, hoping the police officer would be gone when he was done.

When he turned to wash his hands, he noticed the police officer standing at the doorway. He instantly decided to hunch his shoulders, walk in a slow lope and stare at his feet like most of the people around him. He slowly rolled up his sleeves and started washing his hands meticulously. He could see in the mirror that the police officer was still there and seemed to be looking at him—or was his imagination? He picked up his backpack, shuffled to the paper towels; he could feel his chest tighten and then headed for the door, still staring at his shoes.

As he approached the door, the police officer said, "Hey you," in a loud voice and pointed at Rangar. Hank stepped back with his left foot, ducked his head and thrust his bent right arm up as if to deflect a blow.

The police officer had seen the FBI description of Rangar. He noticed this guy as soon as he got off the bus; he seemed different. Now with the guy looking like a beat dog, he wasn't sure why that had been. This Rangar guy was supposed to have bad scars on his right arm but this guy's right arm was in his face and there were absolutely no scars. Now he had to think of something quick. "Relax, guy, I just wanted to let you know your fly was open." The police officer didn't know if it was true but it would serve as an excuse. Hank mumbled something and checked his fly. Sure enough, his fly was open. He leaned over further to zip it up and his backpack almost hit the police officer in the head.

Hank mumbled a thank you as he exited the bath-room. *It's clearly not safe to travel by bus anymore.* He walked out the bus station and headed northwest on 5th Avenue. There was a taxi with the driver standing outside. He asked him for a ride to the nearest truck stop with showers. The driver looked him up and down, noticing his disheveled look. "Hey, man that'll be thirty dollars upfront." Hank handed him thirty dollars. The Pilot truck stop was on the edge of town. It was huge and seemed to sell almost everything. *Perhaps it was time for a new wardrobe.* He grabbed a pair of jeans, a t-shirt, socks and underwear each in his size and went up to the counter to pay. "Can I get a shower also?"

"A shower's five dollars," the clerk said, smacking her gum. She was pretty and slightly built, in her thirties, and had a tattoo of a ring of thorns and roses around her neck. Hank nodded his ascent and paid for the clothes and shower. The clerk handed him a tag with a number on it. "When that number's called a shower stall will be available for you."

Hank headed to the Iron Skillet restaurant section of the Pilot and took a seat in a burnt orange booth. A server carrying a pot of coffee tossed a menu on the table. "I'll be back to take your order in just a minute, sugar." There was a pitcher of ice-cold water at every table and Hank poured himself a glass and opened the menu.

While waiting for his order, he opened his computer and searched for people selling inexpensive motorcycles. He saw one ad that looked promising. It was for a 1985 Honda CT110 for four hundred fifty dollars. More Honda CT series bikes were made than any other vehicle in the world. The CT series bikes were step-through motorcycles with a 105cc air-cooled engine, four-speed automatic transmission, and a dual range transmission that allowed it to climb steep hills with ease. Hank called the number and the owner of the bike picked up on the second ring. Luckily for Hank, the guy seemed to be in a hurry to sell. They made an appointment to meet at the Pilot in an hour.

As he hung up the phone, he felt the server staring at him. He turned and smiled at her. She was at the other end of the line of booths and turned away as if she had been caught doing something wrong. The woman was in her late forties, with the wrinkles of a lifetime smoker on her face. *Why was she staring at me?* She walked to the cash register, where the manager was taking customers' payments. The server waited impatiently for the manager to finish with the customers and then leaned in on her tippy toes to tell him something. The manager, who was wearing a navy blue sports jacket, looked at him and then walked crisply toward the back room.

Hank decided this was just a little too odd. He put his computer in his backpack wondering if the manager was calling the police right now. He imagined police cars racing up with their lights on and the officers getting out with their guns drawn—at him. He started to stand, and almost bumped into his server carrying his order, who gave him a bright smile. "I see you have a shower tag. You get a fifteen percent discount with a tag but normally you have to tell us about it at the time you order. In this case my manager said it was okay to give you the discount but don't forget to tell your server next time." She wagged her finger at him in mock reproach.

His chicken-fried steak and eggs were served to him on an iron skillet, with the toast served on a smaller iron skillet. The shower number sign was displaying sixty-six. His number was eighty-five. *Plenty of time to enjoy break-fast.* When Hank's number came up, he took his clothes and his backpack with him. Afterward, he threw his old clothes away in a dumpster outside the Pilot.

As he started to walk back inside, he saw someone pull up on a CT110 with an old pickup truck following behind. The 'owner' was rail-thin, had long greasy black hair, and burn marks all over his hands. He seemed nervous when Hank introduced himself. Hank looked over the bike. The seat had a split in it but the motor seemed to be running well. The transmissions on these bikes were legendary, so he wasn't worried about that. Hank offered the guy four hundred dollars. The owner licked his lips. "Cash?" Hank nodded in assent and the guy started mumbling something about the title having been in a flood, causing it to be hard to read, as he pulled it out of the back pocket of his jeans. Hank handed him four hundred, the guy signed over the title and handed Hank the keys with a toothless grin. He turned away and headed toward the old pickup truck, where a woman was waiting for him. Hank shivered and turned away.

The CT110 had a rack on the back for carrying equipment. Ideally, Hank did not want to have to ride the bike with his backpack on. He went into the Pilot and bought some rope and some bungee straps. It wasn't pretty but the backpack wasn't going anywhere either. Hank started up the bike, headed south and turned east on Highway 70, which would take him to Knoxville. The CT110 was a great bike but its top speed about fifty-five miles per hour, which forced him to stay on back roads. The trip to Knoxville would take over three hours, which meant he wouldn't be there until late afternoon. Then he had to get to the Great Smoky Mountains National Park, which would take at least another couple of hours.

Hawthorne was standing at a car rental counter in St. Louis when his cell phone rang. He looked at the caller ID and saw it was Nat. "Hi Nat." The clerk behind the counter was a young man with a large pimple on the tip of his nose. He tapped the sign on the counter that said, 'Please, No cell phone calls while in line.' Hawthorne turned his back to the clerk.

Nat had decided the risk that Rangar could track him down was low and he had been drawn to the challenge of unscrambling the clutter of misinformation Rangar was putting out. He thought Rangar might be hiding real information behind the deluge of false information. Nat started looking for events that happened close in time to each other. Most of the information was like his cell phone record from earlier that day. It showed Rangar making a call in Kansas City and then five minutes later making a call in Houston and then ten minutes later making a call from Spokane. In fact, none of the data appeared to be grouped at first.

Nat figured that Rangar was addicted to his computer, just like him. Rangar was probably using a group of proxy servers with a random IP address to access the Internet. These proxy servers needed a MAC address or physical address of the computer to communicate. The physical address of your computer never changed. He knew that Rangar had been in St. Louis early in the morning. So he hacked into a number of known proxy servers and looked at their routing tables and determined if they had routed data to the Wi-Fi at the Greyhound bus station. There was only one physical address that fit this—bingo. He now had the physical address of Rangar's computer. Nat tried to explain this to Hawthorne.

"Okay, enough of the geek talk. What does this mean to me, Nat?"

"It means that I traced Rangar to Nashville." Hawthorne hung up and Nat felt a little put out. *These goddamned cavemen never appreciate the work I do for them.*

Hawthorne knew if he waited for another commercial flight it would take forever to get to Nashville and Rangar would be long gone. He called a pilot friend from his Special Forces days and was in Nashville two hours later. He rented a Toyota Camry and headed for the bus station. Hawthorne asked the ticket clerk if he remembered seeing Rangar. The clerk did but could not provide any additional information. Hawthorne bought a candy bar and flopped into a hard plastic chair. As he bit into the bar, he thought, *I'm not supposed to be a detective, I'm an operations guy.* He ran his hand over his short hair. What the hell was Rangar doing in Nashville, Tennessee anyway? Where was he going? No answers came to him. He pulled in air through his nose and was assailed by the smell of vomit and sweat.

He got up from the chair and quickly found the nearest exit to the street. He started walking up 5th Avenue. A couple of blocks up the way, he went into The Wheel, which billed itself as a cigar bar. Hawthorne ordered a burger and a Coke. After looking over the cigar list, he decided to try a Montecristo Classic No. 5. The server cut off the butt and heated the tip of the cigar. Hawthorne noticed her slender hands and bright red nail polish. He appreciated the slight pepper smell as he held the cigar to his nose.

Hank pulled into a truck stop outside Knoxville. He was tired and he needed something to eat and drink. The truck stop had a Wendy's, so he had a burger and a Diet Coke. While eating, he checked Morris's schedule. He was still planning to go home to North Carolina. He checked the GPS on Morris's Porsche and it was thirty miles south of Alexandria Virginia, crawling along at twenty-five miles an hour. Hank closed his computer, bought some beef jerky, some trail mix, nuts and a pint of water for dinner that night and breakfast in the morning. He also bought a wool blanket. He had to get going; he didn't want to be on the highway after dark. The taillights of small motorcycles are hard to see, particularly when the bike can't go the speed limit and when the driver has had a little too much to drink. It was Friday night, after all, and the hillbillies tended to be binge drinkers who drove fast.

The cars stretched forever along Interstate 95. Morris's mind wandered. He had checked for any obituaries or police reports about Hank Rangar's death and there was nothing. He was so busy at work preparing for his congressional testimony that he had not had time to think about this. But now, with the traffic barely crawling along, it began to gnaw at him. When Rangar had threatened him, he had given him until this weekend. A diesel pickup truck cut in front of him and spewed out a cloud of black smoke that enveloped Morris's Porsche. Goddamned beer-drinking hillbilly. *Why the hell does he need such a big truck? Why is he allowed to pollute my air? Just another example of why people should be forced to take mass transit.*

His thoughts turned back to Rangar. *I'll bet he drives a huge pickup truck. What if he's not dead? The story of my role in AltruMedical would end my career.* He felt some heartburn and pulled his fist up to massage his chest. He wanted to blame it on the diesel exhaust, but he knew it was because he feared Rangar wasn't dead. *I paid ten grand to see his obituary, not have his house burn down.* He decided to call Hawthorne.

Hawthorne was just finishing his cigar when his secure cell number rang. He looked at the caller ID and saw it was Congressman Morris. He let it ring a couple of more times, taking a final puff before setting his cigar down. "Hello, Congressman Morris; how can I help you?"

"Roland, I paid you for a job, but so far there hasn't been any confirmation that it's been completed."

Hawthorne hesitated. "I've got my men on that issue right now." Hawthorne was not about to admit that he knew Rangar was alive. "I think we will be able to confirm he exited this world in that house fire."

"Look, Rangar threatened to end my career by going to the press, and if I go down, I'm taking you with me. Is that clear?"

Hawthorne felt the hair on the nape of his neck stand on end. "Yes sir, I understand completely." Morris couldn't think of anything else to say, so he hung up. When Hawthorne was sure the connection had been cut, he realized he needed a plan to take out Morris if Rangar succeeded in disappearing.

Hawthorne was walking back to his car, regretting that he ever agreed to take on this job, when his phone rang again. He waited for the caller ID information to pop up hoping it wasn't Morris. When he saw it was Nat, he answered, "Nat, tell me you have some good news."

"Rangar used his computer to access the Internet on the east side of Knoxville just over an hour ago."

"What the hell is he doing in Knoxville?"

There was a pause. "How the hell should I know?"

"By the time I get to Knoxville, Rangar will be long gone. We need to figure out where he's going."

"He appears to be headed east for now. I think we can assume he was headed east out of Knoxville." Nat pulled up a map on his computer. "If he continues east at his present rate you should be able to overtake Rangar just outside of Ashville."

Hawthorne stopped walking. "What did you say?"

Nat purposely drew out the words. "I said, if Rangar continues east at his present rate you should be able to catch up to him outside of Ashville."

He's headed to Morris. Shit. Is he going to take out Morris?
He hung up his phone as if to put an exclamation mark on
that thought. Just as he was about to call back Nat, his
phone rang. "Sorry about that Nat. I just realized where
Rangar is going," and with that Hawthorne hung up.

Hank knew exactly where Morris liked to take his
Porsche out for a spin to test its and his capabilities. He
wanted to camp somewhere nearby, not in a campground
and nowhere too conspicuous. His target area was in the
Nantahala National Forest just outside of Whittier.

It was dusk as he headed over to the Great Smoky
National Park on US 441. The air was biting at his
skin and his fingers were numb. By the time he
reached the town of Cherokee, he could barely feel
his fingers. He stopped at Tribal Grounds Coffee
and ordered a hot chocolate from a girl with dark
black hair, who seemed indifferent to his presence.
It was a New-Age place that served overpriced coffee to Americans who had guilty consciences about
living in a wealthy country. A sign prominently
announced that all of their coffees were organic, 'fair
trade' coffees.

He cupped his hands around the hot chocolate until
the numbness was replaced by the feeling of his fingers
being pierced by thousands of pins. Slowly, he felt the
warmth come back into legs and arms.

Hawthorne knew that Congressman Morris lived in Ashville. He needed to get there before Rangar, so he drove the Camry seventy to ninety miles per hour over the mountains on Interstate forty. *Was Rangar going to harm Morris or did he just want to confront him?* He decided it didn't matter, because he had to prepare for the worst. If Rangar intended to kill Morris, how would he do it? Hawthorne knew he'd used a sniper rifle but Rangar did not have his training. He also thought he might slip into Morris's house and slit his throat. But this did not seem to fit Rangar's profile either. Then he thought Rangar might just try to burn down Morris's house and have him die in a house fire—the irony would probably appeal to Rangar and it seemed more like the sort of thing a computer geek would do. Rangar would have to get close enough to Morris to kill him. That would be his fatal mistake.

Hank got back on the CT110 and drove slowly the eight miles to Whittier thinking he was going to freeze to death. In Whittier, he stopped into a gas station/convenience store and bought a paraffin log and some matches. The clerk was in his twenties and wore an oversized, grimy flannel shirt. He looked Hank over with disgust, like a person looks at a vulture eating road kill. "You ain't from around here are you?"

"No I ain't."

The clerk snarled at him, "We don't like smartasses and we don't like Yankees neither."

Hank placed a twenty-dollar bill on the counter. The clerk stared at it for a while and then seemed to decide money was money, rang up the items, and placed the change on the counter.

Great—you're making friends everywhere. He'll probably call up his uncle who's the local sheriff to harass me.

He had to carry the paraffin log under his arm, while he rode. He took Conley's Creek Road south and turned right on Tara Hill Road. An old pickup truck barreled around a turn in front of him. Hank could see the grill of the pickup truck coming straight at him; he swerved right to avoid the collision. The truck skidded in the dirt he could see the front bumper just missed the back of his bike, when he looked up he was headed into a wall of bushes. He braked as he rammed into the bushes. There were lacerations on his arms and face but no real damage.

He pulled the bike out onto the steep gravel road and shifted into the CT110's lower gears. When he reached the end of the road, he found a small footpath and drove the bike up the path a hundred yards until he found a small clearing with a fire circle. He hoped no one would look for him here. There was plenty of firewood lying about and the paraffin log served as kindling. The fire soon crackled and Hank thought about camping with Janine on their grandparent's farm in Iowa. Once he warmed up, he ate some trail mix and beef jerky. He wrapped the blanket around his shoulders and could feel that dew or perhaps even frost had already formed on it. He was tired and set his cell phone to wake him up at 5:30 in the morning. He was less than fifteen minutes away from the spot he had picked out for Morris's accident. The backpack served as his pillow as he lay down to fall asleep. The fire was crackling softly, occasionally spitting hot embers his way. Hank turned on his side to face the fire. It felt nice on his face but soon his hip felt like it was being pierced by a tree root. He got up, scooped up pine needles and dead leaves to form a bed and tried again. The acrid, smoky smell of the fire mixed with the earthy smell of the leaves and he felt himself letting go.

Janine was sitting by the fireplace, a wood fire crackling; it smelled of burning oak. She was wearing an oversized brown and orange sweater, sipping on a mug of hot chocolate. He could see that the leaves were blowing in the yard. The trees only had a few stubborn leaves that still clung. It was overcast and looked like it could snow any second. Tristan and Jess had fallen asleep on the carpet. "They look so content and happy by the fire." Janine turned and smiled at him.

"I wish Mom and Dad could have seen this," she said with soft smile. The steam from her mug was dancing out of her cup.

Hank took a sip from his mug. "Mom and Dad always loved Thanksgiving at the farm. Remember when we were just barely older than Tristan and Jess, and Dad built a maze out of the hay bales for us? We played in there for hours. Mom had to practically drag us in at dark."

"And Mom forced us to drink a cup of turkey soup to warm us up. I can still taste the warm, rich broth."

"Yeah, Grandma made the best turkey soup." Hank gave a mischievous grin. "Not the sort of weak-ass stuff you make."

Janine threw a teddy bear at him. "That's it, no turkey soup for you tomorrow." She sighed, "I wonder how things would have turned out if Mom and Dad were still alive? Would they have moved to the farm or stayed in town? Would Thanksgiving have been at the farm or would they have come to us?" They pondered this for a while, staring into the flames licking up the back of the fireplace.

"Maybe someday you guys will all come out to Colorado to ski for Christmas or Thanksgiving. I think Mom and Dad would have loved Colorado." Neither Mom or Dad had been skiers but Hank thought they would have loved the atmosphere and views. "Mom was pretty athletic in her day. They both would have loved camping with their grandkids." He remembered the horrible call he had received the night they had died. Black ice caused their car to spin out of control and hit a telephone pole. The shock was as vivid as if it had happened yesterday. He could feel his face getting flushed. Janine was staring at him with one of those 'concerned mom expressions.' He turned away.

"I'm sorry; I didn't mean to upset you." She tried to comfort him. Her own eyes were welling up with tears. "It's a lonely world without them. It hurts every time someone at work asks if *the kids are going to see their grandparents. But it's still…" She didn't finish the sentence.*

Hank got up and stirred the fire. "I don't think about if very often anymore, but you're right, it is a lonely world."

"It forces us to think about our mortality in ways that most people get to put off. I am sure they are in heaven smiling at us this moment."

Hank screwed up his face at this last comment. Janine was about to complain when Jess got up and crawled into her lap.

He woke up feeling all of them had abandoned him. No one would worry that his house was destroyed in a fire. No one would wonder if he made it home safely, or whether his business succeeded, or if this assassin killed him. He had no one. He pounded his chest, the pain validated he was alive. He screamed to impose his existence on the world. Now, his own country wanted to wipe him out. His mom and dad would have never understood his decisions. *Perhaps it's better they're not alive.* He doubted they could have absorbed the pain of Janine's death. His parents had always played by the rules, they believed in their country—their government. To see him as a fugitive would have killed them.

Hawthorne arrived outside of Morris's house at 9:33 p.m. He drove past the house and saw lights on. He turned left at the end of the block and then drove down the alley behind Morris's house. After making a loop around the house, Hawthorne was confident Rangar had not arrived. He parked the Camry around the corner from the house, pulled out his SIG Sauer P226, stuffed it in his jacket and headed down the street.

Morris's house was a two-story brick colonial that had a double-story portico held up by four white columns. Hawthorne cut through the hedges on the side of the house. As he pushed aside the lilac branches, a dog starting barking. It was behind him; it was a big dog. He quickly pushed through the bushes, scratching his face, and laid prone. The dog barked even louder. *The damn thing is going to wake up the whole neighborhood.* A door slammed open. "Shut up, damn dog." This seemed to distract the dog. Hawthorne tried to lie as still as possible. He hoped the dog could not smell him. He checked for the wind direction but he couldn't detect any wind. The smell of lilac was overwhelming to him; he hoped it masked his smell. After five minutes of no barking, he could hear the dog scratching at something. Hawthorne slowly rolled over away from the bushes, a twig snapped and he stopped immediately. The dog was still scratching at something.

He crawled on the grass a couple of feet, slowly stood up, and decided to peek into the side windows. Morris and his wife were watching a movie in what seemed to be the family room at the back of the house. Hawthorne walked around the house, looking for the easiest way for Rangar to break in. He noticed his toes were cold and he curled them. Dew on the grass had made his shoes wet. The back door appeared to be the easiest way into the house without being noticed. Hawthorne climbed a maple tree, found a sturdy branch about fifteen feet off the ground, and began his sentry duty. An amateur like Rangar would never think to look for someone in a tree, and neither would nosy subdivision security.

Chapter 26

Hank's phone woke him up. There was a layer of frost on the ground and on his blanket. He stretched and stood up. In the dawn, he could see that the trees were turning color. *Would Morris take his usual drive this morning? What if he has insomnia and gets up early? Better hurry.* He kicked the coals of his fire to spread them out. He urinated on the fire to make sure all the embers were out, ate some trail mix hurriedly and took a slug of water. He put on his backpack, stepped onto the bike, rubbed his hands together and blew on them. Then he kick-started the CT110 and headed out.

Twenty minutes later, Hank found a pull-out on the left side of the road, hid the motorcycle in some bushes and warmed his hands against the engine. Just outside of Great Smoky Mountain National Park, the Blue Ridge Parkway snaked along, cutting through towering granite cliffs. *Car and Driver* had rated this one of the ten best driving roads because of its hairpin turns and beautiful scenery. The autumn day rewarded all of those around the road with a riot of bright red and orange. For every driver traveling the snaking Blue Ridge Parkway, this would be their primary reason for taking this road.

Hank Rangar, standing in the middle of the highway, was oblivious to nature's beauty though. The pungent odor of rotting leaves assailed his nostrils and the frost on the grass was glistening in the sun. Hank checked his watch, the one Jess and Tristan had given him—fifteen minutes before his target would show. He chose a spot at the beginning of a particular pair of those hairpin turns admired by the magazine. The first turn only had a low guardrail between the road and a hundred foot cliff. The second turn that followed slammed against a sheer granite face and hugged around it before cutting back into the deep forest. It would take five minutes to set up the home-made EMP that would disable his target's automobile and another three minutes to cross the road and scramble up the mountainside. This left him with just seven minutes to account for any unexpected events. From his perch, he would watch and wait for Morris to show up, firing his homemade EMP device just as Morris was entering the first hairpin turn.

There was little traffic on the road at this early hour and Hank set down his black REI backpack on the cool pavement. He walked just past the centerline, pulled a pair of fifteen-foot wires from the main pocket of the pack and a package of putty from the left side. He got out a stencil he and Warren had made and laid one edge along the painted centerline of the road. A pair of notches at the far end of the stencil defined the correct distance between the ends of the pair of wires. The road was littered with decomposed granite. He hadn't counted on this. He tried to brush the sand off the coarse gravel asphalt with his cold hand, but this was totally ineffective. He lowered himself down to his stomach and blew across a small patch. Sand stung his face but he had cleared just enough area for the putty. Hank tore off a section of the putty and tested the patch for adherence. Satisfied the putty would adhere, he worked the end of one of the wires into the putty, pulled off another section of the putty and worked it onto the pavement at the other spot indicated by the stencil. Fifteen seconds were lost. He hoped there wouldn't be any other surprises.

He stood and walked to the guardrail, unrolling the ends of both wires. He lined up his stencil along the painted line that defined the shoulder of the road. The stencil included a pair of lines along which the wires should run. The lines made sure that the open V created by the wires was roughly perpendicular to the direction of road travel and that the wires were correctly spaced, with the largest part of the open V on the shoulder of the road. He blew the dust away from the first spot, tore off some putty and worked it into the spot indicated by the stencil. He rubbed his fingers to warm them. The putty was hard to work because it was cold. That had cost him another twenty seconds.

Hank fed the other ends of the wires through an opening below the guardrail. He had been so busy he had not looked over the guardrail; when he did, his stomach dropped and he felt a little dizzy. He involuntarily took a small step back. Of course, he had selected this turn because of the cliff, but he expected a steeply sloping cliff with granite screen, not the almost vertical wall he found. There was a small ledge about eight inches wide a couple of feet below the road surface. These thin shelves continued down for at least thirty feet and anyone who lost their balance here fell to their death. Unfortunately, this was the only place to set up his firing device where it could not be seen from the road.

He took a deep breath, climbed over the railing and balanced himself on the granite ledge. The wires were insulated once they left the road, increasing the breakdown voltage to hundreds of times the level of the bare wires on the road. The technology of EMPs had been around since the cold war. The US had worried the Soviets would explode a bomb in the upper atmosphere, creating a large EMP pulse capable of disabling or destroying the communications and electrical grids across large areas. Hank's system was a miniature version, capable of interrupting the electrical system of a single car.

Standing on the ledge, Hank set his pack down just under the guardrail, unzipped the main compartment and pulled out the firing mechanism, while trying not to think about falling. He attached the end of one of the wires to the firing mechanism. Now he had to balance the firing mechanism on the ledge. He held onto the guardrail with his left hand and held the firing mechanism with his right hand. He looked down at the ledge and felt his head swimming again. *Get a hold of yourself. You are used to being in the mountains.* Hank started to bend over, holding the rail with his free hand, but as he leaned down the fingers of his left hand started to slip. He instantly visualized falling to his death. He stood up. *Damn, this is not going to work. I need some way to balance myself.* He looked at his backpack; perhaps he could use it to balance himself. He climbed back up and looped one of the shoulder straps around the guardrail and held onto the other shoulder strap while placing the firing device on the ledge. Next, he pulled out a set of Leyden jars from his pack and wired the positive terminal of the Leyden jars to the firing mechanism. Leyden jars were a Dutch invention of the 1700s that provided a simple way to store large amounts of static electricity. He attached the other wire to the negative terminal. He moved to the right along the ledge and placed the Leyden jars next to the firing mechanism on the ledge. He climbed back over the guardrail and, making one last check of all of the connections, he grabbed his pack, slung it over his shoulders and cinched the straps. He had lost another minute, according to his watch.

The exact distance between the two wires was critical. Too close and the electricity would arc between the wires at too low a voltage. This would result in an EMP pulse with insufficient energy to disable the seven key microprocessors that controlled the heart of a Porsche 911 Turbo S. Too far apart and the electricity would not arc across the wires and there would be no EMP pulse. He had calculated the ideal distance to be 12.5 inches in the center of the V where the wires met in the center of the road with an angle of five degrees. The arc voltage of dry air was 82,000 volts per inch, so the 12.5 inches would provide about a one million-volt arc. The microprocessors would easily be disabled by one hundred volts across the leads. However, the R-squared losses, the grounding losses, and getting through the electrical shielding all had to be taken into account. He also assumed dry air and he could feel the humidity, which would lower the break down voltage, but he had planned in at least a 3 dB margin; it should be more than sufficient.

The pulse would shut down the fuel injection system and the compression of the cylinders would act like brakes, causing the car to go into a skid. The microprocessors controlling the power steering would stop working and cause the driver to have to steer the car manually. The antilock brakes' microprocessors would also be fried, requiring the driver to pump non-powered brakes. Using the accelerator to regain stability would be the best response in such a situation but the accelerator would no longer work. The driver could then shift into neutral. But this particular driver did not understand physics or engineering. Such was the way with most politicians who were appointed to the US Patent and Trademark Office, an irony which always amazed Hank. Hank was counting on this.

The firing mechanism was a high voltage spring-loaded switch. When the latch released, the double-pull double-throw switch would close the electrical circuit and the one million volts from the Leyden jars would surge through the wires at about 0.6 times the speed of light. Hank calculated that it would take the spring-loaded switch about ten milliseconds to close. He estimated the Porsche 911 Turbo S would be going about sixty miles an hour entering the hairpin turn, which meant the car would travel less than a foot from when he pressed the remote control. The remote control would activate a small solenoid that would then release the spring-loaded high-voltage switch. The solenoid was connected by a pair of wires to a separate Leyden jar through a transistor controlled by the radio receiver tuned to the remote control. This all had to work perfectly for Hank's plan to succeed, which is why Hank over-engineered it.

Even if the EMP device fired correctly, Hank still needed to be sure the EMP device was not discovered and traced to him. To accomplish this, Hank had made his device with Leyden jars made from empty Budweiser beer bottles, aluminum foil and salt water. Everything was built with off-the-shelf parts that you might commonly find on the side of roads across America. Upon pressing the remote control, the solenoid would energize, releasing the spring-loaded switch. The motion of the switch slamming shut would unbalance the firing mechanism and the Leyden jars. There is was enough slack in the wires to allow electricity to flow for at least one tenth of a second,

by which time the Leyden jars would be completely dis-
charged. The electric arc would last a total of ten nano-
seconds, or a million times faster than it would take for
the motion of the Leyden jars and firing mechanism to fall
and become detached from the wires. The heat from the
electricity flowing through the bare wires would loosen
the grip of the putty. The force of the electricity would
scatter wires and jars off the cliff edge. Upon investigation, police would find scattered beer bottles and stray
parts from cars—or at least was what Hank hoped would
happen.

Nine minutes had elapsed during the set up. The cool
morning air made Hank's fingers stiff. He climbed back
over the guardrail and started to walk across the road
when he heard a car. The sound was not a Porsche 911
Turbo S, which was good, but he didn't want to be seen
walking along the road. He hurried across and started
to climb to his perch. He scrambled up the decomposed
granite scree, ducked under a couple of rhododendron
bushes, and continued to climb about twenty yards. The
small tunnel of rhododendron bushes abruptly stopped
against a granite boulder. He scrambled atop the boulder, which had a relatively flat top surface, and perched
about thirty feet above the road. From here, Hank could
see the road for about a hundred yards leading up to the
hairpin turn. He checked his watch; four minutes and
forty-five seconds had elapsed—forty-five seconds longer
than he planned. The Porsche 911 could arrive at any
moment.

Morris had killed more people than Al-Qaeda had on 911, and more importantly, he had killed Janine. It would be one thing if this had just been bureaucratic bungling but Morris had done so with knowledge and indifference. He was being protected by the immoral, self-serving culture of Washington DC. Hank's face flushed with anger.

From his perch, it was highly unlikely any drivers would see him, high up at such a close range taking these particular turns. Hank's anxiety over being seen by the first car was gone but he worried a bit over the putty holding. If the car passed over the median and then the putty, there was a chance the putty would adhere to the tires, pulling it away from the road and releasing the wires. He calculated that his chance of repairing the damage before Morris showed up would be zip shit over infinity. He saw the car, a white Chevy Malibu, moving slowly and erratically; obviously tourists taking in fall foliage pictures. He thought he heard the faint sound of the Porsche in the distance. Engines have a distinctive sound. The S has a high-pitched growl. It was now less than a minute until he expected the Porsche. The Malibu had stopped to take a picture fifty yards from the first hairpin turn. Rangar could hear the tires of the S squealing around the turns and the engine accelerating. If the Malibu were in the way, the Porsche would slow down and ruin his whole plan. He willed the Malibu to move along.

Chapter 27

Stanford Morris woke up early; he was looking forward to driving his new Porsche 911 Turbo S. His house was outside of Asheville, North Carolina and it would take thirty minutes or so to get to the Blue Ridge Parkway outside of Great Smoky Mountain National Park. He wanted to be there before all the tourists showed up taking pictures of fall colors and clogging up the road. He decided to skip his morning shower and pick up a venti cappuccino with low fat milk from the Starbucks drive-through window down the street.

The sound of a car broke Roland Hawthorne out of his stupor. He had spent a cold, uncomfortable night in the maple tree. There had been no sign of Rangar or much other activity to keep him awake. He rubbed his eyes and looked out at the road to see where the noise was coming from. A Porsche was pulling out of Morris's driveway. He saw it was Morris driving.

The sun isn't above the horizon yet. Where the hell is he going so early in the morning? At least I know he is still alive. With the sun coming up I better get out of this tree before someone sees me. Hawthorne lost his grip about five feet off the ground. Luckily, he didn't land on any roots and sprain an ankle but he was getting older and felt the compression in his knees and back, which had done too many parachute jumps.

He heard another car coming up the street, which stopped him in his tracks. It was a police car. The driver was not looking around but braked and then stopped behind his rental car. *Damn.* Hawthorne started walking toward his car. *What the hell does he want?* When he was about twenty yards from his car the police officer got out and headed to examine Hawthorne's car. The police officer did not seem to notice him. He appeared to be around thirty, six foot two, with a little belly. Hawthorne imagined how he could sneak up behind him, break his neck or thrust his knife under his ribs killing him before he knew what happened.

He came up behind the police officer. "Can I help you?" Hawthorne used his best command voice. The police officer jumped a little, turned around quickly and saw a smiling Hawthorne, which disarmed him. He seemed at a loss for words. This was exactly the reaction Roland had hoped for. Roland held out his hand. "Colonel Roland Hawthorne, 82nd Airborne at your service, sir." Roland chose the 82nd Airborne because they were stationed at

Fort Bragg, North Carolina, which he hoped would build a sense of camaraderie.

The police officer shook Roland's hand. "Officer, Jim-Bob Grayson, uh, ah, did you say 82nd Airborne?"

"Yes sir, I sure did."

"My brother's in the 82nd. Two tours over in Afghanistan. Sergeant Gaines Grayson. You wouldn't happen to know him?" The police officer had completely forgotten his purpose—to check out Mrs. Robinson's complaint about a suspicious car parked down the street from her house. Roland said he hadn't had the pleasure to meet his brother but he would look him up this afternoon when he arrived at Fort Bragg. Roland explained he had to hurry to a meeting, jumped into his rental car and drove away before the police officer could ask any more questions.

His back hurt, he was hungry, and he wondered where Morris was headed and where the hell was Rangar anyway? He decided to head the same direction as the Porsche. The trees loomed over the road like vultures. It was deadly still this morning and the houses reminded him of the ones in the movie *Nightmare on Elm Street*. He shivered involuntarily.

A couple of blocks up the way, he saw the sports car pull out of Starbucks. Morris was accelerating like a bat out of hell. Roland was uncertain of his next move; he was tired and angry. *Where the hell had that police officer come from? How had Rangar been able to evade him?* He had successfully completed over one hundred assignments while part of Special Forces and many more since with The Sam Adams Financial Group. It just didn't make sense that some computer programmer was able to evade him. Nat might be right that he was a great programmer but there was no evidence he had any field experience. How was Rangar able to anticipate his every move? Only someone with help could do that. But who would be helping him? Was Rangar working for a foreign government? Could Morris be a double agent? If that were the case, he might be in real danger. He had some enemies at the CIA. This could all be a set up to take him down. He pounded the steering wheel. *Shit—this isn't worth ten grand.*

With a sip of his cappuccino, Morris eased out of town. With no stop signs or stoplights and little traffic, he began to relax and look forward to his drive. It was a crisp morning and there was dew on the fields that glistened in the sun. He loved the way the car's steering reacted to his slightest command. He loved the growl of the engine but what he loved most was the way people looked at him in the car. The pretty blonde girl in the Starbucks looked at him with awe when she handed him his cappuccino.

He turned off his cell phone; he didn't want to hear the piercing sound of email messages. He did not want to think about work at all. *God, I miss being a congressman. The day*

I won my seat, I knew I was set up for life—but it was too damn short. Thank God I got the one hundred twenty-five thousand dollars a year pension even if I served only one day, and the Cadillac medical care coverage is great. It was a hell of a step up from being a district attorney for that shithole of a town in North Carolina. But you had to be a district attorney if you wanted to run for political office. Then state senator, which in both cases paid starvation wages, hardly suitable for a dog. It appeared that the years of self-sacrifice had finally paid off when he won his congressional seat, but two short years later the political tide had gone out and he was stranded on the beach.

He looked up and a fucking semi was going twenty miles an hour in a forty-five zone. He honked and slammed on his brakes. Of course, he hadn't noticed that he was going seventy. *The goddamn Neanderthal shouldn't even be allowed on the road at this time of the day.* Stanford looked for an opening to pass the truck. He was in a Porsche 911 after all. He saw an opening, ignored the solid double yellow lines and floored the Porsche. He was thrown back into the seat, pulled out around the truck, and was almost past the truck when he saw a pickup truck coming the other way. He was pretty sure he would make it—too late to turn back. *Go baby GO… room to spare.* The damn hillbilly flipped him off as they passed.

Hawthorne almost had the Camry floored trying to catch up to Morris. He thought he had caught a break when the Porsche got held up behind a semi with a double yellow line. Then it pulled out and accelerated around the truck and Hawthorne knew he would never catch Morris.

He called Nat and asked if he could track a person's location. Nat told him it was possible using their cell phone but he needed time to hack into the phone system. It would take at least twenty-four hours. That was useful information for the future but would do him no good right now. Then Hawthorne asked if he had any updated information on Rangar—nothing. The car entered a tunnel of trees. They blocked out the sun, there was dew on the road and he felt the tires were not gripping well. *Better slow down, this could be dangerous. Following Morris could be a trap.* The forest was suffocating, he imagined people with RPGs hiding behind every log waiting to ambush him. Morris was out of sight now. He hadn't had a decent night's sleep in over a week. He needed to clear his head. At the next turn out, he pulled over, turned around and headed home to get some rest.

Morris's Porsche was a present to himself for all the bullshit he had put up with. He had sacrificed his life to public service and he wasn't being selfish, but even a saint needed a little reward occasionally. He had really hit bottom when he lost his reelection bid. After all, the odds of a congressional representative losing a reelection bid were less than ten percent. When he lost his seat, he wasn't sure what to do with himself. He couldn't go back to Hickville, NC and practice criminal law. He wasn't hurting for money with his congressional pension but he wanted power. He was too young to become a lobbyist. They were whores with no real power, although it was a great way to get rich as a former congressman. He came to a rolling stop at the four-way and turned right. He stepped on the throttle, shifted into second and was going forty-five in no time. The sun was streaming through the window; it was a perfect fall day.

He and the President were in the same party, so he had set his sights on a job in the administration. He wanted a job with real power, such as a seat on the National Labor Relations Board. The NLRB was created under FDR and everyone knew its purpose was to enhance the negotiating power of unions. It was a great position to build relations with labor unions, particularly the all-important teachers' unions and the public sector unions. These unions not only provided campaign funds but more importantly, they had great grassroots organizations to get the vote out. A perfect position, Morris thought, for his election run to become a senator from North Carolina or a run for governor. When he had approached the President's Chief of Staff, Joe Diglo, he was cool to Morris. While Morris was insulted, he was also persistent and reminded Diglo that he had helped the President carry western North Carolina in the election. Diglo put him off, saying they were looking for the right position for someone of his 'stature' and Morris was beginning to despair that his best option was going to be the lobbyist job he had been offered. Then Diglo had called and said the President had found the perfect position for him—"Under Secretary of Commerce for Intellectual Property and Director of the United States Patent and Trademark Office." The supposed reason for giving him this bullshit position was because of his work on the Patent Reform Bill that had passed while he was in Congress.

There was no one on the road and he was going eighty when he spotted the first hairpin turn of the day. He braked and downshifted. The engine roared. The salesman had explained to him that he should not be in too high a gear entering a turn and he definitely did not want to be pressing on the brake. When the salesman heard he was the director of the patent office, he started explaining the physics of a turning car and drawing vectors on a piece of paper. The salesperson was so excited explaining the physics—it reminded him of the pinheads he worked with at the patent office. They got so excited over the latest technology and always wanted to torture him with the details. He didn't understand their explanations; he didn't even try. *How could these geeks get so excited about inanimate objects? Where was the human drama? What did inventions have to do with life?*

He accelerated up a hill. He could not see over the top and felt the same thrill he had felt as a kid ridding along the country roads in his dad's pickup truck. When he crested the hill his stomach gave that wheee! from the sudden, temporary zero Gs his body was experiencing. There was a quick left turn he had not seen and he slammed on the brakes and slid around the turn. When he came out of the turn he pushed on the accelerator but nothing seemed to happen at first. Then he felt a jerk and he realized he was in too high a gear. That sliding turn gave him a boost of adrenaline—enough cappuccino. It was getting cold anyway.

He turned the patent office job into lemonade. He found out about a particularly promising new technology for heart disease that would save billions in stents, balloon angioplasty and open-heart surgery. Betty Lurie, the beautiful lobbyist for MedCon told him about it. But he was the one smart enough to make millions off it. He'd shown that asshole Diglo—they could try to keep him down but he had shown them he was too clever for that to happen.

For some reason Hank Rangar's angry face popped into his head. He could hear him saying, "You killed my sister." It wasn't his fault; Rangar was a psychopath. The maniac had threatened to go to the police. *Why the hell hadn't the police found his body in the fire? I hope he suffered—I hope he smelt his own flesh burning. They say it smells a little like a pig being barbequed mixed with burnt hair. I hope that is his fate for eternity.*

Morris shook his head. What the hell was he doing! The whole purpose of the drive was to relax him and clear his head. He accelerated; the engine growled. A left turn in the road was approaching; he slowed, downshifted and pulled to the right side of the road. He entered the turn and cut across the centerline, accelerating through the turn. The Porsche handled beautifully. It felt so good to execute a turn with such skill and precision. He thought he was getting the hang of it and accelerated to eighty, flying through a dip in the road and accelerating into a rise. One of those famous hairpin left turns was in sight and he was feeling confident—excited by the challenge of the turn. He downshifted and pulled to the right of the road in anticipation.

The Chevy Malibu accelerated and made it through the first turn, when Rangar heard his target's Porsche accelerating. *Please get out of the way—PLEASE.* He saw Morris doing at least seventy thorough a little dip and rise in the straightaway before the pair of hairpin turns he had selected. The Malibu slowly moved through the second hairpin turn and was now out of the way. The Porsche was approaching the first turn way too fast, Hank thought. He held the remote in his right hand and pushed the button when the Porsche's front tires hit the first wire. Nothing seemed to happen at first. His heart skipped, he could feel the beginning of anger and frustration.

When Hank pressed the remote, the solenoid activated the spring-loaded double-pull double-throw switch. A million volts surged through the Leyden jars into the bare EMP wires and arced over, producing a pulse. It created a voltage overload condition on all seven of the key microprocessors controlling the engine, transmission, brakes, and electronic stability control systems. It took a split second for the compression of the Porsche's engine to cause the wheels to brake and the driver to lose control. Hank's mood changed on a dime.

Morris felt like the master of the universe as he prepared for the left hairpin turn. He knew he was going a little fast and attempted to hit the brakes after downshifting just as the EMP pulse disabled his brakes. The Porsche 911 Turbo S's brakes were hydraulic-assisted. So when Morris pressed on the brakes they still worked, but they were not the precise, quick-reacting brakes he was used to. Unfortunately for Morris, pressing on the brakes at this time was exactly the wrong thing to do. The EMP pulse knocked out the microprocessor that controlled the fuel injectors and the engine was receiving no fuel. The compression of the cylinders acted as a brake on the car. Morris had steered left into the turn, but the sudden deceleration ensured that he was now in a sliding skid. He had no idea what was happening or how to react to it. He noticed the electronic display was not working, but there was no time to think about this. *A guardrail with a cliff beyond it, what do I do?* He thought about how an accident would haunt his political life. He covered his face with his arms.

The right front end of the car slammed into the guardrail, smashing Morris's head into the steering wheel. If the airbag sensors had been working, it would have saved

Stanford's head from hitting the steering wheel and causing him a concussion. The guardrail gave way and the
Porsche jumped off the cliff. The car's front end was
slowed and lifted and the back end moved right past where
the guardrail had been. This resulted in the car doing a
flip. Morris's vision cleared just in time to see the mountains across the valley and then the sky come into view.
This is going to be a bitch to explain to the insurance company.
The car landed on its tail end. A dead pine tree branch
pierced the gas tank. Morris was slammed into the back
of his seat. He lost his breath. The car rolled onto its roof
and slid down the mountain.

Gas spilled out of the Porsche as it slid down the cliff.
Sparks from metal hitting rock caused it to ignite. Morris
was upside down and could see the car slam into a tree and
stop. His right arm had suffered a complex fracture and
his radius bone was poking through the skin. Blood was
smeared all over his forearm. Despite this, he moved his
right hand to release his seat belt. This was excruciatingly
painful. Then he saw the smoke from the fire of the car.
His heart rate quickened.

This was the first time Stanford realized he might
die. At first, he thought it was some sort of metaphysi-
cal joke—he was much too important to die. Then he
saw the sun blotted out by the smoke from the Porsche,
smelled gasoline, his adrenaline surged and he was able
to release the seat belt. He tried to open the door, but
the electronic door locks weren't working. He slammed

his shoulder against the door but this was hopeless. He remembered from some show he had watched on TV that front windshields could be kicked out from inside the car quite easily. He twisted in his seat so that he could get the right leverage; again he noticed the faint smell of gasoline. He kicked with both legs as hard as he could and the windshield gave way. The air fuel mixture was just right so that when the windshield was pushed open it exploded. Morris felt the fire suck the air out of his lungs, searing his air sacs, making it impossible for him to breathe. He smelled his burning hair and flesh just before he passed out and died.

Hank saw the Porsche start to slide, hit the guardrail and perform a back flip. Several seconds later, he saw a plume of black smoke. The Porsche had caught fire. He could not have hoped for a better result. Hank was now a killer. Once he had killed, something flipped in him like a switch.

Chapter 28

Rangar put the remote control in his black backpack, jumped off his perch, and scrambled down the opposite side of the ridge from the rhododendron tunnel. He walked along the road in the opposite direction from which the Porsche had come. A hundred yards down the way, there was a turnout where he had parked the motorcycle. He strapped his backpack on the back of the bike, straddled the seat and lifted the kickstand. The putt-putt of the small engine filled the silence, he smelled the acrid smell of the exhaust, and pulled around, accelerating. There were sirens in the distance. He needed to put some distance between himself and the accident. Three miles from the scene, a fire truck and two emergency vehicles passed him in a blur.

A cold-blooded killer now, he wondered how he felt about this and was bemused to find nothing but resolve to move forward down the winding road. Morris had the chance to do the right thing, and he had refused. Justice had been served for his sister and for those who actually tried to be industrious builders of ideas. If the world had one less evil man in it, whose desires were to tear down those ideas and industries that saved thousands of lives, then so be it.

Sun streamed through leaves glowing golden red and orange. Time flew by with the beautiful scenery as he drove back to Asheville and found the alley behind the late Stanford Morris's house. He stopped at the end of the alley and pulled his bike into a spot between two large lilac bushes. The smell reminded him of his childhood and playing under the bushes. Feeling somewhat concealed, he unstrapped his pack, pulled out his computer, and searched for Morris's Wi-Fi signal. The computer showed a security-enabled network labeled "commander in chief," which Hank knew was Morris's. The house was a conservative, two-story job in a nice suburb of Asheville. The houses appeared to be forty or fifty years old, which was why this subdivision still had alleys. A white wooden fence separated the alley from the house; a portion was indented with a gate. This was where the Morris's trashcans were stored.

Having already broken into Morris's network, the security presented no problem. He had thought of doing this remotely but wanted it to look like the bank transfer had originated with Morris's computer. He logged into Morris's account with Scottrade and transferred five million dollars to an account in the Caymans, using Morris's electronic bill-paying system to make it look like Morris had set this up on Friday night and scheduled the transfer for Saturday. A police car cruised slowly down the street perpendicular to the alley—better get moving. He turned off his computer, put it in its soft-sided case and headed out.

Interstate 40 outside Raleigh was surprisingly busy and Hawthorne thought the drivers aggressive for a Sunday. "...Breaking news..." the radio announced. "Former North Carolina congressman and head of the patent office Stanford Morris has died..." Hawthorne turned his head to the radio and thrust out his hand to turn up the volume. HOOONK. Hawthorne looked up just in time to swerve back into his lane. "Former congressman Morris lost control of his car on the Blue Ridge Parkway near Great Smoky Mountains National Park earlier today. His car tumbled nearly a hundred feet down a cliff and caught fire around 7:15 this morning. He was driving too fast for the conditions, according to authorities... Again, former North Carolina congressman Stanford Morris has died..."

Hawthorne turned down the volume. His vision was narrowing and he felt a little light-headed. At a rest stop, he decided he needed a break and found a parking place near the bathrooms. He turned off the engine and leaned back in his seat. The likelihood of Morris having a fatal accident this morning was too coincidental. He was sure that Rangar or perhaps someone working with him had killed Morris. *How the hell did Rangar elude me? He avoids the house fire and escapes undetected—it was like he knew it was coming. And what was the camera in the tree near his house? Seems more like the work of a planned operation with a support team. The probability of someone escaping that fire was extremely low. Then the guy remembers not to leave an electronic trail. A regular Joe, having escaped from fire, the first thing they would have done was call someone, then they would have talked to the police, then their insurance company. But that's not all, he plants phony electronic cell phone calls. I get lucky in Colorado Springs, with Nat's help, and find he has taken a bus to El Paso Texas but he continues to shake me off. How could he have known I would be there? It's as if someone was tracking me.*

Hawthorne rubbed his forehead. If Rangar was a plant for a foreign government, then they could have tapped his phone and found out about his meeting with Morris. It would not have been hard for them to figure out he was for hire. That might explain how Rangar had stayed a step ahead of him and was able to kill Morris while making it look like an accident. *It doesn't explain how Rangar avoided the fire, but perhaps they set up multiple cameras around his property in anticipation or as a normal precaution. That would make sense if Rangar was working for someone.*

The more he thought about it, the more likely it seemed that Rangar was working as a spy. *Rangar wipes out the Iranian nuke program, killing a number of their scientists, and what does he get? He gets kicked out. Hell, that's how I hired Nat.* Hawthorne almost felt sorry for Rangar. His story was not that different from his own in Afghanistan.

Rangar was probably pissed off about being fired, and if the right people got to him, especially if they offered enough money, well, he probably would have been happy to sell his skills.

The car was getting hot so he rolled down the window and saw a mother dragging her bawling kid by the arm. "If you don't stop crying, I'll give you something to cry about," she shouted as she opened the door to an old red pickup truck and hauled the child in. He felt like going over and slapping the bitch, but controlling urges like that is how you stayed alive in the field. He had seen infinitely worse in Afghanistan and numerous other hell holes around the world. He got out of the car and started walking.

If Rangar is part of a larger operation, we could be compromised. His radar was up and he always paid attention to it. This had kept him from getting killed many times. His client was dead and it was time to think about his and Sam Adams' survival. His operations guys knew how to protect themselves, but their adversary seemed to be an expert in computers and electronic surveillance. If they penetrated Sam Adams' systems, they could gain all sorts of information that might hang them all. He dialed Nat's number. Nat picked up on the third ring. "Boss?"

"Find another place to live and make Sam Adams disappear as much as possible electronically. Send out the code to those in the field. They'll take it from there." Nat started to ask a question but Hawthorne cut him off.

"Your life, my life, and the Sam Adams Financial Group's existence might depend on how well you make us disappear." Nat swallowed hard. He'd never really considered his job dangerous. "Yes sir, I will get right on it."

Hank had two clients outside of Raleigh-Durham, in the Research Triangle. It was the first place to come to mind—the four-hour drive passed quickly. He left the bike in long-term parking at the Raleigh-Durham airport with the key in the ignition. It was midafternoon and Hank turned his face into the fall sun to warm himself. He unstrapped his backpack, went inside and purchased a ticket to the Caymans. His wait for a flight was short; unfortunately, it included a three-hour layover in Miami.

When he exited the airplane in Miami, he was immediately hit with the cloying humidity and stale smell of mildew. People who lived in the southeast got used to this air but to someone from Colorado, it was as if the septic system had backed up. He was stuck in the international building, an ugly, dated version of the more modern domestic terminals. He did, however, find a Chili's restaurant and waited to be seated. The hostess asked, "Just you?" Hank nodded. "Would you like a booth, a table, or do you want to sit at the bar?"

"Booth, please." She led him to the back of the restaurant. The place was nearly empty but it still took the server ten minutes to come over.

"Can I get you a drink? How about a Cadillac Margarita?" The perky server licked the end of her pen.

"No thanks, I'll take a Sam Adams Lager and the bacon burger."

Luckily, the smell of beer and cooking covered up the mildew. The air conditioning was blasting from a vent above his table. This seemed to be the way people in the southeast dealt with humidity. Hank just felt cold and clammy instead of hot and clammy. He wasn't sure which was worse. The beer came in a frosted glass. Beer snobs would have complained it was too cold but Hank thought it tasted great. It was twenty minutes before his burger arrived.

In the meantime he pulled out his computer and transferred the five million dollars to an account in Hong Kong and then back to another account in the Caymans. Even if someone discovered the transfer from Morris's Scottrade account to the Caymans, they could not trace it to Hong Kong and back—he hoped. Then, he closed out the first Caymans account.

The burger was piled with applewood-smoked bacon and came with barbeque sauce. He removed the top bun and ate the burger with a knife and fork, eating the bacon with his fingers. It had a slight caramel coating.

When he finished, he paid with cash. Credit cards left a trail the government could find. Given his recent experiences, he wanted to leave as few traces as possible. The government did not want people to use cash. Credit cards made it easier to tax you and easier to track you down. This was also why the government had eliminated any bills greater than the one hundred dollar bill. Clearly, this violated the First Amendment right to privacy but it was impossible to run a business, comply with the tax code and have any privacy. Hank once asked his attorney how the law reconciled this. After his attorney quit laughing and making sarcastic comments about the government not being logical—only an engineer would expect the government to be logical—he explained the government considered tax code to be a civil law or a contract between citizens and the government. Therefore, the privacy right under the First Amendment did not apply. The logic escaped Hank then and now.

He checked his watch; still an hour and a half to kill before boarding. The TV mounted in the gate waiting area had on Stossel doing another show on big government run amok. The focus of the show was how the FDA had an incentive not to approve new drugs and medical devices. This was denying people choices and even resulted in the death of patients. Examples included even simple applications for smartphones the FDA said they had to approve before doctors were allowed to use them. Stossel asked a guest, "But it's not like there is graft going on at the FDA?" The guest explained that straight bribes did not happen to his knowledge but if you made the *right* decisions at the FDA, you could be assured a high-paying cushy job at one of the major medical companies once you left. Hank wondered about the guest's emphasis on 'right.' *Who came up with these agendas, anyway?*

"Boarding all passengers in rows one through twenty-five for Caymans flight ten fifty-nine," a pleasant female voice announced.

Upon arriving in the Caymans, he inquired at the airport and found a mid-priced hotel off the West Bay Road. His room was on the fifth floor. It had the obligatory two standard beds with a nightstand in between. A digital clock and phone were placed on the nightstand along with a remote control for the forty-inch flat screen TV. The bathroom was next to the door and had a polished limestone tile floor. The shower was a large walk-in but did not have a tub. The other end of the room had a door that opened onto the balcony overlooking the crystal blue waters of the Caribbean. Hank was exhausted. He sat on the edge of the bed and pulled off his shoes. Then he stood up, unzipped his pants and let them drop to the floor. He pulled back the bed covers and fell into the bed, asleep.

When Hank woke, he was groggy, and it took him a second to orient himself. He remembered he was in the Caymans, sat up against the headboard quickly, then realized it was Sunday and the National Cayman Bank would be closed today. Slouching back down in the sheet, against his pillow, he slept for another half an hour. When he couldn't stand the sun's nagging anymore, he decided to get up. Since he could not accomplish anything today, he decided to go scuba diving. The Caymans were one of the best places in the world to go scuba diving, with up to two hundred feet of visibility. The Cayman trench, which reached twenty-five thousand feet in depth, added to the incredible diversity of marine life. He called up the concierge and set up a dive tour.

Hank enjoyed the hot sun, the salt spray and the rocking motion of the boat. Most of his fellow adventurers were older white males, and pear-shaped. A number of them looked a little hung over and the rolling motion of the sea was subtracting color from their faces. They were headed to the USS Kittiwake wreck to dive, a recently sunk ship in fifty feet of water.

The boat slowed and one of the guides announced, "We need everyone to pair up for this dive, so raise your hand if you don't have a partner." Hank raised his hand and so did a lady at the other end of the boat. The guide asked, "Do you mind pairing up with each other for the dive?" Hank indicated he had no problem and the lady nodded her assent.

"Nice to meet you, I'm Hank Rangar with an A." He held out his hand.

She looked a little bewildered and slowly raised her hand to shake his, "Nice to meet you, I'm "Anne—what do you mean 'with an A?'"

"Sorry, a little joke to help people spell my name correctly—it's ranger but the 'e' is—never mind."

"Oh," she responded a little uncomfortably.

Hank estimated she was just under six feet, with blonde hair in a sporty cut, physically fit, cute and a little younger than he was. Probably right around thirty, he guessed. Why hadn't he noticed her earlier, he wondered? She seemed a little withdrawn. They started getting on their diving equipment. Hank turned toward her. "I'll let you lead; I am mainly out for the exercise and the sun." Anne put up a little protest but then relented. They saw snapper, juvenile sergeant majors, stingrays and eagle rays, explored the passageways of the USS Kittiwake and had a thoroughly wonderful time. On the way back, Hank debated asking Anne to join him for dinner. But as the boat docked in the marina, he found himself looking forward to a cold Red Stripe beer on his balcony and solitude.

Hank woke early the next morning, pulled out his backpack, removed the remote control, the left over putty and putty packaging, placed them in a plastic bag and then put his backpack into his overnight luggage. He headed out toward the Cayman National bank where Morris's ill-gotten gains were wired two days earlier, walking because he liked the fresh sea breeze. His white shirt billowed behind him like a sail. The first public trashcan he came to he deposited the plastic bag with the remote control and putty.

It was nice to be outside but the humidity was thick and the sun was very hot on his neck. When he arrived at the bank, he went through a turnstile and was slammed with a gush of frigid air. He wiped the sweat off his fore-head, straightened his shirt and smoothed his hair back. At the reception desk, he explained he wanted to open a couple of safety deposit boxes and convert some funds from his account.

A banker in a tropical suit stood up from his chair in a glass cubicle and came around and shook Hank's hand. They sat down on opposite sides of a glass desk. "Mr. Rangar," the banker said in a deep, soft island drawl. The banker smiled broadly and gestured broadly in a con-ciliatory manner, "Surely this is unnecessary. This will be very inconvenient for you to access the funds."

"I am firm about this. I am uninterested in other options at this time." What he was interested in was how to avoid detection. IRS code required American citizens to report any interest-bearing account. The stated reason for this gross intrusion into the private lives of every US citizen was to stop illicit drug dealers, tax cheats, and more recently terrorists; but the reality was the government used this as a mechanism to stop capital flight.

Every government wanted to be able to use inflation to finance its current bailiwicks and this always resulted in citizens leaving the country. Hank had no interest in helping them further this theft. The banker, well aware of the US rules on reporting overseas accounts, nodded his head, affirming Hank's request. Cayman banks had been under severe pressure from the United States and European Countries to provide information on the people who had accounts. Hank's recent experience with the IRS had given him a new perspective on these excuses for the invasion of his privacy.

He remembered how the tennis star Steffi Graf's father was sentenced to ten years in jail in Germany for tax evasion, when the person who tried to kill fellow competitor Monica Seles was given a six-month suspended sentence. *Western governments are more interested in how they can milk money from their citizens than how they can protect them.*

"Mr. Rangar, I can arrange all the details to purchase the precious metals and place them in a safety deposit box for a transaction fee of two and a half percent."

Hank thought that was a bit stiff—two and a half percent of five million, he quickly figured in his head, was one hundred and twenty-five thousand dollars. He frowned. The banker clearly saw this and explained the reasoning behind the fee—It would be quite complex for Hank to purchase the metals and then bring them to the bank and quite risky. Hank assented to the fee and told the banker he wanted approximately one third in gold, one third in platinum and one third in silver, to be split evenly between the safety deposit boxes.

That evening he walked along the beach just as the sun was setting; a fiery ball of orange on the horizon seemed to be melting across the top of the blue ocean. Streaks of violet and blue rose from the orange sun like steam and dissipated into the clouds. *The sun would set every day as it had throughout time. People would be born and people would die in good places and bad places. What difference can one man make to the inevitability of this powerful truth?* The absurdity of this fatalistic vision of life caused him to laugh at the ocean, the surf loud and continuous.

He had made a difference; Made By Man had made a difference. Made By Man was successful because it was the perfect marriage of virtual and physical and he would now have to find that perfect combination for himself from now on. Men bring physical things into the world first by their ideas and later, built by their hands. Hank knew with the certainty of a life and death truth that these ideas, made into something real and tangible were the reasons why the average lifespan of man had tripled in just the last two hundred years. He was not virtual because he did not owe his life to Janine or Christine or Warren or Will or the government or stinking slime bags like Morris. No, his life was his alone and he would rebuild.

It was getting dark and the sand between his toes was cool to the touch. He started walking back to the hotel. His thoughts turned back to the money; he felt a custodial obligation to the five million. The money belonged to the founders of EWE Technology. *What would be the best way to allow the founders access to the money without it being traceable by the IRS or anyone else, for that matter?* He saw no reason the government should have a claim, since they had been complicit in attempting to cover up the theft in the first place. He also wanted this money to be secure from the ravages of inflation, which was the purpose of buying precious metals in the first place.

He headed to the hotel bar overlooking the ocean, ordered a beer and pulled out his computer. He took a sip of his beer and stared out at the stars hanging over the lapping waves. He realized his expertise in computer security and encryption provided part of the answer. It was possible to set up online transactions where the buyer and seller remained anonymous and yet verify that the seller was paid. Hank decided to set up an exchange bank that he would call Virtue Oro. The bank's assets would be precious metals. The next morning he called the National Cayman Bank and cancelled the safety deposit boxes. Next, he used his computer to set up thousands of accounts with precious metal dealers around the world and transferred the money into these.

Over the next week, he created a routine that moved the assets between accounts in a random manner, so that no government or other thief could fix the location of Virtue Oro's assets at any one time. He created a website and incorporated client software. The client software was a peer-to-peer file sharing system that would keep track of both the bank's assets and every transaction. Each person's account was only tracked by a digital signature. He then posted the website and encouraged people to download the client software and set up accounts with Virtue Oro. People such as Will Devon could buy things with Virtue Oro's currency, called sovereigns, or easily convert the sovereigns into other currencies or precious metals. The bank charged a small transaction fee of 0.001% to fund the website and pay Hank for his efforts. *That was a 21st Century bank and currency. It protected its clients' assets from all thieves for a pittance.*

Hank set up three accounts in the bank for the founders of EWE Technology and sent them emails from the Virtue Oro site notifying them. The email looked like spam sent out to thousands of recipients and was decrypted only when opened by the intended recipients using the noise signature associated with that user's computer.

Will Devon was sitting in his home office paying his bills. EWE Technology had been given a loan for three hundred fifty thousand dollars to fund the animal trials. To get this loan, the three founders had to guarantee it personally. When EWE went bankrupt, the bank realized that Will had almost no chance of paying; and since the economic downturn had wiped out the equity in his house, they forgave the debt. The bank was required by law to report this to the IRS and the IRS had treated the forgiven loan as income. Will had no idea how he would ever get out of this hole he had dug. He was looking at an IRS letter threatening to put a lien on his house. He thought, *Fuck them, I don't have any equity you dumb fucks,* and started to laugh. He felt his eyes moisten and he wiped his arm across them.

He checked his emails and found an odd one. The subject line said 'EWE Technology payout.' *What sort of sick joke was this?* He did not recognize the sender but in the preview panel he saw the writing "Will, THIS IS NOT A JOKE" and it then explained that there was an account with $1.3 million in Will's name at the Virtue Oro Worldwide Bank. The payout was recompense for the theft by AltruMedical and MedCon. The email was signed Houdini and provided instructions on how to access the account.

Will thought it was a joke but his life had become a joke so he decided to play along. If he was worth $1.3 million, he might as well pay off his three hundred thousand dollar mortgage. He followed the instructions to access his account at Virtue Oro Worldwide Bank. Everything looked legitimate, so he went to his mortgage company's website and typed in the information regarding his account into the payment system. Once he had put in the payoff amount of $309,245.64 he hit the enter button and waited for it to show an error. About five seconds later his computer sent him a receipt with a confirmation number and a, "Thank You for Your Payment." Will pinched himself and he felt pain. He padded off to bed and crawled into bed with his wife, sure he would wake up to some sort of error message or the police arresting him for computer fraud.

The new day dawned bright and crisp. He skipped to his office to check on the absurd email he had received. He turned on his computer and opened his email program. As the emails were coming in, he saw one from the bank that owned his mortgage. The subject line said 'Congratulations.' The email told him his mortgage payoff documents would be in the mail and they would be sending out a release of lien letter to the county recorder within five business days. Will shouted, "That's what I'm talking about!" His wife called out, "Honey, are you okay?"

He picked up his cell phone and called Earl Cody.

"Open your email," Will commanded. Earl was in his seventies and in poor health. He slowly shuffled to his computer, while holding his cell phone. "What are you doing?" Will was impatient.

"I'm opening the computer. What is this all about Will?" Earl was irritated.

Will ignored this. "Do you see an email with the subject line of 'EWE Technology payout'?

"Ahh, let me see. No…okay. Yes I do. So what?" Earl asked. Will explained that it appeared to be real and to take it seriously. He had paid off his mortgage. Earl was incredulous. "How did this happen... I mean, who would have done this?"

"Did you see that it was signed by Houdini?" Will asked.

"Yeah. So what?" Earl responded.

"Remember Hank's computer security company's name was Houdini?"

"Yeah, but it's a common name."

"Earl, I don't believe Hank is dead. I think he's very much alive and even though he couldn't do anything for his sister Janine, he is sure doin' something for us." Earl shook his head slowly in amazement as he listened to Will's laughter on the other end of the phone.

Below his hotel, Hank found a table on the edge of a palapa-roofed restaurant overlooking the ocean. He was the only customer and the sunrise was sparkling on the water, but it had not yet reached the sand. He opened his computer, started perusing his emails and saw Warren had written him. Hank had sent him a short email saying he was alive and back in business. Warren replied that Made by Man had an urgent project and needed his help working out how a laser system could be used to determine the effect of wind on the trajectory of a cylindrical object following a parabolic arc with an initial velocity of three thousand feet per second.

The email ended with a postscript that stated Stanford Morris of the Patent Office had died in a horrible car accident and how odd that was. Hank smiled to himself, kicked off his flip-flops, and dug his toes into the cool sand. He pulled out a pad and a pencil and started to think about the problem. He needed a link budget. The target could be modeled as a Lambertian surface. A Hartmann aperture could be used to determine crosswind. He started writing out equations and drawing diagrams.

The server was surprised by the presence of a customer so early in the morning. They mostly served tourists, who were immune to tropical sunrises after a night of partying. She noticed he was attractive, sandy-haired, and broad-shouldered. He was also alone. Perhaps he had just flown in and would be around several days. He had his laptop open and was scribbling something on a pad. He seemed so engrossed that she felt hesitant to interrupt him as she walked up to take his order. He had written impossibly complex equations on the pad. He must be very unhappy to be up so early working on math, of all things. He didn't react as she stood there. "Excuse me, sir." He turned and looked at her with the most joyful, playful smile. Her grin came easily; she couldn't help herself.

"Wow, I should have paid more attention in math class."

Dear Reader, Thanks for reading *Pendulum of Justice.* Reader reviews are the Gold Standard of the modern publishing industry. This is our (yes, this book was a husband and wife team effort) first book and it took us two years to write with vigorous discussion over artistic direction. We have learned a lot, but know we have plenty more to learn. Creating a book with your lover is incredibly rewarding, like creating another child, without worrying about the orthodontia bills! Seriously, your reviews will help us in writing the next Hank Rangar novels and make sure we provide you with a book you can't put down. So let us know what you think, anything that might help us improve our craft.

The authors encourage you to contact them if there is anything you wish to discuss. Dale can be reached at dbhalling@hallingip.com and Kaila can be reached at khalling@hallingip.com. Please put the title in the subject to ensure a prompt response.

If you enjoyed *Pendulum of Justice,* please check out the next book in the Hank Rangar series, *Trails of Injustice.*

Also by Dale B. Halling: *The Decline and Fall of the American Entrepreneur: How Little Known Laws are Killing Innovation*

Authors Note

Published by
Quantum Dot Publishing

Kaila and Dale Halling raised their kids in Colorado where they enjoy camping, hiking and skiing. Both of them grew up in Midwestern small towns where they could bike wherever they needed to go, Kaila in Iowa and Dale in Kansas. They are entrepreneurs at heart; Dale started a water sprinkling business right out of high school. They both share a love of books and you'll often find them, when not in Colorado, writing on the wild beaches of Baja, Mexico. They are passionate about everyday heroes of advancing technology, which lifts the standard of living and quality of life for all. When they are not writing books, Dale is a patent attorney, engineer, inventor, and entrepreneur.

Book Cover

by Keri Knutson

Acknowledgements

Writing a book requires a team and we received help from a lot of people. We received excellent developmental editing by Wordsharp.net, and proof reading by Alexis Arendt. William Greenleaf also provided some very early developmental editing, which was critical. Our beta test readers provided invaluable input and are too numerous to mention individually.

Read on for a sneak peek at *Trails of Injustice,* the second novel in the Hank Rangar Series, coming 2014!

Father Miguel Diaz crossed the cool stone floor of the dias and greeted Maria Louisa. The elderly woman handed him a plate covered with a paper napkin and he bowed slightly as he accepted her offering.

"Padre, your food will grow cold. Please, you must eat, " she gently admonished.

"I am grateful for your thoughtfulness, Senora." He looked in her eyes and saw her soften. As she turned to walk the length of the sanctuary, he made his way to the small anteroom off the sanctuary where he maintained a small office. The tiny room was sparsely arranged with a wooden desk and chair, a lounge and a cupboard. He carefully placed the plate of hot food on his desktop and removed the napkin. Senora's simple fare of rice, beans and stewed chicken would do much to tide him until after Vespers. He sat in his chair and bowed his head over the food, thanking his most generous Lord for the bounty, and the good people of Puerto Penasco. He lifted one of the tortillas, fresh made that morning, as Senora always did, and spooned succulent pieces of the chicken and beans into the middle. He rolled the tortilla and carefully wrapped the napkin around it and tucked it into the pocket of his cassock. Murmuring another prayer of thanks, he picked up the utensil and made deliberate work of finishing the rest. He was to go to Invasión, the poor settlement on the edge of town whose dwellings were comprised of old mattresses for partial walls and sheets of metal for poor lean-to roofs. He had much work to accomplish with his parishioners and one never knew whom the food resting in his pocket might help the most. From the simplest of God's creatures curled up on the sand streets with no owners or a hungry man eager for work in the town, but with no transportation save his feet. This decided him. Today, he would walk to Invasión and stop along the way to greet any who needed a little comfort or were happy to share their cheer and love for the Savior. His people were his blessing.

The sun baked the streets, but turned the sea into a sparkling blue ribbon and it was this ribbon he followed to the edge of town and into the surprisingly organized village of Invasión, next to the railroad tracks that connected Puerto Penasco with the cities in the heart of Mexico. There was a wind that whipped the street sand around his sandal shod feet and slapped the ends of his simple rope belt against the heavy cotton of his cassock. Padre walked with purpose and smiled to the women he saw hanging wash on lines next to their dwellings. Dogs wagged their tails but remained silent and submissive to the newcomer. It was as it should be. Young, restless men nodded in deference, but their eyes were watchful, their lean, strong bodies coiled as snakes prepared to strike. He stopped to talk with a few of them, asking about their families and their sisters. He told them he was praying for more work and encouraged them to resist the army and other temptations. He looked into each youthful, promising face and reminded them God's work required patience and forthrightness. He reminded them that their parents worked hard to never see them bow to the evil forces at work in the world. He caught their attention. Ah, they knew what he was referring to. Penasco was now the training ground for not one but two rivaling cartels. These evil men cultivated armies of young men to aid their unholy wars of drugs and destruction. They were intelligent, good boys, and hopefully, his hamlet would lose few of them to the evil drug overlords who controlled the streets. The Chief of Police had been gunned down with three other officers less than six months prior, the height of the tourist season for their small city. Now, many did not have work. The Norte Americanos were fearful to come to their shores. Easy driving distance from the shining cities north of the border, where there were fewer faithful, but the resources his parish desperately needed to survive and maybe flourish one day.

As cars turned corners and drove up the road, the young swains instantly stood to full height and were watchful. He noticed they would relax as amigos drove by waving and honking. The padre decided to move on up the road. He waved to Miguel whose small store carried fresh fruits and vegetables brought in from the farmers further south. He nodded when Miguel gestured he would have a bag of produce for the parish. He stopped for a moment and bowed his head thanking God for the generosity of the people. He mentally made a note to pick up the bag on his return. He was coming close to the Three Fish missionary. A Norte Americano couple worked tirelessly seven days a week in Invasión, schooling the children and teaching their parents English. He had broken bread with them many times and was grateful for their presence, although they were not of the Catholic faith, the rightful faith of the people of Puerto Penasco. There were children playing soccer in the street with a ball they no doubt got from the missionaries. The children were shouting and laughing, running barefoot in the street as the passed the ball back and forth with quick, agile movements of their feet. Little Carlos, who no longer had his mother and his father was not known, saw him and smiled brightly. His eyes were sparkling like the sun on the water and his dark head moved back and forth from the game to Padre. He felt in his pocket for the filled tortilla and gestured with a grin and a nod for Carlos to come. Carlos was forever hungry and his grandmother worked all day as a maid in one of the vast condominium complexes separating the town from its blue diamond beaches.

The tranquility was broken by the noise of revving engines and tires spinning on a sand road. Padre turned around and saw dust billowing behind several vehicles that must have accelerated to over 60 miles per hour. The children, not realizing the danger were still playing in the street. He ran to them, waving his arms, and screaming for them to get out of the street. 'Carlos, Carlos!" He could not form the words to instruct him. He gestured wildly to his legs and the cassock. The children cleared the street just as three black Suburbans slid to a stop. Carlos hid in the folds of Padres' cassock, trembling. Padre could not see the men in the Suburbans, because of the darkly tinted glass and the sun glinting off the windshields.

Everything seemed too stand still in time for a second and then the door of one of the Suburbans opened, then they all opened and men with bandanas and rifles stepped out of the cars, clearly cartel. Padre hoped this was just a display of force to scare his flock. The Norte Americano man from the missionary stuck his head out of the classroom. Fire spit from a gun and the report caused the padre to flinch. He saw blood spurt from the man's chest as he fell to his knees. The scene was utter confusion, women screaming, everyone running in random direction, pings sounding off the metal roofs, mattresses exploding in front of their faces, and people diving behind whatever makeshift shelter was near. The gunfire seemed completely disconnected from the blood arcing through the air and landing in a million dark dots on the sand. Mi Dios! Some of the boys were lying in the street, crimson circles blooming on their chests and backs their faces contorted in pain. He maneuvered Carlos back, back against the missionary door. Carlos was crying softly. He closed his eyes and prayed to God for guidance and for protection for his people and for the boys he saw lying in the road, the blood flying everywhere. Carlos was trembling beneath his robe and he reached down instinctively to protect him, his legs closing, forcing Carlos behind and against the door. He touched his crucifix praying loudly now for the evil to stop, but he would not cower in front of the devil.

Made in the USA
San Bernardino, CA
19 April 2014